American Rapture

ALSO BY
CJ Leede

Maeve Fly

American Rapture

CJ Leede

NIGHTFIRE

Tor Publishing Group • New York

AMERICAN RAPTURE

Forgiven
Lyrics by Alanis Morissette
Music by Alanis Morissette and Glen Ballard
Copyright © 1995 SONGS OF UNIVERSAL, INC.,
VANHURST PLACE MUSIC and ARLOVOL MUSIC
All Rights for VANHURST PLACE MUSIC Administered
by SONGS OF UNIVERSAL, INC.
All Rights for ARLOVOL MUSIC Administered
by PENNY FARTHING MUSIC c/o CONCORD MUSIC PUBLISHING
All Rights Reserved Used by Permission
Reprinted by Permission of Hal Leonard LLC

Precious Things
Words and Music by Tori Amos
Copyright © 1992 Sword And Stone Publishing Company, USA
All Rights Reserved International Copyright Secured
Reprinted by Permission of Hal Leonard LLC

A Nightfire Book
Published by Tom Doherty Associates / Tor Publishing Group
120 Broadway
New York, NY 10271

www.torpublishinggroup.com

Nightfire™ is a trademark of Macmillan Publishing Group, LLC.

Library of Congress Cataloging-in-Publication Data

Names: Leede, CJ, author.
Title: American rapture / CJ Leede.
Description: First edition. | New York : Nightfire, Tor Publishing Group, 2024. |
Identifiers: LCCN 2024024463 | ISBN 9781250857927 (hardcover) |
    ISBN 9781250857934 (ebook)
Subjects: LCGFT: Apocalyptic fiction. | Novels.
Classification: LCC PS3612.E34895 A83 2024 | DDC 813/.6—dc23/eng/20240603
LC record available at https://lccn.loc.gov/2024024463

Our books may be purchased in bulk for promotional, educational, or business use.
Please contact your local bookseller or the Macmillan Corporate and Premium Sales
Department at 1-800-221-7945, extension 5442, or by email at
MacmillanSpecialMarkets@macmillan.com.

First Edition: 2024

Printed in the United States of America

0 9 8 7 6 5 4 3 2 1

To the librarians,
The animal rescuers,
Every last rebel.

─⟡─

And to my Chupacabra,
forever and ever.

These precious things, let them bleed, let them wash away.

—Tori Amos

You know how us Catholic girls can be.

—Alanis Morissette

American Rapture

HOW TO RECOGNIZE THE LAST
MOMENTS BEFORE THE WORLD ENDS:

You won't.

—⟡—

EMERGENCY BROADCAST.

My entire life I have been told what happens to those who sin. The wicked ones who turn from God's light. The ones who question, who seek forbidden knowledge, who bend to temptation, disobey.

I have always known the consequences for being a girl like me.

EMERGENCY BROADCAST.

But this?

EMERGENCY BROADCAST.

Clothing torn, tears streaming down my face. I drive away from the only life I've ever known.

Covered—dripping—in so much blood.

I tighten my grip on the wheel. Just for a moment, I close my eyes and pray.

HOW TO RECOUNT THE
END OF THE WORLD:

Don't spare any details, no matter what the
cost.

Back up and start from the beginning.

Silent Symphonies

Birdsong outside my window.

Bright midwestern morning. Fresh sun, clear air. Birdsong outside, and silence inside. Dust specks floating, settling, gathering on stuffed animals, crucifixes, Bibles, in the corners of the wooden built-ins my father designed. Paintings of Jesus, of Mary, in their wooden frames. Beige curtains, beige carpet. Silence in my room.

The window before me is sealed shut. Sealed because I opened it the night my brother was taken from our home. The night my world went silent. Five years ago today.

I can feel the season's change is almost here, but I do not yet know it holds the beginning of the end. I do not yet know anything except the inside of this room and the screams of my brother that live in me forever.

Downstairs, bacon sizzles in a pan. My mother calls my name. I pull on my plaid pleated skirt, collared shirt, and sweater. The birds outside have flown away.

In the hall, I press my palm to Noah's closed door, the framed painting of Jesus beside it, one of so many in the house.

I picture my brother, sitting on his bed in the low lamplight. The last good moments, ones that replay all the time.

Our birthday was coming, we were almost twelve, and I had snuck into his room, afraid, like I always was. I never could have known what my being there would do. That these precious moments would become our last together.

We were both homeschooled and took classes at church, but Noah was smart, years ahead in math and science, our mother perpetually embarrassed by it. She said it wasn't godly to indulge in such vanity, said it was dangerous. But when we were much younger, a man in our congregation had seen Noah scribbling and asked him about it. A math teacher, he ran a summer camp at his farm where kids went to tend animals. Because he was in our church, our parents let Noah go. He went every summer, and they had no idea that while the other boys were baling hay and milking, he sat in the kitchen scribbling numbers and learning about the world. I was envious, so envious of it. While I was left at home.

Noah knew things that I didn't, had experiences I didn't have. But in every other way we were equals. We were everything to each other, always. And he always came back and shared with me all the things he'd learned.

Noah across the bed from me, a worksheet in front of him.

"What are you working on?" I said.

"This science project. There's a contest, and the winner gets to go to the Dells." He shrugged. *"Maybe this could be our way in."*

We read about the Dells in a brochure that someone left at church and Noah stole for us, hid under his bed. The Dells were a place where everything was designed to be spectacular. Fun and colorful. Waterpark, a science museum, a bookstore. So many shops, so many adventures. We'd never been anywhere like it.

It was what we wanted for our birthday coming up, more than anything. To go to the Dells, together.

"Think Mom and Dad will ever take us?" I asked.

"Sophie! Breakfast!"

I stand in the hall, alone. I will turn seventeen in a few weeks, quietly and unassumingly beneath this roof as I have every birthday up to now. Noah will do the same in a loveless facility, away from me. Each of us a half person, a half self. There will certainly be no trip to the Dells.

Downstairs, my parents eat.

My father, thin, sweatered, in his signature round glasses, eyes me over the top of his newspaper and says, "You're going to school like that?" The gentle architect, the meek father. He wasn't gentle that night. His hands on Noah's arms. On mine.

I look down at my clothes, the uniform I wear every day. "What else would I wear?"

He turns to my mother, and they share a look. My father says nothing more. His newspaper reads: **PHILADELPHIA, NEW YORK CITY TO CLOSE ALL PUBLIC SCHOOLS TO COPE WITH FLU OUTBREAK**.

My mother withholds the cereal and milk until I've prayed, and when I'm finished she releases the food to me.

The flu, from what I have gleaned reading the back of my father's newspaper and overheard conversations, won't affect us, even though it's bad this year. It's isolated in the Northeast, and they've quarantined that whole part of the country. The priests remind us that we don't have to worry, we are protected by Christ's blood. We invite and accept Him inside ourselves, again and again.

Our home, wood, stone, glass. Careful lines, beige carpet. My father, like every other Taliesin School–inspired architect in the region, designed it in Frank Lloyd Wright's classic Prairie style, organic materials, clean lines to blend into the surrounding nature, a lower story for my parents, an upper story to tuck children away, that only I now inhabit. My father designed our church in the same way. An even larger, more spacious version of our home. Functional, harmonious. Built-ins, shadows across beige walls and beige carpet created by clever window casings and walkways, so many windows, natural light. Architecture that asks for silence, that muffles the world, encourages standing still. Dust specks, floating. My waking hours spent inside these rooms designed by my father, imitating the work of another. My mother likes to say that God is an architect, that we should all imitate Christ, every day. I never say anything.

We eat in silence as we have each morning since that night. I don't want to exist inside this house. I barely want to exist at all. That in itself is a sin. God gifted us this life, these parents, and we are meant to be grateful. We are meant to repent on our knees and receive salvation ecstatically and somberly on our tongues.

One thousand eight hundred and twenty-six days.

So begins, through the taut film of unspeaking, the daily silent symphony that has lived in his place, ever since.

My father sips his coffee, sets it down. My mother sips her coffee, checks her watch. My father flips the page, sips the coffee. I chew.

Sip, place, sip, click, crinkle, sip, crunch, crunch.

The rage and ache in a spotless house. Long shadows over carpet.

Sip, place, sip, click, crinkle, sip, crunch, crunch.

The rhythm of it follows me out the door.

Sip, place, sip, click, crinkle, sip—

My mother shuts the driver's side door behind her, and we are in the car.

Foreston's population is in the single thousands. There are two schools, one for girls and one for boys, both Catholic, and kids come from all different farm towns nearby. My school, St. Mary's, is five minutes from my house. I would walk if I were allowed. As it is, however, I am not allowed much of anything. Including any kind of device to alert my parents to my safety if I *were* to go anywhere without them. No phone, no unsupervised time with the computer. But the town of Foreston is basically the congregation of our church, so there's not much danger anyway. Before this year, I was still homeschooled, but we got a monsignor who was blessed by the Pope, and he told my parents that I needed social interaction. So now I attend St. Mary's. I felt a thrill at the idea at first, a new freedom, any kind of freedom. Until I got to school and realized it was all the same girls from church I had been with my entire life. Beige home, beige church, beige school, beige life.

Still, it gets me away from my mother.

She pulls the car to a stop. I sit up, and she holds out her arm to prevent my exit.

"Your father had a point today," she says. Her sweater is the color of Sunday wine, and she smiles at me briefly, almost sadly.

"What point?" I ask.

"I've ordered you new uniforms," she says.

"What's wrong with the ones I have? We just got them."

"We'll go for a shopping trip, get you some new church clothes too. This weekend."

I can't spend a day with her alone, can't imagine she would ever want to spend a day with me. We don't do this. The other girls make their way into the building, the bell sounding, their overlapping voices, the school chapel's incense wafting to us on the breeze. "Can we talk about this later?"

She turns that smile back on me. From here she will just return to the house, maybe go to the store, to the church events rooms, then home again. I can't fathom what she does with her time, her thoughts. Her hair is like mine, dark and thick, but she wears hers pulled back tight, so that it must hurt, stretching at the skin of her scalp. This austere woman, that pure unflinching smile.

"Don't worry," she says. "We'll get you sorted this weekend."

With this, I am released.

Culver's

Sister Margaret abhors tardiness above all else, as I have been told several thousand times over the course of the semester. "The word of God does not wait for dawdlers!" I do not understand what this means, but it's as permanently etched in my mind as the *sip, crinkle* symphony or the Apostles' Creed. Like the others, it replays itself so often I hardly know where one ends and the others begin.

ThewordofGoddoesnot. Sip. Waitfordawdlers. Crunch. Forgiveness of. Resurrection of.

The class' eyes are on me as I take my seat. I reach in my bag for my Bible and realize I've brought the wrong book, my fingers brushing the copy of *Brave New World* I snuck out of the library instead. Sister Margaret would love to catch me with it. She's staring, suspending the silence in the classroom until I've settled in. Two girls in front laugh. Dark wooden carved scenes of the Last Supper and Judas's kiss hang behind her. Biblical paintings in every corner of this place.

"Sorry, I'll have to share with Ji-Yun today," I say. Ji-Yun next to me rolls her eyes and slides the book two inches toward me.

Sister Margaret levels me with her stare again.

"There is a special place in Heaven for Ji-Yun, and all those charitable souls who help their neighbors in *need*," she says.

And so begins another day in paradise.

My free period falls between Theology and Math, and I spend it reading behind the broken A/C unit in a patch of grass by the back parking lot. Black asphalt surrounded by thick, dark woods, still nearly all green, though some faint yellow begins to peek through. The smell of dirt and maple trees combined with the exhaust venting out the side of the building, the incense still carrying through all of it.

A truck pulls into the lot, loud secular music blasting. I start to hide my book and stand, but it's only some of my classmates. They won't see me, even if they do.

The car slows to a stop in front of me, and I glance up again. A boy drives the green pickup, and Sarah Johnson sits in the passenger seat. In the bed of the truck are two other boys and Rachel Miller. The boys wear St. Augustine's uniforms. One of them smokes a cigarette. I know from hallway gossip that some of the girls steal away with them during school, or after, to go to Culver's, but I don't usually see them. It seems they're becoming more brazen. A breeze blows toward me, and it carries the fried cheese smell of their food.

I'd forgotten. The feel of fried breadcrumbs against my lips, the pull of cheese, grease dripping down my fingers that I bring to my tongue, sucking them clean. Fried food. Delicious food. My family hasn't eaten foods like this since before Noah left, our home and life undergoing a strict and purifying transformation to the most ascetic, unpolluted environment possible.

And maybe it is the day and all its memories, maybe it is a rare moment of witnessing a brazen act. But I am struck, suddenly—profoundly—by them.

My classmates, the boys. The casual way the boy holds his arm around Rachel's shoulder, how carelessly she rests her hand on his knee. The scent of the decadent, forbidden food on the wind.

Their contact, skin to skin.

It's not that I haven't learned, or surmised, what men and women do behind closed doors. I'm sheltered, I'm not an idiot. Even children who do not sin or read illicit books know these things here. Livestock is a daily part of life for nearly everyone at some point or other, and livestock copulate. And fornication is written all throughout the Bible.

But seeing girls my age, and boys, together . . . witnessing their carelessness, their *want*.

It's real.

Suddenly this makes it *real*. Makes them seem realer than reality, as though they are hyperpigmented and I, like the rest of our world, am something dull and fading.

The boy jumps out of the truck and helps Rachel out after him. On the pavement, he pulls her body to his—one hand around her waist, his other in her hair. Their hands that have been smeared with grease, that have been licked clean.

She lifts her face and, as if it were the most inconsequential thing in the world, tilts herself forward to kiss him.

Kiss him.

If the Sisters see her, she'll be suspended, and every family's form of punishment is different. But she doesn't care. *She doesn't care* about the consequences. All Rachel seems to care about is the boy whose lips are crushed against her own, whose chest and stomach and hips meet hers. His fingers on the bare skin of her back where her shirt rides up.

Rachel and this boy. Here, in the morning, out in the open and against every rule, earthly and divine. Sharing more than their skin, more than their heat. I can't look away. I don't want to, even as my heart threatens to burst through my chest, adrenaline lighting every part of me.

Because in this singular moment in the parking lot at our school, in the middle of the day, I think maybe they have accomplished something I've never even dared to dream possible.

They might have miraculously, incredibly, solved the riddle of how to be not just living, but . . . *alive*.

The air stands still around me. A crackle, electricity.

Leaves shudder at the edge of the woods.

The driver says it's time to go, and Sarah drags Rachel toward the school. The other boy in the back tosses his cigarette to the ground. Sunlight streams in through the passenger window so that I can't see the driver, until his head lowers and his face blocks the sun.

He has the darkest eyes I've ever seen. And yet, somehow they glint golden-black in the light. His skin and hair too, darker than most in this town, smooth and perfect. His hand grips the steering wheel, assured and casual. I've never looked at the hands of a boy my age. Not like this. The curve of his fingers, the outline of tendons along the back. The sunlight as he flexes them, just so. A stirring of some kind, a . . . *curiosity*. Maybe . . .

"Hey!"

The voice brings me back. The kissing guy is looking at me. I am sitting on the grass staring open-mouthed at a stranger. At all these strangers.

"Maybe you should join us next time! You and me, baby, we could party!" He and his friend in the back laugh and gesture in ways I don't understand. Rachel comes back and slaps him, calls him a pig. Then she kisses him again, long and deep, the front of his shirt fisted tight in her hand. My heart, still thudding, still—

She turns, gives me a pointed smile. "Aw, cute, she likes you! Todd likes them virginal, don't you, Todd?"

My cheeks flush hot.

The cigarette guy, Todd, directs an upward thrust of the chin at me and says in a low voice, "Sup."

The driver turns his head away, the sun streaming once again around his face so that I can't make out his features anymore. If he saw me or noticed me at all, he already has forgotten. Not that I want to be seen. Noticed. I don't. I really don't. Leaves rustling.

The driver starts the truck. The girls disappear inside after another joke made at my expense.

The parking lot is empty once again.

I sit where I sat before, the same book in my lap and the same life at my disposal. And—

A huge gust of wind hits me from the side.

I gasp. Dirt and small bits of debris pelt my arms and legs. I shield my face and brace against it. A cold wind, violent and sudden.

And then it calms, the air returning to normal.

My heart is pounding, breath coming too quickly. That wind blowing from the woods. I turn to them. The hollow space between the trees dark and deep. Stretching, beckoning.

Nearly a whisper, something watching.

The hairs on the back of my neck lift. The now-gentle breeze against my skin.

As though the Devil is saying hello.

As though I can feel his touch.

HOW TO FAKE A FEVER:

Raise your body temperature naturally with movement, spicy foods, hot beverages.

Run the thermometer under hot water, if digital. Shake from side to side, if mercury.

Spritz your face with water to mimic perspiration.

Think forbidden thoughts.

The Talk

I spend Friday night teaching myself how to tie knots after a visit to the library, where I find a book on the subject. My father gives me rope and string to practice. Tasks can carry you through many hours of a life otherwise too empty to contemplate. And *books,* the right ones, can nearly make you forget what it is you're trying to forget in the first place.

It is too difficult, I realized years ago, to borrow anything from the library I actually want to read that I will also be allowed to, as the books I am permitted are limited to select preapproved middle-grade books, how-tos, and, of course, religious texts.

I've read nearly all the how-to books the Foreston Public Library has to offer, and Mrs. Parson, the librarian, special orders more for me. I show them to my parents, and they are none the wiser to the fact that I am pulling others simultaneously. Meanwhile, I pick up a new skill or two every week. A real win-win kind of situation.

My room is now full of these Friday night experiments. Handsewn animals, refurbished furniture, homemade candles, Rube Goldberg machines, a little robot I built and programmed to walk. Sometimes I imagine they make their own symphony, each contributing its own sound, breathing life into the space around me.

I lean against my bed and reach underneath it for the small compartment Noah and I built there. We put one under his bed too. Our secret place where we left notes for each other, small items, sneaking into each other's rooms and keeping our most precious treasures hidden from our parents. I never would have thought that anything kept there would take my brother away. That he might have secrets, even from me.

I open mine now, full of colorful origami with notes written on the folded paper. It makes a difference, even if it's a small one, to know there is a part of Noah here that isn't closed away behind his bedroom door, locked and left shut since he left.

It's easy to shut people out, I've learned. You don't even need a door.

I wake to my mother standing in my room, her low-heeled foot on the constrictor knot I made the night before. With a lurch, I pull my blanket over the book next to me in a way I hope looks nonchalant. It's the *Divine Comedy*. If discovered, it might be more accepted than the others, but I still don't want to find out.

I blink the world into focus. She never comes in here.

"Mom?"

"Sophie, good morning. I'll see you downstairs," she says, and she turns to leave.

I don't understand, but then,

I remember. Our shopping day. I groan and fall back to my bed.

We arrive at the mall in the next town over, a place I've only been a handful of times, and not in many years. The echoes of my mom's church organ music from the drive still cling to us crossing the parking lot. The wind brushes against our backs as we step through the sliding automatic doors that whoosh behind, seal us in.

We are in a department store. Scents of perfume and cleaning products and new plastic. Soft music, voices. My mother and I traverse the shiny white linoleum aisles between appliances and linens, the lights harsh against our skin. She has not told me what we're doing here together, why I needed to come with her. Why it couldn't wait.

We enter the main atrium, and we are assaulted by food smells— decadent and greasy, sweet, salty, spicy, fried—lights, bright white, yellow, multicolored, mannequins posed in revealing shockingly bright-colored clothing. Kiosks with keychains and jewelry and hair styling tools and even an ear-piercing booth where a young girl holds her mother's hand as a teenager approaches with a metal device. A secular world bustling and carrying on while pop music plays on the speakers and shoppers yell and talk and eat and children laugh and cry.

It's dizzying.

"Stay here," my mother says tightly, and walks toward an information desk. A bored-looking young woman stands behind it wearing all black, the heaviest eye makeup I've ever seen, and a medical face mask. A bottle of hand sanitizer sits on the counter in front of her. My mother has to wait in line behind an old man, and she eyes the masked girl warily. I see a number of medical masks on different people milling about. I don't know if this is normal in the secular world. Everything is so . . . chaotic.

Not far from the information desk and in front of a luggage store is what looks to be an art installation, some kind of interactive map of the state. My eyes catch on it. The glowing bright saturated color, bouncing around in a mesmerizing pattern. I glance at my mother. She's still waiting her turn and watching the girl in judgment. She's not paying attention to me.

I step over to it. A large neon-lit map of the whole of Wisconsin with cities, forests, parks, even the Dells. My heart constricts. Noah in the lamplight, sitting on his bed.

Different sections light up in different moments, the rest of it going dark, all the complexities of the lit-up region highlighted as they're shown. Its movements hypnotic.

This land, this vibrant version of it.

I identify Rusk County, where I am, and Waukesha County, where Noah is. Two hundred fifty miles away. I touch my fingers to it, studying the roads in between, thinking of the few times we've visited. Wishing more than anything that we could get in the car from here and head that way, that I could just see him even for a moment. To know what he's doing right now, or thinking.

Waukesha goes dark. Another county is illuminated, one that is far away and I don't care about. I am left staring at the reflection of my own eyes in the dark as the map moves on. I don't know most of these places, don't really know this state at all. But I know two points, and they're the only ones that matter.

Another set of eyes appears, right in front of mine.

I jump back.

The eyes blink.

I—

Oh. It takes me a moment. But then I understand.

Someone is standing on the other side of the installation. It's two-sided, and as the light shifts into different sections of the map, the rest of it is left dark but translucent, just enough to see through if two people stand very close to it on each side. I take a step to the left where the neon light has traveled, illuminating another county, trying to think if I've ever seen it. Then the light shifts again, and the eyes reappear in front of mine.

I step to the right.

The map shifts.

There are the eyes, again.

And I start to move away, but . . . I realize I know them. I've seen them before.

I step closer. I know I shouldn't. I don't know why I do it, nerves lighting up my body.

He steps forward too, a face in the dark. Then he stands to his full height, and I have to tilt my head up to meet his eyes, looking down at me through the screen.

The boy who was driving the truck at school. He's here. Here where I am. Seeing me through the map.

I am not breathing. My chest and stomach tighten. There must be less than ten inches between us, on either side of this screen. And the expression on his face. He's looking at me like he wants to see me. Like I'm something worth seeing.

He reaches forward and touches his hand to the screen.

And on this side, my side, as if in a trance or a dream or as if I were someone else entirely, I reach my fingers up to meet them.

"Yo," a male voice, "Ben, you coming, or—"

The screen goes dark. All of it. The map has finished its neon circuit, and I see through it completely. Everyone does.

The boys from school are here. I lower my hand, step back. Todd and the kissing boy both look up. And Ben, the driver, still standing there, right in front of me. Still, just . . . looking.

"Sophie. What are you doing?"

I whip around. My mother is here, furious. Her eyes rake over me. "I told you to stay where you were," she says.

I hear the boys' laughter and turn to look back, but the art installation has started up again, and I can't see through to the other side.

The little girl at the piercing booth screams. Her mother says, "Great job, baby, you did it!" The teen has shoved the needle through her ear.

"Come on," my mother says. "It's this way."

"What about this one?" My mother beside the rack holds up a dress identical to the one she has on. It is long, with short sleeves and a deliberately undefined waist. I shrug and agree.

I can't shake the confusion, the turmoil in my chest, thrumming through my blood. The jolt that came when my eyes met his. *Ben*, the other boy had called him.

The embarrassment and shame when they laughed.

My mother is agitated, but is making an effort to be gentler with me than usual, and I don't know what to make of it. The dread sits heavy. Dread and . . . what is the other feeling? A crackling. Something I know I should not feel.

I follow my mother into the changing room full of dresses we've pulled. The sales worker who helped us watches the news on an iPad outside our fitting room, and its sounds carry to us inside. Something about the flu outbreak. My mother stands and pulls the curtain back.

"Excuse me, would you please turn that down?"

I don't see, but the volume lowers, and my mother closes the curtain again.

Now, with only the soft department store sounds around us, in the blandest, most austere store in this mall, I am trapped inside this tight room with my mother, and I don't know what to do with myself. I should undress, I guess that is what's expected, but my mother hasn't seen me without clothes since childhood. No one has.

"Let's try this one first," she says, and I force myself to begin, keeping my eyes down.

She rattles off an upbeat string of chitchat about upcoming church functions and Father James this and Monsignor West that as I slide off my clothes and try to keep myself covered. She's trying so hard today. I glance around the space, searching for something to look at that isn't her.

My eyes catch on the mirror. On me in the mirror. In my bra and underwear.

I feel a little sick. I don't know how to feel.

But I know why we're here now, I understand.

Why my mother would pretend for today that our life and our family are okay, at least enough to share a room with me for an extended period of time.

The overhead fluorescents shine in the mirror just as the sun did behind the boy at school. The boy I just saw. The one who saw me here, like this. Have I looked like this this whole time? Is this how everyone has seen me?

I had some soreness in my breasts and bled for the first time a year ago, but these things don't matter to me much. The body is just another cage, like the house or the family or the church or the town. We don't have full-length mirrors at home, and the ones in the bathroom at home and school only show my face. But it has all just been unimportant. Until now.

I don't look like a girl anymore. I mean, I do, but I also don't. I've worn bras for some time, and maybe I've noticed them feeling tight, but I haven't realized how tight this bra is. I thought they were all meant to be uncomfortable, restricting.

I have breasts, fighting to break free of the fabric. I have a stomach that is taut with lines where there didn't used to be any, as if the softness somehow melted away. There is a new curve to my hips. And my face. Now that I really look at it, it doesn't look like me, doesn't look like the face of a child anymore. I am somehow more defined, a little sharper, as though I am just now coming into focus.

It's a terrible thing to admit, a sin within itself, but I am sparing nothing in this account, so here it is.

Somehow, while I've been looking the other way, while I have been waiting for time to run its course, for life to present me with anything worth pursuing, my body and my face and my whole outward self has turned into something not extraordinary, but maybe not ordinary either.

I understand why I'm here.

Beauty is dangerous. It is temptation and sin, something to be hidden and pretended away, for safety, for propriety, for the grace of God. Women's beauty draws the darkness. It *is* the darkness.

I look to my mother. It wasn't always like this. When I was young, she would kneel beside me, elbows sinking into my comforter at night, and we prayed and sometimes even laughed, but only when Noah hadn't caused trouble for a long time, when he was tucked into his own room, quiet. She would tie my hair into a careful braid, fingers slow and gentle and kind, wrap her arms around me and squeeze me so tight because I was the one who would let her. And because, I think . . . she loved me.

Now, here, in this dressing room, despite myself, I want to ask her something, something real, but I don't know how to do it. She lived a life before me, she has experienced so much of what I will experience, and she could teach me things. I don't have to be alone, not in this one thing. The day Noah left, I revoked the title from her in every way I could, and I have made myself forget what it is I am even missing. These moments, when they come, are the worst. The wanting. I want so much.

I think of my father noticing the change in my body and am hot with shame. My mother has stopped talking. She watches me in the mirror, sees me seeing. She sighs and rests the dress in her lap, and I know she is about to say something important. Something real and meaningful. A feeling sprouts in my chest. Hope, maybe. Maybe I will blink my eyes, and it will all be rewound. Maybe she and my father never did what they did, and maybe I have a mother here I can allow myself to love and grow close to and ask for guidance when I need it. Maybe there is a way to move forward, and this life is not the loneliest thing imaginable, just counting minutes between phone calls to my brother.

"Mom," I say, and my voice holds everything I am thinking and more. After a moment, she speaks.

"It's a burden, my love, and it's real."

I must look lost still because she reaches over and squeezes my arm. Pain is written on my mother's face. A look that flashes there periodically, only ever breaks briefly through her serene exterior. But for once, she doesn't try to hide it.

"My girl," she says.

I stiffen beneath her touch. I don't mean to, but I am not used to it, not used to anyone's.

Disappointment flashes. She releases me and folds her hands in her lap. She takes a moment, and when she looks up, it is now in a frank and dry way she has never looked at me. Gone from her eyes is any mothering distance, any Catholic piety. This is a new woman, one I've never seen.

"You're so like me," she says. "I'm sorry for that."

Goose bumps erupt, up and down my arms and legs.

"I saw those boys, you know," she says.

I hold myself very still.

"Do you know them?" she asks, danger edging her tone.

I shake my head. I cross my arms over my bare stomach. She makes no move to hand me the dress, just watches my face.

After a moment, she accepts what I've said.

"You know what the most valuable thing you carry is."

I nod.

"You know you can only give it once, and then it is gone forever."

I nod.

"You know that after that, you are stained, marked. Soiled forever. Unless it is within a divine union, and unless it brings forth children into the world. You know that until that day, you have to guard it with your life."

I nod again.

She watches me longer, tries to find something.

"The world is different now," she says. "Things have changed, for a lot of people. You can be religious and less strict, can go out with friends and boys and move through the world nearly the way secular people do. I'm sure you see other members of the congregation living this way. I know you've noticed. I know that you resent the way we live, the way we've raised you."

I stand, nearly naked, my heart pounding.

"I know you resent me the most."

The faint sound of the employee's iPad on low volume, of other shoppers somewhere off in the store. I find my voice. "I don't—"

"Yes, you do," she says, taking in a deep breath that seems to hold all the weight of the world. She squares her shoulders and smooths her hair down. Bracing herself.

"Mom, could I just get dress—"

"The way your father and I met," she says.

It takes me a moment to catch up, but I say, "Um, yes, at the chapel. But—"

"You remember the story." Of course I do. They used to tell it to us all the time, when we were young. Our mother was in religious studies, and our father was an architecture student, and he fell in love first with St. Paul's Chapel, and then eventually with the girl he met in it. He would say it was the beautiful Catholic girl with the soulful eyes who showed him the ways of the world, who showed him all the light. It was a repeat story back then, like any of the Bible verses. *Soulfuleyes, showedmethelight.*

My mother in the dressing room nods, just slightly. "There is . . . more. To the story." She draws in a deep breath and lets it go, touching the scapular that hangs always around her neck. Two rectangular pieces of heavy, uncomfortable cloth held together by a string, one piece resting on the chest, and one down the back. It is antiquated, and hardly anyone wears them now, but my mother wears hers every day since that night. It causes discomfort, is meant to remind her constantly of her devotion to her faith, to ensure a good life, a good death, and entrance to the Kingdom of Heaven. She is always clinging to it, or to the rosary in her purse.

"There's more to that story," she says, "and I think maybe it's time you hear it.

"I was the first in my family to go to college," she says, "the first, as far back as anyone can remember, to ever leave the state of Wisconsin.

Growing up on the dairy, I just . . ." She flashes me a wry smile, another look I haven't seen before. "I always felt the world must be so much bigger," she says. "*Wilder* than our rolling hills, the sunrises and sunsets that always came, always in the same way.

"I always knew I was going to leave. The schools weren't great up north, so I worked hard. I entered competitions, won awards and scholarships, read everything I could get my hands on. Until finally it was time to apply to college, and with the funding I'd received, I could go.

"I was going to move to Madison, get my degree as an English major, read all the stories I could. And then I wanted to teach. Somewhere new and exciting, wherever a professorship would take me. I would need a graduate degree for it, but I was a hard worker, and I knew what it would take, even coming from nothing. I worked at one of the dining halls, in the dairy store, scraping windshield ice for professors, bringing the elderly their groceries in the snow. I studied as hard as I could. A year in, I was offered the opportunity to travel to Ann Arbor to be an assistant to a professor in the summer school there. My parents didn't want me in a new state alone, but they had family friends on a farm about an hour outside of town. So they called them up, and I was told I could go stay with them.

"I was so . . . *happy*." So much in the word as she says it. Freedom, sorrow . . .

Hatred.

"I . . . got loose and liberal with my clothing and my lifestyle. I smiled more. I made friends in classes who I went out with after and drank beers. I was so proud. So vain. So vain about my successes, my achievement. So pleased with everything I'd done. And all this time, I was so involved in myself and my own vanity that I did not realize what was happening. I did not notice the ways in which my wanton behavior affected the couple I was living with. I did not see how the man had begun to watch me, how the woman began to resent me. If I had only . . ."

She takes a shaky breath and then steels herself, fingers pressing tight to her scapular. Then the flat leveling look returns to her face, dimming her again.

"One night . . ." She pauses a long moment, staring at me and not at all. She opens her mouth and closes it, then opens it again.

"One night, when I got back from teaching and spending time with my friends, I parked my car beside the barn. I found him . . . waiting there, for me.

"He said there was something he wanted to show me. So I followed him inside. There was nothing except the animals, the tools, and the hay," she says. She fingers the scapular, clings to it. And any trace of the wild curious young woman I'd just caught a glimpse of is gone, completely.

"He did what he did to me in a cow stall."

It takes me a moment, to put the pieces together. To understand. I suck in a breath.

"No, just—" She clears her throat, touches the cloth. "I have to finish." Another breath. Heartbeats. My mother, here before me. Telling me this.

"It went on for a long time," she says. "Long enough for me to think about things, once I stopped struggling. Long enough for me to . . . realize. With my face pressed to the dirt and this man, so much stronger than I was, moving over me. Moving in me.

"I had thought I was so clever, that I could achieve so much. That the world was a big waiting beautiful place of adventure. But I was not a clever girl. I was not anything special at all. I was nothing more than the basest thing, an animal. Reduced to nothing more than the swine and cows that crowded the barn around us. I had been brought low.

"He left me there a while, I don't know how long. Long enough for me to understand. And I did. I understood in the dirt and straw and manure that *he* didn't make me that at all. *I* had entered this man's home and walked around with bare legs and tight shirts. *I* had paraded temptation before him every day for months. And he was only a man. Men can only ever be what they are. I *forced* him into adultery, into grave sin, and by my vanity, by my pride, *I* condemned us both."

Her words. My naked flesh. This too-tight room.

"I . . . could not face my parents in my shame," she says. "So I returned to Madison. I would not go home until I was the devout girl my mother had always wanted me to be. And now I understood why. Why she had always been right. She had been protecting me.

"I changed my major to Religious Studies, and I volunteered at St. Paul's Chapel at the school. When I met your father . . ." She falters for a moment, clutches her scapular tight in her graceful fingers. "I was so tarnished by shame, marred and broken by the sin of what I had done. I was not the unadulterated virgin he deserved, that any man would. But somehow, he wanted me anyway. I couldn't understand it. But what I learned is that if we choose Christ, He is with us, and I knew Christ again. I was pious and penitent, and because of that, despite all my sins, I found a good man, one who is far too good for me. I still sometimes . . ." There are tears in her eyes now. She does nothing to stop them.

"Here is what you have to understand, Sophie, what you must see. It is perhaps my greatest sin. You and Noah . . . you came out so perfect. So *beautiful*. Since the day God delivered you to me. I knew when you arrived that there would be consequences, because I was so enchanted by your beauty, both of you. I had been a vain girl, and now had become a vain mother. I should always have known there would be a consequence for that, just as there had been before. I let myself forget the sin I carried.

"Noah was so difficult, Sophie. And you don't know what he's—" She shakes her head. "But it was my fault. My sin brought that into our house. *I* did it to us by my vanity. You can't ever let yourself believe your beauty is anything but a sin." She reaches up now and swipes the tears from her eyes. "Womanhood is a burden. We must know our great responsibility, or it will be taught to us, and not gently. It is our duty as women to cover ourselves and hide these bodies so that we don't tempt others to sin, or fall into vanity or lust ourselves. Not for flesh, not for knowledge or, like a stupid young girl, the *world beyond*. God gave us all burdens. And this is yours."

She takes another breath without looking at me and picks up a dress.

"Here," she says, wiping the last of the tears away with the back of her hand. She returns, in a terrifying instant, to the woman I know, fortifying herself behind her piety.

"Try the blue."

The iPad volume turns back up as we leave. There are more reported deaths in the Northeast from the flu, and now it has spread to the Midwest.

There is at least one confirmed case in our state.

The Music Room

I roll out of bed and get ready for church, slipping on one of my new dresses. My parents and I, with the rest of the parishioners, will break our fast with donuts in the gathering space after mass, the whole of the congregation milling about, asking each other the same questions as any other week, repeating the same condolences for sick loved ones or the recently departed. I will be allowed the sugar-free ones. The food will sit in our stomachs with His body and blood, churning, decomposing together.

Monsignor West preaches from behind the podium over the bowed, reverent heads of the congregation. Parishioners show varying degrees of attentiveness. One man won't stop rubbing his nose every time Monsignor uses the word "adultery." Some of the children sit coloring biblical coloring books, but most are not allowed this small kindness and stand tight-lipped in their dress clothes and dress shoes, thinking about all that's to come in their Sundays and all that they are not at present doing.

Noah and I were five years old when our parents first told us that God, Jesus, demons, and the Devil are always watching, that they all know our every thought. That the Devil sits beside us at all times, breathing hot breath onto our necks, into our ears. Snaking insidious ideas into our minds. To Catholics, thoughts are sins as much as actions are, and our thoughts do not belong to us alone. We are never safe from the eyes of God, from any of them. They hear it all, see everything. Maybe the children think of that. Maybe they think of the donuts.

Before us hangs Jesus.

Other Christians revere a whole and healthy Christ, a living or resurrected one. But Catholics worship the crucified. In youth choir we sing a song from His perspective in which we can count each of our ribs, blood oozing and crusted on our hands, on our face and in our eyes from the crown of thorns, dripping down from our nailed-in feet, falling to the earth. We sing another song of how He carried his own cross to the site, the thorn crown already fixed upon his head. Catholics are no strangers to darkness and violence. We fill our churches with it and worship it every day. Christ died brutally for us because we are full of sin, because we *are* sin. God gave us Paradise, and we proved that we didn't deserve it, so He took it away. We spend our days repenting so we may one day finally, *maybe* know the light again. We humble ourselves to one day deserve Him, and the kingdom He built for us.

Burned benzoin resin, beeswax, pew wood, old carpet must. The otherworldly tones surrounding us, suffusing the air and the floor with their vibrations. High pipes built into the very foundation of the church, climbing its walls, up toward the stained glass through which the light reaches us, the hollow fixed spine of the building my father designed. No sound in this world as utterly beautiful and terrifying as an organ dirge and choir echoing through a Catholic church.

Next to me, my mother and father stand, eyes downcast, hands resting on the pew in front of them, inches from each other's, but not touching.

In our home are old photos of my father and mother. I can see that he might have been somewhat handsome, once, when he was not so hardened, not so adult. And she had been an English major. I can hardly imagine it. No books live in our house besides a few coffee table books on architecture and the Bible in each room. But in her head must be hundreds of stories, hundreds of ideas she never lets free. I wonder if they are still there, sustaining her, or if she has buried them someplace forgotten and deep.

Monsignor says something about the flu and something else about Corinthians.

I think of Rachel Miller and that boy behind the school, the closeness, the casual intimacy. I think of my parents and how I have not seen them touch since Noah left. I think of my mother in a cow stall. I cannot think of it. Her story. What happened to her.

Itwentonforalongtime.

I shiver. I am sick. No, I won't—

I am responsible for this distance, this life stuck inside with strangers who don't have to be strangers at all. I know if I forgive my parents, it will be there for me. Love, family. But it is too much. I don't want to, I *can't* examine it. I cannot see my mother in this way, with compassion and love and desperate need. I cannot hold the truth of her past and the truth of my hate simultaneously. So I choose. For my brother. For me.

I have one friend in this life with whom I am intimately acquainted and who will never be taken from me, the same friend of every Catholic girl in this world.

The guilt, as always, is writhing in my gut.

Movement tugs at my field of vision. The son of a family we see every Sunday sits a few rows from where I sit with my parents. My age, or a little older. He is looking at me. I touch my face to see if I have something on it, but I don't find anything. I look back at him again, and he holds my eye this time. Does he know I'm different, that I don't belong here? That I have such sinful thoughts? Such hateful thoughts? It isn't until his father clears his throat that he returns his gaze to Monsignor West, and I am released.

We take our seats, and I try to sink further into myself. Maybe my parents are not the strangers. I am the foreign one, I am the one that came out wrong.

My eyes flash up to the sculpture of Christ, the crown on his head. Nails sunk deep in emaciated flesh. This carefully rendered starving bleeding moaning Lamb of God who died for our sins. For our salvation.

His palms are red with it.

Monday morning, the *crinkle, crunch,* the newspaper page flipping.

FLU STRAIN SHOWS SHOCKING NEW SYMPTOMS IN MIDWEST.

My father doesn't let me read the paper, says there's no reason for me to concern myself with current or world events. My parents striving always to prevent hysterics in their emotional daughter. I'm late for school.

I find myself feeling painfully conspicuous in the halls. I wear the same uniform I've been wearing all semester, the one I now know is too tight and too short, but the new ones don't come in for a week. I sit down under Sister Margaret's hard stare and listen to her preach about Revelation. The guilt is making itself known today. My mother's story. I can't think about it. I can't think about anything else.

In this body, I feel grotesque and exaggerated. A plaid-skirted imposter. Temptress. Sinner. Serpent. I am a danger, to others and myself. I don't want any of this. But even still . . .

I had felt it. A little thrill, the slightest taste of admiration for what I saw in the mirror. Vanity, Envy, Wrath. My mother's story. I am falling into darkness more every day, and I hate myself for it.

If all the aspects of being a chaste and virtuous Christian elude me, this one does not. I've never needed a scapular. Self-abasement comes easily.

I wait in the bathroom until the halls are clear to return to my reading place outside. Once the school is quiet, I set off. Mary watches me, Jesus watches me, Paul and Michael and Joseph. All the demons. Like always.

Halfway down the hall I pause.

There is a sound. A kind of mewling or the groan of an injured person. I backtrack and find it is coming from the music room.

The room is dark, and the door has been left slightly open, just enough so I can look in, but not enough to fully illuminate the space. I lean in, my head just beyond the opening, and my eyes slowly adjust.

On the edge of the platform, in the middle of the room, our makeshift stage for choral recitals, I see a girl's plaid-skirted backside. She leans over the platform, one foot on the floor and the other bent, slightly, at the knee as if she is reaching for something in front of her. The rest of what I see I can't make sense of. It's . . . none of it is quite right. I push the door open further, and it creaks.

I freeze.

Whatever is happening on the stage continues. This sound, this movement. She hasn't heard me.

And then . . . another form on the stage. Two tanned limbs on either side of the girl's body. Legs, both bent at the knee, ending in school-approved sneakers.

This fused-together four-legged creature in plaid, writhing before me. The sound I heard from the hall, a rhythmic panting.

My brain begins to make sense of what I'm witnessing, and a number of things become clear:

> *1. I am not supposed to be seeing this. Whatever these two girls are doing, and I am not totally sure of the mechanics of it yet, I should not be here.*

> *2. They should not be doing this here, or anywhere, but* especially *not in this place.*

And

> *3. Finally, most importantly, I should* not *feel* any *kind of thrill at witnessing something, standing in the room with it, that is so absolutely, categorically sinful.*

I can't move. I can't—

And then my legs work. They take me outside. I sit down, or collapse. I pull out my book. I try to make sense of what I've seen, try not to think of it and to just read, try to make sense of it again. Two girls, and they weren't just kissing. One of them with her legs spread, her skirt lifted to expose all of herself, and the other exploring, her hand finding the exposed girl's breast. Her mouth on the other girl, in that forbidden place. Both of them, *churning.*

And something down deep, lower than my gut.

Strange pulsing heat.

Something that feels, shockingly, terrifyingly . . . like *want.*

An announcement comes halfway through my next class. Someone has fallen ill at school, and the whole of the student body is released early. We are reminded to say our prayers and keep our hands clean. We are given no further information.

I step out the front doors into the light of early afternoon, girls streaming out around me, some whispering, words catching my ears only in fragments. *Fever. Spread. Here?* Out of the corner of my eye I spot Sister Margaret handing Sister Anna a large bundle of bloodred cloth. Sister Anna taking it quickly and stowing it under her arm. I duck my head before either can spot me. The air is tight and crackling the way it was the day Noah was taken. Again, or still. I don't know. Something isn't right. The tree line shivers in the wind. Everything charged, alive.

I walk myself home, yellowing leaves blowing around me. How did they change so fast?

Nothing is as it should be, everything is changing.

And I wonder if it is me.

HOW TO CLEAN A WOUND:

Wash hands thoroughly with soap and water.

Stop the bleeding. Apply gentle pressure.

Rinse under running water for five minutes.

Cleanse with soap and alcohol-free saline or water.

Remove debris from the skin with sterilized tweezers.

Apply topical antibiotic and sterile dressing.

The Flu

My mother's car is not in the driveway, and I let myself in with the key from under the mat. Inside, the house is as quiet as it is when we're all here together, but I am struck by the fact that without the *crinkle, sip* symphony, the silence is not so oppressive. It is almost comforting. Almost. I make myself a snack and sit down at the table, trying not to think about what I saw in the music room. Or my mother's story.

It's Monday. I glance at the clock. I have an hour. I clean my dish and am shouldering my backpack to head upstairs when I catch sight of something.

My father's newspaper from this morning. I hesitate only a moment before I drop my bag to the floor and open it.

September 23rd

The Centers for Disease Control and Prevention issued a warning this past Saturday in regard to a recent outbreak of a previously undocumented viral infection which appears to have originated from the outbreak of North American respiratory syndrome (NARS-CoV) in New England. The two strains were thought to have been unrelated, but experts now say the midwestern strain, classified as human parasyphilan virus (HPSV), may have mutated from the Northeastern NARS-CoV, although the late stage symptoms diverge drastically, raising alarms in the healthcare community and beyond.

"We knew NARS had a high propensity to jump species and mutate, but we didn't expect this. This thing is volatile and unpredictable. We need to take this seriously, and I am worried," Emily Robertson, Professor of Medicine at Columbia University, tweeted on Sunday. Robertson, and other healthcare professionals, urges Americans to wash their hands and remain vigilant in following WHO and CDC guidelines for prevention.

Over the last two weeks, thousands of infected individuals have been reported in Minneapolis, St. Louis and surrounding areas. Now sixteen cases have been confirmed in Wisconsin. Twelve deaths were reported in inner-city Milwaukee, all elderly members of a local retirement community, Verdant Pastures, the same retirement home known for its 2016 outbreak of trichomoniasis and chlamydia among residents.

Symptoms of HPSV include headache, high fever, nausea, irritability, increased appetite and, in new fatal cases, "manic or erratic" behavior in the final stages, along with a male-presenting red rash on the palms.

I set the paper down. The last two weeks? It's hard to believe I wouldn't have heard about this before now.

But I *have* heard about it, of course I have. It's just that it didn't seem like anything to worry about, and old people die from the flu all the time. But this feels different. It's here, near my family. Near Noah. Dust specks float in the kitchen around me. Jesus watches from his painting beside the refrigerator. The sun streaming in is too bright, too focused. This peace built on the memory of Noah's screams.

I fold the newspaper and place it exactly as it was on the counter. I run through the basic steps of breathwork as outlined by *Relaxation for Dummies* to focus my mind. The book caused some controversy in my house when I brought it home from the library as it veered dangerously close to meditation which is, naturally, sacrilege. But ultimately it was let slide, and I find myself returning to the breathing often.

Upstairs in my room, my mind is calmer, and I remember once again that I am in an empty house, a rare luxury. I flip through some pages, but nothing sticks. My brother lives in an environment not so different from a retirement home in size and shape. Sure, retirement homes are full of old people, and Sacred Hearts is a place where children's spirits are sent to die, but he is in equally close proximity to others as those old people would have been.

I return to Dante's *Inferno*. Again my mind works against me. I am back in the doorway of the music room. Watching the girls, the one so exposed, the other taking advantage of that exposure. That vulnerability. Tanned skin in a dark room. Her fingers on the other girl's breast.

A feeling I am not familiar with spreads through my abdomen, and my heart picks up its pace. And as soon as the question forms in my mind, I know it will not be worth the effort of a fight. Because once I allow myself to wonder what it would feel like, I know this with absolute certainty: I won't be able to let it go until I find out.

To know thyself is a virtue.

Dante is kind of a downer anyway.

I check again that my parents haven't pulled into the drive, and I shut the door. I lie down on my bed. I stand again. Jesus comes down off the wall. Stuffed animals spin around, Mary in her frame is turned to face the corner. Even without their eyes on me, I am still watched, always.

But my mother and the flu and the boy in the truck and the girls at school and my body and Noah's screams. It's too much, all too much, this anxiety.

This is just . . . a question.

I set my hand on my stomach, beneath my shirt. My skin is warm. I won't think about the consequences. Just for a moment, I won't think about anything. A question.

I slide my hand farther, over each of my ribs, hard and sharp in contrast to my stomach, up to the elastic of my bra.

I feel everything. My heart pumping blood, my lungs drawing air.

I let my hand travel upward, keeping the thin fabric of my bra between my palm and my breast. My chest rises and falls beneath it. I move gently at first, lightly, my other hand gripping the blanket beneath me. I feel everything there is to feel in these new additions to my body.

My touch grows firmer. More confident. A warmth spreads through me, and my body begins to respond in places I am not touching. And I am on fire. A spreading flame that I ignited, that I control and don't. Even through the fabric of my bra, I can feel my nipples get harder, and I don't know if they're supposed to do that or if it is normal, or—

It feels good.

Alarmingly good. Eyes half open, I turn my head, continuing my exploration, this reprieve from . . . everything.

My brain half-registers the Bible and crucifix on my bedside table. But I—

A hard wind gusts against my window.

Hissing in my ear. Sulfur on my tongue.

Jesus isn't the only one watching.

I bolt upright, pinning my arms to my sides.

I am sweating. My chest heaves, and my heart is pounding. That dangerous, glorious, sinful warmth now replaced by what I know should have been there all along.

Guilt.

A forked hissing tongue.

Ourdutyaswomen. Temptation. We must not—

In the Beginning

"Noah, I'm scared."

He looked up, sitting on his bed with his worksheet in the low lamplight of his room. His room that I wasn't supposed to be in at night. His room that was locked each night after sundown so he wouldn't get up to any trouble. But I'd stolen a key, and when I was afraid, I went to him. I was always afraid. I was always seeking comfort from my brother.

"Nightmare?" he said.

"I think . . ." I didn't want to say it out loud. Didn't even want to think it. But, "Demons," I whispered, "in my room." I strained to speak quietly, as we always had to at night. But my breaths were coming fast, uneven.

Noah looked at me calmly, even a little sad. "I told you, Soph, they're not real," he said.

I sat down across from him, still shaking, and he looked at me, face open, laid entirely bare for me and me alone. I did the same for him, showed him my fear. It was how we always shared with each other, how we read things that weren't said. Only for each other, and no one else.

I whispered, "The wind, it was so strong—there was lightning, and the wind came inside, and I think it brought—"

"You had your window open?" His mouth tilted up at the corner.

We weren't supposed to open our windows at night, for fear of what could get in. For what watched young susceptible girls, what waited to tempt them. But I had done it.

"Why?" he asked.

Because I wanted to know. Because Noah wasn't afraid to be curious.

Because I wanted to be like him, and I didn't want to be like me. Because . . .

The night wind. I don't know. I just wanted to feel it. Just once.

"I'm serious," I said. "I think something . . . *called* to me."

"It didn't, I promise."

"How can you promise that?"

"Because demons aren't real."

"Yes, they are."

"Something that can hear all our thoughts, all the time? That waits for us to think something bad and then climbs inside us to use our bodies? Or make us sin?"

"Shh," I said. "You shouldn't say that. You know what will happen."

The thing about demons and the Devil was that the more you thought or spoke about them, the more you drew them to you, the more you opened yourself up to their power and control. Invited them.

Noah didn't believe the things we were taught, and I would never understand it, even if I so desperately wanted to. I wasn't like him, I couldn't ignore what they told us every day, the images stained in glass and etched into every page of every book. Hellfire, skin burning and bubbling in boils and blisters, melting from our body every second for eternity. Creatures with long jagged teeth and tongues, wide eyes, and horns doing unimaginable things. Clawing or pecking out our eyes, tongues, fingers, and worse. Taking what they wanted from us.

"Noah," I said. "The wind got scary. Do you hear it? What if a demon did come in through the window? What if one came in and I got possessed and I did something terrible? What if I tried to hurt you?" I swiped tears from my face. Tried not to feel the cold, lingering touch of it on my skin. The sinful wind I invited in, that I wanted to feel until it came. I closed my eyes tight against the whispers, the hiss. "I smelled sulfur!"

"Sophie, you would never ever hurt me. And it's a storm. Lightning smells like sulfur."

I pulled my arms in tight across my chest, tears falling to his bed.

Noah said, "It's just a storm. See?" He put one hand on my arm and pointed up with the other. "Just storm wind and lightning." It took me a moment to hear the rain on the roof. But he was right.

It was just a storm. After a moment he said, "Do you remember the ants?"

I shook my head.

"When we were little kids, you were really afraid to step in the grass. Remember? Mom and Dad thought it was because you were afraid of the ants and bugs touching you. You always yelled, *No, ants!* But it wasn't. You were afraid of stepping on them because you didn't want to hurt them. And it's impossible to walk through grass without stepping on something."

I looked up at him.

"You wouldn't hurt anyone," he said. "You wouldn't even step on a bug."

I sniffled, and the rain poured above us.

Noah watched me, then when he knew I was okay, he said, "Rule breaker." That smirk was back, and I could see the teasing in his face and also the pride. He was impressed. I sniffled, and I couldn't help it. I smiled a little too. I was pleased to have impressed him. He was everything.

"What are you working on?" I said.

"This science project. There's a contest, and the winner gets to go to the Dells." He shrugged. "Maybe this could be our way in."

"Think Mom and Dad will ever take us?" I asked.

He didn't say anything to that. We both knew the answer.

"Can I see the brochure again?" I asked.

Noah nodded and stood, bent down to reach for the secret compartment beneath the bed, and then paused.

"Turn around," he said.

"What?"

"Turn around."

"Why?"

"Just do it."

I didn't understand. We never kept anything from each other. What could he not want me to see? It hurt my feelings. But I closed my eyes.

I heard Noah reach beneath the bed, and that sulfur smell returned, the room growing cold. Did I close my window when I came in here? I thought I had, but now . . .

I shivered. I could feel the cold tendril of a breeze snaking down my arm, still. Could feel it whispering.

Noah rustled through papers. I wanted to open my eyes, but—

Bang!

I jumped, turned. Noah's bedroom door was thrown open. Lightning flashed in the sky, casting light over the figure in the doorway.

Our father.

Whoosh! I turned. Noah spilled and scattered the contents of what had been hidden in the under-bed compartment. Papers slid out in every direction beneath him.

There was a magazine on top of the pile. One I didn't recognize. Noah was shaking. I'd never—

Thunder boomed, cracked through the whole of the house. I turned back to the door, to where our mother now stood, crying out—I thought at the storm, but . . . no.

Her eyes were fixed on the floor. On the magazine.

Our parents in his room because I had snuck in. Because I had opened my window, and I had been afraid.

Noah looked up at me from the floor, an expression on his face I had never seen.

Pleading. Terrified, embarrassed, devastated. Vulnerable, angry.

Afraid.

For once, Noah was *afraid.*

And it was all my fault.

At our designated weekly time, I pick up the phone and call my brother.

I endure the hold music, harp plucking beneath a saccharine female voice.

Thank you for calling Sacred Hearts, a spiritual sanctuary for families afflicted with challenged children and teens. Please hold. A caretaker will be with you shortly. Thank you, and may God's love shine on you always.

"Sacred Hearts. How may I help you?"

I exhale. Nurse Dana is the only one who works in this place who is not an actual vulture. "Hey, it's Sophie. Is Noah there?"

"Hey, Sophie. Yeah, he is. But he's on probation, so you've gotta keep it short."

A shuffling and a beep, and after a moment,

"Well, well, who could it be?" Noah's voice, buoyant and teasing.

While I have turned to hatred these last years, he has found humor, found better ways to survive. Though with all his pranks, it still gets him in trouble.

"Noah," I breathe, "it's so good to hear you."

I hear him pause, cut himself off before his next joking line. "What happened?"

"Mom and I had a mother-daughter day," I say.

"Whoa. What was that like?"

I clear my throat. "How are you?" I ask. "What'd you do this week?" I can't talk about it. Can't think about it. I'm not even sure he'd believe me if I told him anyway.

"My probation? I just played a little prank on Nurse Dolores."

"Do I want to know?"

"You probably wouldn't approve, if that's what you're asking."

"Well . . . she always deserves it."

"She really does."

"What's the penance?"

"Oh just about two thousand Hail Marys and six hundred Our Fathers. Supervised."

"Worth it?"

"Definitely. And they're still letting me run."

Noah's one nonreligious pastime he is allowed at Sacred Hearts is physical exercise, and he loves it. He's always been fast, but now that it's nearly all he's allowed to do, he has gotten very good. For a while they suspended him from it because he tried to run away from the facility too many times. But he got so depressed without it that he wouldn't eat, so they eventually broke and let him start it up again.

"I'm guessing we don't have time for a book this week," I say.

"No, maybe not. She said I only had a few minutes."

Each of the illicit books I check out and read, I relay the stories to Noah through the phone. The same way he used to relay everything to me that he learned at his math camp. I try to remember as many details of the books as I can, try to paint an exciting picture in our limited time. Next time I'll make sure it's a good one.

"Miss you, Soph," he says. Some of the pain in me softens. "Hey, I'm down to five-thirty," he says. He means his mile running time.

I smile. "That's amazing! How did it feel?"

"Like heaven." It's a joke he makes a lot. He doesn't believe in Heaven. Or mostly he doesn't believe that the people we are taught will make it there will.

"Wanna hear something crazy?" I ask.

"Always."

"I heard Sister Josephine fainted during choral rehearsal and fell on Mr. and Mrs. Henricks."

"Remember that time Mrs. Campbell's hair caught on fire taking eucharist?"

I laugh. "Could never forget it."

A moment of companionable peaceful silence. When we're together, we never feel the need to talk too much. Now, with such limited time and with it only over the phone . . .

"Things have felt different lately," I say. "Do you feel it?"

A pause. Heartbeats. A bird tittering outside my window.

"Yeah. Things are definitely weird. I was actually going to ask you a favor," he says.

"What?"

Two birds, again, singing in the branch of the tree.

"This flu. Do you know anything? Have Mom or Dad said anything about it?"

"You know they don't tell me anything. But, um, I read Dad's paper today. I know it's bad in the Northeast, and I know they've got some cases here now. I don't know anything else."

"Sophie, I don't think it's just *some* cases. I think something big is happening."

"Why do you say that?"

"Little things Nurse Dana says, the way everyone's been acting. There's a new guy in here, Tyler. He made some comments on the first day. Said some towns are all sick people now, that those hospitals are filling up and they even have to turn people away. I think this is worse than they're telling us."

"Who, Mom and Dad?"

"Mom, Dad, Foreston, the congregation, Sacred Hearts. They don't believe in things like this, or they think they're safe from it. But I don't know, Soph. I just . . . I think we need to find out. I'm telling you, something's up. I just have this feeling we need to pay attention."

"So what can I do?"

He laughs. "What do you mean? Use the computers at school, or the one at home, and get more information for us or steal Dad's newspaper."

"Either way we're at the mercy of the adults."

"We don't have to be."

"Noah."

"Sophie, I can't do anything from in here, and definitely not while I'm on this probation."

I am quiet, that anxiety spreading. The wind against the window.

I'm ashamed, but it's the truth. "I'm afraid."

"Of getting caught?"

"No. I'm—I've been . . . slipping. I don't know. I'm just . . . scared."

He's quiet for a moment. "You sound like them." His voice is soft, but the accusation in it hits me like it's meant to.

"Well what if they're right?" I say. "You've always dismissed it, but I can feel it here, like something's stalking me. I don't—"

"So you think *I* was slipping? You think I was slipping and I got possessed?"

"No, I don't think that."

"Don't you?"

"No," I say. "But this—I feel something. The darkness, this wind, there's—"

"Wind? You sound crazy."

Again, that pang of hurt. We don't do this. We don't fight.

"You know I'm not," I say. "And you're being mean."

"Well I can't do anything, but you can and you won't because you're too afraid."

"Of course I'm afraid. I'm alone here, with Mom and Dad and every major consequence, every *eternal* consequence, for my every action, and I am failing at every step of the way to be anything good, and I am terrified that I'm going to damn us all, that—"

"So, what, you're blaming me for being gone? For leaving you alone with them?"

"What? No, Noah, I'm blaming *me*. I sinned, and I can't stop sinning, and I don't know what's wrong with me." I am crying now. Shaking. The wind is blowing outside again, this wind, pushing at the walls, clawing them. I am clinging to this phone like a lifeline.

"Sophie, you know that's insane—"

"I'm not crazy!" My voice is loud and rings out for a moment. Neither of us says anything. Then, he says,

"I know. You're right. I know, I'm sorry."

"I'm sorry too. I'm so sorry. I miss you so much."

"I miss you too."

"And . . . I know I'm afraid all the time. I'm trying. I—I don't know how anyone deals with this fear. How anyone can stand it?"

"I don't know."

No. He doesn't know, because he doesn't feel it. Because he is so much stronger than I am. Because he doesn't believe.

"Noah, are they listening?" I ask, after a moment.

"I don't think so."

"Today, at school, there were these girls, they were . . . I think they were . . . touching each other." My voice is soft and raw as I say it, as I pose the question I can't actually pose.

Silence, for a moment. Then,

"They were *what*?" he asks. Tension in his voice, a warning. My heart pounding.

"That magazine, that night. We never . . . Do you still—?" I don't know why I ask, don't know why I need to know, why it's taken me so long. Because it's the only secret between us? Because I just want to understand?

"I don't want to talk about that night," he says. And he means it. He doesn't want to talk, and I know I've messed up by asking. I know I shouldn't keep going, but—

"Noah—"

"Time's up, Noah. You gotta head back to prayers. I'll give you one more minute."

"Please, Sophie," Noah says, none of the teasing there now. "Just do that thing for me, okay? Get us some information. I'm telling you, it's been . . ."

"Yeah, okay, I will," I say. "Noah, I love you."

But the line is disconnected.

My mother, father, Noah, me. The magazine and the night that changed everything.

Our mother called the priest. Our father gripped Noah harder than he'd ever taken hold of anything. He shook him, yelled inches from his face, spit flying. Noah cried. My brother was crying.

Thunder, sulfur, wind, tears.

Noah's tears. Mine.

The priest came with altar boys, bigger and older than Noah, stronger than him. Our father threw Noah over, passed him to them like he was glad to be done with him, like he couldn't stand to touch him. Like Noah wasn't even a person at all.

"This isn't your home," our father said. "You're not welcome here, not like this."

I ran for Noah. I fought against the altar boys and even the priest, yelled and fought and pleaded.

Please! No! What are you doing? Noah!

Our father held me back. Held me back while they dragged Noah through our living room. Kicking, crying, begging forgiveness. Screaming.

I'm sorry! I'm sorry, I repent, I won't—

Past the dining table, out into the stormy night. My brother, the rain soaking his pajamas.

His eyes, terror in them. For the first time in his life, afraid. I screamed, fought against our father. His fingers dug in tight to my skin, bruising me.

Noah, crying, reaching for me. The wind battering the house. Thunder booming, nearly rattling the windows.

Sophie!

Noah's eyes on mine, Noah calling my name.

Both of us screaming, fighting to reach each other. Both of us ripped apart.

Our mother standing there, watching it all. Silent tears streaming down her face.

She had called them. She had done this.

And I knew. Even through my sobs and my screams and the terror that was being ripped in two.

I knew in that moment looking at her, as the front door slammed and I heard the van doors shut outside, taking my other half from me.

Even if it was deepest sin. Even if I would burn for it for all time,

I *hated*.

I hated my mother's tears more than anything. She didn't deserve them.

I knew in that moment that I would hate her forever.

In her hand something glossy. The magazine from Noah's room.

The magazine from Noah's room. With two shirtless boys kissing.

The Photograph

By Friday, three students are out sick, and two more leave during the day with fevers and headaches. I think of Noah, and what he asked me to do. But in my free periods, Sister Anna supervises the computers, and there is no way to get around her.

It's raining, hard, dark sky looming over us. I find a quiet corner in the cafeteria to finish my book. I still wear my too-small uniform and drape a sweater over my legs so that no one can see up my skirt. I wonder if Noah will notice the change in me, whenever I see him next. It fills me with shame again that my father noticed. An unclean, sick feeling.

Because some students are missing from my class, Sister Anna asks us to move forward. In front of me are Sarah and Rachel plus two of their friends. Sister Anna breaks out into a coughing fit as she begins to lecture, and when it doesn't cease, she steps out to the hall, the door closing behind her. The moment she is gone, the girls converge on Rachel's phone, whispering. Sarah's jaw drops.

On the screen is a picture, taken from the front, of a boy's torso. Like the ones on the magazine cover. He is covered in a sheen of sweat or maybe oil. I can't see his face, just the region between his shoulders and hips. His shoulders wide, hard muscle on strong bone. The curve of that muscle rippling through his arms, over his chest, and on his abdomen makes my own stomach tighten. I can't even see him up close, but I still feel that pulsing warmth spread through me, so quickly it comes and takes root. It's intoxicating. Dangerous. And yet—

"He *sent* this to you?" one of them whispers.

"Yeah, and this is like the tamest one. You won't even believe—here, I wasn't going to show anyone, but I can't not. It's just too much. But you absolutely *cannot* tell!" She pulls up another photo, one that is zoomed in on something else. Before I can get a good view of it, she looks up and sees me standing next to them. She hides the screen against her chest.

"Um, excuse me. This is private."

"Oh, sorry. I was just . . . stretching," I say.

The girls laugh and whisper as I sink into my chair, Sarah glances back at me and stage-whispers, *"She's so weird!"*

Sister Anna returns, her eyes watering and sniffling against a hand-kerchief. "Now," she says, "let's begin."

I don't listen to her lecture.

I am preoccupied—Noah, the girls in the music room, the flu.

The music room girls. I couldn't see their faces, couldn't even really make out the exact color of their hair, and half the school is blond anyway. They could be anyone in here. The sky outside the window is so dark. It feels important, somehow. I don't know. I'm restless. Noah's magazine has always been an open question, the one secret between us, even now.

Before I think better of it, I say, "Sister Anna?"

Sister Anna looks up. All the girls turn to face me.

I hesitate, now with everyone's attention.

"I have a question," I say.

Sister Anna raises her brows.

"It's about, um . . . homosexuals."

The girls erupt. Laugh and lean into each other, whisper. *"Is she se-rious?"*

Sister Anna's face goes white, whiter than usual. That look, almost like . . .

Then it's gone. Why would *fear* show there anyway?

"Settle down, girls. Settle," she says. "Sophie, we're talking about Job, you can't possibly—"

"I just don't understand."

She sighs. "What don't you understand?"

"Well, like in Sodom. Why did they do that? Why would men choose men?"

Again the girls laugh, and Sister Anna regards me for a moment.

Then she says, "Why does anyone sin? They allowed the Devil in, bent to temptation."

"But why were they tempted? How would the Devil benefit from that?"

"Because by choosing perversion, they turned their backs on God and earned a place in Hell."

"But if men who choose men, or women who choose women, know that it will earn them a place in Hell, if they know it will break their relationship with God, what do they get out of it? Why do they choose it?"

"Because they are wicked."

"But that doesn't—"

"We're not discussing this," Sister Anna says. Her tone is harsh, the words swift. Weighty. Something in the way she fidgets with the chalk in her hand.

I don't understand. I still don't understand. But then I think of the two girls in the music room and the feeling that ran through me. It was dangerous and bad, and I knew it. But a part of me . . .

I shake my head. Maybe I'm not any closer, or maybe I understand it more than I want to. But what I do know is that Sister Anna is wrong on one point. And it's such a vital point, such a profound incorrectness that as I sit here in this classroom, the wind scraping against the windows, I feel something maybe. Just slightly. A shift within me.

Noah is the farthest thing from wicked.

Thunder booms outside, and rain pummels the windows. The lights flicker off, then on, and I stare out into the dark. The dark in the daylight. The woods.

The whisper, and the wind.

HOW TO DEVELOP A
PHOTOGRAPHIC MEMORY,
BY THE METHOD OF *LOCI*
(CICERO'S MIND PALACE):

Construct your mind palace. Preferably a
familiar building, one you know inside and
out.

Fill it with characters. Obscene, grotesque,
funny, tragic. Memorable. Attach what you're
trying to remember to them.

Take a walk through it.

Practice often. Memory improves with repetition.

The Library

My mother drives me to the library after school. The rain comes down even harder now, that same crackling electric feeling underlying everything, suffusing the air. It's so dark it almost feels like night. I hold my bookbag close to my chest and run through the downpour to the doors. My mother always brought Noah and me to the library when we were kids. But after he left and I refused to interact with her the way I once did, she started waiting outside while I found everything on our list.

Inside, I pause. This warm place. This welcoming, peaceful, sacred place. When I am here, nothing beyond these walls matters. This place more home than home.

I shake the water off and dry my shoes as much as possible. This, a house I don't want to profane. The rows of wooden tables and shelves under the yellow lights, the rain sliding down the glass windows, the smell of old dusty books and new plastic-covered ones. There is nothing complicated here. Just stories, just acceptance, just life.

I glance over at the main desk where Mrs. Parson usually sits, but it's empty. I'll find her tagging or shelving somewhere in the stacks.

One time, in the year after Noah left, I was here, and the loneliness had been particularly crushing that week, the nuns particularly cruel, and I'd always liked the library, always felt safe here. And I didn't mean to. But as I was reaching for a book, I just broke down crying, right in the children's section. I sat on the floor, and I cried and cried into my hands.

"It must have been a really awful book," a woman said.

I looked up, sure I was going to get in trouble. But the woman standing in front of me was like an angel. She had dark skin and hair and eyes, and I had never seen a face so symmetrical, so lovely and perfect. It was like she wasn't real. And she was so open, kind, smiling in a bright pink sweater. I realized she'd said something to me.

"What book?" I sniffed, wiping my eyes with the backs of my hands.

"Whatever made you cry like that."

For a moment, I sat there, uncomprehending. And then I understood. And . . .

I laughed. I had forgotten what it felt like to laugh.

"That's better," she said. The way she said it, the way she knelt down beside me and took in my face. It was like she really cared about me. And I knew she couldn't because she didn't even know me. "So if this wasn't a book-related tragedy, what kind was it?" she said.

I shrugged, sniffed again.

"Let me guess. Kids at school?"

"The nuns."

"Ahh, I see."

And I don't know why I said it because I didn't know her at all, but, "I miss my brother."

"Did something happen to him?"

"He doesn't live with us anymore."

She watched me for a moment and then nodded her head.

"You seem like a smart girl," she said. "Are you picking out books for yourself?"

I nodded. She looked around the children's books, furrowed her brow. "Is reading easy for you?" I nodded again, quickly. She smiled. "I think I may have just the thing."

She stepped away and came back with a book in her hand. "I'm Mrs. Parson, by the way. I'm the new librarian. And you are?"

"Sophie."

"Nice to meet you, Sophie. Have you read this one by any chance?" She held it out to me. *A Wrinkle in Time*. I shook my head, no.

"I think you might like it."

"I'm not allowed. I can only get the books on my list," I said.

She bent down and studied me again, seemed to read everything about me in that one look. I saw it. Understanding. She put out her hand, and I took it. She helped me up to stand.

Mrs. Parson winked. "I won't tell if you won't."

I grab the mercifully dry books and slip them into the return slot at the front desk. A shiver runs through me, in my wet clothes, and I begin my walk through the aisles. Sliding my fingers over the books and their little tabs. I love the way they feel, slick plastic, dimpled leather, crinkling paper. I take in a long, deep breath.

There are too many books in the world, so many that it would take countless lifetimes to read them all. So I've devised a system. And there is only one rule: I choose at random, and no matter what I am delivered, I can't put it back until I've read it cover to cover.

I close my eyes and reach out my hand. I slowly move down the aisle until the moment feels right. When it does, I stop and let my fingers move closer to the shelf. I pause, enjoying the moment, and extend them toward the nearest spine. Time is suspended. All my worries momentarily gone. I am about to meet a new friend, explore a new world, become a new me, if only for a short time.

My fingertips brush up against it.

"Excuse me. I, uh, hate to be the bearer of bad news, but reading generally requires keeping one's eyes *open*. Unless, of course, you're looking for the braille books. If you are, you're in the wrong section."

I spin around.

Ben.

From the truck at school. From the map at the mall. And now he's standing here. In the library, no screen between us.

"It's you," he says. Then his face colors, as if . . . embarrassed? He straightens and says, "You, uh, you go to St. Mary's."

My brain stutters. My mouth, strangely, says, "Did the uniform tell you?" It's an absurdly childish response, and I am not sure why I am suddenly annoyed. He is so beautiful I can barely breathe.

I blink, shake my head. Where did that thought—?

"Uh, no, but now that you mention your uniform, do you want a towel or something?"

His eyes travel from my wet hair down to my collared shirt and stick there momentarily. He clears his throat and looks away. And I am now, suddenly, acutely aware that my shirt is soaked through, completely. My hair, pulled to one side and dripping down, is only making the situation worse. I am wearing an old bra, and it doesn't cover the tops of my breasts, which shouldn't matter except that the white fabric of my shirt now clings to my skin there. Everything is visible. My face grows hot. I pick up my bag and hold it in front of myself as a shield.

"No. Thank you." I glance around and wait for him to leave.

"So, uh, you were at the mall too, right? It was you I saw there?"

"Oh. I—no. Probably someone else." I don't know why I say it.

"Oh. Huh. Okay then, um, so how can I help you?"

"Help me with what?"

"With finding books. This is a library."

I glare at him. "I know this is a library. What are you—where's Mrs. Parson?"

The boy leans against the shelf and crosses his arms. His eyes are as fascinating as they were before. His skin just as tan and glowing. I am like some kind of cave creature next to him. This boy who has freedom and fun and friends. And there is the other thing about him, perhaps the worst thing, painful to stand in the presence of. Somehow, he seems to just radiate *goodness*. I am certain of it, watching him. I am certain that for every moral deficiency in me, there is something bright and shining in him. And I think I hate him for it.

"She's not feeling well," he says, a shadow passing over his face. He quickly adds, "But it's nothing, I don't think. I think she's just tired. Or like, at worst, a cold."

"Oh. I hope she gets better."

He shrugs. "Yeah. Thanks. She will." There's a lot in those words, and I want to ask more, but I can tell he doesn't want to talk about it.

As he shrugs, the sleeve of his T-shirt lifts, and I see there's a tattoo on his upper arm. I can't make out what it is. I can't imagine getting a tattoo. I wonder what could matter so much to him that he would get it permanently etched on his body. His arm, his muscle, there beneath the skin. I swallow.

"So why haven't I seen you here before, if you're here all the time?" I say.

He squints, smiles again. I think that maybe he is laughing at me. "Didn't we just see each other twice last week?" He knows it was me at the mall. I have no idea why I lied about it. I'm acting insane.

"I usually have practice today," he says, "and Mom only needs help early in the week."

"Mrs. Parson is your mother?"

"Yeah. She's the best."

Now that I think about it, he looks just like her, and both of them with that same easygoing *goodness*. But this annoys me too. Mrs. Parson is one of the few kind adults in this world, maybe the only one. And now I have to share her with this boy? He is like a bobcat or a lynx, all confidence and pride. His eyes try to hold mine, but I don't want to look at his eyes. Not with the feeling they bring. I don't want to look at his eyes or his tattoo. Or his forearms. Or his hands, or chest. I want my heart to resume its normal pace.

"But you're not a librarian," I say.

"No, but I know this place as well as a librarian, and I can help you find whatever it is you're looking for."

The way he says that last part makes me think he is talking about something other than books, and I want and don't want to examine it. Something stirs inside me that is not hatred and not fear or guilt, that sets my insides alight. I shove it down.

"I'm fine. Thank you. I have my own system." I turn and walk away. My heart *pounding*. I shake my head to clear it.

"Yeah, I noticed," he says. He walks with me. "I'm Ben, by the way." He holds his hand out. I look at it for a moment, then reluctantly give him mine . . . because it's polite. We stop walking.

Our hands touch. His is warm and strong, so much larger than mine. Callused. Whose hands have I ever actually touched? My parents' during prayer, my brother's when we were younger, adults with whom I've had to shake hands at mass. *Peacebewithyou.*

But there is nothing formal or familial about his handshake. I look up at his face, let myself for a moment. A sharp nose and full lips. His eyes are . . . but they are nothing compared to his mouth. What is wrong with me? I am about to say something. What is it? I don't want to let go of his hand. I want to slide mine up his arm, over his shoulders, to his neck, to touch more of his skin. I want—

Ourdutyaswomen. Temptation. Sin.

I pull my hand away. He looks down at me, failing to suppress his smile.

He clears his throat again. "And, your name is . . . ?"

I take an irritated breath and glance around again. The library is empty, other than the two of us. I'm not sure if it is a good or a bad thing. "Sophie," I say, refusing to meet his eyes.

"Sophie."

A chill again, at my name on his tongue, in his voice. This time I think it has nothing to do with the wet clothes.

"It's nice to meet you," he says. "I guess I'll let you get back to your search."

Finally.

He turns and walks away, out of my view. I check again to see if he is really gone. Not that I care where he is, as long as it isn't here. I want to be alone. I am here for new books, not for him. Not for the librarian's son who probably doesn't really even know anything about books and just says he does. Who drives around with girls from my school and probably kisses them all the time. At this unwelcome thought, I am even more agitated.

Slowly, I start back down the aisle with my hand in front of me.

I am about to stop when I feel it arrive at a book sticking out farther from the shelf than all its neighbors. I open my eyes.

Standing in front of me is Ben, holding the other end of the book in his hand. He doesn't try to hide his smile now.

"It's my favorite in the section. I think you might like it."

I scowl at him. I hate that I'm acting like such a child, but this is my Friday library visit, the one happy uncomplicated thing, and he is complicating it. I have to take this book now, whatever it is. Those are the rules, even though he interfered with my system. Who is this guy, anyway, to ruin this? "How do you know what I like?" I say.

"I've seen you reading when I drive by the school. You read the same kinds of books I do. A couple weeks ago you read Ursula Le Guin, and before that, *Fahrenheit 451.*"

I don't know what to say to this.

"This one's good. I think it's more for girls, maybe, but I read it in like two days. And it's a whole series. This is actually book two, but the first one is kind of a downer. Still really good though."

"Well, thanks," I say. "I'm gonna go look for more books now." I turn and walk away, wondering if he is watching me leave.

I pick up the only two *For Dummies* volumes in stock that I haven't read. On my way to the circulation desk, I walk through nonfiction on an impulse and pick up, using my method, uninterrupted this time, a book about Cicero. I head toward the check-out desk, where Ben is waiting for me. I place my books down in front of him and look around the room, anywhere but at him. He seems to be intentionally taking forever to scan each book and place new stickers in them. There is no way he can be this slow by accident. I lift my head to say something.

Once my eyes are on his face again, my mind is totally blank. And then I am very aware that the table is the only thing that separates us.

That deep and steady pulse starts again south of my belly. The ever-present guilt, shame, fear.

But I don't care much about those just now.

He holds my eyes for a moment and then glances down at the book he is scanning. "*Auto Repair for Dummies.*" He brings his dark eyes back to mine. "What kind of car do you have?"

"I don't. I don't have a car." My voice sounds thin and breathy, foreign to my own ears. I can't look away. I bite my bottom lip. His eyes slide down to my mouth. I stop biting and close my mouth. He looks down at the next book, *Raising Chickens for Dummies*.

"Chickens?"

"No, no chickens." I've let the bag drop down to the table. After scanning the Cicero, his eyes make their way back up to mine, stopping for the briefest of instants on my shirt and the places it sticks to my skin. I can feel the line his gaze traces, from my stomach over my chest, up my neck, over my mouth, and back up to my own. The tingling heat it leaves in its wake. I shield my chest with the bag again.

He looks down and scans the book he picked out for me. This time he smiles and meets my eyes straight on. "You're going to read it," he says. "I really think you'll like it. I—"

"No, please don't." I put my hand on top of his, over the book, the one he pulled for me. He seems as surprised by my hand now as I am. I take it back and feel my face grow hot again. How stupid could I look? How stupid could I be? "I . . . haven't looked at it yet. Don't tell me."

His eyes travel back down to my mouth as I speak, then back up to mine. Holding them there, he nods slowly. He scans the rest of the books as if he is moving through honey, slow and deliberate. My breathing is difficult and quick, and the seconds feel long, stretched out, but in a way that is full of promise. He holds his hand out. I look at it and then back at him.

"The bag?" he says. "For your books."

I hand him the bag, but this time he doesn't look at my chest. He moves his eyes carefully away from mine and on to his task. When he is finished, he hands it back to me, heavier now. We stand there for a second. Suspended. Out of time. Then he asks, "Do you need anything else?"

"Oh." Right, I forgot. "Um, yes. I just need to use one of the computers, quickly." I turn. "I'll just—"

"They're down."

"What?"

"Well, this one is working, but the rest of them aren't. I think it's because of these storms."

"Oh."

"Do you . . . want me to look something up for you?"

"Well, actually, do you know anything about, um . . ." I feel stupid for asking, feel certain Noah is blowing something out of proportion, though I'm not sure why. "Do you know anything about this flu?"

"You mean NARS? Or like the mutations?"

"I . . . guess both?"

He stares at me as if I'm telling a joke. "Like you just want the latest updates, or . . . ?"

"You know what, actually it's fine, I don't need anything."

"No, here, I want to help," he says. I am staring at his mouth again. He asks, "How much do you know? I can try and pull some articles up or just fill you in myself."

"I just . . . I told someone I'd get them some information."

"Right. Well." He looks down at the computer screen and starts typing, "do you want to come around? I can show you, or you can read through."

I hesitate, and he seems to notice it. "Here," he says, and turns the desktop around to face me. "So there are a lot of articles. I don't know where you'd want to start. Do you want to know more about the Northeastern strain, or statistics? My mom says the CDC and WHO websites are good, but it's still kind of confusing. There's a lot of stuff about what the government is doing and the flu shot and these religious groups.

And the whole 'Sylvia' thing, but most people say that's fake even though some of the videos people have been sharing from some of the cities are wild. I think it's gotta be fake though."

My eyes race over the screen. All the articles, all the news reports. There's so much here. I don't understand half the things he's talking about.

"Has this been going on a long time?" I ask. "Are people . . . does everyone know about this?"

Again, that look like I am from another planet. "Yeah. For months. And this new mutation and the Sylvia rumors, that's been going on for weeks. That's why everyone's so crazy right now, the government and scientists and everyone said they'd be able to keep it isolated, around New York and Boston, but it's gotten to other cities. Nobody can fly there, and they quarantined that whole area. But now like Minneapolis and Detroit and Chicago are getting quarantined too. And then the Crusader people who've gained a wild amount of traction on TikTok of all places. It's . . . You don't know any of this? Really?"

I shake my head.

"How is that possible?"

I don't know. I don't know how. My mind is racing. Too many questions, too many thoughts. "Um, would you mind printing some things for me? Anything you can find, anything that's easy. Is the printer still working?"

"Yeah, or I could email a bunch of articles to you."

"No, I'll have no way to read them."

"Right. Um, are you Amish?"

"I don't know what that is. Could you just please print . . . anything?"

"Yeah," he says, staring at me, "of course."

He clicks something, and I hear the printer start up. I watch him move, as I try to parse out any of what he just said.

A horn honks outside in the rain.

My mother in the car.

Standing here before this boy. This boy with the lips and the eyes and my shirt soaked through, and—

"I have to go." I grab the bag from him. He starts to say something, but my mother honks the horn again. I step away.

Before I get to the door, I turn back. Ben is staring at me as though he has no idea what just happened, as though no girl has ever walked away from him before. Or maybe he is thinking how strange I am. Sophie the loner. Sophie the freak. Sophie who knows nothing.

"Tell your mom I hope she feels better," I say. "I really hope she feels better."

The wind picked up while I was inside, and the rain blows in all directions now. I jump in the car, soaked yet again.

My mother reads her pocket Bible. "What took you so long? I was about to come in there and get you."

She looks up, and her eyes go wide when she sees me.

"What's wrong? You look like you have a fever." She reaches out and touches my face. "Your skin is hot. Do you feel sick?" A brief look of panic in her eyes before she hides it. She is worried. She knows about all this, the flu.

Noah's right. Something is happening.

"I'm fine," I say. "Just a little tired."

After a moment, she nods and starts the car. I turn away from her and watch the library grow smaller out the window.

Maybe I am sick. Maybe that's why I keep feeling so strangely, why I am a magnet for sin and lustful feelings with this new body I didn't ask for. Can you tell when you've become possessed? Can you feel it? Are there warning signs, or hints along the way? Maybe this is all a test. Maybe every woman goes through this, and I am just doing a worse job than everyone else.

If it is a test, I am definitely failing.

HOW TO CARE FOR CHICKENS, THE BASICS:

Check water and food and clean/refill as needed.

Collect the eggs. Keep nest boxes fresh.

Clean the coop.

Give them roosting space and light for winter.

The Valley of Horses

A t night, I sit down on my bed and open my bag. I lay my books out in front of me and end with the one Ben chose. It's called *The Valley of Horses*. I lie down, holding it to my chest, and turn to face the wall.

I replay our conversation in my head. The flu. All I've learned is how much I don't know and that something's going on, something my parents are keeping from me.

Then there was the other part.

Ben. Ben and me.

Our words were innocent, normal. But it was the things we didn't say, the things I thought and the way he looked at me. The air around us that we somehow generated. All of it making me feel unclean and unworthy and ashamed and also something else entirely.

I wake Monday morning with *The Valley of Horses* open and my face pressed to one of its pages. I stayed up the last three nights reading it, and when I finished, I went back and reread my favorite scenes, my skin on fire. Jondalar teaching Ayla what their bodies can do together, what *they* can do together. And the way he makes her *feel*. He reveres her, worships her even. With his words and hands and ... I didn't know men could revere women like that. Women anticipate the needs of men, care for them, gift them with their virginity and childbearing and submission and accept the men's protection and guidance in exchange. I've never seen anything like this. Jondalar holding her needs even before his own. Her . . . pleasure.

My heart races thinking about it. About how much trouble I would be in if my mother found out. About how Ben read this book, how he gave it to me. About how I imagined so much more than I can even admit to myself now in the light of day.

And I know it's not real. All these books I read with these alternative lives and lifestyles, with relationships that don't play out the way they do in real life. They're fiction, and they don't reflect any kind of reality I've ever known. I understand that they're separate.

They're just . . . ideas. Hypothetical.

But this weekend, for three nights with a flashlight below the covers, I got to pretend. I got to live in this book and this world and not the one I am stuck in. And Ben gave that to me.

Breakfast passes as it usually does, though without the usual *crinkle* of the *sip, crinkle* symphony, as my father says he doesn't feel like reading the newspaper this morning. There's a tightness to my parents' shoulders, more than usual. My mother checks my forehead for fever.

"You're worried about the flu," I say.

My mother pulls back from me. "You look different," she says, scrutinizing.

"We should go get Noah." I avert my gaze from her, will her not to see me. "If people are getting sick. He's in tight quarters."

My father says, "The media's been blowing it out of proportion. He'll be fine."

"What media?"

He doesn't answer. My mother shoots him an angry look.

"Go get in the car. You'll be late for school."

More students are absent today. I realize at school that girls are talking about it, that they all know about this. I catch words here and there, *NARS, Sylvia, hospital.* It occurs to me that maybe I've been hearing these for a while, but I have been so checked out from what anyone at school says for so long that I just didn't pay attention.

I wait in the school library until Sister Anna has to use the restroom, and I sprint over to one of the computers. I do a quick search and click on an article that says **MIDWEST BRACES FOR NARS-COV SURGE.**

It says that due to rising case numbers in Chicago, Detroit, Minneapolis, Cincinnati, and Milwaukee, all midwestern cities should anticipate high numbers of infections.

I put *What is NARS-CoV* in the search bar, and just as I click enter, a throat is cleared behind me.

"School computers are for schoolwork only," Sister Anna says.

I turn around and look up at her.

But—

She's so close. Too close.

Leaning in so that I can feel her body heat through her robe. No one stands this close to me, ever. And she's . . .

Sister Anna is staring at me almost as though she wants something. Her eyes are glassy, and she coughs, once into her arm. Inches from me.

"Sorry, Sister Anna," I say, trying to lean back, away from her.

I turn the computer off and move to stand, but she's so close to me, I can barely shift without brushing up against her.

"Um, do you mind if I just—"

"You shouldn't be asking those questions," she says.

"I . . ."

The way she's looking at me . . . I don't know how to interpret it. I'm going to get in trouble for this. That's what is happening, I'm in trouble for researching this on the computer. For the questions I asked her in class.

"I'm sorry, I just—"

Sister Anna reaches out, and touches my cheek.

Sister Anna touches me.

I am motionless. Her breaths are loud and hot, and she looks like she is here and not here. Adults don't touch other people's faces. The nuns definitely don't.

Sister Anna touching my skin. "Shouldn't ask those questions in class," she says again, this time nearly in a whisper.

She strokes three fingers down the side of my face. Her eyes follow the trail. And they land on my mouth.

I don't know what this is. My brain isn't working.

But one thought comes through.

I need to get up.

My legs move. I slide myself out from beneath Sister Anna, away from her touch. As far from her as I can get. Even so, I have to brush what I think is her thigh, and—

I mumble another apology and nearly run from the room.

The wind is strong, but the rain has stopped, dark clouds looming. I step outside and try to think, try to clear my head.

I still feel her fingers on my skin. Sister Anna's fingers. Sister Anna's fingers on me.

I crack open my book, but I'm distracted, unsettled. More than that. I can't get the feeling of her skin off mine.

A car pulls up.

I look up, my body confused, all over the place. I wipe off the side of my face where Sister Anna touched me. I prepare myself, try to, to see Ben.

But this is not the truck I saw them in before. There are only two boys here, and neither is him. I recognize them, though. They're the same two from before, the same ones I saw at the mall—Todd and the kissing guy. Sarah and Rachel step out and head back into the school, smiling and whispering to each other.

I return to my book, trying not to feel disappointment that Ben is not here. Trying not to let myself think of Sister Anna again. That awful feeling on the side of my face. I expect the sound of the car starting and rolling away. But it doesn't come.

I look up. The boys are still there.

They are watching me.

This time Todd drives the car, and the one who was kissing Rachel, the one who sent her the photograph, leans against the side of it, a look on his face that makes me want to hide, or make myself smaller. He smiles, and I smile back, a little, to be polite. I return to my book. They still don't leave.

"What, you don't like us?" the kissing boy calls out. Cold wind, dark sky.

I place my bookmark and prepare to go inside. But he's waiting for an answer, so I say, "I don't know you."

He walks toward me. I stand, maneuvering to keep my skirt from showing anything. By the time I do, he is beside me.

"Here, let me help you with that," he says, and he reaches for my bag. I hesitate, but I let him take it. He shrugs it onto his shoulder. "I'll walk you inside," he says.

"Okay," I say, but it comes out softer than I mean it to.

With the backpack, the bottom of his shirt rides up, and I catch a glimpse of a tanned defined stomach I've already seen, one I could never forget. This is the boy from the photograph on Rachel's phone. To know what this boy looks like beneath his clothes, to have seen it without his knowledge. To remember every inch of his skin, now so near me . . . I tear my eyes away. He smiles at me as if he somehow knows what I'm thinking.

I clear my throat and walk toward the school, my heart pounding.

"You're always by yourself," he says beside me. His gait is confident, like Ben's, but if Ben is a bobcat then this boy is a tiger. His is a prowl and slink.

"Um, yes."

"Why?"

"I like reading," I say.

"I don't like books so much."

"Okay . . . What do you like?"

"Pretty girls. Like you."

We arrive at the door, and I reach for the bag. My hand is shaking a little. "Well, thanks. Um, for carrying that, I mean."

He hands it over, his eyes holding mine, like Ben's did. But he is so different from Ben, and I don't even know his name, and he doesn't know mine, and he is with Rachel, but he is looking at me with such *intent*. Terrifying warmth spreads through me again, my body betraying me. I try to speak but nothing comes. I reach for the door handle.

He shuts the door. It takes me a moment to register that it's happened. His arm extended in front of me, muscular the way I know and shouldn't know that the rest of him is. I take a step back, but he's turned so I turn, and now my back is against the door. The door he is still holding closed.

"Um," I say, "I need to go back inside."

"I bet you can steal just a minute." He is closer to me now. Our chests nearly touching. I try to back up further, but I can't. And maybe I don't really want to, but I do. I need to. "Can't you?" he says.

I've forgotten the question, even as he asks it, I can only focus on the space between us.

He reaches up and takes a strand of my hair in his fingers, his eyes locked on mine. Nearly like Sister Anna did. What am I—

"You're too hot to be alone all the time," he says.

"I—"

"Are you really a virgin?"

"What?"

"Rachel said you were, and Ben agreed. I don't believe them. I think you've got a side to you. Naughty. I can see it. You can always tell when it's there in someone."

Ben said that about me? He talked about me like this? Shame. White hot, through my belly. "I don't think—"

"What I think is that you sit out here because you want someone who's not too chickenshit to come and give you what you want."

"I don't want anything."

"That's not what your eyes are telling me."

He steps even closer, closing the distance between us. He presses his chest against mine, his hips on my hips, just as he did with Rachel. He smells of sharp cologne and sweat. This boy sweat, repulsive and not at all. I am hurt, mortified, even though I don't have reason to be, and I am angry that I let myself think about Ben for a whole weekend, that I got caught up in him. And I am terrified, and I feel—

I know I can't be here. There is fear, but there is also the hardness of this boy against the softness of me, and there is something extending out from between his legs, and the feel of it shocks me and sends that heat spreading faster, but the panic is rising in me too, and alarm bells in my head. They grow louder. The wind crashes against us, leaves swirling in the air.

My mother's story.

Alarm bells ringing.

They're not in my head. I look up. So does he. The bell is ringing.

Voices and shuffling sound inside. Sister Margaret speaking through the door. I can't be caught here with this boy, not like this. I use the momentary distraction to duck beneath his arm, grab my bag, and run toward the front entrance of the school, my chest rising and falling, cologne and sweat still filling my senses.

I don't know what I'm doing to draw this attention, don't know how they can sense the sin on me. But it has to stop. The Devil and demons find the weakest among us, worm their way in through poor defenses.

I am slipping.

In the next period, all the girls whisper, but it's not about the flu.

I walk down the hall, and faces stare.

Freak, one of them says. *Whore*, says another.

I step into Sister Anna's classroom, and everyone falls silent. Sarah raises an eyebrow and clicks her tongue. Rachel smiles.

"Well, well, if it isn't our favorite virgin. Trying to get that cherry popped by my *boyfriend*?" She speaks loudly enough for the whole room to hear, and girls laugh, wait with bated breath, eyes hungry. They've been anticipating this. One whispers to another. They all watch me.

"Will just texted and told me what you did. How you made a move on him outside even though you knew, and he reminded you, that he is with me."

"That . . . that didn't happen," I stammer.

"You think we don't know what you're doing sitting out there with your ass and tits on display every day where *our* boyfriends come to see *us*? How pathetic can you get?"

"I . . . what?"

"You act like you're too good for everyone here, but you don't have friends, and no one likes you. Especially not my boyfriend. Okay?"

I stand, stunned. I want to turn around and leave, but I can't make my legs move.

"I said, okay? You got it?"

"Yes," I say, finally, "I got it."

At this, the rest of the girls laugh. One of them says *Slutty Sophie*. One of them says *Jezebel*. I take slow and purposeful steps forward to my seat.

Rachel has received another photo, and I am sure it's from that boy, I guess his name is Will. More whispers, shocked faces, devouring eyes. I don't look at it this time. I play the silent symphonies, and I try to make myself smaller in my chair. This day is almost over.

Rachel turns. "Oh, you wanna see? You wanna see the photos my boyfriend sent me?"

Sarah laughs. "Show it to her. Show her what she can't have."

Rachel's eyes narrow. "You'd like that, huh, Sophie? You'd like to see Will's—"

"What's this?"

Sister Anna's voice. Rachel starts to put the phone away, but Sister Anna says, "Rachel Miller, you give me that this instant."

The girls' faces are white enough that I know the image is of something worse than a bare chest. Silence descends over all of us.

"It's Sophie's phone. It's disgusting, I mean, she was trying to show it to all of us, and we told her to stop and put it away but she just kept—"

Sister Anna holds up a hand for Rachel to stop talking. The hand she touched me with. Her eyes dart to me, and I know she is remembering. I don't know what to do. I want to throw up. She takes the phone and drags her eyes from me to Rachel. "Let's see what was so much more important than our lessons today." She pulls out her glasses. And she glances at me once more before looking at the screen.

Her breath catches.

She stands eerily still, save for her eyes which occasionally flit up or down the image. No one moves, no one breathes.

Minutes pass. Rustling in the room, shifting in seats. One girl to the side whispering to ask another girl if she knows what's on the phone. Sister Anna's tongue emerges from her lips and wets them. A minute gesture, but slow. A light sheen of sweat appears above her lip, on her brow. Her eyes are glassy, and her nose is red as though she's had a cold or been crying. She still does not move, just stands there, breathing.

A blur of black and white outside the classroom door, and Sister Margaret backtracks to peer in on the frozen woman at the front of the room.

"Sister Anna," she says.

"Sister Anna," she repeats, louder. And this time Sister Anna jumps, eyes tearing from the phone and focusing on Sister Margaret in the hall. She blinks rapidly.

"Yes, Sister Margaret," she breathes.

"Is there a problem?"

"No, no, there's not," she says and walks over to shove the phone into her desk drawer. She closes and locks it with a little key on shaking fingers. "We were just getting started."

Class resumes.

The sheen of sweat never leaves Sister Anna's face.

Sacred Hearts

I can't reach Noah. I have to call three times and hear the recorded message all the way through before someone answers.

"Hello?" A man's voice, hurried, distracted. I don't recognize it.

"Um, hi, I'm calling for Noah Allen."

"For who?"

"Is this Sacred Hearts?"

"Oh. Yeah. Are you family? Of one of the patients?"

"Yes."

"Didn't the facility call you already?"

"Call about what?"

"We had to move everyone. One of the kids was infected. We've got 'em moving to a hospital here."

A breath.

Everything, paused.

"They're all sick? Noah Allen is sick?"

"I don't— Look, I just work for the building management company. There's a lot of chaos right now, and I don't know much beyond what they're telling me."

"What hospital?"

"What?"

"What hospital did they take them to?"

"St. Joseph's over in Waukesha."

"Did you say Sacred Hearts called all the families?"

"Yeah, I mean they were supposed to."

"And you moved *all* of them?"

Noise in the background, voices and shuffling. "Hey, look, I'm sorry.

You can call back, but we gotta take care of things here. You know where to find him."

He hangs up. It doesn't make sense. Nothing makes sense right now. But one piece breaks through.

Didn't the facility call you already?

I run down the stairs. My parents both sit in the living room, my father poring over his drafting table as my mother, apron on and cooking timer nearby, flips through a Christian living magazine.

The words bubble up out of me before I even set foot in the room. "Noah is in the hospital and you didn't tell me? Why is Noah in the hospital?"

"Sophie, calm down," my father says.

"Is he okay? Is he sick?"

"He is with trained professionals who are well versed in the ways to—"

"Is Noah sick?"

"No."

"Why would they send kids who are not sick to the hospital?"

"They're just there as a precaution, and they'll be able to go back to Sacred Hearts in a few days. He's fine, Sophie."

"This virus seems serious, we—"

"Where did you hear that?"

"We have to go get him. We need to bring him home."

"This isn't his home, Sophie," our father says.

I take a step back, and then another. I can't breathe. I am so full of hate, am blinded by it.

"Of course this is his home," I manage to say.

"No, it's not. Not anymore." Hanging on the wall above him, *What Would Jesus Do?*

"He's your son," I say.

"Sophie—"

"Have you ever loved either of us? At all?"

My mother flinches, and my father stares at me with a fury I haven't seen since *that* night. A muscle twitches in my mother's neck. She turns to me, slowly and deliberately closes her magazine, and sets it beside her. When she speaks, her voice is quiet and a little raw.

"Sophie, your brother *is* sick. Not with the flu, but something worse. We haven't been forthright with you, but we will tell you he can't come back to this house, not with what he's done. Not with who he has chosen to be. Your father and I pray for him every day, but that's all we can do." She coughs, once, into her elbow. She touches the scapular.

"He's not sick," I say. "You know that. You both have to know that."

"Not all illnesses are of the body, Sophie. There are far more maladies of the mind and spirit than you can even imagine. The Devil hides behind all of them."

"How am I even related to you?" My voice has risen to a fever pitch, and I am nearly screeching, but I can't help it.

"Sophie, you don't know—"

"What I know is that you're not doing anything! You're sitting here baking bread and reading the newspaper as if everything's just great in the world, as if you deserve some kind of parenting award for having given up on a kid that you chose to make in the first place. But as long as things look good to everyone else! As long as we have a picture-perfect family to show the church so you two look like you have something in your miserable lives to be proud of!"

My father stands from his chair. "Sophie, you stop this right—"

"Noah is the best thing either of you has ever made, and you don't deserve him. You never have, and you never—"

A loud slap.

Silence. It takes me a moment.

My father is still standing by his chair in the corner.

But my mother has moved. She stands before me, holding her hand like she doesn't know what to do with it. Her eyes are glassy. My face stings. My ears are ringing.

There is blood in my mouth from my teeth breaking through the inside of my lip. My mother hit me. She hit me hard. My mother in her apron. I take a step back from her, bring my fingers to my lips, touch the blood there.

"Well now you're parents of the year," I say.

"That's enough!" my father's voice booms through the room and shocks me into silence. My mother's eyes have started to fill, and my father looks angrier than I've ever seen him. There's a light sheen of sweat on his forehead. He points at me. "Don't you speak to your mother that way! Don't you ever speak that way in our house! You are a child, and you know nothing."

I stand there, seething, afraid, exhilarated. Full of more guilt and hate than I know what to do with. It is terrible, powerful. And it fills me. I stare into my mother's eyes and hope, just for a moment, that it shows there as clearly as I feel it. Her face is ashen, and she looks confused, as though she doesn't know me or even herself. She looks young in this moment, and frail.

I think of her story.

I see her, lying there, with the animals.

I suddenly don't feel powerful at all.

I feel as though I am the adult and my mother is someone I am meant to take care of, and I have failed.

"Mom—" I say.

"I said that's enough, Sophie," my father says. "Go to your room. It's enough."

I want to scream or cry or throw something, or for my mom to hug me or yell at me or hit me again. I don't know what I need. I feel too much and want too much and can't handle the look of shame on my parents' faces. But I can't stop. Even with the guilt and shame and all the feelings I cannot name surrounding my mother's story. I can't stop. Not now. I'm not sure that I even want to.

Holding my mother's eyes, I say, "I'm nothing like you."

The timer dings from the couch.

I turn and walk up the stairs. My mother starts to cry.

HOW TO RECOGNIZE THE LAST
MOMENTS BEFORE THE WORLD ENDS:

You won't.

Confession

My father locks me in my bedroom so I can't do anything. I can't get the number for St. Joseph's Hospital. I can't try to steal either of their cell phones to get more information. My bedroom window has been sealed shut ever since *that* night, so I can't even climb out.

I don't sleep. I don't even read. I lie awake all night, praying to God that everything will change, that this is not the life Noah and I have. That we can find some way to be together again.

I drift off in the early morning hours, and when my alarm finally sounds my door has been unlocked. I head downstairs for breakfast and find a note on the table next to my cereal bowl:

> *Your mother isn't feeling well, and school is closed today.*
> *Mrs. Ingles will pick you up and take you to confession.*

It's my father's handwriting. It doesn't say where he is.

I read the note twice more. School is closed. I've never gotten a note from my parents. They have never not come down for breakfast. The coffee maker isn't even on. I consider knocking on their door, but then I remember my mother's face last night. I am not ready to see them yet either.

My lip is swollen, and since I am not permitted makeup, I can't do anything to cover it up. I tell myself with each step out the door that I was right to say those things. I was right.

So why doesn't it feel like it?

Mrs. Ingles, our next-door neighbor and a member of the church, is waiting outside already when I step out. She speaks little to me, something I have learned to value in adults. But today it's unsettling. In the back seat of her car is the same bloodred fabric that Sister Margaret had in the school parking lot, thick like a blanket or robe. At the church, she sits in one of the pews, and I trudge to the confessional, step into the small space, and kneel down.

After a moment the window opens, and I can see the outline of Father James's face. I tense. I never like being in here. I make the sign of the cross and look straight ahead. "Forgive me, Father, for I have sinned. It's been one week since my last confession."

My tight clothes, my feelings of hatred toward my mother, the two girls in the music room, touching myself, Ben at the library, *The Valley of Horses*, Will, Sister Anna, everything I said. My mother's face last night. The note at the breakfast table. What comes out instead is, "I disrespected my parents. For this I am truly sorry."

Father James replies, "Is that all?"

"Yes." I feel a little sick. I can't stand the guilt that overcomes me just sitting in this space. This tight room with this man, determining my eternal fate with his judgment of my sins. The confessional is meant to remind us of what we are. Wicked, suffering, base. In need of absolution. And it does it. It strips away the world and leaves you only with the priest and yourself. With all your endless faults.

"Are you feeling alright?" he says.

"What do you mean?"

"You sound troubled."

"Maybe," I say. "I don't know."

Father James breathes a ragged breath. "I haven't been feeling myself lately either. But Sophie, the blood of Christ is on us. In His love we are safe, and we need not fear. How's Noah?"

I jerk my head up, try to see him through the small cutouts in the wooden screen. I can just make out his old-man face, the slight white stubble on his chin. Have my parents said something?

He coughs into a handkerchief. "*Such* a troubled boy," he says.

I bite my tongue, as hard as I can. I close my eyes. I scream inside, loud enough to drown out the prayers I have to say, the words that do nothing to bring my brother back to me.

Hail Marys, the Prayer of Contrition, the Prayer of Absolution. I feel sure that he can see through me as easily as I can see through the screen. For once, I don't care.

"Amen," I finish automatically.

"Your sin is forgiven. Go in peace. And send Noah our prayers." He falters on the last word. I eye him through our divider. Sweat dots his forehead, and he is wheezing.

I leave the confessional, peering into the space as he opens the door on his side. His palms shake as he rubs them together.

They are as red as if there is blood on them.

Mrs. Ingles takes me to do volunteer work, which in this case is cleaning the Sunday school and choir rooms. She watches me the entire time, so I can't sneak off and try to find a computer. She even follows me to the bathroom. I scrub and scrub again, down on hands and knees.

Hours have passed and I've hardly felt them. Questions, swarming. Everywhere.

We pull into my drive with a basket of get-well-soon items for my parents that we picked up together at the store. I take the basket and my backpack through the door and into the kitchen. On the car ride over, I practiced what I will say to them. I will use the opportunity to start a dialogue. To bridge a gap. Or try. The idea turns my stomach, but I know it's right, and might be the only course for change. And . . . I want it. Change. Dialogue. Something. I want us to go get Noah.

A sound emerges from the silence of the house.

Coming from the living room.

Gooseflesh prickles my arms. The sound at first is not quite human, but familiar.

A rhythmic panting, and a grunt. Like the girls in the music room.

This time, though, there is one female voice and one male.

And though on later—involuntary—reflection I will realize that I should have known exactly what was happening, that I should never have taken one single step toward that room or I would regret it for the rest of my life, at that moment my only thought is,

Are my parents okay?

The question carries me into the living room, heart thudding in my chest, where I drop the basket on the floor.

There, on the off-white carpet, beneath the stone mantel my father designed, supporting a painting of an ever-watchful Jesus, are my parents. Completely naked.

Pushing, pulling, *clawing* at one another other in a steady, unapologetic rhythm.

Infection

My first thought is that it's my fault. I sinned and somehow brought this into being. This is my punishment. My second thought is that there has to be something firing wrong between my eyes and my ears and my brain. There is no way this is happening.

My parents are fevered and sweaty, their eyes bloodshot. My mother's hair sticks to her face, and my father's glasses are crushed beneath their bodies on the carpet.

These are not my parents. They are strangers, and they are all wrong. All of this is wrong.

I close my eyes and open them again. This cannot be happening. In years, I haven't seen my parents so much as share a fleeting kiss, and now . . .

My mouth goes dry. I don't know what to do. I think I need to put a name to it, and I don't want to, and my heart is racing, and the word comes to me, and I don't want it to. I don't want to acknowledge it, but they don't stop, and I—

Copulate. Copulating.

Bile claws its way up my throat. My parents *copulating* on the living room floor. Right in front of me. And I am standing here watching.

My legs feel like Jell-O. I think I am going to be sick. Even with me standing here, even with their bodies and depravity on full display, they just continue. Pulling and clawing, *writhing* against each other. My mother's nails digging into my father's shoulder, his naked shoulder, my father's naked shoulder, and—

I run.

I am out the front door. I don't feel my legs. I don't feel anything. My head is spinning, and nausea threatens to overwhelm me. They are possessed, they have to be. It wasn't them. Possession would be preferable, anything would be, to . . . *that*.

But there was the article, and the flu. *Erratic behavior. Manic behavior.* I am dizzy and unwell, and there is an immediate and pressing need to get as far away from my house as possible.

My mom's car sits in the driveway. I was required to take my driving exam when I turned sixteen, and I got my license, but my parents don't allow me to drive. I've never done it on my own.

I run to the sedan and try the door. The car is locked, I'm stupid for not thinking of it. The keys are in the house.

I fight down panic and tell myself it'll be no problem. I'll go back inside and quickly grab them. Maybe I'll realize I never even saw what I thought I did, and life can return to normal.

I take a deep breath and head back up to the front door.

I open it slowly. Set one foot into the house. I can't see the living room from here, but I can hear, and with a fresh wave of nausea, I realize that what I witnessed before is still taking place. I did not imagine it, did not dream it up in my sinner's brain. I gag.

I can do this. The keys are in my mother's purse, and it is just there on the other side of the kitchen. I'll have to pass by the same open hall to the living room through which I saw them before, but I can do this. I just won't look.

I take careful steps over the wood. I don't let myself see what's happening. I can still catch motion from the corner of my eye, but I will not let my brain put together what it is. I reach the bag and open it, carefully. Inside are my mother's keys, along with her wallet and other small items. I take the keys. I turn, keeping my eyes down and my focus on stepping lightly.

I am halfway back toward the front door when I notice. Something has changed.

My heart beats once, twice.

There is no sound.

The house has returned to silence.

I turn my head toward the living room.

Just in time to see my father, naked and snarling. Running straight at me.

I move. Don't think, throw myself into action.

The kitchen, ragged breaths. My father's breaths. And—

My mother comes at me from the side.

I lunge, surge forward. Her fingers reach, grab hold of the arm of my sweater. I'm almost at the front door. She pulls the fabric, and I shrug out of it, her fingertips brushing my skin, and my father is almost on me, and—

I jump through the open doorway and slam the door shut on both of them. On my parents who are chasing me, naked and insane.

My back against it, I feel a thud and buckle. I don't want to, but I turn my head, just enough to see inside through the stained-glass cutout behind me.

They shove and slam their bodies up against the wood. I can see them through the glass. Fevered eyes. Their rage or hunger or whatever it is that is so unlike the only parents I have ever known. I don't know what they want from me, but I can barely hold the door against them, and my mother snarls at my father, who shoves her aside. *Shoves* her, hard, so that she falls, and I can't process anything except that I need to get in the car, and that the second I let go of this door they will come for me.

These are not my parents.

I grab the metal cross that sits on our porch, my other arm and back straining to keep the door closed. It opens a little, my father's hand pushing out into the daylight.

I turn and slam the door on it. His palm is red and blistered already, as if he's held it to a stovetop. He lets out a yell, and tears blur my vision as I slam the door again and again. Until he pulls his hand back and I can finally shut it.

I shove the cross through the handle. I don't know if this will work, if a brace only works on one side or both, or even at all. They pound against the door, and I know this flimsy attempt won't hold. A cross and my bare hands between my parents and me. Drool trailing down from my mother's mouth, her eyes someone else's.

I turn. Run for the car, but I don't even make it past the porch.

The front door bursts open, cross clattering, broken in half. I trip, catch myself against the porch rail, and stand. My father staggers out, still naked. Roaring with rage I've never seen or heard.

And there between his legs is something far too horrible to contemplate. But it's there, and it's the thing that was pressed up against me by Will at school. It can't be here on my father. Here pointed toward me. I am paralyzed, and I am going to be sick.

And then—

The world tilts.

I'm down. Tackled to the porch, breath knocked from my lungs. My father, my own father, on top of me. His naked body on top of mine.

He pins me down so that I can't get free, no matter how hard I writhe. His breath and skin are hot, nearly burning, and he is sweaty all over. I can't be touching my father's skin or sweat.

I struggle, and blood leaks from his hand where I slammed it in the door. He is not there in his eyes, his face without glasses unrecognizable. It's not my father, this hungry sweating thing hovering above me. Something else is in there, and he is gone. I make myself believe it.

I seize the cross and shove the sharp end into his shoulder. He rips at my shirt with his red palms, and I scream and shove the cross in again, piercing his skin, blood spraying over my chest. Drool on his lip. His eyes unfocused. He reaches down and tugs at my skirt.

I cry out, thrust the cross into him harder. He takes it from my hand as though it is nothing, tosses it into the yard.

I can't move. I can't do anything. My legs bare on the front porch of our house, afternoon daylight, and my father's skin hot against my skin.

I close my eyes, tears falling, and I start to pray.

Our father, who art—

His weight lifts.

I open them to find he is no longer on top of me.

My mother has ripped him away. How was she strong enough to do that? I suck in a gulp of air, scramble back.

Her eyes fixed on mine, she lunges for me.

My father grabs her hair and yanks her back. My mother shoves him, harder than I thought was possible, against the porch rails.

He throws her back against the house. Her head collides with the metal porch light with a crack, but she just shakes it, and staggers back up to standing. She is disoriented, stumbling, but she rights herself. She runs at my father again, tripping now as she goes.

The keys are on the grass. I don't let myself think. I get my footing and sprint for them, and then to the car. Across the grass, over the driveway. I open the door, throw myself in, and thrust the keys into the ignition, locking it, making sure every door is locked.

Only now do I look up, now from the momentary safety of this vehicle. My parents have forgotten me.

On the front porch, for all the world to see, my mother on top of my father, her head thrown back as if she is broken. My father's blood covers them both. Because I stabbed him. I stabbed my father, and they are pushing and pulling at each other.

I pull out of the drive. Mrs. Ingles stands on her own front porch. Her mouth wide open. I don't know how long she's been there, if she watched me screaming, my parents attacking me, and made no move to help. She turns at the car's motion. Our eyes lock.

And I know. She did see. She saw and did nothing, would have done nothing, even if it had continued. We hold each other's eyes.

Then I whip the car around, tires squealing over the asphalt, and I leave my home, my parents, and Mrs. Ingles behind.

I don't turn. I don't look back, even for a second.

I don't know where I'm going, only that I need to get away from the house. I have to swipe at my eyes because the tears haven't stopped, and as I drive these streets I know so well but have never navigated alone, these streets I have traversed in the back seat and passenger seat of my parents' cars for the whole of my life, I can't clear the images from my eyes, can't shake the feeling of my father's body on mine and the sound of my mother's skull slamming against the side of the house.

I shake my head, my hands unsteady on the wheel. Nausea bubbles up again. Splinters are lodged in my legs and back, from the porch. Splinters because—

I turn on the radio. My mother's favorite church organ. I turn the dial and land on a rap and hip-hop station. I don't listen to this kind of music, have never been allowed to. But it is loud. Loud enough to drown out my thoughts and obscure the insidious images that I. *Cannot. Get. To. Stop.*

I'm not paying attention to where I'm driving. All I know is that my house is behind me, and the road is in front. The other cars are going the speed limit, but it's too slow for me, too slow for what I need. I come upon a ramp leading to the freeway. I've never been allowed to drive on the highway, it's too fast, too dangerous. I see my parents again. On the floor, sweating, panting, writhing. I feel my father's body on mine, and something like a sob escapes my throat.

I veer left and take the ramp.

The car accelerates as my foot presses down on the gas. My heart is pounding. The music blasts through the speakers. I drive. Time doesn't mean anything. There are only the images and this car, and me trying to keep myself together. I turn the music up as loud as it can go.

I find that the brain is an incredible thing. Incredible that with each mile of road behind me, the images obscure.

I didn't see it. I didn't feel it. None of this is happening. I am just a girl who is alone, driving seventy miles per hour down the freeway in my mother's car, and I am okay.

For the first time maybe in forever, I feel totally and absolutely . . . I don't even know the word for it. What do I feel? Not panic, or terror, or revulsion, or dread or guilt or shame. For once, not those.

Maybe I feel momentarily, insanely, a little bit *free.*

I floor the pedal and surge forward. My heart still pounds, but now in a way that thrills me, makes me feel alive. I am in control of one thing in the world, and it is this car. I realize with a laugh that this is more control than I've had over anything, maybe ever.

I drive for what feels like days but is probably more like an hour. I drive until the adrenaline drains from my body, and my brain's miraculous departure ceases.

I drive until I am just a girl in her mother's car, alone in the world, and my shirt is sticky with my father's blood.

My palms sweaty on the wheel. My father's palms so red. Sliding over my arms, my legs, up my—

The cars around me are going too fast. I'm not in control. I don't know how I ever thought I could be. Every mile is farther from my house and farther from my life. I don't even know where I am.

I flip on my blinker and try to pull into the right lane to exit, but there is a car behind me that I didn't notice, and it has to brake and swerve to avoid me. Its honk peals through the air, a crying accusation that I should not be here, should not be manning this vehicle or doing any of this. Should not be out in the world alone. I swerve back to the left, but there is another car there now, and we only miss each other by a fraction of a second. The horns honking and music blasting and the inhuman cries of my father and mother. Loud, louder, everything so loud I can't think.

I am at an exit. I turn the wheel, hard, and veer off onto a feeder road, spot a gas station over on the side. The car swings wildly, skids over a curb and into the rest stop grass patch, comes to an abrupt and violent stop. My shaking is uncontrollable, my shirt drenched in sweat and blood.

I take a few uneven breaths, wiping my forehead with the back of my hand. I tell myself everything will be fine, but I am not convincing. I have a quarter tank of gas. It should be enough to get me . . . somewhere. Where can I go?

I could just turn around. Anyone who can actually help me is back in Foreston. Except I don't trust anyone there besides my parents and Mrs. Parson, and the one person I most trust is in . . .

The interactive map at the mall. The roads leading to him.

I push my hair back out of my face and reach to turn off the radio. Of course. I can't believe I—

I have a car. I can get to Noah. I can see my brother. I can—

A sound blasts out from the speakers. Long, loud, and deafening in the small space. I push the nearest button, all the buttons, anything to make it stop. I switch to a new station, but the sound is on all channels. Every single one.

The long beep, and the message:
EMERGENCY BROADCAST.

𝔔uarantine

*EMERGENCY BROADCAST. EMERGENCY BROAD-
CAST. BEEEEP. BEEEEP. EMERGENCY BROADCAST.
IMMEDIATE QUARANTINE IN EFFECT FOR ASH-
LAND, BAYFIELD, CLARK, JACKSON, JUNEAU,
MARATHON, MILWAUKEE, MONROE, RACINE, RUSK,
SAUK, SHAWANO, AND WAUKESHA COUNTIES.
VEHICLE MOVEMENT RESTRICTED. ROADBLOCKS
IN EFFECT. ALL ARE REQUIRED TO STAY IN HOMES
UNTIL FURTHER NOTICE. THOSE WITHOUT AC-
CESS SHOULD REPORT TO FOLLOWING MUNICIPAL
SCHOOLS . . .*

I stare at the radio as the message repeats itself. My brain moves at half speed. A quarantine. Rusk County, where I live. Waukesha County, where Noah is. Two hundred fifty miles between. I haven't been to St. Joseph's Hospital before, but the guy on the phone had said it was in Waukesha, so they must be close by each other.

I check the glove compartment for a map. Mints, the car's manual, a pocket Bible. I try to think about signs I might have seen on the highway. I close my eyes and breathe.

Then I realize. I know the signs I passed already. I know the direction I'm going because I have traveled this way before, not as much as I'd like to have, but enough. I am already on my way to Noah, more or less. Heading, at least, in the correct general direction. A noise bursts out of me that is a laugh or a sob. I should fill up the tank, but there's no money in the car, and I didn't bring any. A spike of panic at this new discovery, but a problem I can deal with later. I know where I need to go.

The radio repeats its message on a loop, and I let it play. It propels me forward, back onto the highway, but with purpose this time, with direction. Encouraging me toward my brother. *WAUKESHA COUNTY UNDER IMMEDIATE QUARANTINE.*

The traffic thickens.

I barely make it ten miles before I am forced to a complete stop.

Three lanes going in one direction, grass on either side of us. I'm in the middle lane, and beyond the highway and grass are trees and woods and billboards.

The closest billboard on the left says **FALL BECOMES YOU, VISIT WISCONSIN!** A woman with autumn leaves for hair smiles out at us, holding a mug of cider, her shape outlined above the top of the billboard. On our right is another black background and red thick letters that say **LUST DRAGS YOU DOWN TO HELL—JAMES 1:15.** *Christian Radio.* Flames lick at the bottom of the words, and Jesus' torso floats, arms outstretched, untouched and pure in a giant cutout, above the words and the flames.

Horns honk. Cars try to inch forward, but there's only so much space. Yelling. People stepping out of their cars to ask questions. Everyone making calls, taking photos, furiously typing on their phones. I roll down my window, just a little, to see if I can learn something, but it's hard to decipher what anyone is saying. The wind carries a sharper bite now than it did even yesterday, and even with the chaos, I hear and feel the leaves shaking on the trees on either side of the highway. I shiver, consider approaching someone, asking what they know. But I've never been on my own before. I'm not sure where to begin. Strangers surround me, an entire world of them. Adult strangers. Cars stretching as far as I can see, in either direction.

The sun glows in its final hour, shines golden on the cars, the billboards suddenly silhouetted in front of it. The **FALL** woman's head and the leaves transform in silhouette, the two largest of them on either side of her forehead like horns. Her smile still bright even in shadow, her eyes aimed down at us. Jesus on the other side.

I sit for so long in the same spot that I finally turn the car off to conserve gas. I close my eyes and cover my face with my hands. All I can think is that they're going to block Noah off from me. No one has any idea where I am, not one person in the world.

I try to remember something, anything, other than the events of the last few hours. How-tos. How to caramelize sugar, how to sew a French seam. My heartbeat slows. I riffle through the glove compartment again, but there is nothing useful. I turn to the center console. Papers, coins, a pen. And then, black on black, almost invisible in the early evening light, an actual miracle.

My mother's cell phone. I look up briefly to billboard Jesus and send a prayer of thanks.

I hesitate, my fingers hovering over the buttons, and then I do it. I dial my home number, praying to God and Jesus and anyone else who is there for my parents to answer. Praying that I am crazy or possessed and that none of what I think transpired did, or even if it did, that they have some kind of explanation, and they will tell me that it's okay and I can come home now and everything I am afraid of will amount to nothing because I am not alone in this world.

The phone rings once. Twice, three, then four times. It goes to voicemail.

I call again. A third time.

I do not let myself panic. I do not let myself cry. I dial the only other number I know.

"*Thank you for calling Sacred Hearts, a spiritual sanctuary for those families afflicted with challenged children and teens. You are calling during our non-office hours. Please call back at a later time. Thank you, and may God's love shine on you always.*"

I end the call and try to use the search function to find the number to Noah's new hospital, but service isn't good enough. The map app isn't loading either. I think for a second, force myself to take in my surroundings. I have read enough survival how-tos to know this is an imperative step. I must remain calm.

The woman in the car to my right holds a baby who cries loudly enough for me to hear. She wears a medical mask. The man in the car to my left won't stop honking his horn. He's a foot or two past me, and I lean forward to see him through his window. As I do, he catches my eye, flashing me a grin that makes my palms sweat and my heart beat loudly in my ears.

A red Camaro sits in front of the honking man, and its driver rolls down the window and yells obscenities and threats at him. From the Camaro's passenger window, a woman's red-nailed hand taps to the rhythm of a very loud song. All their windows are open. A family in a camper van behind me with Packers helmets hanging from their mirror sing a song all together, but even through my rearview I can see the worry on the parents' faces.

The sun sinks lower, red and orange filling the lower half of the gray swollen sky. I try the radio a couple of times, but I'm not getting any information beyond the emergency broadcast.

The man in the car to my left continues to lay on his horn. The guy in the Camaro gets out, slams his door, and goes to the honking man. He yanks him from his vehicle, and punches him in the face.

I try to make myself smaller in my seat as I lock the door for the hundredth time. I look to see if anyone else has noticed what is happening. Everyone is trying not to look, but they are still watching. Of course they are. The honking man, shorter, blond, in a Milwaukee Brewers sweatshirt, stands suddenly very still, as though he didn't just get punched. The Camaro guy, bearded and wearing a jean jacket, sees the honking man's face and takes a step back. He takes another and says, "What the fuck." He backs into the center lane in front of the car just ahead of me, and the honking man follows, turns, so I can see his face. So I can see the smile there, the glassy eyes.

His red palms.

I want to yell, want to do something to stop what I know is coming. But as soon as I open my mouth, the honking man—the infected man—has lunged.

He grabs the back of Camaro's head, hits so hard and fast with his full weight that they both hit the ground. In seconds, the infected man straddles Camaro, pins his arms. Camaro in shock, struggling against him.

The infected man bends down and shoves his tongue into Camaro's mouth. Camaro is much larger, he should be able to fight him off. But somehow, the infected man holds him down. The strength my parents had on the porch.

He reaches down with one hand, his other forearm pinning Camaro in place, and undoes Camaro's jeans. Camaro calls out, bucks, thrashes, trying to free himself. He rips his arm loose and knocks the infected man in the side of the head. He kicks and wriggles back, turns over onto his stomach and starts to crawl.

The infected man is there.

He jumps on top of him, digs his knees into the backs of Camaro's thighs. Drool trails down from the infected man's lip, and he pulls Camaro's jeans down. Camaro yells again.

The infected man grabs for his boxers next, rips them open, exposing Camaro fully in the night.

The Camaro woman opens her door and steps out, seems to just now see or understand what is happening. She screams. Screams as the infected man reaches down and unzips his own jeans.

She turns, pulls a tire iron from the car, and runs to them.

She lifts it above her head and swings it down on the skull of the attacking man with a scream. Metal and bone collide with a *crack*.

The infected man doesn't stop moving, doesn't stop trying to dominate, and he's exposed himself now, that awful *thing* there between them. Sticking out from his body.

Camaro yells, strains with every muscle. The woman bashes the infected man's head, again and again, blood spraying over Camaro on the ground.

The infected man drools, grunts. He fists one hand around that thing, that body part he has. He aims it toward Camaro's backside.

The woman swings the tire iron again, this time with the whole of her might, tears streaming down her face. She brings it down with one final *CRACK*.

The infected man stills.

He rolls off Camaro. Drops, lifeless, to the asphalt.

The woman goes to Camaro. She's still crying. Hysterical almost.

Long moments before Camaro stands, before she gets him up, taking her hands for help. Pulling his pants up, fast, stumbling a little. Dazed, he looks down at the other man. He silently asks her for the tire iron with an open palm, closes his fingers around it.

He sends her back to their car and rears back and beats the infected man twice more. He swears, wipes his mouth. Shaking. He looks like he's going to be sick, turns like he doesn't know what to do with himself. He spits on the man's body.

When he returns to his car, to the woman, hysterical, standing beside it, Camaro touches her face to see if she is okay, tucks her hair back behind her ear. He holds her tight to him and says something over and over as she cries.

But I can see his face. The terror. The shock of being overpowered, the near-miss of it. If you can consider it a miss at all.

The sun meets the horizon, and streaks of pink, red, and orange slash through the lower half of the sky. The upper half heavy and dark as it has been.

Camaro gently closes the woman into their car. He returns to the man on the ground one more time. Kicks his body off to the side so all I can see of him is his arm and head peeking out from behind the car, jerking each time he's kicked. Blood pooling beneath him. Camaro looks around then, at all the windshields of all the cars. To see who witnessed this.

He meets my eye, and he holds it.

The way I looked at Mrs. Ingles.

"What the fuck is wrong with you people?!" he yells, to all the cars, to me. "Huh?!"

After a moment, he shakes his head and swears. Runs his hands over his face. He gets back in his own car, and all the windows roll up. The music stays off.

The woman with the baby cries, and the parents in the camper point at something in the distance to distract the children. The father keeps glancing at the place between the two cars where the man now lies. As he urges the kids to look somewhere, anywhere else.

I hit the lock button again. Cars all around me are honking, louder and longer now. The woman in the car in front of me abandons hers, just slams her door shut and walks away from it with a backpack into the woods.

The sky darkens.

The FALL BECOMES YOU billboard illuminates with yellow, artificial, upward-facing light, the woman smiling down over us, her eyes large and knowing, her nearly horned head. On our right, the LUST billboard lights up as well, red on the flames. And Jesus himself half pink and half green in the neon light outlining his shape. I've never seen anything like it.

Glowing, flashy, and provocative. So unlike the Jesus I know.

The colors bathe us all, cast the night in an unnerving, otherworldly red-pink-green haze. I want nothing more than to be reading under the covers in my own bed. I don't even need to be reading. I would take just being in my own house. The cage that was a prison until I had to run from it.

I search the car. There is no charger for the cell phone and nothing new in the center console. The phone's battery is at fifty percent. I call Sacred Hearts again. Same message. I call my house again. Still no answer. The browser still doesn't work.

Half an hour passes. I strain to see something up ahead, anything that will give me a clue as to what is happening. I turn the car back on and try the radio. My eyes dart up to the FALL sign, and a thought occurs. I flip to the Christian Radio station. And here, finally, it's not just the emergency alert. Someone speaking, a radio show host my parents sometimes listen to, and a guest with her, a male voice.

"So just let me get this straight," the host says. "This thing, it's jumping from person to person, it is taking over people's bodies, *possessing* them, making them *fornicate* in public places, outside of sacred unions, compelling them to commit sodomy, rape, all manner of immoral acts. And no one can just call it what it is. We're clearly looking at a situation that's either demonic or angelic, and either way the sinners are going to pay. It's pretty simple."

"Well, it's an interesting question, Carly," the guest responds. "It certainly seems to be spreading faster in major cities, and we know there are fewer Christians in city centers these days than ever before. But I suppose the question is, why? Why now, why like this? This country has lived in sin for a long time, why this moment?"

"God's work has always been mysterious."

"That's right, of course, but—"

"All I'm saying is maybe it's time. Christians are getting tired. I'm tired of it. The whole nation is tired. And why? Because we've abandoned our values, we've lost everything that we were founded on, we're a nation of baby killers, perverts, idolators, and something is happening here. I just think Reverend Ansel is saying something meaningful, and we should—"

Movement in the corner of my eye. I turn my head, silence the radio. At first I don't understand. And . . .

No. I must be seeing things.

The man on the ground, the dead man who was hit with a tire iron countless times, the man whose skull I heard crack.

He is moving.

His arm jerks toward his body. He rolls—actually rolls—onto his stomach.

A moment in which nothing happens. In which I think I must have imagined it, or it was a trick of the light. Even though he's clearly turned over.

Then he plants his hands under his shoulders in the pool of his own blood. The dead man, the broken one. He pulls himself forward to push onto his knees. His movements are horrible to watch. Convulsive, contorting. He takes a long, labored breath, plants one foot on the ground and stands, stumbling only a little. He seems dazed, but he swivels his torso around, taking in his surroundings. I catch sight of his face.

A slick of sweat covers his forehead, alongside the blood. His jaw is broken, bent and hung open, and blood pours from his nose. His arm is bent backward, and one of his eyes is swollen and blue-black. Even so, I know the look. I've seen it, inches from my face, on my mother, and father.

The man searches from where he stands. Scenting the air, like an animal. That thing between his legs. It is still out. Jutting from his pelvis. The end of it is glistening.

Nausea. The world spinning.

The man's head tilts.

He takes a jerky step forward. Toward the front of my car.

I hold as still as humanly possible.

Another step. He's coming toward me.

No. No, he's—

Then another.

He's in front of me.

Another step. He sets his hand on the hood. My hood. He closes his eyes. Inhales. Blood drips from the side of his face, landing on my mother's car.

Plop. Plop.

He twitches as though something is broken in his brain as well as his body.

Plop.

He slowly turns in my direction. I am frozen.

His tongue emerges from his unhinged jaw, tasting the air in the pink, green, red light. He takes a lurching step forward. Another. Toward my driver's side window. I can't move.

He stops beside me, his hips at the level of my eyes, that *thing* there. I am paralyzed. I am not thinking of my father, I am—

He reaches for the door handle.

I unbuckle my seatbelt with shaky hands and shove myself backward, into the passenger seat. He leans down and gropes along the edges of the door and the window, clawing at the metal and glass with his fingers. His blistered flesh smears pus and blood in its wake.

He grunts. Wet thick breath heavy enough to hear from inside the car.

I fumble until I find the cell phone beneath me. I dial 9-1-1. Put the phone to my ear as the man pulls at the handle again, shakes it. He grunts, and a spray of blood paints my window.

"Nine-one-one. State your emergency."

"I'm on 53, and there's a man trying to get in my car. We've been stuck here for a long time. I'm, I'm alone."

He rears back and slams his elbow into the window. "Please send someone. Please—"

A crackling of static, then the half-clear words of the dispatcher.

"Hello?"

Static.

The man shoves his elbow against the glass. The car rocks.

"Hello?!"

Silence. He backs away.

"Hello! Can you hear me?"

He runs and body-slams the car. It rocks, creaking on its wheels. I scream into the phone. "Please!"

The line goes dead.

He rams the car again. Rocking it with a terrible screech. The thing between his legs moves back and forth as he throws his body sideways.

I scream for someone to help. I climb into the back seat and bang on the rear window for the father in the camper van, but no one responds. There is nothing in the car I can use to protect myself, nothing I can do but wait as the man tries to force his way inside. I could go out the other side and run, but this car is my only safety, and I saw what happened to Camaro. Maybe he won't get in. Maybe . . .

I draw my knees into my chest and cover my face with my arms, eyes squeezed tight in the back seat. I want my parents. I want Noah.

The rocking stops.

The only sound my own ragged breathing.

I am afraid to lift my head and open my eyes. I am a coward. So I clasp my elbows and stay pulled in tight to myself, waiting for the worst.

A long moment passes, and nothing happens. I cautiously lift my head. I open my eyes.

The man isn't there.

I sit up very slowly and look around all sides of the car. I glance over toward his car, but don't see him anywhere near it either.

There is a full minute of silence.

I think . . . I might actually be okay.

I think I'm—

His skull smashes into the windshield.

I scream and throw myself against the back seat. He slams his forehead into the glass in front of the driver's seat. His head already bloody, disfigured. Again and again. The car rocks, the dull thunk of bone on hard glass. Again and again, he pounds and throws himself into it.

The glass begins to fissure and spiderweb. The bone of his skull shows where his skin has split open. Blood sprays from his head, spurting over the windshield. The bulge between his legs still prominent and visible.

With one great slam, he breaks through.

Glass and blood rain down. I throw my arm up, squeeze my eyes shut. Then I hear him coming. I open them in absolute terror.

I try the doors from the back seat, but I locked the car from the front. My mother keeps the child lock on. I can't get out.

He thrusts his head through the hole. Shards lodged into his skin, blood dripping into his eyes. He props one knee up on the hood to crawl his way inside, the car bowing and creaking beneath his weight.

And then he stops.

He tilts his head, sticks his tongue out again. Tastes and sniffs the air. And he shoves off my car.

He jerks and lurches, faster than anything humanly possible. A demon from Hell speeding through the night, crooked, thrashing, raw. I try to track him through the back windows, but all I can see is the top of a woman's head peeking out from behind a car, hoping to find out what's going on.

And then the man is on her.

Her screams are the only sound for a long time after.

No one goes to help.

I mentally go through the stages of rewiring a lamp. When I get to the final step, I can breathe again. I don't know how long it's been since the woman stopped screaming.

The sky has darkened into full night in the multicolor glow of the billboards and the few headlights people have kept on. I can't sleep. I'm not sure I'll ever be able to sleep again.

The wind rages in periodic gusts, each one crashing into the LUST billboard with neon Jesus, making it creak and sway. I curl up in the back seat. Last night at home feels like a lifetime ago, and I wonder if maybe I have died, and this is Hell already, and I am finally paying the ultimate price for being the kind of person I am.

Another scream. Male. Howling.

I reach forward and turn the radio back on, but it's back to the emergency broadcast.

"Sophie?"

Noah in my doorway, eight years old, carrying his stuffed animal.

"Yeah?" I said. I'd been crying into my pillow, but I didn't want him to know that.

"Did you have a bad dream?"

I nodded.

"Thought so. Me too."

I scooted over, and he crawled into bed with me, the stuffed animal between us.

Our mother read us the Bible every day as part of our homeschooling. That day she had told us the story of the Levite and his concubine. They were traveling and had to spend the night in Gibeah, but no one would take them in except an old man. Late at night, bad men surrounded the house and demanded that the old man hand over the Levite because they were wicked and unnatural and wanted to fornicate with him. The old man offered his own daughter to them instead, and the bad men refused. So the Levite sent his concubine out to them. She was raped all throughout the night, repeatedly, and was dead by the time he came out in the morning. He took her body home to Ephraim and chopped her into pieces that he sent to the twelve tribes to start a war and punish the bad men.

Our mother said it was a scary passage but that what mattered was that it was about chaos and lawlessness. Chaos was bad, and people need a strong ruler. Without one, bad men will be able to get away with bad things. This is why we choose Christ and why we follow God. It is why we respect our fathers and our governors and the pope and priests and the president. Rulers are important. Hierarchy and respect. They know more than we do.

The bad men in Gibeah were punished, and there was a war. But the old man did not get in trouble for offering his daughter, nor did the Levite for handing over his concubine.

"You know why I think it was fake?" Noah said to me.

"Why?"

"Because there was a whole village. She was outside in the square, and a whole village heard. I think someone would have stopped it. Someone would have helped her. I think people are more good than Mom says. When it really counts, people take care of each other."

I let my tears fall and whisper to the car.

Our Father, who art in Heaven, hallowed be Thy name.

More screams. A loud thunk, another crack of metal on bone.

Thy kingdom come, Thy will be done, on earth as it is in Heaven.

Horns honking.

Give us this day our daily bread, and forgive us our trespasses.

More voices. Screaming.

As we forgive those who trespass against us.

The baby crying.

And lead us not into temptation, but deliver us from evil.

The night stretches and gapes. Neon Jesus and the horned woman of FALL.

And I am alone.

Amen.

The Highway

The rumble of bikes growls through the night. I'm not sure if I am half asleep, or if I've just stared open-eyed at the same place on the dash for so long that it seems only minutes have passed. I bolt upright. A police motorcycle weaves through the traffic behind me before stopping three cars back to talk to someone. Another cop passes by the empty car on my left as he makes his way farther up the road.

I turn the ignition on but keep the headlights off and open the car's moon roof just enough so that I can stick my head out. I climb up slowly, making sure no one is lingering around my car, and emerge through the roof into the night.

It's cold, the wind pushing against the car, the Jesus billboard creaking. I inhale. The traffic stretches so I can't see an end to it. Lights flash up ahead in three different places, red and blue.

I steady myself with my hands on the leather seat backs. My palms are sweaty, and in the wind I can feel the places on my neck and face where I am still wet from tears.

The camper van behind me blocks my view, but I can still make out that the traffic extends as far back as it does in front. A number of rows back, there's been a collision, one car slammed deep into the back of the other, wedged there now, unmoving.

One policeman stops his bike and talks to the drivers near the wreck, peering in their windows with flashlights. After speaking to each of them, he moves on, as though he's looking for something or someone in particular. He shines his flashlight over the pavement, and I see red just as he does. Blood on the ground, shining in the beam. He pauses, says something into his radio. He gets back on his bike and speeds off back in the direction he came from.

"Hey!" I yell. "Hey!" I wave my hands above my head.

Another set of headlights suddenly flickers on.

I drop back down into the car as quickly as I can. I close the moon-roof, shut the car off again. A helicopter blasts through the night sky, and a voice booms from a speaker, repeating one phrase:

PLEASE REMAIN IN YOUR VEHICLES, AND KEEP YOUR DOORS LOCKED.

The woman with the baby is sleeping when I catch the first sign of movement. Four or five cars ahead. People who got out of their vehicles, despite the warning, now climb back in.

I turn my car on. The woman still sleeps. I honk the horn. She wakes, looks my way, then faces forward as though she hasn't seen me, as though she is afraid to.

I've taken the back floor mats to sit on so my body won't touch the crazed man's blood and I used them to sweep most of the glass to the floor. It crunches beneath my sneakers.

In a few moments I am finally able to roll forward as well. The man's car next to mine is still empty, as is the one in front of me. Slowly, cars maneuver around them. I imagine it from above, rocks stuck in a riverbed.

The honking intensifies. Neon Jesus creaks and sways. I am so relieved to be leaving this spot behind. I get around the stuck cars after a few tries and travel another ten feet. The woman with the baby looks young, in her twenties. Her baby is sleeping now, but the car seat has been moved to the front.

Slowly, so slowly.

Don't you speak to your mother that way.

"Noah, do you believe what the priests say about sinful thoughts being as bad as sinful actions?" Noah, on his bed, in the lamplight. Wrinkled pajamas. Noah and me in his room.

"No, it makes no sense. I think you worry about the wrong things."

"But . . . what if . . . how can you know if you're a good person?"

"Sophie, you are the only good person."

"Noah, you know I'm not."

The red and blue lights are now so near that they color everything in my field of vision, overtake the pink and green. A policeman speaks to the driver in front of me. Cars honk all around.

The cop motions me forward. I roll down my window and pull up to meet him.

"Officer. What's happening?" I might cry from relief.

He wears a bandana over the lower half of his face and has on latex gloves. He shines a flashlight on me and around the car. His name tag says **VERGES**. "Jesus. What happened?"

I clear my throat. "A man, he tried . . ."

"Did any bodily fluid enter you?"

"Excuse me?" I say.

"Spit, blood, semen. Did any of that enter you, or come in contact with your skin?"

"Um, no."

"You're sure."

"Yes."

He shines his light on my shirt, covered in blood. He stares at it for a moment. He sweeps his flashlight beam into my eyes, holds it there so long I have to blink and pull away.

"I don't have a fever," I say. "I feel fine."

He looks for another tense minute and then lowers the beam.

"Are you alone out here?" His voice is deep and tired. When the spots from the flashlight clear, I can see he is young, for a cop, and looks like he hasn't slept in days.

I nod.

"How old are you?"

"Seventeen," I lie. I will be soon anyway.

"Where's your family?"

"Waukesha County," I say.

The police officer swears under his breath. He picks up his radio and mumbles, "Got another one. Any more room on the bus?" The person on the other end responds immediately, "Can't take any more. Got another"—*pause*—"infected here. Evacuating and sealing."

The cop, VERGES, swears again, louder this time. He rubs his eyes with the back of his free hand and lifts his hat to smooth his hair down beneath it.

Horns honk behind us. The loud creak of the billboard in the wind.

He looks back at the gridlock of cars and then around to the other cops nearby. His attention returns to me, and I think he's sizing me up somehow. He touches his hand to my door and says, "Wait here."

He steps over to one of the other cops who wears a medical face mask and is busy reading things off a clipboard to drivers. Beyond them, there is so much open road.

A brief image flashes in my mind. The road ending ten feet ahead, spilling over in a waterfall. I see myself just about to drive forward, over the threshold of the world, along with the rest of these poor souls. Down, down deep into someplace dark and roiling.

Dizziness passes over me again. My abdomen burns. I lean my head back against the seat. After a long minute the cop appears by my window. "Listen. We can't—there's not a lot we can do for you. You're a minor, so I can't leave you alone out here, but I need to deal with these other cars and get the road cleared and get people back into their homes."

"What is it that's infecting people?"

He shakes his head. "We're gonna clear a spot for you to pull over and park near us. You're gonna have to wait. I don't know how long, as long as this—" He gestures back toward the cars stretching behind me. "—takes. Then we're gonna find somewhere for you to go, okay?"

"I need to get to my family. I'm not far, I know how to get there."

"Listen, ma'am, uh, girl—" He rubs his eyes again.

"Sophie."

"Sophie. I need you to move your car so I can deal with the rest of these people."

"But—"

"Goddamnit!" He pulls his hat off his head and tilts his face skyward. "I will force you out of your car, put the thing in drive, and move it myself if I have to. Do I need to do that?"

I flinch. He looks as though he himself is on the verge of tears. I start the car. I do not let his word repeat in my head. *Goddamnit.*

He points me toward another officer and says, "If you feel so much as a sniffle, alert one of us immediately. You understand?"

I nod and put the car in drive. The other officer directs me as I park on the edge of the highway, facing the traffic and the back of neon Jesus. The cops nearest me move their bikes so that I am blocked in, and then resume their duties. I watch them talk to driver after driver and direct them.

I am stuck, and I don't know where Noah is. Not really. I know he was at that hospital, but I don't know if he's sick or if—no, he's not sick. He can't be. I would know. I would feel it.

One of the cops is speaking to someone through a car window. She unsheathes her radio and calls in backup, but the radio clatters to the ground. The driver, a woman my mother's age, suddenly thrusts her torso fully out the window while two of the cops fight to restrain her. They wrangle her out of the car, push her down to her knees on the pavement. She thrashes beneath them.

After a moment, she stills. Hands cuffed behind her back and head slung forward, she does or says something that has the female cop leaning in closer, the one without the face covering. She says it again, and the cop leans down even—

The woman on the ground strikes, catches the cop's bottom lip between her teeth. She bites down.

The cop jumps back from the infected woman. Blood pours from her mouth. Half her lip is gone. Someone yells, "EMS!" into a radio, and the other cops back away from her, watching her warily as her face gushes blood, trying to keep the infected woman restrained. The bleeding cop screams.

Forgivemefather.

I unbuckle my seatbelt, reach for the door handle, and open it just enough. I slide out and silently let the door close behind me.

I lower myself down to the ground and press my stomach to the asphalt. Disobeying an officer, breaking laws. I am like the crawling thing in Eden. I am, with every choice, stepping farther from goodness and grace. But closer to my brother.

From beneath my mother's car, I see the officers' feet and frenzied movement. More horns, yelling, helicopter blades in the air. All of it comes from behind me. In front sit two unattended cop cars and miles of now-open road. And somewhere beyond that, there is Noah.

I once read that the average person runs a hundred feet in thirteen to sixteen seconds. I take a breath and steel myself. Like Noah does. I'll run like Noah.

I push to my feet and go.

One.

Heart pounding.

Two.

Ears ringing.

Three.

Fingers numb.

Four.

Legs aching.

Five.

ThewordofGod.

Six.

Sipcrunch.

Seven.

Noah.

Eight.

Noah.

Nine.

"Hey! You! Stop her!"

Ten.

Lights.

Eleven.

Sirens.

Twelve.

EMS trucks.

Thirteen.

Strong hands throw me to the ground. Skin tears from my knees. My hands cuffed behind my back.

My father holding me back from Noah. Noah screaming. My father holding me down on the ground.

Feet pound on the asphalt. Someone above me asks, "Another one?"

Someone else says, "I don't think so."

I stare out at the road stretching in front of me, the one that leads to Noah.

It's all I see as I am locked in handcuffs. All I see as I am deposited in the back of one of the cars I was so desperately trying to reach.

My first night in the world on my own, and I am trapped, held captive once again.

Another great gust of wind blows, and the neon Jesus breaks in half. He comes crashing down to the highway.

HOW TO INCREASE RUNNING SPEED:

Interval Train

Hill Train

Tempo Train

Just train, at all, you stupid girl.

Maro

H ey, uh, excuse me, Sophie. Miss. Kid. Could you wake up?"
    I open my eyes to gray early morning sunlight, burned rubber,
and gasoline. I sit in the back seat of a police car. Someone has covered
me with a jacket. My wrists are raw and tender, and when I try to move
them I remember it's because they're handcuffed.

A policeman stands at the open door next to me, a little awkwardly,
and a few more of them talk nearby. My hands are cuffed behind my
back. My mouth is dry, and I have to pee more than I've ever had to in
my life. This is the same cop from last night, I can tell even with the
medical mask now on his face. Verges.

Other than a few cars scattered around the expanse of highway
in front of us, the road is mostly empty. Another cop car behind and
one motorcycle. The billboard cutout that crashed to the ground. My
mother's car parked to the side of the road, windshield shattered.

I sit up.

He asks about the blood on me, what happened with the man on the
road. I tell him. I leave out what happened with my parents. He takes
it all in, is unsurprised.

"Um, can I . . . ?" I turn and show him my wrists.

"You gonna run?"

I shake my head. He considers me and then uses a small key to un-
lock the cuffs. I roll my wrists and rub feeling back into my hands.

"How are you feeling? Any coughing, any sign of fever?"

I shake my head again, no.

He nods and produces another set of gloves from his pocket. "I
don't have another mask," he says. "Sorry."

"Is the virus spread through the air?"

"Look, I've been out here all night."

I don't know what to say.

"I gotta go to Waukesha County, to report there. You can wear that jacket," he says to me, and I glance down to the one that some-one laid over me while I slept, the one I now realize, seeing his bare arms, is his.

"Oh. No, thanks. I don't need it."

He's going where Noah is.

"Suit yourself," he says. "You hungry?"

"Yes," I breathe.

"Let's go."

I sit on the back of Officer Verges's motorcycle, my skirt tucked be-neath me so it won't fly up in the wind, my body as far from his as I can make it. One of the two police cars, the one I was sleeping in, had to go elsewhere, and the other was full of blood in the back seat, so they said the motorcycle was my best bet. I hesitated to put my arms around him, this man, this stranger. But he told me I would fall off if I didn't. My legs nearly touching his.

Garbage litters the highway asphalt, blows in the early morning wind. A plastic food container flies and brushes my bare leg. Billboards appear on the side of the highway, new ones. A beer garden with a woman's breasts as the prominent image. **ERECTILE DYSFUNCTION A THING OF THE PAST** with a man and a woman kissing. Cellulite removal, a pic-ture of a woman's lower half in a bikini, from behind. One that says **TAKE MY HAND, NOT MY LIFE, STOP PLANNED PARENTHOOD NOW**. And one with just the words: **MILK, AN EASY CHOICE!**

Half-torn-down pumpkin and cider stands, corn crops. This land-scape, foreign. As if I've never really been here before, in this state, in this world. I am cold in the rushing morning air, in only my skirt and torn polo. I should have taken him up on his offer of the jacket. I reach in my skirt's pocket with one hand.

My stomach drops.

I don't have my mother's phone.

No. How could I not have it? It was in my hand when I . . .

When I ran.

How stupid could I be? How could I not keep track of one thing, such a valuable vital thing? I am so furious with myself I can hardly breathe.

Cornfields rolling behind fast food restaurants and storefronts. Roads and fields stretching in every direction. Still the brightest greens of summer, but yellowing leaves have arrived, in a dusting here and there beneath trees like the one outside my bedroom window, orange beginning to break through. Fall leaves, trash on the highway, broken glass.

Freedom. What I've always wanted.

My stomach churns. I hold on tighter.

Officer Verges parks in front of Millie's Supper Club with a blue neon **SORRY, WE'RE OPEN** sign hanging in the window.

Two cops step out of the car next to us, a man maybe in his forties and a younger woman who from the look of her has seen much better nights.

Officer Verges stops the motorcycle. I jump off as quickly as I can, adjusting my skirt. Something is shoved to my chest.

"Might be better if you put that on," he says. His jacket. I don't argue this time.

He introduces the other two cops as Harold and Vick and tells me to call him Maro. The hostess knows them all and shoots a suspicious glance at me before seating us.

Vick sits down and mumbles a *Thank fucking God*. I flinch.

The only people in here, besides me and one other couple, are policemen. Every square inch of the wood-paneled walls is covered with photographs of cops, some black-and-white, some in color. Red-and-white Ws and **AMERICA'S DAIRYLAND**, old flaking signs for Lake Monona, Lake Mendota, and the U.P. Posters with all kinds of beer, half-nude women holding giant mugs of it. All the color, words, images, the vibrant clutter of them, such a stark contrast to the spare tans, beiges, and wood of our home, our church, the school. My life.

With her elbows propped on the table, Vick drops her head in her hands. I'm seated next to Maro, across from the others, and the battle-worn exhaustion they share is different from my own. I feel I am intrud-ing. I try to lean closer to the window. They pass around hand sanitizer, and we all use it. They tuck away their gloves in their pockets.

Only the hostess and one waitress work the dining room, and the air is filled with the promise of bacon and pancakes. I eye the menu, trying not to faint from gratitude, and a new reality sets in. Food costs money. I don't have money. I've never been to a restaurant without my parents, and I've never really paid for anything on my own.

I take in the three adults I share the table with. Exhausted, fright-ened, angry.

I ask Maro if I can scoot by and use the restroom.

On the way, I pass another table of cops. One of them says, "We got the call, and it took two guys to get him off of her. She was shaken up, but what could we do, ya know?" His voice falters. He clears his throat. "We sent her off with the EMTs. I mean, it was a fuckin' rape. Now she's probably got it too. Just fuckin' spreading this thi—"

I wash my hands and stick my head under the faucet, drinking in water for a full minute.

Rape.

My mother's story.

My mother.

I sway and catch the counter. Splash water over my face again.

I raise my eyes to the mirror. I still don't recognize the person standing there. I slide off the officer's jacket.

My too-tight polo and plaid skirt. The former covered in blood and ripped at the neckline. By my father. Blood spattered on my skin. My chest, and my neck. My left breast half-exposed in the old bra, my hair falling out of a messy braid. Without allowing myself much thought, I shake it out and rebraid it, my eyes fixed on the girl before me.

Honorthyfatherandmother.

Rape.

Goddamnit.

A sign on the wall says:

GOD CREATED MAN BEFORE WOMAN BECAUSE HE DIDN'T WANT ANY AD-VICE ON HOW TO DO IT.

I wash my skin with the pink diner soap and dry it with a rough paper towel. I rinse my mouth out and swallow another huge gulp. I know I can't stay in here forever.

My hands still shaking, I wash again.

Back at the table, in front of my seat is a plate of eggs, sausage, pancakes, hash browns, and toast. The officers each have their own plates and silently eat. Maro notices me first, and he moves so I can sit.

"Ordered for ya," he says.

I swallow with some difficulty. "I don't have money."

Maro shakes his head. His arms bare because I wear his jacket.

He nudges a cup of coffee and a glass of orange juice toward me.

I pick up my fork and look to the other two. Harold is staring out the window, nearly catatonic, but Vick is watching me. "You may as well then," she says.

I eat every bite of food and down the orange juice. I sip the coffee, my first time having any, and at first it is bitter and unpleasant, but they bought it for me, so I drink it. By the end, I think I like it. I drink it all down anyway. When I finish, I raise my head to find Vick and Maro watching me. Vick laughs, sort of. "That appetite. You fifteen?"

"Seventeen," I lie.

"Your family on the inside?"

"Waukesha."

"You heard from them? Been able to talk at all?"

"No."

"Does anyone know where you are?"

"No, but—"

"You gonna take her to Eli's or no?" This is not directed to me, but to Maro, who is finishing his toast.

"I need to get to Waukesha," I say.

No one says anything.

My voice comes out softer than I want it to, but I finally force out the question burning its way through me. "What's happening inside the quarantine zones?"

Silence, Maro's chewing.

I should be sitting at the kitchen table right now with my parents. I should be hearing the *sip* and the *click* and the *crinkle*.

"I am so grateful that you bought me breakfast," I say, "but please, my family is in there. Please tell me. I've had maybe the worst twenty-four hours of my life."

Vick raises an eyebrow at me. "*Maybe* the worst?"

Noah, dragged, screaming, through our home.

"Please," I say. "I can handle it."

Harold's hand comes down on the table, shaking silverware on plates and knocking over the salt shaker. His voice booms through the space. "No one can fucking handle it."

He presses his forehead to his palm and then stands so fast he almost takes the table with him. He doesn't wait for Vick to move but steps right over her, rocking the table on his way out, orange juice sloshing over the sides of the plastic diner cups. The door slams behind him.

The diner is quiet for a moment. Then talking resumes, silverware, a deep fryer sizzling.

After a long minute, Vick says, "Harold's family is in there—his wife and his kid. And they got the flu. The virus. Whatever. They got sick before he went on duty. Had to wait and see if he was sick too. Can't go back in now, not even him."

"So, all of this is NARS?" I say.

"Well, not anymore."

"What do you mean?"

"You know what?" Maro puts his fork down. "We gotta finish breakfast, make sure Harold is fit for duty, and then *we* have to get back to work."

"But I need to go. I need to get to my family. I can't stay here."

Before I realize it's coming, Maro's hand is on my arm, and he is looking me right in the eyes. "You are *not* going in there. You clearly somehow don't know what this thing can do, and if you do and still want to go in, then you've got bigger problems. We all have people we love in there, but unless we're talkin' to them on the phone, for all we know, they're already dead."

He sees me flinch at the word. I don't quite comprehend it.

"Yes. *Dead.* People are dying. You are one of the lucky few who might survive, if any of us do." He tosses his napkin on the table. "We've let too fuckin' many die already."

He lets go of me and waves the waitress over, tucking some folded bills into her hand with a *Thank you. Stay safe.*

Thunder sounds in the distance. No one seems to notice.

HPSU

Outside, Harold sits in the passenger seat of his squad car. "We ready?"

Vick nods and slides in. They pull out, Harold giving Maro a cross between a salute and a wave as they drive away. The red and blue lights flash on again, and I watch them grow smaller in the distance.

Maro stands on the gravel of the parking lot, hat crooked on his head.

"Where are we going? Where in Waukesha County do you have to go?" I say.

"Well," he says, fiddling with a toothpick in his mouth, "*we* are going to Eli's. And then *you* are going to stay there because I have to work to help try to get this nightmare under control."

"Who's Eli?" I cross my arms.

"Buddy of mine."

"A *buddy* of yours? You're taking me to stay with just some guy? You said you would take me to my family."

"I told you that I have to go to the same place you want to go, not that I would take you there. Eli's a good guy. I can vouch for him. I promise, I wouldn't leave you with someone who isn't safe. Also, you're covered in blood. You need to be monitored for signs of infection."

"What—where are all the other teenagers? Surely I wasn't the only one driving by myself in all that traffic. Where did you send them?"

Maro's jaw tightens on the toothpick, snapping it in half. He spits it out on the ground and reaches for his keys in his back pocket. "Johnson Municipal School. Walton Road."

"Okay. And . . . ?"

"And what?"

"And why am I not going there? If I can't go home, at least that makes more sense than your *buddy* Eli's house."

"No one can go there now." His hand messing with something in his pocket.

"Why?"

His jaw tightens as he lifts up his hat and smooths his hair down. A vein throbs in his forehead. Like the one in my mother's when I screamed at her.

"Why can't I go there?"

"Fuck it all," Maro says. He sits on the curb and pulls a pack of cigarettes out of his pocket. He sticks one between his lips and lights it on shaky fingers.

How to Build a Fire: 1. Dig a small hole and surround it with rocks.

Maro takes a long, deep drag, his eyes half closed. After a few more pulls, he sees me, still looking at him. He closes his eyes and exhales in what I know to be frustration, something greater. Grief. Fear. All of it. After a moment, he says,

"Someone got infected—or was infected—inside. They got a few kids out, but it's all quarantined now too. I don't know if a single one of them is alive."

"Oh. Isn't there some kind of protocol, or—"

"Honestly, kid, at this point, it's all gone out the window. We're just tryin' to get this thing under control, and cases like you, we take 'em as they come. There's no precedent for this. The White House tossed whatever plans they made for this kind of thing, and I'm not sure those would even account for this anyway, so we're doing our—" He grinds his foot against the gravel, gritting his teeth. "—guldarn best. Okay? Now, I am going to finish this cigarette because I fuckin' started it, and then we are goin' to get you to Eli's so I can do my part in this cluster."

I try to stay calm. If I can somehow convince him to let me join him, or steal another car, how easy would it be to get through the barriers they've set up at the county lines? I shiver again, goose bumps on my legs. The cold doesn't seem to bother Maro. He stares up at the sun, now fully risen, bright and yellow-gray through the clouds. I watch it too. That thunder still rumbling in the distance.

"So, the infected people, they act kind of . . . um, funny?" I say.

He snorts a laugh and inhales again but doesn't answer me.

"I'm serious. People being . . . you know, aggressive. Like on the highway. That's because of the virus?"

Demonic, Christian Radio says.

"Wait, you're actually not joking. Kid," he turns to me, "how do you not know this?"

"I'm learning that I'm pretty sheltered, I guess. Will you please tell me?"

"I mean, it's been on the news for months. It's been the only thing. Philadelphia? Detroit? The schools and hospitals?"

I shake my head. "Not allowed TV," is all I say.

"Oh shit."

My entire body goes on alert. "What?" The way he says it.

"Do you know what happens to people who are infected? Do you know how big this thing is? Before, inside, I thought you just— Seriously, how do you know nothing about this?"

"I don't know. No one told me. But last night, the man attacked me. And he jumped on this other man and this woman. They were screaming." *And I think my parents are infected too, and I want you to tell me that they weren't, that they aren't, that maybe it was demons and the priest could come, and maybe we can fix this.*

He sighs, drops his cigarette, smashes it underneath his boot. My eyes catch the motion, but I keep my gaze forward, afraid that if I move I will break this tentative sharing between us.

He shakes his head. "I don't even know where to start."

"What are the symptoms?" I say.

A long pause, then Maro pulls out the pack and lights another.

"Well, we don't know everything. I mean, we know basically nothing. But there are two things, NARS-CoV and Sylvia. Sylvia mutated somehow from the NARS virus in the Northeast, and there were some cases in the past months, but not here, and they were few and far between. Some people thought it wasn't even real because what they were saying was so extreme. I mean, a virus that makes people . . . do *that* to each other, it just like . . . who would believe that?" He lets out a laugh. "No one ever expected it to get here so fast, or hit so hard."

His voice is raw. "It starts out like the normal flu, just like the NARS virus—aches, chills, fever, runny nose, breathing stuff. But if it's NARS, that's all that happens. You get better, life goes on. If you've got Sylvia, HPSV, then that's only the beginning. You feel better for a couple hours or a day, almost normal, like you've gotten over it. Then the fever comes back fast, way worse than before, sometimes with a headache, sometimes not. Real glassy eyes, sometimes confusion. And a rash, on the hands, but only for men. Red and blistery, kind of shiny. Now they're sayin' the flu part is happening even faster, the whole timeline speeding up.

"Then people get—well, sort of really, uh . . . sexual, like every part of their brains has shut off except the one that wants 'em to . . . The virus allows for this thing to take root, hijacks the brain. I don't totally understand it myself. And Sylvia, it's new. I mean, I guess we're just figuring it out, or just trying to, but it's spreading fast, and changing fast, and . . . Anyway, that's the gist of it. Oh, I mean, and then . . ."

"Then what?"

"Well, the fever kills them. It usually takes a couple days, but not always."

An American flag waves at full mast on the road. Beyond it another billboard for a restaurant called Twin Peaks.

Thefeverkillsthem.

The fever kills them.

"That guy, who attacked you on the highway. It can take some time before the symptoms start. We need to watch you to be sure, but I won't put you with the other infected unless you show definitive signs. That'd be just about the same as drafting your death certificate."

He throws his cigarette butt on the ground and stamps it out with his boot. "Let's go."

It's a long second before I can speak. "Wait, Maro."

He looks up.

"It doesn't kill everyone, does it?"

I feel the desperation in my voice. He must hear it too, see it on my face. He gives me the most terrible look of all. Pity.

"I'm sorry, kid. I don't know about your family, or . . . It's . . ." He clears his throat and takes a deep breath. "What we know is if they get to the, you know, *sexual* stage . . . they die. People aren't surviving. It's why there's a quarantine, and I mean, do you know how much it takes for the government to step in like they're doing? And this fast? This is massive—"

I don't hear anything else.

I don't hear anything.

The air quivers around me like smoke over a fire. My lungs constrict. I can't breathe.

Strands of my hair blow in the wind, my skirt flaps around my thighs, a fly buzzes near my face. Rolling hills and the flag flying high.

No. He must be wrong. He has to be. What does he know?

More than I do. Before this, I didn't know anything, thought that it was a rough flu season on the East Coast, far away from here, and nothing more. My father was right. I know nothing.

I turn and run, unfeeling, unthinking, back into the diner. Just past the door lies a stack of newspapers, dated from two days ago. I pick up the top one and stare at the headline until the words unscramble and form something comprehensible.

DEATH TALLY RISES AS VIRUS HITS MIDWEST
October 1st

The HPSV death tally has risen to over 3,000 in the US. 643 deaths have been reported in the Midwestern region alone since last Wednesday, the 26th. The Wisconsin and Minnesota state governments, with the Centers for Disease Control's help, have enacted extreme quarantine measures in order to control the spread of the virus. Any infected individual MUST report to Emergency Medical Services, and will be relocated accordingly.

An inside source from within the CDC's Special Pathogens Branch reported that clinical trials on simian subjects are currently in progress. So far, these trials indicate that roughly 80 percent of individuals infected by the virus will eventually exhibit behavioral changes including, but not limited to, sexual mania and fervor, and the male-exhibited hand rash. While concrete data from human subjects is limited, in all 109 studied human cases of late-stage HPSV, characterized by intense sexual mania and fervor, there are no reported cases of survival.

If you see anyone exhibiting signs of infection, it is your civic duty to report them to the nearest law enforcement official and protect yourself by any means necessary from contact. Infected individuals must quarantine immediately. Please do not expose your neighbors and loved ones to this virus. Minimizing exposure is the state and country's number one priority.

My leaden legs carry me out of the diner and into the parking lot. Maro is waiting for me. I stand there, saying nothing. Maro climbs onto his bike. I get on behind him, unconcerned this time with my bare legs or our proximity. This stranger.

Thefeverkillsthem.

We pull onto the highway. Still empty, save for the trash. Empty and eerily quiet.

My parents are infected. They have the fever. They were copulating on the floor in front of me. They attacked me, and they were going to do it to me as well. And my father's hands.

My parents are infected.

They are . . .

Maro and I drive northeast now, away from Noah, away from my parents, away from everything I know.

I open my mouth for words to escape, but they don't come alone. I feel the hate so strong in me, it fills everything. This terrible hate born inside me that I have been carrying and nurturing and feeding for years, hatred for them. And now—

"It's stupid that you're taking me here when you just have to turn back around after!"

Infected.

"Do you hear me?!" I yell.

Thefeverkillsthem.

"This is stupid!" I yell even louder. "It doesn't make any sense! Take me to my brother!"

I hit him. Use my hand to strike another human being. It feels good, releases something.

I hit him again. He doesn't turn, and he doesn't stop.

My hair whips in my face, and my eyes water from the unrelenting onslaught of air.

I'm angry that he doesn't have helmets. I am angry that my skirt won't stay down, I am angry that he—a total stranger—won't let me see my brother who might be in danger, and I am angry that Noah is anywhere other than where I am, that he ever was.

My parents are infected.

They did this, separated Noah and me and made me love them anyway. Attacked me and hurt me and forced me out of our home and now they have abandoned me to this nightmare.

They left me to this, and now I am alone with this man I hardly know, and I could be infected now. I could be infected now from my father and mother, from that man on the road, and all I want is to be with them and tell them I love them and tell them I am so unbelievably sorry.

This is my fault. It's mine.

All the times we fought, all the times I seethed in hate and shame. And now they're gone.

I will never see my parents again. Never. My brain sets the words on repeat:

Gone. Neverseethemagain.

Thefeverkillsthem.

And even as I fight it, even as I push the thought away and strain against it with all my might, as I hit the stranger in front of me over and over again, the policeman who could arrest me for it, the adult who could punish me, it forces its way in and settles in my gut.

This is real.

This is my life now.

I am Sophie, and I lost my parents.

When I was sixteen, my parents died.

This is my story now.

Not just my story. Noah's too. And he doesn't even know. He has no idea.

My eyes have filled, and my throat burns. I open my mouth as wide as it can go, and every frustration and every fear and every horror I have witnessed in the past day and week builds until it pours out of me, escaping in a scream that originates in my belly and fills my whole body like a flood. It gushes from my lips and reaches only the vacant highway.

The wind whips my voice away to nothing.

Hell Hound

Eli's is a solitary farmhouse on a dirt road, framed on either side by cornfields. A rusted tractor sits beside the house along with a woodchipper and a giant freezer. In front of the house is an old white truck and a chicken. The windmill squeaks. Dark clouds gather on the horizon.

The motorcycle slows, crunches over the dirt and gravel, scaring the chicken off into the field, a flurry of feathers and squawks. The air smells of manure and the faintest hint of pesticides. I did farm chores when I was younger in community-building projects with the church, and I never minded the way the manure smelled, like earth and something ancient.

Maro pulls to a stop in front of the house. With the engine off, it is quiet. Crows cawing overhead, the steady creak of the mill. I step off the bike, and Maro follows, stretching his legs and putting his hat back on after the ride. He lights another cigarette. He never put his mask back on.

"Feel better?" he says.

I don't know you. My parents died.

"Listen, as soon as I'm finished at the Waukesha County border I'll come back and get you, and we'll figure out what to do next. You'll be safe here until then," he says.

"I want to go with you."

He sighs and smooths his hair back under his hat, exasperated. "It's not safe for you there, and it is here, and I can't babysit you while I'm doing my job. Okay? Let's get inside."

He brushes past me and takes the steps up to the house. The screen door slams shut behind him, but he leaves the front door open. I glance back to the bike. The keys are still in it. Did he really just leave them? I turn back to the house. It's quiet. Maro is presumably with Eli, and I won't be stranding him because there is a truck here. I watched him before, the way he started it.

I move toward the motorcycle, eyes on the front door of the house. I swing my leg over, feeling for the first time the huge weight of the thing. Okay, I did watch him before, but now that I'm on it . . . I flip the switch behind the red button. Yes, right, Maro did that both times he started it. I can do this. I brace myself.

A sound cuts through the morning. A loud crash. Maro's voice, guttural. I prepare to rev the engine, thinking he's spotted me. But then—

It's not anger in his voice.

It's . . .

Fear.

Before I can think better of it, I jump off the bike and run to the porch. I stop at the closed screen door and listen. What I do not expect to hear, following his anguished cry, is a dog's growls and barks. Maro yelling obscenities. A broom lies on the porch, and I pick it up near the straw end. I open the door as carefully as I can and peer inside.

While from the outside the farmhouse appears to be falling apart, dusty and half-dilapidated, inside it is lovingly and carefully furnished. Floral fabrics and paintings of exquisite otherworldly scenes, in deep, rich colors. There are books. Tons of them, on shelves built into the walls. Lamps spaced all around for reading. Fresh flowers in vases.

I close the door quietly behind me. To my left is a tiny kitchen, to my right another room, but I can't see into it yet because the living room wall blocks my view. The sound is definitely coming from there. I skirt around furniture and tiptoe to the edge of the wall. I can just see inside.

"Fuck you, motherfucker!" Maro swings a chair at what I can only think at first is a monster. Huge and covered in fur so black it is like the absence of light, its head looks like it would reach my shoulder. Not only the largest dog I've ever seen, but larger than I thought possible.

It bares its massive teeth at Maro. Maro holds his arm oddly, and when I peer around farther, I can see where his sleeve is torn, and there's blood on it. The dog's muzzle dangerously close to him, even with the chair brandished between them. It paws at it. Maro pulls back again, and the beast crouches low to attack.

I step into the room and yell, "Hey!"

Its massive head swings toward me, slobber dripping from its jaws. The growling grows in volume.

"Kid, goddamnit, get out of here!"

I stay where I am. I hold the broom out in front of me, positioning it between us horizontally. I angle my body to the side and keep my eyes down. *Make yourself a smaller target.* I need to slow my breath. If I am afraid, he will feel it. If I am angry, he will feel it.

"Go," Maro says.

I raise a hand to Maro, the other still holding the broom. I keep my eyes fixed on the ground between the dog and me. Even with my heart pounding in my chest, I count each breath. I can feel the beast's hot breath even from here, can smell his urine in the house. *In 2-3-4, out 2-3-4.* The dog's growling quiets, just a little. *Stand your ground. In 2-3-4, out 2-3-4.*

We stay this way for a long time, the dog, the policeman, and me.

Eventually, the dog loses interest and pads back over to the corner it was defending.

I lower the broomstick and whisper, "Are you okay?" I shoot a glance to Maro. He looks as though he's seen a ghost.

"How did you do that?"

Keeping my voice low, I ask, "What is he guarding?" The dog stands over a big, cloth-covered heap on the floor. Flies swarm, and I realize the smell in the room is not only urine. The dog paces, sniffing and licking the cloth. He nudges it with its nose, whines, paces again.

Maro shakes his head. "We need to go."

Maro sits on the edge of the front porch cradling his head in his palms, as he has done for the last half hour. A crumpled piece of paper sticks out from his hand. I stand awkwardly between him and the bike. I can't stop my brain from calculating what it would take to jump on and drive away and what my first steps would be if I made it clear of the farm. But taking in the man in front of me, so pitiful and beaten down . . .

I let him have a minute, and then when it becomes too unbearable to watch I ask again, "What happened in there?"

Maro looks up at me as if he has forgotten I exist.

His eyes on me. I start, flinch a little. It's the first time we've just actually looked at each other, I guess, since the highway or the diner, since he was just some adult in a mask.

He has blue-gray eyes, brown hair, a tight jaw. Haunted, worn down by the world, maybe even before this. But . . . there's something else too.

I know it doesn't matter, nothing could possibly matter less. And maybe it's because I am in shock, because I am losing everything. But it's there.

He's . . . well . . . *very* good-looking.

I take the thought back. He's an adult, and it's not—But I can't. I mean, it's just his face. I've never seen an adult who looks like this. And he's studying me, maybe searching for something, maybe remembering. I can tell he's thinking of someone else, not really seeing me, but even so . . . adrenaline, coursing through me. Maybe it's residual from the dog. I am, strangely, very aware of my body, the space it inhabits.

I feel . . .

His eyes return to the paper in his hands. I am released.

My breath slows, a little. Shame, confusion, I don't know. My arms in his jacket. He reaches into his pocket for a cigarette, but his fingers shake enough to make the feat almost impossible. Finally, he fishes one out.

"That was Eli," he says.

"What?"

"That was my friend. In the corner. We—I was here a week ago." He clears his throat and steadies his voice. "He told me if he got infected he was going to . . ." He takes a long, shaky drag on the cigarette. "He has a girlfriend been livin' here with him, maybe she got him. I don't know. I don't know who the fuck's dog that is."

"You should feed him." My words come out breathless, strange.

"What?"

"The dog," I say, and I shake my head. "It'll help. Help him trust you."

"Oh."

"What's on the paper?"

Maro stares at it and shakes his head. "He always did have a flair for the dramatic. Suspect this was some kind of joke."

I wait, and by the end of his cigarette, the last of the smoke clearing his lips, he reads aloud. "*Hell is empty,* it says."

I whisper the rest, tearing my eyes from his face, from the way it makes me feel.

Thunder sounds again.

"All the devils are here."

Maro digs a grave out back near the single large tree that grows there, and I sit obediently on the front porch watching the corn sway, counting the mosquitoes who land on me and feast. He told me that under no circumstances was I to go back into the house.

He took the keys from the bike when he went to radio someone and tell them what happened to Eli. The officer on the other end said not to touch the body, but I understand that this is his friend. And orders only go so far. Maro also took the keys for the truck. I know how to hotwire a car. Well, I at least know the steps. Every second I am here is another second something could happen to Noah.

The dog is whining, inside the house. It's been going on for as long as I've been sitting here—twenty minutes, I don't know. The sound is making me crazy. Dog training instructions blow through my mind like the wind in the corn, moving alongside the other words.

Ourdutyaswomen. ThewordofGod. ForgivemeFather. Virus. Infected. StandYourGround.

I stand and head toward the truck.

I am only a few paces beyond the house when a thought catches up to me. Then another. Questions I don't want.

Where did my parents die? Have they died already, or is it happening now, right this minute? Have they crawled their way back into the house to breathe their last breaths beneath the eyes of Jesus in the home they made, or are they still on the front porch where anyone could see them, naked, painted in blood because I stabbed my father, *I stabbed my father.* And how long will they stay there? Will someone come?

Will their wishes be honored, to be buried in the plots they bought in the Catholic cemetery? Or will the hospital tag them and shove them in freezers or incinerators and dispose of them the way they would any other corpse of the secular world?

My mother wearing that scapular every day to try and ensure she would have a peaceful death and receive last rites. They won't have last rites. Which means . . . after a lifetime of servitude, after everything, after holding Christ above all else . . .

Will my parents not even make it to Heaven?

The dog's whining reaches a fever pitch. I curse myself and turn back, open the screen and the front door, and stalk into the room to the right. When the dog sees me, its whines morph again into a growl. Its muzzle pulls back, teeth exposed and muscles flexed under that black fur. I can't tell what breed he is, but his head is massive. Maybe some kind of mastiff mix, maybe Great Dane or Newfoundland. His fur is short, and he seems to have been bred to look as terrifying as possible. I don't have the broom with me, I left it outside. It was supposed to say to the animal *this is my space, and that is yours, and we can each have our own.* But I don't care about the broom, and I don't care about Maro's rules. I just need the whining to stop. I see where Maro left a bowl of food by the door, and I take a little in my right hand, grab hold of the bowl in my left.

I take a step toward the dog. It warns me with a nearly deafening bark and snarl. I pause, then step closer, keeping my eyes fixed on his. It's not safe to challenge him in this way, it's not in the instructions. But I hold the dog's eyes anyway.

I move closer. There are now only three feet separating us, and he is even larger than I realized. If he strikes, he could kill me. Still, I take another step.

I reach my right hand out to him, palm down, food in it. He snarls again.

I wait.

He growls, low and steady, slobber dripping and pooling below him. But he takes one step toward my hand, lowers his face to it. His teeth inches from my knuckles, his hot breath wetting my fingers. I stay still, and I wait.

He sniffs. I let my fingers unravel slightly, turn my palm upward, showing him the food. He slowly stretches forward and takes it from me.

I start to move toward him. He rears back and snarls.

I still. After a moment, he comes closer. This time, tentatively, I brush the side of his jaw and the soft fur of his ear with my knuckles, holding the bowl up, offering him more food with my other hand. I graze his face and the top of his neck, moving my fingers carefully and slowly over the dog's giant head. The rumbling in his throat slows, and then eventually quiets all together.

And then the whining again. He looks back at the lump on the floor and then up at me, wanting me to do something. He paws at the figure, nudging it with his nose, looks up at me again.

"I know. I'm sorry, I can't do anything. I'm so sorry."

Then, faster than I can track, the dog spins his body sideways and throws his whole weight into me, taking us both down to the floorboards, the bowl and its contents clattering to the floor. He sits on my legs and stomach and presses the side of his head into my chest. He whines and drools as he licks my arms. I wrap one arm around his neck and run the other over his back and belly, back and forth. My head comes to rest on top of his. He whines and whines and leans into me, and I hold him as tightly as I can.

I know, I know. I'm so sorry.

We stay on the floor in the living room for a long time like this, rocking back and forth. I whisper to the dog, his whines rising and falling, drool slipping down my arm. I close my eyes. Physical contact with another living being, the kind I have never been allowed. After a while, I hear Maro calling for me outside. He swears, loudly enough to hear through the walls, and the screen door slams against its frame. "Kid! Goddamnit, kid, are you in here?"

The dog growls again against my chest. I whisper to him and hold his head close. Maro bursts into the room. I sense him stop short behind me. The dog lifts his head, warning him. The growl rumbles through my body, but I hold him tight and stroke his back, whispering to him still.

"What in God's name—"

I flinch at Maro's choice of words, and the dog's warning grows.

"Shh, it's okay. He's a friend, it's okay."

"You think that thing is a friend? Kid—I told you, you can't be in here. You could get infected. We don't know if—"

I keep my voice deliberate and low, refusing to turn toward him. "I am telling Barghest that you are a friend. If you don't want him to attack you, you should calm down and introduce yourself."

"Barghest?"

I slowly extricate myself from beneath the dog's massive frame and move to his side, petting him all the while. "He has a tag. Stay where you are. I think I can do this."

I keep petting him as I stand. Barghest follows suit, looking from me to Maro and then back again. I try to encourage him to walk toward Maro, but he won't leave his post next to the fallen body on the ground.

"Okay. Come over here slowly."

Maro shoots me a look. He steps forward but stops a few feet away from us when Barghest growls again. Maro has wrapped his arm in a long-sleeved shirt to stanch the bleeding.

"Hold out your hand," I say. "No, not like that. Gently."

I grab his fingers and pull them toward Barghest's face. The dog sniffs at them, looks up at me, sniffs again, and then licks. Maro lets his breath out in a long, slow exhale. I drop his hand and rest mine on the furry head beside me. Barghest does in fact come up to my shoulder.

"Are you sure this wasn't Eli's dog?" I ask. "He seems to be protecting his body."

"I knew Eli better than almost anyone. He was the one who got me into the force. We were partners. He definitely did not have a dog. Fuck, you can't be in here."

"We've both been in here. You're going to carry Eli's body. We're sharing a motorcycle. If it's airborne, then we both probably already have it."

Maro deliberates. Barghest presses into my side, and I have to lean back into him in order to keep my balance.

"I finished the grave."

It takes a few tries, but I am able to get Barghest to move a few feet away from the body—not far, but far enough for Maro to have some room to move him. The fabric covering the body is the same curtain fabric that still hangs in one sheet on the rod above. Eli must have grabbed and ripped it down, covering himself at the last minute. Flies buzz, and the breeze that blows through the house since Maro left the doors open makes them swarm even more.

I sit on the floor and hold Barghest's head against me. I try to angle my body and position his so that he can't see what's happening with Eli's body. I peer over his head and watch Maro pull the curtain back to reveal his dead friend's face.

I see it at the same time he does.

He drops the fabric. Stares down at the heap on the floor, the one that we can now see is not one body, but two. Four arms and four legs, wrapped and tangled around each other, a woman's hair fanning over the man's chest, both naked and now exposed to the flies.

My parents on the living room floor. My mother beneath my father.

I shake my head. The man and the woman, her body mostly on top of his. A silver pistol resting on her back, underneath his right hand, and a pair of matching, red-and-black oozing holes—one in his chest, and one in hers. Blood from their wounds has streamed out and crusted over Eli's torso and arms. Their hands are clasped together.

I don't know how long we stare at the bodies. I expect Barghest to make a run for them, to lunge for Maro standing over them, but he only leans into me. I tell him the best lie there is.

It's going to be okay.

It doesn't take long for Maro to expand the grave to accommodate two. But getting the woman's body—Maro said her name was Fiona—into the plot behind the house isn't easy. Barghest almost attacks both of us when we try to move her. When Maro starts piling dirt over her, Barghest runs around her grave in circles, whining and pawing at the earth, howling.

I walk through the house, so full of life and love and stories. So *full*. It makes me want to cry. My eyes catch on a piece of art in the living room. A gold frame, title: *The Lovers' Whirlwind*. A dark scene I remember from *Inferno* in Dante's *Divine Comedy*. Great wind tunnels beneath one shining sun, not quite bright enough to illuminate the rest of the scene. Darkness. Pain. So much longing. And those twisting, turning funnels, entirely full of bodies. Naked bodies, writhing bodies. A woman's, and a man's, their hands outstretched, reaching for each other. Even as it is clear they will never touch, will be stuck forever in the torrent.

"We're not taking him," Maro says definitively. He is on the bike, keys in the ignition, ready to go. I stand between the house and the bike once again, but Barghest is now at my side.

"We can't leave him here."

"We can't take a dog on the bike."

"We'll take the truck."

"I'm taking my bike."

"Then I can't go with you."

"What, you want to stay here?"

"I'm obviously not going to stay here. I am going to get in that truck with this dog," I say.

Maro's radio buzzes. He clicks it on and gets an order. *Report to Waukesha County line.*

I hold his eyes a little longer, then turn and head for the truck. Barghest follows. I let him into the bed—the backseat of the cab is too small for him to fit—and then sit myself down in the passenger seat.

Barghest growls at Maro when he opens the driver's side door.

The three of us pull out on the highway.

𝔐𝔞𝔤𝔞𝔷𝔦𝔫𝔢𝔰

I am half lying down in the tight backseat of the pickup. I must have fallen asleep. I sit up, push my hair out of my face, and make sure I am covered by the little bit of skirt I have. Maro drives, and Barghest in the bed pants out at the road behind us. The wind has picked up again, whistles against the windows, ruffles Barghest's fur. The clock on the dash is broken, but it appears to be late afternoon.

"Where are we?"

"Near Augusta. You've only been out for a half an hour."

"He probably needs water."

"The dog?" His eyes catch mine briefly through the rearview mirror. His eyes, his attention on me. My heart picks up again. What is wrong with me?

I realize in this moment that I know nothing about this man, and he is the only person in the world who knows where I am. Other than his departed friend, I know nothing about this person I am traveling with.

I force my eyes off his face and nod.

"We gotta fill up pretty soon anyway. I'm sure we can find something. You hungry?"

"No."

Maro emerges from the gas station with two sandwiches, bags of chips, two packs of cigarettes, and a huge bag of dog food. While he was inside, I let Barghest out to walk around and found him some water. We sit together in the bed of the truck, his head in my lap. Maro drops the food in the cab and lights another cigarette. The wind is blowing hard now. It takes him a few tries.

"Was anyone in there?" I ask.

He shakes his head no. I jump down from the truck.

Inside, I grab a bottle of water. I stop for a moment at a magazine rack and pick one up, setting the bottle down on the counter. I've never been allowed to read these. Of course not, after what happened with Noah.

The pages are glossy and smooth beneath my fingers. I flip through. Women in bikinis, in underwear, in short tight dresses and leather pants and jewelry and makeup. There are men too, shirtless, suited. Not like the church suits, not like any I've seen, but ones that make me take notice of the lines of a shoulder, the length of a leg. There are tips for applying makeup and finding the best pushup bra and PLEASING HIM AND YOU.

I am struck, once again, by how little I know of the world outside Foreston, and the few other places I've been. I've never seen women like this, and I wonder if they can possibly be real, or if they are only an idea of something, a distant work of fiction. It's terrible, realizing how much I do not know, more it seems at every turn. I am helpless, and I don't want to be. But somehow, I don't think the answer is in this magazine. There aren't any here with two boys on the cover anyway.

I set it back on the rack and smooth my hands over its cover, once more.

The women's bathroom is down a long corridor that ends in what looks like a supply room, a red and yellow neon sign by the door that says NATURAL AMERICAN SPIRIT. In the hall, the buzz of a flickering fluorescent light seems to bounce off the walls. The flies over Eli's and Fiona's bodies.

I try the door for the women's room, but it's locked. A sign hangs sideways on the wall saying the key is with the cashier, and a search around the cash register proves fruitless.

On the other side of the hall is the door to the men's bathroom, slightly open. I look around. No one is here. Surely the men's bathroom can't be that different than the women's. I've always been told it's wrong, but I have to go.

I push the door open with one hand and fumble for the light switch with the other. I feel around for a moment but can't find it. There's no switch in the hall, so it must be farther inside. Holding the door open to allow in as much light as possible, I step into the bathroom.

I place my foot down.

I slip, try to catch myself, but my foot slides out completely from beneath me. I scramble to take hold of the counter, but it's too late, it's happening too fast.

I fall, hard, tailbone on tile. The door slams shut.

I am engulfed in darkness.

I try to push up onto one elbow, but it too slides out from under me. The same substance I slipped in. I've fallen in something wet and sticky. Globs of it. On one of my legs, under my arm, seeping in to wet my side through my shirt. The room smells heavily of chlorine and a little of human waste. Bile rises in my throat, and I will myself to breathe. *Probably soap. It's just soap.* I press myself up with one hand, and feel the substance there as well, viscous, that tangy, acidic smell. I reach around in the dark until my fingers find the door handle. I pull myself up to stand and throw the door open. Stumble back into the hall.

I won't look down. I can't. I refuse, in the fluorescent light of the store, to see whatever is now covering my body. I wipe any wet areas of skin on my shirt and skirt, keeping my head up. Everything is fine. *It's just soap.* It's just soap as long as I tell myself it is.

I walk down the corridor, the wetness under the sole of my left shoe causing it to squeak. *Just soap.* I am about to reenter the main part of the store when I hear breathing. Breathing that is not mine.

I don't want to look. Like the slime, like so much of this, I just want to close my eyes and open them again and find that none of it is real. I want to walk calmly out of the store and get in the truck with Maro and continue on to my brother.

But someone is breathing behind me.

I turn.

At the end of the hall, a man emerges from the supply room. He stares down at his feet, moving slowly, and he somehow hasn't noticed me yet.

I take a step back. He doesn't notice. I take another, with my left foot. My shoe squeaks on the linoleum, just loud enough for the man's head to snap up. For his eyes to lock on mine.

I know this look. It is the look of the man on the highway, of my mother, my father. His forehead is beaded with sweat, and I don't need to see his palms to know they are red.

I run.

My left foot slides on the floor, and I have to slow down to keep from falling. The man's feet pound on the tiles behind me, and his ragged breathing is the only thing I hear. I swerve around the aisles, the man's steps drawing closer. I can feel and hear and smell him closing the distance between us, that chlorine stench on him as well, everywhere, on everything.

His hand catches the back of my shirt.

I reach for the closest item on the nearest shelf, a wizard or Santa Claus figurine, and slam it into the side of his head. He lets go just long enough for me to pull away and sprint the final five feet to the door. I scream for Maro.

Outside, I run for the truck. The man bursts through the door behind me.

Before I know what is happening, Barghest is out of the bed and racing toward me. Maro steps out from the driver's side, gun in hand, but the dog is in the air, a great flying beast. He tackles the man to the ground. Has him locked down beneath his massive body, growling only inches from his face.

"Sophie, call the dog!"

I open my mouth to call his name, but it's too late.

Barghest's teeth clamp onto the man's neck and rip out his throat.

Barghest's low simmering growl, his mouth dripping blood. A spraying, gushing gurgling from the man. His body, beneath the giant dog, spasms, chokes, a blood bubble rises up and grows from his open throat until it pops. Droplets spatter the pavement.

Barghest's growl doesn't quiet until the man is completely still, until every shudder and spasm has ceased.

Maro positions himself between Barghest and me.

"Did he touch you?"

I stare at Barghest, at all the blood.

"Did he touch you?"

"Um, my shirt. But I slipped on this stuff in the bathroom, and it's all over me, and—"

Maro's face as he sees what's on me. "Take your clothes off, now."

"What?"

"I'm serious, get them off *now*!"

"I—what? No! No way!"

"Goddamnit, I won't look! You have to get out of those clothes, and you have to get that off your skin. Do you hear me?"

He runs to the bucket near the pump that holds the windshield squeegee and starts dipping paper towels into the soapy water. He turns back to me.

I am paralyzed.

"Hey! I'm serious!"

"You said you wouldn't look!"

Maro drops the paper towels, throws his hands up in the air, and closes his eyes. He covers his face with his hands. "I am not looking! *Please,* get that stuff off you. I'm going to turn around and get you a blanket out of the truck. I'll keep my back to you."

I am in a parking lot in the middle of nowhere. I will be naked *outside*. With a man and a dog and another man who just tried to do Lord knows what to me. Barghest ripped a man's throat out. He sits on his haunches beside him, looking at me as if he's brought me a prize.

I take a deep breath and finally lower my eyes to my body and the substance covering it.

There is no choice.

I peel off my polo, careful not to let it brush against my face or mouth as I do, and toss it on the asphalt. Maro waits behind the truck with his back to me, and the man on the ground is dead. There isn't anyone at the gas station, and the road is empty. A billboard across the road says **PROTECT FAMILY VALUES**.

I work to undo the buttons on my skirt. The longer I think about what might be on me, the faster I go. It drops to the ground. The wind ruffles the tiny hairs all over my skin. The viscous off-white slime is on one arm, one leg, and, I want to cry, it's seeped through to my bra as well. I look over at him again: he still faces away from me. My heart pounds, and that all-too-familiar shame-guilt churns in my stomach.

I run to the window-washing bucket and, with my back to the truck and Maro, unhook my bra and scrub my skin as quickly as I can manage.

Any panic I felt regarding the sticky mess that just covered my body gives way to a new desperation when I realize I have to walk over to the truck, and Maro, in only my underwear, to get the blanket. I stand near the pump, shivering with my arms over my chest, the wind whipping against my skin, and call to Maro, "Um, can you just lay the blanket over the side of the bed without turning around and then maybe get in and just wait?"

"Did you—" He starts to turn his head toward me as he speaks but stops himself and faces forward again. "Did you get it all off?"

"Yes."

"Are you sure? This is really important."

"Yes! You think I want that stuff on me? Can you please just put the blanket down?"

He does as I ask. The wind blows even harder now, and the blanket threatens to fly off the truck. I have to do this. I sprint for it.

I reach the blanket and wrap it around my body as fast as I can. It's a woolen scratchy thing, and I think I have never been happier to be covered in my life.

"Are you dressed?"

"I mean—kind of?"

"Can I come out?"

I nod and then realize he can't see me. "Yes."

Maro steps out, and I try to hold my head a little higher. I am a sinner. I just bathed in windshield-washing fluid, and I stand in nothing but an old blanket in a gas station parking lot, in the middle of nowhere. But I am alive, and that stuff is no longer on me. At least I think.

"Are you okay?" he says.

I nod.

"Okay. You should probably just wait in the car. It's gonna be a minute."

He walks around the truck to where Barghest sits, licking his paw, next to the man's dead body. His teeth drip red, and a piece of skin hangs in the fur of his snout.

Barghest saved my life.

It's just blood.

"Do we really drink Christ's blood, Mom? His real blood?"

"Yes, but it is and isn't his blood."

Is and isn't.

The blood between Eli and Fiona.

My parents' bodies pressed together. My father's hands.

My parents.

Mom.

Dad.

Gone.

Dead.

Nothing.

I double over and vomit on the asphalt.

HOW TO SET UP A BOOBY TRAP:

Attach the body of a keychain siren to the top of your door.

Tie fishing wire around the alarm pin. Make a strong knot.

Screw a hook above the top of the doorframe, and attach the fishing wire.

If hooks, screws, wires, and keychain sirens are not available, marbles on the floor can be quite effective. And quite dangerous.

Another Life

From the front seat, I watch as Maro takes the tarp covering the ice machine in front of the store and lays it over the dead man. He leads Barghest to the same window-washing station where I rinsed the slime off, behind what used to be my school uniform. I watch as Maro uses the water and paper towels to gently clean Barghest's face, speaking to the dog, too low for me to hear. It makes my heart race for some reason. And Barghest sits perfectly still, trusting him.

This moment between them, this trust. I am reminded of the one thing that really matters. I look out over the expanse of open road and try to imagine what Noah's doing and thinking right now. Where he is. He is healthy, and alive. I tell myself he is. He has to be.

Maro settles himself back into his seat next to me, and a wet Barghest pounds on the metal floor of the bed behind us. I pull the blanket tighter.

Maro threw away the gas station food. We weren't sure what the man might have touched.

"Feeling okay?" Maro asks. "Any signs of it?"

I shake my head no. My naked body against the blanket, my heart pounding.

"Hey, are you feeling okay? This is important."

I clear my head. "Yeah, I feel fine. But you should get a first aid kit," I say, glancing at his arm.

He stares at me.

"Dog bites can get really infected."

He seems to recognize I'm right about this. His brow furrows. Then he gets out of the car and heads back inside to get one.

"So we're going to Waukesha County?" I ask when he's back.

"We've been through this. You cannot under any circumstances go inside those quarantine zones."

"Then where are we going?"

He is silent for a moment, then says, "We'll figure something out."

"Why don't we just find a car somewhere, and Barghest and I can go find Noah, and you can report to duty. I mean, it wouldn't be—"

"Goddamnit, you are not getting this! I am a policeman. I am not going to help you steal a car right now, and I am not going to let you go off by yourself."

"You stole from the store."

"I stole chips and cigarettes. This thing that's going on, kid, it's serious. A quarantine is just an *attempt* at keeping something under control. If things change, people will need their cars. They may not get far, but we can't take that chance away from them. And you've seen what this virus does. If you get infected, you're not gonna get to your brother anyway. I mean, look at Eli. He *chose* that, because it was a better way to go than the alternative. You're staying with me until I can drop you somewhere safe, and we're not gonna talk about this anymore."

He pushes some buttons on the radio, but it's broken, and he can't get anything to play. He swears and hits the steering wheel, then reaches for another cigarette.

"You're gonna run out of those," I say.

"Yeah, well, probably better that way."

He drives. We don't say anything. I wish Barghest could fit in the cab. He is infinitely better company than this angry man beside me. The air feels electric again, staticky. I think it might deliver rain soon. I picture it falling on the tarp covering the dead man in the parking lot, his blood sliding over asphalt, diluting until it's gone.

Maro turns off the highway and onto a dirt road.

"Where are we going now," I say.

He doesn't look at me, and I can tell he is in an even worse mood than before.

"Get you some clothes."

A red and white ranch-style sits a mile down the road. Like Eli's house, there is little else in sight. Open land. Grass, grains. Maro pulls into the driveway. There are no cars anywhere, but smoke climbs from the chimney, and the tracks in the dirt are fresh.

The sky is too dark for afternoon.

Maro pulls to the side of the house, and the second the truck stops, Barghest bolts out of the bed and into the grass. His tail wags wildly, and he sniffs in a great circle around the house.

Maro reaches behind his seat and takes hold of his gun. "Stay here."

He goes to the front porch and knocks on the door. Nothing happens.

He opens the screen door and knocks on the wooden one. When there is still no answer, he turns the knob and opens it. "Police! Anybody here?"

He disappears inside.

A long minute.

Barghest is somewhere behind the house, circling, Maro somewhere inside it. The wind is a living thing, beating at the car and the boards of this home. I shiver in my blanket. It is eerily quiet, aside from the wind, away from everyone and everything.

I free my hand from the folds of the blanket and find the door handle. My bare feet touch down on the dirt. I leave my sneakers on the floor and the truck door open. I make my way to the house, the wind pushing at my back. It's been too long. I haven't heard gunshots or yelling, but Maro shouldn't be this slow in returning.

I step up to the porch, a small creak. Cows graze in a nearby pasture, and they huddle together. I've read somewhere that that means something, but now I can't remember what it is. The air holds the expectant feeling of singular possibility and almost certain danger. The slow receding of a mother's palm before it collides with a daughter's face.

Something is coming.

I push the front door open.

The farmhouse is dusty and old, but lived in. Nothing as lovely as

Eli's, but comfortable. The front door opens into a living room with a denim chair and couch set, hand-knitted quilts draped over them. The wood underneath my feet is splintered and scuffed, most likely from the many pairs of boots stacked near the door.

A scream, sudden and shrill.

My head whips to my left. I take in the room, furniture. Movement.

It's steam, issuing from a stovetop teakettle.

I take a tentative step forward, craning my head to see the far corner of the kitchen.

Empty.

A large window on the far wall looks out onto the field behind the house. I see no sign of Barghest, just grass. A horse in the distance.

To my right, a hallway leads to the rest of the house. I hear nothing. Not the sound of Maro's boots, not his voice. I am nearly naked and fully unarmed. Not that I've ever been armed before, but . . . A metal poker leans against the fireplace. I take slow steps toward it.

I feel safer with the weapon in hand. Kind of. My other hand clasps the top of the blanket above my breastbone, and I tell myself that I've made it this far. I creep down the hall, heel-arch-toe pressing down softly on the worn boards. Framed photographs line the walls, horses and steers, twin paintings of George W. and his father with American flags behind them. A family, father, mother, and a young girl, all in denim. They look happy.

To my left, a door is slightly ajar. A beam of dim light creeps through the opening, making a line on the floor right in front of my feet.

Holding my breath, I reach the hand with the poker forward and peel open the door, bracing for the worst.

It takes half a second for my eyes to adjust from the dark of the hallway. When they do, I see the bedroom is empty. Of people anyway.

The room is full of color. Clothing strewn here and there, art, and posters. On the corner of a desk, a framed photograph. A girl my age leans into another girl, her hip cocked, arm slung over her friend's shoulders. They are both smiling as though they've just shared a secret. One of the girls is clearly the one from the family portrait in the hall, but older here, with her friend. They wear ripped jeans. One of them has on a midriff-revealing tank top, the other what I think is a band or movie T-shirt, though I don't recognize the name. Again, like the magazines, the sense that there is so much more color to these girls, to their lives, than my own.

I turn my attention to the rest of the desk. Cluttered with rainbow pens, coins, to-do lists, jotted-down notes on scraps of paper, highlighters, stickers. A University of Wisconsin red hoodie draped over the chair. Photographs, drawings, ripped homework pages, clothes, and more variations of lip gloss than I would have thought existed. This is the bedroom of a teenage girl. Mine is that of a child.

There are no crosses in this room. There's no framed painting of Jesus, no stuffed animals or Bible.

Next to the bed—purple silky bedspread and pink puffed pillow—is a crinkled photograph of a boy. A boyfriend. His arm around the girl in the crop top from the other photo, the girl whose room this is. His arm hangs around her in possession, and pride. I think the sweatshirt is his.

I go to the dresser, its top two drawers slightly open. I let my blanket fall, just a little, to see what's inside.

My eyes catch on it.

Purple lace. A purple lace bra. I've never seen anything like it, outside of that magazine at the gas station. This beautiful delicate thing, the fabric-wrapped wire, the little purple flowers with tiny flecks of blue in them. It's soft, much softer than the stiff white lace of my communion dress or the yellowing fabric that hangs in the windows of Mrs. Ingles's house.

I run my fingers over it, imagining.

The door opens behind me.

I freeze, tighten the blanket around me. I turn.

I hold my breath as the door creaks slowly wider.

There is a man in the doorway.

He steps into the room. I scream. The poker flies from my hand.

It flies through the air. Falls and bounces off the bones of my foot, clatters onto the floorboards.

"Oh God, are you okay?"

Maro. Maro in the doorway, and Barghest pushing in beside him. And then the pain. I am blinded by it.

I hop on my other foot, holding the blanket shut, eyes squeezed tight, unable to make a sound. I bite my lip and give a quick nod. Horrified, I realize I am holding the bra still, and I turn and stash it in the drawer. I am hot with shame and in more pain than I have ever been in my life, and I realize my face is wet because tears are streaming down it, and nothing exists except the fiery hell that is my foot.

"Here, let me take a look."

"No, no, it's okay. I'm fine." I try to take a step on it. I cry out, catch myself on the dresser.

"You're not fine—you're bleeding."

"What?" I somehow say.

"Look, you're bleeding. Will you let me help you?"

My foot is hideous. Already purple-blue and cut open, blood pouring out.

"How did it cut me?"

"It's a poker. It has prongs. We need to bandage it."

"Um . . ." I start to come back, start to regain my vision.

"Kid."

"Yeah, okay. I'll just . . ."

Maro seems to register why I am uncomfortable. He takes in the room, and his face colors. He keeps his eyes off me. "Oh, um, so this works out well. Why don't you, uh . . . get some clothes on and then come in the living room and I'll help with it. Can you manage?"

I nod.

"Okay, great. Just us here, so. Yeah. Okay. Good."

He stands there for another second, his eyes down and shoulders tense, and then removes himself from the doorway, shutting the door behind him.

I breathe. When the wave has mostly passed, I think through my next moves. The room has one window. I hop over to it and close the blinds. I go to the dresser again and open the other drawers. The girl who lives here is taller than me, and maybe a little thinner. The clothes won't fit perfectly, but it should work. I wonder what happened to her. Maybe she will be back any moment and will find me riffling through her things.

I find a pair of jeans that are more or less my size, just a little long. I pull them over my hurt foot as best I can without getting any blood on them. In the shirt drawer, there seem to be only tank tops and T-shirts that will probably be too tight on me. I find the largest of them, a shirt that says КоЯп. I don't know what that is, but it seems fine enough.

In the underwear drawer, I eye the purple bra, my fingers hovering over it. I go with the plainest one I can find instead.

Maro sits in the big denim chair in the living room, two steaming mugs of tea on the table in front of him and a small box in his hand. A fire burns in the fireplace, crackling loudly.

He stands when he notices me. It's a nervous stance, an awkward one. Once I saw an image of a boy asking a girl to prom in a poster at the library. I don't know why that flashes before me now. I don't know why that image brings so much heat to my face. Why looking at him does. Probably because he just saw me in only a blanket.

"First aid kit was a good call," he says. "Do you need help?"

I avert my eyes, make my slow way to the couch. I sit, prop my bleeding and now markedly swollen foot up on the coffee table next to the hot tea.

"I'm an idiot," I say.

He seems not to know how to respond to that.

"So, uh, do you mind?" He gestures vaguely to my foot.

I shake my head.

He gets to work taking things out of the kit, and he sits on the coffee table next to my leg, pushing the mug out of the way. The table creaks slightly under his weight. His hands brush against my skin, and I can feel that they are callused, more than Ben's in the library. More than mine, even with my Friday night projects.

"Do you do woodworking?" I say.

"What?"

"Your hands."

"Oh," he says. Looking down at them like he's never considered them before. "I . . . sailing, in the summers. And you know, I guess just the gym?" He asks it like a question, as if I know anything. "Is it . . . are my hands making it worse?"

"No," I say.

"Okay. Good. Sorry, I'll make this quick."

"So you were the one boiling water?" I say. The dizziness comes again, a new wave. I squeeze my eyes shut and grip the couch cushion. My brow beads with sweat, I can feel it.

Maro notices the sweat and goes rigid.

"I'm not . . ." I say, but can't finish the sentence. "I mean, I don't think . . ." He still hasn't moved. "It's just the foot," I say. Or it could be a fever, it could be—

He nods but eyes me. "Uh, no. No, I guess the owners of the house must have left in a hurry. But it was boiling so I thought I'd take advantage. Can you bend it? Does that hurt?"

I reflexively pull my foot away from him, which makes the pain so much worse. Through gritted teeth I say, "Yep. That hurts."

A crash in the kitchen.

"What was that?"

"Barghest."

In response to his name, the dog lopes into the living room, brushing past the Green Bay Packers curtains, his wagging tail knocking the antenna off the TV.

He approaches the couch and curls up on the floor by my good leg, placing his giant head in my lap. I scratch his ear and breathe through whatever torture Maro is performing on me.

"I've broken a bunch of bones in my life," he says. "This isn't broken, but you're probably gonna have nasty bruises for a bit."

I let my head fall back against the couch. "Thanks."

Maro finishes bandaging the wound and walks over to stand in front of the window with his mug. One hand in his pocket, one bringing the tea to his mouth as he surveys the fields. This living room. This house. We don't belong here. Sitting on a stranger's couch, in a stranger's clothes, drinking from a stranger's mug. Maro is a stranger too.

"You said no one's here?"

"No one."

"But the teakettle—"

"Like I said, they must have left in a hurry. They left a radio on in the main bedroom. My guess is they heard about the quarantine and had somewhere else they wanted or needed to be."

"But why would they have heard about it so late?"

He shrugs, gestures out over the fields. "It's isolated out here. If they didn't have the radio or TV on, how would they know at all?"

I nod. My foot is bandaged neatly. I know how to bandage small wounds from my how-to books, have read about it plenty of times. Maro did a good job.

"Thanks. For helping with my foot."

He shrugs again and looks back out the window. The sharp cut of his jaw. The bob of his throat as he swallows.

"Now you," I say, looking down. Away from him.

"Now . . . ?"

"Barghest's bite. We have to disinfect it."

"Oh. I can do it." He steps back over to the coffee table, starts to unwrap the shirt from his arm, dried blood and slobber pulling from the wound. He sucks in a breath through his teeth.

"Let me help," I say. I lean forward and take the first aid kit. He hesitates, then sits back down across from me. I open the small bottle of rubbing alcohol. "This is going to hurt," I say.

He nods, and I know I'd be yelping if it were me. But he holds himself still. I pour the whole bottle in the puncture wounds. I have to touch his arm to not spill it everywhere. His skin is warm, and his arm corded with muscle, tensed, in this moment. I've never felt a man's arm, I don't think. Strange. "Where were you when I came in the house?" I say. "Why did it take you so long to find me?"

"Oh. They have an attic."

". . . Okay?"

"I was trying to see if anyone was here. I saw the attic door and thought they might be up there. When I went and looked, I got . . . distracted."

I try to read his face. Thoughts of the worst kind force their way into my mind. Maro killing the inhabitants and stuffing them in the attic. My mother's story. Maro bringing me to this house to . . .

I close my eyes. When did I start thinking this way about people? About *anything*? Maro is a policeman. He would never do that. And there's no car outside. Whoever lives here is gone.

I finish what I can do for his arm and lean over Barghest's head to take my mug. Maro stands again, giving me space. I push the suspicions from my mind.

I think of the girl whose clothes I wear. With her parents, presumably. That girl doesn't have any crosses or rosaries or looming pictures of Jesus, and yet she probably got to keep her parents. I sip the tea. The hot water travels down my throat and warms me from the inside. The sky is darkening further. Dead bugs visible on the window that weren't there when I first sat down. The wind howls stridently, a thirsty dog licking at the house. Pawing at it.

I set the mug down and stumble trying to stand.

"What do you need?" Maro asks.

"Water. More food. For Barghest."

"Already has some."

"Oh. Thanks."

"Yeah."

Neither of us speaks. He rubs his eyes and turns to me. "Look, um, I know it's kind of weird, being in this house and everything. But I'm thinking we should spend the night here. I don't know what's going on with that wind, and no one else is here, so . . . We should try and sleep a little, I think. While we can."

While we can. I think about it. After a moment, I agree, my desperation for a real shower temporarily prevailing over guilt and any misgivings. I need to get to Waukesha as soon as possible, but I am exhausted, really exhausted. Sleep isn't a bad idea.

Maro insists on wrapping a plastic bag around my foot and securing it with a rubber band. He helps me all the way to the bathroom door. I try not to lean too much on him, try not to let too much of our skin touch. So far he's been nothing but nice, nothing but helpful, but . . .

"Hey," I say, and he stops, looks at me. "Um . . . I know it's your job to help people, but . . . why are you helping me? I mean I know you have to go report for duty, but don't you have friends or family to get to?"

"I . . ." His eyes glaze over, pain shadows his face. He opens his mouth, closes it, runs his hand over his head, his jaw. Seconds. A minute. Then, "I'm gonna find us something to eat."

In the bathroom, I lock the door. I find a bottle of aspirin, and take three tablets, and undress. The shower has a seat, so I sit and turn the handle. The water sprays down, hot and fast over me.

I take in my body. Limbs accounted for, if battered. Three times I've been attacked by the infected. How long does it take for symptoms to show? Or are they showing already? My heart racing, skin growing hot, just looking at Maro. The way I can't stop watching his face. That can't be normal, right? Or maybe . . . I think again about the Christian Radio.

I can't help but feel that it's all connected. There hasn't been wind like this since the night I opened the window, the night Noah was taken from me. And my thoughts growing ever more impure, the hatred filling me, my body betraying me, becoming this magnet for sin, this vessel that only *wants*, against every logical thought.

In the Bible, God's wrath is delivered on the wind, in great decimating gusts. He demolishes civilizations, razes entire histories to the ground. God controls the elements. But spirits can carry on the wind, the Holy Spirit, lesser ones. Including demons. I don't know what to think. There is a virus. There is something powerful at work. Great and terrible and full of wrath. The Devil or God or something in between, I don't know. But I do know I feel a stirring in me. It is danger and it is hellfire, and it is there, with the fear and the pain and grief and shame and guilt and self-hatred. A demon can lie dormant in a body for a long time, can influence a person's life in small ways for many years until it is ready to do worse. I have harbored something dark ever since Noah was ripped from our home—hatred, but maybe . . .

Maybe I let something in that night through my open window, and maybe it's been inhabiting me all this time. I am so afraid, so desperately afraid.

In the hot shower spray, in someone else's house in the middle of nowhere with a bloodthirsty dog and a stranger, I pray.

I pray for Noah. I pray for my parents. I pray for Eli and Fiona and the people on the highway and the woman with her baby and Vick and Harold and their families.

Deliverusfromevil. Ourdutyaswomen. Don'tyouspeaktoyourmotherthatway.

I pray that this isn't all my fault.

𝕷𝖆𝖘𝖙 𝕾𝖚𝖕𝖕𝖊𝖗

I hop inelegantly out of the shower, reaching for anything that can stabilize me. The clothes I wore earlier are crumpled on the floor not far from where I stand at the edge of the sink, and I drip water on them, on the bra and underwear at the top of the pile. I sigh and towel myself off, try to keep the rest of it dry.

At the dresser, I tug the underwear drawer open again.

The purple bra sits on top. I search for something else.

But . . .

In this room, no eyes watch me from paintings or images. Jesus and the Devil are always with me, I might hear the demons and feel their claws on my neck, but . . . I don't see them here.

I pick it up, this delicate little thing that is so dangerous. I'll just try it on and then take it off, just to see how it feels. Just because I'm here. I slide each arm through the straps and fasten the clasp.

Maybe a garment shouldn't make a person feel transformed. But priests wear robes, little girls wear white for purity, as do brides. I look again to the photograph of this teenage girl who does not look like she has guilt anchored in her stomach or shame stamped on her brow. I imagine her in these T-shirts, the lace underneath only known to her. Now I, too, harbor this secret. I am afraid of the way it makes me feel. Afraid, and yet . . . This freedom, this choice. I locate a matching pair of underwear and slip it on. I run my hands over my breasts, just once, to see what they feel like in this adornment, this new vessel. My new skin.

I sit on the bed and slip the jeans and T-shirt back on, the sweatshirt over. In the hall I am met with the most glorious smell. A feast sits on the dining table. An impossibly delicious-smelling meal of po-tatoes, broccoli, baked chicken, and corn bread.

"Where did this come from?" I say. I lean on the wall for balance, arms crossed over my chest. I am sure, suddenly, that the lace under-wear and bra were a terrible idea, that he can see them on me, and my stomach clenches, my face hot again. But he doesn't look at me any differently.

"The fridge was pretty full. You were in the shower a long time."

I stay where I am, unsure of what to do. Barghest is sprawled on the couch, his head propped up on the arm, eyes glued to the food on the table.

"Hungry?"

This time I nod. Sleep can wait. I make my unsteady way to the table, conscious of how the new undergarments brush against my skin as I move. Still, Maro doesn't seem to notice.

"You don't look good," he says.

I surprise myself by letting out a quick laugh. "Thanks."

"No, I mean, the foot looks painful."

I shrug. "My fault. It was stupid. How's your arm?"

"It's okay," he says. "Can't blame the dog for protecting her."

He puts food on a plate for me, as though he knows exactly what and how much I want. Something about the gesture, familial and care-taking, sets me on edge. I don't like it from him.

"I can make my own plate," I say.

"Oh, do you want to? I can take that one." His voice is low. I didn't really notice before, but now with him so close to me, it's almost like I can feel it vibrate through my own chest. Again, I take in the hard planes of his face, the sinful and dark in me surfacing, and—

"No, I mean it's fine, I just . . ." I ask again, "Why are you being so nice to me? And where did you learn to cook like this?" I didn't mean to ask the second question, but I caught the scent of it, and it just hit me.

He pauses. "My sister taught me. But the corn bread's from a box."

"You have a sister?"

He pours himself a glass from a bottle of wine. My parents don't—didn't—drink, and I've obviously never had any alcohol other than communion wine. He catches me looking.

"You want some?"

I immediately shake my head no.

"Actually, it might help dull the pain in your foot a little. Don't know why I didn't think of that first thing."

I eye the bottle hovering over the table, tilted in Maro's hand, waiting for an answer. Another dangerous thing, this bottle, the blood-colored liquid within it. Another sin.

Maro sets the bottle down. "Oh, sorry. I forgot you're—I obviously wasn't trying to pressure you to drink or even—" He clears his throat. "Yikes. God. Sorry."

"No, actually I want some," I say. As if someone else is speaking through me. I wonder if the underwear is actually transforming me, taking possession of my voice and appetites. I wonder if something else is. This too-terrifying possibility.

Maro looks uncertain. Then after a moment he says, "Yeah, okay. Here."

He pours the liquid in my glass.

"Thanks. I just need to . . ."

I bow my head, close my eyes, and begin a silent prayer for my food.

But saying Grace without my parents, without my father voicing the words we all repeat, without my mother's perfume blending with the smells of the food—it feels impossible, somehow. Like sacrilege.

I swallow back a lump and pick up my fork.

And for the first time in my life, I begin my dinner without an *Amen.*

The food is delicious, and the wine, sipped tentatively at first and then without much thought, relaxes me. A blush creeps into my face, I can feel it, but it is warm and calming, not at all the awful burning of embarrassment and shame that I am so accustomed to.

I know I should feel guilty about drinking wine with a strange man, but I somehow don't. I actually feel kind of great. Guilt is a sitting baseline, and its absence, maybe its first real absence ever, makes me feel buoyant, light. Giddy, even. And Maro is right, my foot does feel better. I ask him if I can have a second glass. He hesitates, then agrees.

"How old are you?" I ask.

"Twenty-four."

"Oh. You're not much older than I am."

"I don't know about that," he says.

"Seven years." Eight years.

"Those are a big seven years."

"Are you religious?"

"Excuse me?"

"I mean, you know, do you believe in God?"

He shrugs.

"Well, do you go to church?"

"I did as a kid. But . . . I don't know. You finished?" He stands, begins clearing the table.

"I didn't mean to offend you," I say. "My family is very religious. I'm religious. We—" I start laughing, a little, and it feels strange. "They would be so horrified to know that the person I am with right now doesn't believe in God!" I laugh. I can't help it. It's the funniest thought in the world.

"I know what it's like." Maro sits again, our two glasses and bottle of wine between us.

"What?"

"I—" He clears his throat. "Sorry, it's—I'm not good at talking about it. I didn't mean . . . earlier, when you asked. I know you don't know me. And this whole situation is . . . I just . . . I'm not good at talking about it."

He's looking somewhere else now, somewhere far away, and so I watch him. I let myself, objectively, like he's a saint in a painting. Like he's not real, sitting before me. His jaw, his Adam's apple, his stubble. His long eyelashes and slightly crooked nose. I don't know what it is. He's not perfect like Ben at the library, not flawless. But I just want to look at him, just find it hard not to.

"I lost my sister," he says. "When we were in high school. Amy, she— she was the prettiest girl. God, I hated the way all the guys looked at her, but even though she was my sister I kind of couldn't blame them. Some people are just like that. Just, you know, shining."

His words wash over me with a delay, the wind beating against the house.

"She was in with the cool crowd. They liked to go diving out at this one spot under the bridge near where we lived. She was out there with them, and they didn't know the water level was low, and . . ." He rubs his eyes a little. "She was the only one who jumped that night. Guess it just takes one to know . . . And it was her."

A long silence, both of us staring in different directions. The clock on a side table in the living room has begun a small silent symphony with Barghest's light snores.

"When I saw you in that car, on the highway . . . You had the same look in your eyes that she used to have. And I had just sent all these teenage kids to this place, and they all ended up getting infected. I mean, I as good as killed them, and I just . . . I just needed to save one. We saw so many people die, and . . ." He runs his hand through his hair. "I just want to get you somewhere safe, with someone who can look after you. Then I'll have done my job, and maybe you'll be okay in this world, and grow up to live your life. Just . . . you know. One."

The wind howls.

I lean forward, grab the bottle, and pour another glass for each of us, emptying it completely. I lift my glass toward him.

"To family."

Maro looks at me with surprise and something else. Maybe admiration, though I can't imagine for what. And maybe his eyes sweep over my face now, take me in the way I just did with him, the way I can't stop doing. Not remembering something from before, just . . . seeing me. Maybe for the first time. I don't know what he sees. I only know that even through the wine, even with the wind still battering the walls, I am sure he can hear my heart, the way it pounds in my chest.

He lifts his glass, and it clinks against mine.

After dinner Maro searches the house and comes back with a crutch that we adjust for my height. I am desperately tired, but I find myself making excuses to stay up with him, to be in the same room. I can't bear the thought of being alone. And also, his nearness distracts me. From the grief and fear. Being beside him, tracking his movements. It makes my heart race in a way that is terrifying, but is also addictive and exhilarating and hopeful. I am intoxicated, in more ways than one. When I sleep, we will wake and leave this place. And we'll part ways. I may never sit in a room with this person ever again. So I just . . . stay.

Cell service is down, and now so is the TV. He turns on the radio periodically in the other room, but there's not much we can do tonight. I turn on Christian Radio briefly, but it brings back the bad terror, and it doesn't give new information anyway. We've opened a second bottle, and I sip slowly. I wish Noah was here. What I would do to transport him. Show him this secular family's house. He would love Barghest. He would love all of it. The guilt flares, that I am not actively searching right now, and I feel sick for a moment. But the wine dulls it. Maro's presence dulls it.

At some point in the night, we find ourselves sitting in the living room again, my crutch beneath me on the floor, Barghest snuggled next to me on the couch, my foot propped on the table. Maro rests on the floor, his back against the denim chair, surveying the dark field in the back through the window, now plastered with flying things, more arriving by the second.

"What's sailing like?" I ask.

He thinks for a moment, closes his eyes. "It's like . . . you have to attune yourself to the sun, the waves, always the wind. You feel for it, on your neck, feel for the direction it's blowing. Everything else just . . . falls away. When you dial in, when you start moving with the wind and sea, you become a part of it. It's freedom."

Freedom.

"Is it nice, being an adult?" I ask.

He snorts a laugh and meets my eyes. "No, not really."

"Oh," I say, disappointed.

"Being your age, it's the best and the worst. You know what I mean? Like, everything is so intense, so extreme, and it all feels life or death, even when it's not. Everything does. Exams, friendships, first love. But that's what's so great about it. You just feel so alive all the time. You just *feel.* On the adult spectrum, I'm young. The guys at work, like I'm the baby in the group. But even now I can see, life just starts to weigh on you, and new experiences don't really light you up the way they once did. You don't always get that same intensity." He takes a sip. "And here we are, in a *very* new experience. Maybe I . . . Careful what you wish for, I guess."

"Did you . . ." My skin is so hot, my heart going haywire, but, I ask it anyway, here with the fire crackling, the wind howling. I ask, "Did you have a first love?"

His eyes meet mine. And he tries to read something in me. His mind seeming to war with itself. But there is a thread, a . . . tie. Alive. Thrumming between us. I wonder if I am imagining it. But I don't think I am. It's there. A recognition, maybe. How can I feel like we know each other already, or some part of each other? Or is it that I just want to?

He smiles, a little, an unsure smile. "Yeah, I did. But I don't know . . ." He frowns, looks down at his glass. "Maybe we shouldn't be talking about this. I don't really . . . we've had a lot of wine, and things are crazy, and you're like—"

"I could die tomorrow," I say. "What if my last wish was a story and you said no?"

"I think you're a little insane," he says, brows furrowed. But it doesn't hurt my feelings like when Noah said it. His expression, he's teasing. I think he thinks I'm funny. But something is bothering him too.

I shrug.

"Laura," he says.

"What?"

"Laura. My first love."

"What happened?"

"She was that girl that just marched to the beat of her own drum. She was in the band, played the violin, but she would play it like a fiddle, make up goofy songs. She dressed funny, sometimes she'd just wear like pajama pants to school with some kind of fancy shirt, or a candy necklace or a strange hat. She got made fun of for it, but she never cared. She was just interesting, and most people just kind of . . . weren't. It took me ages to get the guts to ask her out, and by the time I did, she was with somebody else."

"So what did you do?" I say, keeping my voice even.

He shrugs again. "Nothing. She was happy, and her boyfriend was my friend."

"But you loved her?"

He laughs again, more to himself. "Yeah, I was crazy about her. But sometimes it's like that. That's what I mean. I felt like my guts were ripped out every day looking at her in class, knowing she loved someone else, thinking about her every second. That's being a teenager. That's the beauty of it."

"That sounds awful. And that's a terrible story."

He laughs again. "Maybe you're just a bad audience."

"No, I love stories more than anythi—"

A huge crack of lightning flashes through the sky. Thunder booms seconds later.

Noah. That night.

Barghest's snores. The clock ticking.

"I was so scared as a kid, of storms," I say.

"Really?"

"I was terrified that God would send another flood because we weren't good enough, and we would be wiped from the face of this earth. A night like this . . ." I trail off, take another sip. "I would have been so afraid." I *am* so afraid. But with the wine . . .

He turns. Looks at me. I can feel his eyes. "You're not scared now?"

I think about it. "Not of weather. My brother, he would let me sneak into his room on stormy nights, because he knew. And he'd distract me, tell me or teach me things. He taught me how to make an origami bird, because birds are always chirping after a storm, always telling the world we've made it and we're okay. That's what he said."

"Sounds like a great kid."

"Yeah. He is."

A long, tired silence. Then we both start to speak at the same time.

"Oh—"

"No, sorry I didn't—what were you saying?"

"No, no, nothing, I don't even remember now."

We sit for another moment. If it wasn't for the constant *tick, tick* of the clock counting metronomic time, I wouldn't know whether seconds or hours were passing.

"What about Eli and—" I begin.

"Fiona?"

"Yeah, what about them?" I ask.

"What about them?" He takes a big swig from his glass.

"What's their story?" I say.

He shrugs. "Was that this morning?" He rubs hard at his eyes. "God, it's crazy, that he's just not there now. There and then not. It's crazy how that can just happen. It never gets easier."

I say, "Maybe if you tell me their story they will live on, kind of—you know, through it. Like Paolo and Francesca."

"Who?"

"It doesn't matter."

Cold winds. Lustful souls.

Another long pause.

Tick.

Tick.

Tick.

CrinkleSipCrunch.

Thefeverkillsthem.

Maro's face.

I drink again.

"Not much of a story, really," he says. "Think they met at a bar, she worked there. Her husband's bar, actually. Eli was there a lot after he retired. He got stabbed during a drug bust, so he stopped working while he was still pretty young.

"He'd go and sit there and drink sometimes in the middle of the day, never when it was crowded. Eli doesn't really like crowds . . . *didn't* really like . . . So, I think they, you know, got to talking and hit it off, and one thing led to another." He smiles, but it doesn't reach his eyes. "Actually, it turned out we knew the guy who owned the place, the husband. Used to be the DA, nice guy. Eli felt bad about it, but not bad enough I guess, 'cause he kept seeing her. I only met her a handful of times, they kinda kept to themselves."

He stops for a moment, looks as though he is concentrating hard to remember something. "Anyway, it's like I said, not much of a story."

Barghest's back rises and falls as he sleeps, his leg occasionally twitching.

I wonder where Fiona's husband is now. If he's infected. I wonder what it means that she chose to die with Eli instead of him. It seems impossibly hard to reason. I can't help but picture some poor man on his couch, wondering when his wife and dog are going to get back from the store and then hearing about the quarantine. He might still be wondering where she is.

If they had been given the choice, would my parents have chosen to die together like they did? Did they love each other as much as Fiona and Eli had loved each other? They would have hated the knowledge that they had been on the ground like that the last time anyone saw them, let alone their daughter. That they had done what they did.

But maybe they got to die together, and even if it was horrible, maybe they were happy, even if only for a second, to be in each other's arms. I hope so. I so desperately hope.

Will I ever love someone, or be loved, like that?

I might not even live to love at all.

Maro stands. "You should sleep."

"I don't want to." It sounds more petulant than I mean it to.

"Well, I'm not your father. You can do whatever you want."

At his words, a tension snakes into the room, swift and sharp. The sentence cutting through whatever thin veil of comradery and ease we have found. Neither of us likes it, I see it in him too.

But just like that, the spell is broken. I am tired. I'm in an unfamiliar house with a stranger, drinking alcohol and wearing illicit clothing. My brother is in danger, and I need to be in good enough shape to get to him when it's safe and light out.

"Yeah. Okay, I'll sleep," I say and try to stand.

"Here. Let me help you."

"No, no, I've got it, it's okay."

"Are you sure?"

"Yeah. The crutch helps."

We stand now, five or six feet from each other. My heart beats. His neck and his jaw and eyes. "Okay, then," I say. My voice sounds different, like it doesn't belong to me. "So . . . thanks for the food, and the foot, and everything." His hands in his pockets, bandaged arm. His arm that I bandaged. His skin that I touched.

"Yeah. Thanks for the, uh, company." He swallows, stands up straight.

"Yeah," I say. "Good night."

"Sleep well. I'll be out here if you—"

"Yeah, okay. Thanks."

"Hey, Sophie."

I turn, my heart racing. A strange sort of hope rushing through me. I don't know what I hope he'll say. But I really hope it, almost desperately. It's insane, but him, standing here before me—

"You're gonna make it through," he says. "You're gonna find your brother, and have your first love. You're gonna make it."

In the girl's room—I find her name is Kelly from a homework assignment—I crawl under the sheets. It feels like a violation, sleeping in someone else's bed. Barghest tries to get up on the bed, but we can't both fit so I take one of the blankets and set it on the floor beside me, and he curls up right away.

Maro's words. The way they disappointed me, the confusion taking over. Lying in bed, I wonder if he will sleep tonight. Lying in another bed in this house. I wonder what he will wear, how his chest will rise and fall. I wonder if he'll think at all about me. Then I stop wondering because I shouldn't. And because of course he wouldn't.

And all my thoughts are overlapping, melting into each other. Words changing the colors of images, my mother's face and the library stacks and empty highways littered with trash. All those girls in the magazines, on the billboards. *The Lovers' Whirlwind.* **LUST WILL DRAG YOU TO HELL.**

Hell is empty.

Cold. Gray and cold.

Standing on the edge of the ranch house's porch.

Naked. Where's my blanket?

The vast expanse of land stretching in front of me, peppered with thousands and thousands of crows, black specks littering the land. Dirt spilled on a canvas.

And cows. Cows gathering. The sky is green.

My mother's voice.

It's coming.

What's coming? Where are you? Mom!
You should have confessed your sins.
I'm so sorry, Mom. Please, where are you?
It's coming now.
Sophie.
You have to wake up.

Barghest barks loudly, crouched between me and the door. A roaring fills my ears, and my head feels thick and not quite right. I shake it, but it doesn't help, and the noise only grows louder.

Hell is empty.

A crash from somewhere out front.

I catapult out of bed and remember only after I put weight on my foot that it's injured. Pain radiates through my entire body, and I scream, fumbling in the dark for my crutch.

I open the door to the hallway, Barghest glued to my side. I limp down the hall, disoriented, unsteady.

I reach the end and look out. Into a green-black sky. I think it's still night, but this . . . it's strangely bright, and the kind of green that only comes before . . .

I know a green sky.

I know why cows huddle. Now I remember.

They do it when there is a storm coming. A big one.

The Wind

Maro!"

Roaring wind. Debris crashing through the fields, into the side of the house.

His voice comes from behind me. "Hey, I'm here!"

"Where were you?"

"We have to go," Maro yells over the wind.

"What?"

"This house is right in the storm path."

I hesitate. From what I know of tornados, we should stay put. From what I've read, leaving is the worst idea.

"Trust me. We have to go now." He knows something. He doesn't give me time to argue.

Maro hurries me through the door and out onto the front porch, Barghest right behind us, tail between his legs, body crouched low.

Maro runs ahead to get the pickup started, sparing a look back every second or so to make sure we're following. When we get to the truck, it takes a minute to coax Barghest up into the bed. He is whining, and the green sky has lost its temporary brightness, now, in seconds, has shifted almost entirely to black, the air volatile and alive. Maro tells me to get in the cab. And by the time he closes the truck gate and gets in his own seat, I am just buckling my seatbelt.

The wind shoves up against and underneath the truck so that it rocks on two wheels. The wheels come down, and Maro reverses and spins. Barghest slides in the back and hits the side of the bed. I turn and see him scrambling. His paws struggle to find traction on the metal. I am convinced I can hear them scraping, scratching, even though the wind blocks out every other sound.

Maro floors the pedal, and we are flying down the road at a hundred miles per hour. Barghest slides and hits the side again. He looks up at me, his dark eyes pleading.

Noah's eyes as he was taken from me.

Our voices screaming out for each other.

I don't think. I crawl into the back seat, my foot on fire. Maro yells, and the wind rips at the truck. I slide the back cab window open and pull myself through the small opening, careful to grip the siding while steadying my body against the corner of the bed.

My position is awkward, the wind pummeling, whipping my hair into my eyes. But Barghest sees me. He scrambles forward, trying to reach my outstretched arms.

"Come on, buddy, you can do it. I'm right here." I don't know if he can hear, I can hardly hear myself. This wind scrapes at my skin and my eyes, and I am nearly drowning in it.

Maro hits a bump in the road, and Barghest skids even farther back. We pick up speed, and the tailgate lock buckles. If it opens, there will be nothing between Barghest and the road behind us. I can feel more than see that the funnel is there too, just miles beyond the end of the truck. Far enough for us to still be on the ground, but I'm not sure for how long.

The tailgate lock shakes.

Noah calls my name.

I fling myself toward Barghest, landing on top of him, my arm reaching over his giant body and holding on to the side. I try pulling us both farther forward, every muscle straining as I fight the wind, our speed, and the dog that weighs as much as I do. I hook my good foot into a groove, and I find a handhold on the side. Just enough to keep us here. I hope. I pray.

Trash and debris torpedo through the air above our heads. The truck shakes and bumps as we gain even more speed. The storm is coming closer, I can feel it. I strain with everything I have. The sky impossibly inky and dark, holding no stars, no moon, as if God never uttered those four seminal words. As if he means to blot them out now.

And coming from its center, a protrusion dropping down from its infinite black belly,

The funnel touches the ground.

I press my face into Barghest's fur, his nails scratching at the metal of the bed, my own fingers raw and clinging with everything I have. I inhale the scent of beast, of blood, of electricity, and dark. I breathe it all in and wonder again if maybe we are not dead already.

Barghest.

Noah.

Youaretheonlygoodperson.

And just before it all goes black,

A whisper in my ear. The wind like fingertips, grazing my neck.

HOW TO SURVIVE A TORNADO:

Take shelter in a cellar. If unavailable, a
closet or bathroom will do. Keep clear of
windows. Stay low to the ground.

If inside shelter is unavailable, lie down
flat in a ditch or low field.

Do not attempt to drive. Do not attempt to
outrun it.

Fiberglass

I open my eyes to black. It moves up and down, rhythmically, and there is texture to it. A thick earthy musk, radiating heat.

Barghest.

I breathe him in, wonder at the fact that I am breathing at all, that I am here. I want to reach out, stroke the fur so close to me. But I can't lift my arm.

I roll my head and take in my surroundings. It's dawn, or almost. Dark but with the faint blueish tinge that tells me we've made it through. I lie on grass under a wide-open sky, a jacket laid over me. I try to sit up, but I can only lift my head and then have to lower it again. Everything hurts. I try again. This time, with a groan, I am able to push up on one elbow.

I lie in a field surrounded by giants. No, beasts. Demons? I close my eyes and open them again, the world swaying a little. But they're still there. I did not imagine this.

All around us in the grass sit giant creatures. Giant, horrific, unnatural creatures in the predawn night.

Enormous figures in shades of gray, all in various states of decay. Elephants, cows, alligators, skeletons, cowboys, buffalo, bears, samurai, sharks, a giant buck-toothed mouse, a devil. Teeth, claws, fangs, ears, wide staring dead eyes, in all directions. A hundred of them, at least. All with nightmare faces. All empty and lifeless.

Maro sits twenty feet in front of me, smoking a cigarette, studying something in his hand. He sits on an overturned life-size elephant, half-buried in the ground, another broken one beside him. I open my mouth, and a strangled sound comes out.

He stows the small item in his pocket and turns to me.

"You're awake." His voice holds an edge to it.

"What is this place?"

For a minute he doesn't say anything, silently surveys the field.

"Weird, right?" He looks me over again, then says, "We're behind a fiberglass factory. These are the used molds, I guess. For like amusement parks and roadside attractions and fast food signs. I don't know. Don't know why they don't just throw them away."

The creatures surrounding us are not all that mars the grass. Trash is strewn everywhere, small bits of fast food wrappers, grocery bags, building materials.

"Tornado?" I manage to say.

He nods. So much passes over his face. I can't read it all. I'm not all here, I don't think.

"What town?" I say.

"Sparta. Tornado blew us off course."

"Are we going to Waukesha?"

"Well, I got radioed. Now I'm supposed to report somewhere over in Plainfield, and I'd like to find somewhere for you to go before I go in."

"Go in." I try to sit up. Pain flares again, my arms, back, chest, abdomen. "You're going into one of the quarantine zones?"

"I gotta go where they call me."

"But you'll get yourself killed."

"Not if I can help it."

"So you're allowed to go in and I'm not."

"Yes."

"Why?"

"Because." He's really angry. I can feel it, the way I felt the tornado, growing in power. "You have no idea what it's like inside. I am a cop, and I am trained, and this is my job. You've got a messed-up foot, and people are dying left and right, in the worst ways possible. You've already been attacked, more than once. And you seem to have a death wish. That is why."

"I'm not a child, Maro. I don't need help."

"You *do* need it!" He stood up. "You *are* a kid, and there is fucked-up shit out there, and you need someone to protect you."

"What, like you?"

"Sure, like me."

"You have to report to duty. And I have someone I need to get to. I'm not just going to sit around as though I'm helpless while my brother is alone out there."

"But you are helpless. You make terrible decisions, and it is frankly a fuckin' wonder you're still alive. I have known you for *two days,* and I know this."

"Terrible decisions?"

"Yeah, like the one you made to get in the bed of a pickup truck in the middle of a fucking tornado! For a *dog*! A dog that we watched *murder* someone!"

"He murdered someone to save me. And what do you care? You don't even know me. You think you have to save me because you couldn't save those teenagers, and you couldn't save your own sister, but guess what, Maro? I'm not her!"

The words are out of my mouth, and they are poison, and I am poison. There is silence. Maro, Barghest, me, a graveyard full of giants.

I can't take them back. They hang in the air in the fiberglass-mold graveyard, come to shatter whatever trust we had left, to obliterate it to nothing.

"No," he says quietly, keeping his eyes away from mine. "You're nothing like her."

We don't speak again until we're in the truck, and even then Maro only mumbles, because he feels he has to, asking if I need anything before we get on the road. I shake my head.

The land has been ravaged. The funnel branded its path clearly into the earth, and detritus litters the horizon, as far as I can see. Wood, rocks, garbage, clothing, car parts, pieces of homes. Broken signs and billboards. IT'S OKAY TO DROOL AND DRIVE: WISCONSIN STATE CHEESE.

You're nothing like her.

My last words to my mother. *I am nothing like you.*

"How did we get out?" I say.

He gives me a sideways look.

"I mean, out of its path."

"We drove for a long time until its path wasn't the same as ours anymore."

"Shouldn't we have stayed? I mean, the house—"

"It's gone."

"What?"

"Tornado blew through a number of years ago, and they had to replace one whole side of the house. That storm wasn't nearly as big as this one."

Guilt gnaws at my stomach at the way he's now speaking to me, clipped and wary, and I can still feel those terrible words in my mouth, in the air between us. But then his words sink in, and I turn to him. "Maro, how do you—"

"Approaching white pickup, approaching white pickup, please pull over. I repeat, pull over." A megaphoned voice stops me from finishing my question. *"Do not, I repeat, do not attempt to exit your vehicle. Stay inside until a uniformed official gives you clearance."*

Before us, a makeshift wall has been erected to block access to bigger roadways, and a combination of policemen and some other type of uniformed officers control the perimeter. There stands above the wall one elevated tower from which the megaphone-wielding guard yells down to us. The light in the sky grows, the sun just starting to peek out from behind the horizon.

A tan Jeep drives out to meet us. A man stands on its back, holding a rifle trained on our windshield. The car stops thirty feet away from us. Two men jump out, both keeping their guns fixed on us as they approach. They split off, one going to each side of the truck. One yells for us to roll down the windows.

"Do not move. If you do, we are under orders to shoot. Is that understood?"

He waits until we nod.

"What is your business here?" His eyes sweep over us, his fingers white on the gun. The man on my side is just as nervous, and he leans away from me.

Maro answers before I can say anything. "Sir, Officer Maro Verges. Sauk County PD. I've been radioed several times requesting my presence. I'd like to show you my badge."

The man gives Maro a long look, then says, "What were you doing outside Sauk County lines?"

"I was visiting friends when we started getting the calls. Was told to report to a station first in Waukesha, now Plainfield. Helped direct traffic on 53, been trying to get back since."

The guard weighs Maro's words. He motions to me with his gun. "What about her?"

"Minor. Her family lives not far from here, in the quarantine zone. Found her alone with her dog in a broken-down car."

The guard turns his attention to me now. "Well, it seems you got pretty lucky, young lady, having an officer find and protect you during all this."

"Yeah," I say. "Very lucky."

"Have either of you come in contact with any infected?"

I open my mouth to answer, and Maro interjects again. "Not directly."

The guard nods, peers into the truck one more time, and says, "Stay here."

The sun clears the horizon, casting light on the wall, on the world. It glints off the guns.

The man on my side of the car remains where he is, rifle fixed on me. I look straight at him. "What do you think I'm going to do?"

He averts his eyes as though I am something best not to be looked at.

"Soldier, what's wrong with you?" The first guard is back.

"Nothing, sir," replies the man outside my window.

"You see something?" He reaches for his gun again, now slung on his back.

"No, sir, I just—teenage girls make me nervous . . . Sir."

The guard squints his eyes and says, "Jesus Christ, get yer shit together. Dismissed, go do something else."

"Sir, yes, sir."

"Sorry. He's—" He's more relaxed now, tired like all of us. He's got a paper in his hand. "Well, he's an idiot. But it's been—I mean, you've seen what it's like out there." He gestures to the wall. "In here, it's . . . You wouldn't believe the numbers. So many bodies . . . we don't even . . ."

Maro nods. "We get it."

"Are we going in there?" I say.

He raises his eyebrows. "In there? No, ma'am. No, we can't let anyone in there, and you don't want to, promise ya that. But there's a station nearby. You been vaccinated yet?"

"No," Maro says. "There's a vaccine already?"

"Yes, no. Few days ago was first we heard of it, but I guess they been doin' it in the Northeast for a fair bit. Government is setting up vaccination centers all over, stations outside the quarantine zones. They're workin' fast. There's one real close, just outside Plainfield, a high school, called somethin' queer, Bright Futures, Bright Light, I dunno.

"You two should report there, get the shot. We don't know yet if it helps, but they won't let you report to duty now till you've got it. Bunch of cops out there so they might just station you there. Take this with you, you'll be able to bypass a buncha BS going in."

Maro looks at the paper. *"Clean Bill of Health Granted by the National Guard.* Huh."

The man shrugs. "We've lost a lot of officials. Doctors, mayors, sergeants. At this point, if you're not jumpin' on me and trying to rip my clothes off, that's good enough for me. Not sure I ever thought I'd say those words. You let the cops at Bright Whatever know that we're with 'em. That we're all on the same team."

"I will. Thank you." He puts his hand out to shake the other man's.

The guard pulls back.

Maro says, "Oh. Right. Sorry."

"Shit world, where you can't shake hands. You two stay safe out there."

Just as the guard said, the vaccination center is set up in the gym of a high school not far from the wall, Bright Beginnings.

Chaos outside. A mass of people cordoned off in different areas by fences, all trying to avoid getting too close to each other. Three paramedic trucks are parked, along with five or six police cruisers, off to the side of the gym.

The school was relatively untouched by the tornado in terms of damage, but trash and debris litter the grounds, the wind sweeping the garbage around and into the throbbing crowd to join in the confusion.

Maro parks the truck near the police cars. No one notices our arrival in the midst of everything. He grabs his jacket from the cab and reattaches his badge to it before helping me locate my crutch. I put one sneaker on my good foot and carry the other one by the laces.

One line going out of the facility leads to portable bathrooms set up to the side of the gym bordering the parking lot. There is a large area that I would guess is where people wait before they receive the vaccine, fenced in on the soccer field. This group is particularly frenzied. People trying not to touch each other, fights breaking out anytime someone makes contact with a neighbor, which only serves to throw them into each other more.

I start to make out their faces. Sweaty, afraid. A woman stands holding a small child on her hip, screaming at a nearby man and trying to get away from him. Another child, a little older, holding on to his father's hand with both of his, pressed against the metal of the fence, eyes wide. I scan all of them, looking for Noah, for any sign.

Maro leads Barghest and me to the front of the holding area. Only two officials stand between the fenced-in mass of people waiting to get vaccinated and the entrance to the gym. But large guns are slung on their backs.

One holds a clipboard and rubs his eyes with the back of his hand. The man, fair-haired and freckled, notices us approaching and holds his hands out. "Stay right there. New arrivals?"

The other man, tall and thin, turns to us. "Maro? Is that you? Holy shit, we thought—"

"Charlie. Shit, it's good to see you." Maro reaches out to shake the cop's hand but drops it just as fast, nodding instead. "Ope, this is, uh, Sophie, and the dog's with us too. Sophie, this is Charlie, Officer Nicks. And, sorry, I don't think we've met."

The first cop says his name, which I can't hear over all the commotion. His uniform says he is from a different county's police department. He looks distrustful of us.

"We can't have dogs in here," he says.

"He's a service animal," Maro replies before I can say anything.

"You got paperwork?"

"Dude, we don't have anything. She needs him. It's medical."

The guard isn't convinced, but he doesn't push it further.

Charlie says, "Maro, I'm so glad you're here, and that you're okay. We've got pretty strict protocols, though, and since you've been in infected areas I don't know what we can—"

Maro produces the paper from his front pocket. "Does this help?"

Charlie looks it over. "Haven't seen one of these yet, but National Guard has actually been pretty on their shit, so . . ." He folds the paper and tucks it in his own pocket, marks something down on his clipboard, and looks at me. "Your name is Sophie . . . ?"

"Allen."

"Sophie Allen. Alright. Maro, they'll want you to report inside—" He swears, his eyes on the crowd.

The blond cop leaves us to take care of a fight that's broken out at the front. People are yelling because we skipped the line. Charlie raises his voice to Maro over the noise. "This isn't a place for little girls, man. Shit's crazy in here. People are—" He gestures to the fight in the holding area. "You know." In the holding area, a man throws another man to the ground and gets on his knees to punch the downed man in the face. I still don't see Noah.

Someone has scratched words into the building paint behind the officer. I squint my eyes and try to make them out.

Maro says to his friend, "What else are we supposed to do?"

Charlie gives me a long look and says, "That dog as vicious as he looks?"

I hesitate then say, "He can be."

He nods. "Keep him close."

As we pass him to enter, I am just able to read the words.

Abandon all hope.

Sylvia

I nside, people everywhere. Sound reverberates through the space, off the high white ceilings and the shiny floor to the walls and high-up windows. The gym still waking up, it seems, everyone bleary-eyed, pouring cups of coffee. Overhead lights warm the space some, and long white sheets hang from the rafters. Banners hang down too, from the ceiling, the windows. **GO MINOTAURS**. A glowing backlit image of a red, horned half-bull, half-man glares out at us, overseeing it all.

As we make our way in, I begin to get a better sense of the organization, if one can call it that. The long sheets divide the huge space, as do ropes tied between the folded-up bleachers and hooks attached to the walls.

Barghest is nervous and leans his body into mine so it's hard to walk. He whines softly, and I try to reassure him.

I identify the vaccination area on the left side of the gym first. Plastic chairs are set up for those waiting while mask-wearing nurses and a few people in plain clothes inject a clear fluid into arms. The orange biohazard bins and sterilization station mark it as the most official, and I would guess most important, of all the areas inside the gym.

Signs are posted on some of the sheets, saying things like **POST-VACCINE WAITING AREA; OFFICIALS ONLY BEYOND THIS POINT; SLEEPING BARRACKS A, B, C, D**. I follow closely behind Maro, who somehow seems to have an idea of where we should be heading.

People watch us pass, eyes drifting from Barghest at my side down to my injured foot, up to Maro. Someone yells, *They're letting fucking dogs in here?*

Maro doesn't slow his pace, so I don't either.

I scan every face I pass on the off chance something has changed and Noah has ended up here. They all are desperate, nervous, tired, and afraid. None of them are my brother.

A policeman stands guard at the entrance to each area, and a large group of cops huddles together off to right side of the gym, across from the med station. Maro leads me through the crowds until we reach them.

Their faces change as they notice us. Calls of "Oh my God!" and "Holy shit, Maro!" "You're alive, dude!" "Fuck, how did you get here?" ring out to join all the other sounds. He strides to greet them and then pauses a few feet away from the group. One of his friends sets down her coffee cup and says, "Fuck that, I gotta hug you. Come here."

She's pretty, and his age. And when they hug it is clear they're very close. My stomach does something sour watching it. Maro gives the altered, official version of how we made it here. Then he introduces me.

"You get the shot yet?" she asks him.

"No, neither of us has."

She introduces herself to me as Officer Pike and leads us over to the nurses' station. Maro tells me they went through their training together, that they've known each other more than a decade from home. She points out different things along the way, but she walks with Maro in front of me, so I can't hear most of what she says.

When we arrive at the med area, Officer Pike asks Maro if we stopped through Neillsville. A pained look crosses his face.

"Yeah. They were gone already. I was hoping they'd made it here?" He says it as a sort of question, hope in his eyes. That desperate hope I know well.

Pike shakes her head. Maro rubs his hands over his face again, swears softly, and then reaches for the cigarettes in his pocket. Pike sets her hand over his. "Not in here."

She introduces us to a nurse who says that Barghest has to wait outside while we receive our shots, but by outside she just means outside the curtained-off area. These constructed borders, such flimsy grasps at normalcy. Pike has to physically restrain Barghest from following me. I touch my forehead to his before I go. He licks my throat, once. Maro tenses, probably remembering what his tongue has recently touched. Okay. We won't do that again.

The nurse sits me down on one of the plastic chairs and asks a series of questions from a clipboard, beginning with my name and where I'm from.

"Have you come into contact with any infected individuals?"

Maro catches my eye from the table next to mine and gives me a subtle but sharp shake of the head.

"No," I say.

"Have you experienced any of the following symptoms: fever, sore throat, respiratory distress, nausea, severe headache, dizziness, or increased arousal?"

I flush what I'm sure is bright red and shake my head quickly.

"Ma'am, I need a verbal confirmation, yes or no."

"No."

"When was the last time you had sexual relations?"

I think I might actually die.

"Um . . ."

"Have you had sexual relations in the past seventy-two hours?"

I shake my head and then, in response to a piqued look from the nurse, clearly say, "No."

She takes my arm and swabs it with an alcohol-soaked pad.

"How did you come up with a vaccine so quickly?" I ask. "I thought this virus was new."

She nods. "We haven't. This is the NARS-CoV vaccine. No Sylvia vaccine yet."

"Sylvia," I say softly.

"HPSV. Human parasyphilan virus. Causes lesions in the Sylvian fissure in the brain, so 'Sylvia.' Not the scientific term, but easier to say. And the internet seems to like it."

She sticks me with the needle and uncaps another syringe.

"What's that one?" I say.

"Benzathine penicillin G."

"What is it for?"

"Syphilis."

"I don't have—"

She waves away my words. "*Parasyphilan* virus. Means *like* syphilis. Brain lesions, swelling in the frontal cortex, that's how it hijacks the host, gets them to propagate it by fluid swapping. Also the hand rash, classic secondary syphilis symptom. Big difference, besides being viral, is that the timeline for Sylvia is about a thousand times faster."

"But you think this will work?"

She sits back, the syringe in her hand, her face unreadable.

"Yeah," she says, but she holds my eyes. Imparting something, but I'm not sure what. "Be careful in here."

She shoots the liquid into my arm.

"Now, let's take a look at that foot."

The nurse next to me asks Maro the seventy-two-hour question. *Have you had sexual relations?*

He hesitates, then responds, quietly, "Yes."

We wait for Maro to get his dog bite sterilized. He assures Pike it was inflicted by another dog, but I can tell she doesn't buy it. Then Officer Pike ushers us into another curtained-off space: **SLEEPING BARRACKS A**. We are told that since we're not able to shelter in our homes, we need to remain here for forty-eight hours, until the shots have started to work their way into our systems, and we can only leave to use the bathroom, or in my case to let Barghest out. My foot is bandaged and wrapped to excess to prevent any chance of infection. "Fluid sharing" is a term I've heard more in the last minutes than in my whole life up to now.

Maro had . . . in the last seventy-two hours. That means right before he met me on the highway. Where had he been? He said something about visiting friends. I don't like it, I really don't.

Sleeping Barracks A is a curtained-off makeshift room with cots, set up between the fabric dividers and the far wall of the gym. I would guess there are maybe thirty beds in all. Most of them are taken, either claimed with articles of clothing or occupied by anxious, shocked, devastated humans.

The sheets only give the barest illusion of privacy and fail to pose any kind of real boundary. If anything, this place seems like a breeding ground for contagion. The air is so thick with tension and fatigue, I can nearly taste it. Barghest, still whining beside me, feels it too.

The vaccination nurse made me sign a contract saying that I understand that while I stay in this facility any sexual activity is prohibited.

I agreed to abstain from "fluid sharing" as well as sharing food or drinks, and promised to disinfect my space with the provided sanitation products daily. I signed the form as if my whole life hadn't been an unwritten contract ensuring my abstinence anyway. As if my whole value as a person, a future wife, a mortal girl and woman who hopes not to burn in eternal hellfire doesn't lie largely in my intact virginity. Anyway, I don't even know what it would be like. Clearly good enough to risk incurring the wrath of God, at least for some people. But how could anything be that good? How could anything be worth it?

Ayla and Jondalar in *The Valley of Horses*. Eli and Fiona on the ground.

"I guess we should find a place," Maro says. He still won't look at me, after what I said. I don't blame him. I couldn't blame him if he never wanted to talk to me again. He owes me nothing, and that's fine. Because it's the same for me. So why is my chest burning?

We move down the aisle, passing beds on either side, all taken. Some people sleep, others read or check their cell phones or talk in hushed or loud voices. Some cry. Barghest leans into me. There are no sheets or pillows or blankets. A few people have jackets covering them, but otherwise the cots are bare. Thin mattresses on metal frames.

Some people have stowed purses or backpacks underneath their cots, but for the most part no one has much. Families huddle together, and one couple has scooted two cots together so there are only a few inches in between. They hold hands, the woman dozing, the man holding on to her as if she is the only thing keeping him connected to this world.

Officer Pike stands watch near the edge of the room. Her eyes are trained on the couple.

"How are they doing food?" Maro asks her.

"MREs, twice a day. Breakfast will be coming soon."

She directs us to the far end of the aisle and tells us that Barghest can sleep on the floor as long as he stays with one of us at all times and doesn't cause any trouble. She lingers on the word "trouble" until I nod agreement.

There are three unoccupied cots in total, two on one side of the aisle and one on the other. Beyond the empty cots, a group has taken the five beds nearest the wall, what I would guess is prime real estate with its one side of real privacy.

We consider the cots. When neither of us makes a move, I say, "You don't need to sleep next to me. I mean, I'm fine if you want the one over there."

His gaze travels over the group near the wall playing a card game, the two free cots on our right by an empty one with a jacket on it, the single free cot on our left, the large man sleeping next to it. I can tell none of them want a dog around. They stare at him, and us.

Maro shrugs and mumbles something that sounds like *Whatever you want*. He removes his jacket, reattaches his badge to his shirt, and claims the lone bed.

I take off my hoodie and choose the cot farther away from the group, the one with the mystery neighbor. This way Maro isn't directly across from me, but diagonal so I can see him if I want to but don't have to every time I look up.

On the one hand, it feels unwise having the only person I know not next to me at all times, especially after all we've been through in the last forty-eight hours. On the other hand, I can't imagine sleeping so close to Maro. Maybe I feel terrible for what I said to him, and maybe I am terrible. But there was our fight, as stupid as it was. And the fact that he answered yes to that question. And that thing he said last night, his words hanging in the air between us, my name in his mouth. Maybe I can't imagine sleeping next to him because it terrifies me, fills me with shame and guilt because maybe a small part of me, a bad, unhelpful, potentially eternally damning part, wants . . . *what?*

The family discuss the vaccines. I can't be near him right now. I can't trust myself to be near anyone. Is there a chance I could actually be sick? I take quick inventory. But physically, other than the bruises and my foot, I feel fine. Maro sits on the edge of his cot, facing my bed. I stand.

"Um, excuse me, Officer Pike," I say.

I limp toward her as she looks up. "Hi, um, so I'm looking for someone. A teenage boy, my age, and we look a lot alike, brown hair, green eyes, he's a little over six feet, and his name is Noah Allen. Have you seen or heard of anyone like that?"

She takes measure of me, clearly sensing the desperation. "No, not yet," she says.

"What about in the holding area outside? Can I go ask around?"

She sighs, then nods. "No, you need to stay here, but . . . Noah Allen?"
I nod. "Thank you."

I feel Maro's eyes as I return to my cot, facing my mystery neighbor's space and all the beds beyond it. Facing this way so I won't have to look at him. Because there's something wrong with me. I call Barghest to curl up on the floor next to me. I close my eyes, just for a moment.

"No! Stop! Stop him!" An old woman's voice. A scream.

I fling myself upright, Barghest growling beside me. I must have fallen asleep, and it takes me a moment to remember where I am. Voices, movement, confusion. Maro vaults from his cot and down the aisle. Officer Pike runs to meet him.

"He's infected!" the woman screams. She looks to be nearing eighty. In the bright chaotic space, the infected man pulls her to him by her sweater, holding her frail body to his so hard that she can't even struggle.

Panic ripples like a wave, down all the cots, across the gym.

I watch, heart pounding, as Maro and Pike try to wrench the infected man, tall and young, off the older woman, staggering beneath his weight, as everyone else in the barracks backs away. Everyone stopped, mid-movement, mid-thought, knuckles white, breath held. Not helping. Maro touching an infected person. Maro too close to him.

The infected man elbows Officer Pike in the nose, and her blood spatters the floor. He lunges again, grabs hold of either side of the old woman's face, and shoves his tongue in her mouth.

But it's not just his tongue, I realize, nearly sick. He's biting her. Biting and licking and pulling and chewing, and there's blood, the old woman's blood. Even as Maro and Pike fight him, he attaches himself tighter to her. They pull at him, but he is clamped around her, as though he is trying to burrow inside her.

A curtain falls, large metal hooks coming down with it, striking with a clang against a table. The old woman screams inside his mouth. Muffled, gurgled. As the man tears at her face, as he tries to push himself deeper inside it. As he devours it.

Another officer joins, pulls at his arms. Finally, the seal is broken. And they are able to wrench him off her, blood spraying.

The woman's face though . . . an open wound, lips torn and chewed, a chunk of her tongue missing. She is crying, and screaming. There's so much blood. The officers holding him shove their way through the curtain opening, the infected man kicking and growling like an animal.

Nurses come in and take the old woman.

We hear her screams for minutes after.

Then nothing.

The glowing minotaur sign. His red horned face glaring out over all of us. The wind blowing against the side of the gym. The Christian Radio announcer repeating in my head: *You're telling me this isn't demonic?*

Maro returns to his cot, smelling of industrial-strength disinfectant and cigarette smoke, only glancing briefly at me as he passes. I watch him, but he won't acknowledge me. He doesn't want to. I feel the same pit in my stomach as when the girls at school called me a slut and freak, but this is worse. For some reason it's so much worse with him. I hate him being mad at me, not being able to look at me. Still, he's not hurt.

I lie down on my side, my face pressed into Barghest's fur. I hold him tight.

And looking around this room, all the bodies, all the people, I think anyone could be infected. Anyone can be attacked during the night. Or the day. Anyone could already have it, including me.

Within the hour, breakfast is delivered in plastic containers that say **MEAL, READY-TO-EAT** along with bottled water. I eat mechanically. My foot sends constant pain signals to my brain, and my body is bruised and stiff. Maro and Barghest made it through the night. I did. We survived a tornado. I need to use the restroom, haven't gone since last night at the farmhouse, but I don't want to talk to anyone to figure out what the protocol is. After the gas station, the thought of a public restroom is worse than discomfort, at least for now.

I eat silently, giving Barghest half my meal. He'll need more food, but I'll have to find it later. I let him lick the meal container clean and then pour half my water in it for him to drink.

I glance up to find Maro is watching me, but as soon as I catch his eye he looks away. He hasn't touched his food. He monitors the rows of cots and the disheartened people in them. His shoulders are tense, even more than before. He's thinking about the old woman. I know by now that he is the kind of person who takes responsibility for any bad thing that happens around him, whether it's justified or not. Which is why what I said was so particularly cruel.

I need to do something. I want to know whose house it was that we stayed in and why he kept it from me. I want to know who he had sexual relations with before he saw me. I want to know if he was thinking about that when we were at the farmhouse. If he's thinking about it now. I have too many thoughts, too many feelings, new ones, bad ones, strange ones.

I was cruel before, and selfish. He doesn't deserve that. And maybe I also selfishly don't want him mad at me. Maybe I . . . I can't sort out the rest now, but I can apologize. I'll apologize to Maro and then search around this place and see if anyone knows anything about St. Joseph's Hospital in Waukesha.

I take a breath and turn to him. "Maro, I'm—"

But a voice sounds behind me, and I am cut short.

"Sophie? Oh my God, is that you?"

Ben

B en.
 Ben is here.

Ben from home. From school and the mall and the library. I try to calculate how many days it's been. Six, I think, since I saw him last. But it feels like a lifetime. My parents died since then.

My parents died.

Ben stands over me, and he says, with a pained smile on his face, "Can I . . . hug you?"

"What?"

"You have no idea, Sophie. No idea." He doesn't wait for me to move but takes hold of my hand and pulls me up into a tight hug.

Every inch of his body pressed against mine. I can't even think. His arms, his chest, his—I'm not sure I've ever been hugged like this, by anyone. His body, so warm. He must feel how quickly my heart beats against him. I clear my throat, and just like that, he releases me.

He keeps his hands on my arms and sweeps his eyes over me.

"You have no idea how good it is to see you. Just to see anyone. I've been . . ." He trails off, and I take him in too. This boy I've met only a few times, but who now is my closest tie to home. I know enough to see that he is different. Even in so little time, he's not the same boy I met in the library. Heavy circles beneath his eyes, and a long cut down the side of his neck, very fresh and recently stitched. A wildness in him that tells me he has seen things he is trying to unsee.

"Your family?" he asks.

I shake my head.

"I'm so sorry."

"Mrs. Parson?"

His look tells me the answer.

"I'm . . ." I want to fall to my knees. I can't—Ben still hasn't removed his hands from my arms. He holds my eyes for a long minute. "I'm so sorry. I can't believe . . ."

"Well, listen," he says softly, such deep sadness in his eyes. Mrs. Parson. I can't fathom it. "We've got each other now. So neither of us has to be alone."

A throat clears beside me.

Maro is standing there.

I'm steps behind. Mrs. Parson. Ben and Maro, these worlds colliding. "Hey," Maro says.

"Hey," I say back. I wonder if he can see the things I am feeling, my heart and my body. Mrs. Parson gone. He and Ben introduce themselves. I look on in a daze.

Ben had said she was sick before, I should have realized.

Maro looks to me. "You okay?"

I nod.

He tilts his head toward Ben. "Old friend?"

"Something like that," Ben replies. A moment passes between them, between the three of us. I don't know what to make of it. Barghest senses it because I hear him stir behind me, a low growl building in his throat.

Maro nods. "I gotta go take care of some stuff."

"Okay," I say.

"It's probably best not to touch." He looks once at Ben and then back at me.

When he leaves, Ben says, "How do you know that cop?"

"Oh, um. He's been helping me."

"Huh. God, I can't believe it." He sits down on the cot next to mine, the one with the jacket. "Whoa, who's this?" Barghest stands beside him, sniffing, hackles raised.

"Also a friend. He's sweeter than he looks." It's mostly true, anyway.

Ben reaches up slowly to pet him, and Barghest allows it.

"Is that your cot?" I ask.

"What? Oh this one? No, but it's my friend's. I mean, you get to know people here pretty fast. But she's cool, I'll ask her if we can switch."

My stomach does something at the idea of Ben sleeping next to me. Is that better or worse than Maro?

I don't know how to respond, so I lower myself to the edge of mine. I smile, a little, my hand on Barghest's back. His weight leaning into me. "This is Barghest. He's . . . he's mine now, I think."

"How did you guys end up all the way out here?"

"Oh." I shrug. "It's kind of a long story. Not very exciting." My eyes meet his, and I feel his body pressed against mine again in that hug, the hardness of it, the heat.

"What about you?" I say, my voice cracking a little.

"Oh, man." He lies down on his friend's cot, on top of her jacket, and kicks his feet up. I can imagine him doing the same thing on a couch after coming home from sports practice, or whatever it was he did in his spare time before all this. Mrs. Parson's house. He turns on his side and props himself up on one elbow. His face darkens.

"Well, Mom was sick a little bit ago. She . . . we went to the hospital, actually right after I saw you, that night. The hospital was . . ." He trails off, stares for a minute, and touches his neck where the long cut is. He shakes his head. "It all went downhill fast."

"She was always so kind to me," I say. I hope he feels how much I mean it. "She was the kindest adult I've ever known."

"Yeah, she was the greatest."

I catch the muscle twitching in his jaw, the way he swallows back the feelings that threaten to erupt as he accustoms himself to the cruelty of the past tense. I watch him reminding himself that it is real and it is happening.

"I went to be with my dad down south because I had nowhere else to go. But before I made it, the quarantine was in effect, and some army guys redirected me here. I've seen no one else from home. It's all blocked off, you know. All of Foreston."

"Yeah, I heard."

"We're lucky, to have gotten out," he says. But he drifts somewhere dark again.

We are silent for a time. What can I say to someone who just lost everything? What can he say to me? I'm dazed, and there is so much volume in this place, so much movement.

After a few minutes he says, again, "I'm so glad you're here."

I am not sure who he thinks I am. This boy who watched me reading and occupied my thoughts in a previous life, a life that existed last week, a life that never will be again. Will he be disappointed by who I am, or does who and what I am not factor in at all? Maybe all I need to be for him is a reminder that life before did exist. Maybe that is enough.

I scratch Barghest behind the ears and say, "Me too."

"You look like you haven't slept enough," he says. "You probably should, while you can. It's kind of the one thing this place is good for. Well . . . till now, anyway."

I open my eyes. A girl sits on the cot next to mine with Ben. Backs to me, they play some sort of hand-slapping game, the girl exhaling softly through her nose in what I think is a laugh every time Ben's hand touches hers. Soft hair, bare shoulders. I push myself upright. Barghest has moved from my side to sit near Ben, who at every break in the game reaches over and pets him.

Barghest is the first to notice me. He walks over and licks my face. Surely it's been long enough since licking infected blood that it's okay. And surely dogs can't carry it . . . right? He looks up at me and I reach around and pull him to me, lean on him. The girl has just begun to say something to Ben when he turns around and says, "Sophie, you're up."

He angles his body toward me. That boy body he carries with such thoughtlessness.

"Sophie, this is Helen. Helen, Sophie."

"Hey," I say. "Nice to meet you."

"Yeah, you too," she says, but she doesn't quite meet my eye.

Helen is beautiful, almost alarmingly so. She has light hair, tan skin, large blue eyes, and is probably only a couple of years older than me. She wears a pink-and-red dress that makes me self-conscious about my own ill-fitting T-shirt, too-long jeans, and dirty bare foot, even if her dress is torn and marred in a way that tells me her getting here was just as difficult as anyone else's.

Maro returns to his cot from somewhere, the movement catching Barghest's attention.

"Maro," I say. "Where were you?" I don't know why my voice sounds accusatory. As if I have a right to know.

He says, "Around. Helping, trying." He notices Helen, who is watching him.

"Hi," she says. She stops, surprised at herself, she didn't mean to say it. Her face goes red, and she blinks. She is noticing his face, how he looks.

"Hi. Um, I'm Maro . . . Officer Verges." He's distracted, tired, glancing over at his cot.

Helen's eyes dart up to his and back down once. "Helen. Nice to meet you."

Annoyance shoots through me. He's handsome, but he's not that handsome. Ben's way more perfect, younger, taller, has an easiness to him that Maro probably has never had, at least not for a long time. Maro's just . . . Maro. He doesn't even glance at me before excusing himself to talk to the new cop on duty. I tamp down the agitation. It doesn't matter.

Helen's eyes follow him as he walks away and then return to Ben. "You know these two from home?" she asks. She does not address me.

"Yeah, Sophie anyway. Actually, I was gonna ask you if we could switch cots, but I guess I didn't realize there was an empty one right there." He gestures to the free cot on the other side of me. "I should go get my stuff."

I watch Helen's face as her eyes travel between Ben and me. "Yeah, okay," she says.

When Ben leaves, Helen doesn't say anything to me. She sits, smoothing over her hair and then her dress. A large man wearing a shirt that says FLAT EARTH ARMY on another cot near us stares at Helen's bare legs, the smooth skin of them. I do not envy her dress.

"How long have you been here?" I ask.

Helen doesn't look at me when she answers. "Almost two days. Same as Ben."

"Are you, um, do you go to school?" I say.

"I graduated this year, took some time off. Starting at UW next fall." She pauses, considers what she said, probably wondering what next fall will look like. But she doesn't want to speak to me. She pulls out a phone and starts to scroll.

"Oh," I say. "Um, is there any news?"

She exhales, annoyed.

She says, "I was gonna watch this. You can . . . if you want." She still doesn't look at me but gestures at the phone as she taps on a video. I lean in closer as she turns the volume up enough for us to hear.

A shiny-looking man my father's age in a red sweater and a priest's collar sits in front of a stone fireplace in what looks to be a warm, cozy living room, addressing the camera. A fire crackles behind him. He smiles.

"Hello there," he says, and his voice is soft and pleasing. A holy man's voice. Trustworthy and persuasive. "If we haven't yet had the pleasure, I am Reverend Don Ansel, and I'm so glad you're here. By now, you might have noticed that God has sent change surging across our land with a swiftness and brutality that can only be attributed to His awesome might. And our great nation is now facing a crisis of the utmost severity. But the question we may ask ourselves, as friends, neighbors, loved ones succumb to this terrible plight, the question that plagues all of us in this time of crisis is *why*." His smile doesn't falter.

"Do you know him?" I ask Helen. "Is he your reverend?"

Helen pauses the video and looks at me. "God no. But—you haven't seen this guy?—he's got over a million followers. He's been like everywhere with these videos, in all the politicians' photos? You haven't seen?"

I shake my head.

"Oh. Okay. Well I guess he's been saying for years that a time will come when he and his followers will be *called to action*. And now he's saying it's time or something. I don't know, that's why I'm watching."

"Who are his followers?"

"Um, Christians of different types all over the country. Evangelicals, Catholics, Baptists, others. He's somehow unified all these people from different sects. Made it political, got all the craziest ones on board. I don't really know. It's all . . ." She waves her hand as if to say . . . something. I don't know. It seems as though I maybe should.

"Oh," I say. And maybe I remember the Christian Radio mentioning his name back on the highway.

Helen presses Play again.

"I can answer that question for you," Reverend Ansel says, "if you're willing to listen. This *viral mutation*—as the secular world insists on calling it—as we know was seen first in New York City, but grew to its current strength in the Midwest, starting in Chicago. This summer in New York City was the highest on record for secular and liberal protests, and just one week before the first reported supposed *mutation* from the *'flu'* to this 'Sylvia,' one week before this plague appeared, was the great librarians' summit. Fifty thousand librarians gathering to protest the banning of pornographic, unnatural, and immoral books from our children's schools. Fifty thousand saying they oppose erasure while fighting tooth, nail, and claw to keep the Bible, the one True book of our history and our salvation, *out* of our children's education.

"And Chicago, three days before the first report of this '*Sylvia*,' what bill had just passed? That men in women's clothing—sexual, depraved—these perverts and sodomites would gain and retain irrevocable rights to perform *for our children*, prey upon their innocence. Even while other states had justly revoked their ability to proselytize their perversion. And thus ensued the largest known gathering of 'drag queens' in American history, swarming Chicago's streets. Three days before this 'Sylvia' appeared. Right there."

Helen makes a sound in her throat, and I look up. She looks furious, or maybe like she wants to cry. The video plays on.

"Christians have faced more oppression and erasure in recent years than ever before. And the world has paid for it. Storms, terrorists, increased violence, confusion among young people, so-called gender politics, the dark world of social media, infanticide, men and women choosing to turn their noses up at God by indulging in same-sex 'relationships,' forsaking God, blaspheming, at every turn. We are lost. And what has God done every time we've lost our way? What does He do in the Bible again and again?

"This nation, once mighty and moral, just, honorable, has descended into depravity. Senseless madness. Our vices, our wickedness, our degeneracy, like Sodom and Gomorrah and Eden itself, have infiltrated our communities so completely that many haven't even realized it was happening. We have tainted this great land. It's the simplest truth, and the righteous among us know it. What does God do when we have fallen into wickedness and sin, when we have succumbed to darkness? In His mighty righteousness, wisdom, and might, time and again?

"He *reaps.*

"But it's not too late. If we continue to band together now, if we—"

Helen exits the video. "I'm sorry, I can't," she says. She is so upset she is shaking. "I can't look at this anymore." She scrolls another moment through what she says are people's reactions. There are lot of supportive ones, saying Reverend Ansel has been right this whole time, that we need to arm ourselves, speaking about the immorality of the secular world. Helen skips past all of those and clicks on one reply, which is a linked video and text that says, *Mic drop.*

In the video, a woman speaks on a red carpet to an interviewer. She has more makeup on her face than I've ever seen, makeup that's more like art, or painting even, than actual makeup. She has blond hair and wears a pink dress, and she's furious. "Stats on drag queens being pedophiles: zero. There's no drag queens being arrested for sexual assault of children. That doesn't happen. Do you know where that happens? The *church* . . . This whole country mollycoddles Christians, and I'm fuckin' tired of it! Do we have separation of church and state or not?"

"Who is she?" I ask.

"Trixie Mattel."

"Is she an actress?"

"Well, she's more of a personality. Like she does drag, but she sings and writes music and is really funny, and she's done some cool things for Wisconsin. She's from here."

I don't totally understand what a drag queen is, but it's not the most important question I have just now. Helen seems to be finished scrolling, is going through just for the sake of it.

"Hey, um," I say, "is there any way . . . would you mind if I maybe used that for a minute? When you're not using it, I mean. I just want to check up on something."

"Oh, uh, yeah." She picks it back up and looks at the screen, then says, "The thing is I'm at twenty percent, and I don't have a charger so . . ."

"Right. Well . . . maybe someone . . ." I turn to the other people around us. "Does anyone by any chance have a phone charge—" I don't quite finish the word as I land on the creepy man in the FLAT EARTH ARMY shirt two cots over and across the aisle watching us, holding a charger up in one hand.

"Oh," I say, "um, thanks." I awkwardly pull myself up onto my good leg and the crutch and limp over to him. Barghest stays beside my cot, sleeping. The man stands, towering over me, his gaze traveling down my body. I hop back a little to get space from him, and he leans forward. I take the charger and say, "Thanks, I'll just be right back." I turn and move away as quickly as I can, scanning the area for an outlet and trying not to feel his eyes on me.

There's one on the wall, and I ask the woman sitting there if she'd mind. I sit on the floor and plug the phone in, opening the map app. I type in *St. Joseph's Hospital* and see the various routes I could take. My parents used this function the handful of times we left Foreston, to go to Holy Hill where the holy water spring is, or to visit Noah. The map doesn't show what areas are blocked off though, where the quarantine lines are drawn. I put a search in the browser for quarantine zones in Wisconsin. I click on a few things that aren't helpful before finding a map of the counties with certain lines drawn. I click, and it starts loading. If I can know what's blocked off, I'll be able to put together the route to get to Noah, find a way around the barricades.

The gym goes dark.

Everyone pauses what they're doing, looks around.

The power went out.

I click on the map, but now it doesn't load. I try again.

There's no Wi-Fi signal. And—

The commotion starts all at once. Everyone with a phone asking the others.

Is yours working? Do you have service?

"Service is down?!" someone says, panicked. "Are you serious?"

I stare down at the phone, this little device that was almost the key to Noah, that was almost everything. I wait a long moment, a minute, a couple more. But nothing happens, nothing changes. So I limp back to Helen and hand her phone back. I walk over to the FLAT EARTH man. "Here," I say to him. He's sitting now, leaning back on his elbows on the cot, sprawled so his legs hang off the sides, knees wide open. "Thanks," I say.

He makes no move to sit up or stand again, just lies back looking up at me.

"Um, I'll just leave this here," I say, leaning over on the crutch to drop the charger on the floor by his foot.

"Luke," he says.

"Sorry?"

"My name's Luke."

"Oh right, okay."

There's still no sign of Maro, and I feel Luke's eyes on me like greasy fingers, and I'm sure Helen is watching this, and I don't know why that makes me feel shame, but it does.

Wi-Fi and cell service are out. Everyone's antsy, the rise and swell of it palpable, noisy, charged. Somehow, insanely, the giant red minotaur still glows over everything. I can't understand it. With the rest of the lights off, it's even more unnerving, casting us all in an otherworldly red haze. I stand here, and I don't know what to do. The school should have computers, but if the power is out, then they won't be any help.

Officer Pike peeks her head in through the curtain at the end of our barracks, face half-lit in red. "Sophie," she says. My heart pounds. Barghest is up and standing, towering over Helen. I call him over to me and limp to meet Officer Pike. She meets me halfway down the lines of cots. Her face is tired, gaunt, and sad. "I asked around, about your brother. Maro says he's your twin?"

I nod, praying, hoping—

"I'm sorry. But just because he's not here doesn't mean you won't find him. We don't know where this thing's gonna head, and—"

I'm sorry.

I knew it was a long shot, almost impossible, but I hoped for it. I hoped for it so badly and I didn't realize it, and the creepy man and Helen and that reverend and the power outage, it's all too much. Tears burn the backs of my eyes again, and I am so sick of being this helpless, at the mercy of everyone and everything. So sick of crying so easily. Voices on all sides, discussing what this could mean, the power, cell service. Too many voices. I need to move, I need to get out of this space. I thank Officer Pike, and the tears push in.

I start toward the end of our barracks, passing people, living bodies, every person a risk. Barghest pants heavily. I could slip underneath any of the hanging sheets, avoid the accusatory stares, but there already is

so little privacy, and so little order, that to violate what tenuous struc-
ture they've managed to put in place here seems wrong. I can't afford
more wrong, not until it really counts. And I feel like that might be
coming. A woman cries into her knees. A boy, maybe ten, just stares
straight ahead at nothing. A thirty-something man with a beard near
the entrance points to my borrowed KoЯn shirt and makes a devil
horn gesture with his hand. I finally make it to the makeshift sheet
door leading to the rest of the gym.

Maro stands at the med area just outside our barracks, holding a
phone flashlight up for a nurse who stitches a wound. He looks up at
me, asks where we're going. "Bathroom," I say without looking at him.
If I look at him he will know I am not okay, and it's so stupid, and I just
need to get out of here. I just need a minute for myself.

The red glowing minotaur looms huge in front of me.

"Sophie! Hey, wait up!"

Ben runs up to me. The tears, panic rising.

"I'll go with you."

"I'm just going out for some air," I say. My voice shakes.

"Hey, are you okay?" he says, gentle, concerned, and it's too much. I
shake my head, and my stupid embarrassing tears start to fall.

Maro is watching us, and I want to disappear, to be anywhere but
here. Ben steps between me and the rest of the room, instinctively or
purposefully blocking my face from view.

"Let's get you out of here," he says.

He steers me away from our area, and more people comment on Barghest. A child screeches and runs from him, the mother glaring at me.
My tears keep coming, faster with every second. Ben ushers me past all
the people, through the chaos and noise. Someone yells at a nurse. Music and shows play from different phones even without service. Every
few steps, Ben tilts his head down to see if I am okay. It makes it so much
worse. I wish I could disappear. He leads us through a heavy curtain
that I am sure we're not supposed to go through, on the other side of
which is a wall. We continue between the curtain and the wall until we
come upon a door that is hidden from the general public's view, behind
the stacked risers.

"My first day some pretty gnarly stuff went down, and I had to get
some space. Found this," he says, and opens the door.

The wind is a wall of force, and we have to lean into it to push through and get outside. It changes the course of the tears on my face, and I reach up with my free hand to wipe them away.

We stand on a patch of grass to the side of what probably used to be a parent drop-off area. Ben makes sure the door won't lock behind us, and Barghest sniffs in the grass. From this side of the gym, we can't see anyone, not the holding areas outside the main doors, not the bathrooms. No one walks out here, and it is such an immense relief to have the space to ourselves that my tears fall harder.

"Can I?" he asks. He holds his arms out. I nod, I think I nod, through the tears that I am so angry are still here, and Ben steps forward and wraps his arms around me. I press my face into his chest, and he stands, holding me, this person I barely know, my tears absorbing into his shirt, and I am mortified, and I am grateful, and I am so afraid. The wind claws at us, and I cry until my tears are spent and I can smell and feel the boyness of this—stranger? friend?—who hasn't stopped holding me. And he's warm. He's warm and firm and I feel . . . Not so much a feeling as it is a *want*. A need. A deep pulsing imperative. I am a gaping hole of a person, and I am suddenly full of a surety that he could fill me up. He could make me not feel any of this. He could fix it, I could fix it. Or at least not feel it, at least—

Eli and Fiona, two naked bodies entwined in blood.

I might be infected.

I push away from him. Take in gulps of air.

He's staring at me. But it's not accusatory, and he's not afraid. He looks confused.

"I'm sorry," I say. I don't know if I mean for the crying or my thoughts or endangering him or stepping away, but he seems to remember himself now too, this new world. He runs his hands through his hair.

"Yeah. I'm sorry too," he says. "I forgot for a minute."

Maro is back, standing on the other end of the barracks, speaking with another cop. The little boy is still sitting and staring at nothing, no one with him. I stop and crouch down when we get to his cot. A man and a woman perpetuate a loud and heated conversation nearby, their voices overpowering.

"You were the one who wanted to drive here."

"To see my mother."

"To see your mother in a fucking pandemic."

"She's my mother!"

"Hi," I say to the boy. "I'm Sophie." He stares straight ahead. "What's your name?"

He still doesn't register me, so I gently place my hand on his arm. He jumps, terrified.

"Oh, I'm sorry," I say.

He pushes away from me and slides back on his cot.

"No, no, I'm so sorry. I didn't mean to scare you."

He stares at me, eyes wide. Then his gaze falls on Barghest, and he trembles.

"This is Barghest. Do you want to pet him?"

The boy shakes his head. He is thin with brown hair and a dirty striped shirt. Jeans, checkered tennis shoes. Bruises all up and down one of his arms. He looks so much like Noah did.

"Well, she's fucking dead now!" the woman in the couple says. The cop Maro was talking to steps in, asks the two to lower their voices.

I turn back to the boy. "What's your name?"

He stares at me again and then finally whispers, "Wyatt."

"Wyatt, are you alone here?" I ask.

He takes us in for another moment and then nods yes.

"This is Ben," I say, "and we have two other friends over there." I point to Helen's and Maro's cots. "Do you want to come sleep by us? I'm sure we can get people to move around."

He stares but doesn't say anything. Moments pass, so long I think he doesn't understand what I'm asking, and I'm about to ask again when Ben's hand touches my arm. He shakes his head. I bring my gaze back to the boy, but it catches on Maro down the line. Maro watching us, Ben's hand on my arm, this little boy. I return my focus to Wyatt. Alone and terrified. He still doesn't answer, so after another long minute, I nod and stand.

"If you change your mind," I say, "you know where to find us."

He squeezes his arms tight around his knees.

The couple makes up, the man holding his crying wife. The officer makes them separate.

The police stationed at the entrance and the medical staff in the vaccination area continue working through the night with a handful of flashlights. The green and red of the exit signs have stayed on—someone said they were powered by tritium, whatever that is. No one knows how the minotaur is still glowing. The intake and medical stations are located on the other side of the gym, but in the cavernous space with the shiny floors, their words, cries, questions echo to us as though they are both very near and very far. Muffled, but all-encompassing. The wind still assaults us, battering the building's defenses. An echo chamber of fear and grief. Insulated, self-perpetuating.

My neighbors cry, whisper, snore. A new guard has replaced Officer Pike, and this one made the couple scoot their cots as far apart as everyone else's. I think Pike, like Maro, is someone I can trust. She is not one of these cops who thrives on enforcing rules or revels in their power. She seems like she's actually trying to do good.

Ben sleeps next to me, Helen on my other side. I can just make out the sound of her whispered breath, and I think she is praying. She hasn't cried in front of us, but earlier she excused herself suddenly and returned with a red, splotchy face and hands that trembled less than they had before. Now she lies beneath the jacket that I suspect belonged either to a boyfriend or a brother. Her bare legs shine in the red and green light of the exit signs, the glowing minotaur.

Barghest sleeps on the ground between my cot and Ben's. We had to scoot them farther apart to accommodate him. Even so, I find myself lying next to this boy, the boy who belongs to the world where we both had parents and read books and went to school and never thought about death.

I prop myself up on my elbows and turn to sneak a glance at Ben, stroking Barghest's fur while I do. He sleeps fitfully, head resting on his arm. He wears a blue T-shirt and jeans, his sneakers on the ground beneath him. It's warm inside with all these bodies, even with the power out. It probably won't stay warm for long. But he still shivers every now and then. One of Ben's feet hangs off the end of the cot, gray socks, and his hair is tousled.

His face is so perfect, not so different from the way I've pictured the faces of boys in books, the ones we are supposed to love. Would his skin be warm, if I reached out now? Is it soft like mine, or is his male skin different? The boy at school, Will. He told me that Ben had speculated with him as to whether I am a virgin.

Would Ben really say that? Would he think about me in that way? My eyes drift to his lips, and I feel my own part, just a little.

Sound assaults us.

Maro is up. The other cop too, and they both run through the sheets. Ben's eyes open. Helen wakes. Barghest growls. Everyone sits up, wakes up.

Screams.

Bloodcurdling screams. Coming from outside. More than one voice. Two, three, more.

Pop, pop!

Gunshots. Gunshots?

All hell breaks loose.

Cops run through the gym, calling to each other. Everyone jumps up from their cots.

The screams outside grow, sound spreading, moving, stretching in all directions.

We can't see, but we hear it. A cop runs in and shouts to us, "Don't move! Stay here!"

Just outside the gym now, at the entrance on the other side. Screams Inhuman growls. Animals, monsters. Demons.

Officers yelling, swearing. *Another one!*

Over here!

Shit, there's—!

A huge gust of wind rips through the gym, billowing the curtains so we can see beneath them. There's a teenage boy there, my age, across the gym. It's so hard to see. But I think . . .

He has dark brown hair, he's about six feet tall.

He's—

Noah.

He backs into the gym from outside, a woman running at him, an infected woman. Running at Noah.

He stumbles back over a table, falls with a clatter and a bang to the ground, his legs up on the overturned table, body on the gymnasium floor. "Keep her away from me!" he yells. "Get her—!"

I am up, and I am running, limping, trying to run.

"Sophie!" Ben's voice.

I don't stop. My world right now is the teenage boy across the gym. He yells, still, calls for someone to get her off him, pushes back from her. But she is so fast, so strong.

I trip, catch myself. Trying to clear the obstacles, trying to get—

His voice stops. Is cut off. Cut off because she is on him. Her knees hit the floor hard as she straddles his body, pinning him to the ground.

She grabs the sides of his head, her fingers latching onto him, and she thrusts her tongue into his mouth.

He thrashes beneath her. So many bodies running in every direction. I am closer, almost there. Dodging bodies and curtains and tables and purses and shoes and—

Noah screams.

More voices outside, inside. More gunshots.

Someone shoves at my side, and I trip, right myself. Push forward. The pain in my foot enormous as I try to run through the dark. He is yelling, and—

His yells are muffled. I can't see, can't see his face. I skirt around the dividers and I don't even know what, it's too dark and too much movement, too many voices and bodies.

And then I am there, between them and the front doors of the gym. I stand beneath the exit sign, and I see them in the red glow.

As the woman plunges her tongue in his mouth again. As she reaches down and splits open his pants, tearing the zipper open. He should be stronger than her. It doesn't make sense that she can hold him down. He yells again, and I am closer. Six feet away. Five.

And I stop.

Two thoughts at once.

It's not Noah.

And she is ripping the skin from his face with her teeth. All of it. It sounds like thick paper tearing.

He screams. The squelch of the movement of his jaw with his skin removed. I can see his cheekbone through a hole she has made. She bites into him, presses her face into his like she can't get close enough, like it will never be enough.

He tries to fight her, but she laps at the inside of his face, driving herself beneath his skin. Licking and plunging in the side of his cheek, into his nose. Tongue probing every cavity, ravaging him. His blood painting them both. Her hand in his jeans now. She moves her underwear aside, touches herself there, rocks her hips back and forth. All of her for everyone to see. Blind, drooling ecstasy on her face. He calls out for help, his face and throat open and exposed, and—

A large body shoves me. I fall and land on my elbow. New pain tears through me. A policeman rushes her to pull her off the boy. But she is clamped on. The cop calls out, and another runs past, shouts to me, and others who are too close, "Move!"

He and the other cop remove her from him, hoist her in the air with her lower half exposed, kicking. She opens her mouth, and releases a roar, inhuman, disgusting, blood spraying, gurgling down her neck. Leaking everywhere out of the boy's face. She grunts, spits, thrashes.

I back up. She flails so wildly, I can't get around them. She lets out another screech, a sound I have never heard a human make I shuffle back until I hit the door. The boy sits up. He brings his hands to his face. Skin hangs from the side of it, and he tries to stand, tries to move. His pants still ripped open. I don't look. I turn and open the door.

I throw myself into the wind.

Outside, it is darker.

I take a gulp of air and stumble onto the grass. The screams and gunshots come from below, the fenced-in holding area we passed on the way in.

I don't know why I do it. Because I can't face the boy inside, I can't see him discovering what's happened, what they will do or where they will take him. Because I did nothing. Nothing to stop her. I could have tried, but I just stood there.

I move toward the noise. I limp and shuffle, dazed, half-blind. Until the holding area is in full view.

A single car's headlights illuminate it, only from one side, only through the beams. On the other side, red and blue from one police light.

Some of them are naked. Some are bloody. Some unmoving.

But the rest—

Human beings. Mutilating, mounting. Clawing. Ripping apart. Human beings tearing, biting. Licking, sucking. Moaning, grunting, groaning. Human beings, still and quiet, the ones riddled with bullet holes, and the ones who were overpowered. The others digging into them, trying to bury themselves inside any way they can. A living, writhing mass of flesh.

"Hey, get back inside, it's not safe!" someone shouts.

But I stand there longer.

I stand there in the night wind.

All the bodies roiling together.

The teenage boy is gone, as is the woman who attacked him. I don't know where they went. We hear more gunshots. A lot of them. Too many to count.

Ben, Barghest, Wyatt, and Helen sit between three cots. They've put Wyatt on mine in the middle, and Ben and Helen sit on the ones on either side of him, Helen keeping Wyatt calm, Ben holding Barghest. When Barghest sees me, he whines and yelps, runs to me, and my heart constricts.

"Thank you," I say to Ben, leaning into Barghest, holding him to me, scratching his ears. I take all of them in. "Are you okay?"

"Yeah, are you?" Ben says.

I nod.

"Maro?"

"I don't know," Ben says. "I haven't seen him."

I sweep the barracks, but he's not here.

"You sure you're okay?" Ben asks.

"I . . . saw. Outside."

"What happened?"

"I think . . ." I close my eyes against it, but it's there. Maybe always will be. "I think everyone in the holding area got infected. Or enough of them anyway. I think the cops shot the rest."

We check my sweatshirt for blood. We don't find any. We give it to Wyatt to use as a blanket. With the doors open and the power still out, it's getting colder.

"Take my cot," Ben says. The gym is as repaired as it can be with limited officials and no real light. The blood is mostly gone. Many cops are still out there, somewhere in the night. Doing things we probably don't want to know about.

Maro's still gone. I don't see Officer Pike either.

"Thanks, I'd rather just lie here with Barghest on the floor," I say.

After a while, Ben accepts this and lies down. Helen on her cot, Wyatt on mine, Barghest and me on the floor. Ben turns away from us on his. I watch, feeling suspended in time just as I did with him in the library, as his breathing turns from quick and uneven to something steady and soft. Wyatt's breathing has also evened out, his small hand resting on Barghest's back. All in the glowing red minotaur's light. Barghest watches me, as if to ask if I am okay. I touch my forehead to his. Where is Maro?

The wind on the windows. The of the other people. Breathing, crying, whispering, snoring, existing. This could be it for me. For any of us. This virus that takes us over and turns us into the most base and vile versions of ourselves. Could Eve have been sick in the Garden? Is desire an illness in itself?

Or is God turning our sin against us, sweeping His almighty wrath across the land in these winds the way Reverend Ansel is saying?

As if knowing I am thinking of it, the wind surges again against the walls. And I feel a whisper. A pull. The same I did in my bedroom the night Noah was taken. The same I felt in the tornado. The call of something that does not feel like God. It feels darker. It feels like death.

For the first time, it occurs to me. Truly. I might not make it past sixteen.

That teenage boy won't. He won't even make it through the night.

And how unlikely it is. The idea that I can actually find Noah. In a world without power and cell service, a world full of raping, flesh-burrowing demons. He has no idea where I am, and I only know of a hospital where he may have been at one point last week.

It occurs to me how unlikely it could be that he is even alive at all.

I've always thought, always felt, because we're twins. Because he's my other half and I am not even half a person without him . . .

But maybe I wouldn't know. Maybe I will hold on to this empty hope forever, spend my remaining days searching for someone who doesn't exist anymore. Who I didn't even get to be with for so much of our lives. But my mind won't even process it, won't really believe. It's Noah. He's foundational. Like the sun, he's an indelible part of my reality.

Time passes. Maro's cot remains empty. He still isn't here.

Barghest watches me as I quietly get up and go to his cot. As I lie down on it. I'm not sure what I expected it to smell like, maybe cigarettes and the farmhouse we stayed in. But it smells of disinfectant like everything else in this place. It holds no warmth or trace of him. I shiver in the night air.

I lie in the dark for a very long time, waiting for him, waiting to know he's okay.

All the bodies of all the people. And there is that wind again, battering the siding, whispering. Noah out there somewhere. Noah, who has to be.

And I think, as I drift off in this gym, we are all just dry tinder.

And eventually we will all burn.

Dawn

I jerk awake to the smell of coffee and a room full of voices. An entire gymnasium full. I sit up and rub at my eyes until my surroundings come into focus. Gray light streams in through the windows.

"You okay?"

Ben sits upright in his cot across the aisle from me, two cups of coffee in his hands. I am in Maro's cot. Wyatt sits on Helen's, the two of them playing Chopsticks with their fingers. Noah and I used to play it.

"Do you drink coffee?" Ben asks.

I nod. The night comes back to me, all of it. I want to ask about Maro, need to ask. But if he's not here, if he's not okay . . .

"Um, thank you," I breathe.

"Yeah, no sweat." He hands me the cup. "Power's back, but Wi-Fi and cell are still out."

"Barghest?" I ask. My voice raspy and thick. The teenage boy from last night. It wasn't Noah. I tell myself again, it wasn't Noah. Still.

Barghest stands at the other side of Ben's cot and walks, tail wagging, toward me.

"When I snuck out this morning he followed me, so I let him out. Hope that's okay."

"Thank you. But you didn't have to. I mean, he's my responsibility, I should take him out." It's still hard to breathe, hard to focus. Maro still isn't back. I lean into Barghest, and he licks my face.

Ben's eyes crinkle as though he is smiling, but he looks exhausted, more than before. "You may be many things, Sophie Allen, but I don't think you're helpless. I just thought he probably needed to go. He's pretty well trained."

I pause. "Did I tell you my last name?"

He sips his coffee. "It was on your library card."

"And you . . . remember?"

"Of course I remember. It's been a week. And I mean it's not a big deal. I just . . . like you." He shrugs as though that is the simplest thing in the world.

Movement at the front of the barracks. Officers step through the curtain to deliver our breakfast.

Maro steps through.

Maro is alive.

My chest, my throat. Tears burning again.

Maro is alive.

He has a black eye and is walking funny. Something is hurting him. In this moment, I can see how young he is, for an adult. Compared to the other ones here. All this responsibility, all this running around, trying to keep people safe from something that is clearly so much bigger than all of us, and he's really not much older than I am.

He carries three containers of food, and his eyes automatically sweep down the line of cots. They land on me. I know it, I feel it. It is there. That strange knowing, that pull. That deep recognition. And then he looks away again. He stops at Helen's cot. He hands the first tray to Wyatt, and the second to her.

"Thank you," Helen says, as if she has been waiting for this, expecting it. Maro doesn't acknowledge me. I don't know what's happening. Is he mad at me still? Does Helen remind him of his sister? Helen is older than me. Does he *like* her?

All the bodies in the holding area.

We made it through the night. Maro, Ben, Helen, Wyatt, Barghest. All of us.

"Here," I say, standing, "take your cot." I want him to look at me.

He does then, looks up as if only just noticing. As if I am nothing. He says, "Thanks."

I stand, and we shuffle around each other, two limping bruised people. We both sit on our respective cots, and he starts quietly eating.

Ben says, "So, I hope this isn't moving too fast for you, I know we hardly know each other, but . . . I did get you breakfast. I hope this doesn't ruin our friendship." He's trying to lighten the mood, to bring some peace. Maro refusing to look at me.

I produce a smile. "Thanks," I manage and take the food.

My eyes catch on a new woman, sitting on a cot two away from Maro. She must have arrived while I was sleeping. She is tall with dark skin. Hair in small tight braids bound all together in a bun. She is stunning. Not beautiful the way Helen is, not the way my mother is, but *more,* a wilder sort of beauty, vibrant and alive. She holds her shoulders back and her head high, wears tight red pants and a black leather jacket, gold jewelry on her ears and throat. She is like the women in the magazines. She is like a queen out of a book, not quite real. Her eyes are closed, and she listens to something on her headphones. Her fingernails are gunmetal gray, rings on fingers, traces of lipstick on her mouth. She wears a sparkling red gem at her throat. She opens her eyes then, catches me admiring it. Catches me admiring her. I look away.

An official at the front holds up paper towels and cleaning spray and instructs us to sanitize our spaces.

Maro eats only half his food and sets the rest of it down in front of Barghest. He has to step toward me and lean down close to me to do it. I can smell him, feel his heat. I hold myself very still. I make myself hold very still. He doesn't look at me.

But I see the moment he turns and notices the woman in the red pants. I don't think he means to. But he pauses. The same way I did. Takes her in. Then he straightens and walks out of the barracks. I feel sick, from which part of everything I don't know. All of it.

Luke sits on his cot, watching Helen, and me. He catches my glance as I look over, and he holds it. Smiling. Slowly forking food into his mouth. Like he knows something. Like he can see what I wear beneath my T-shirt and jeans. The stupid purple lace.

I turn back to Ben, to Barghest. Helen and Wyatt still playing, even while they eat. Ben who I watched sleeping last night, Ben who when I look at him even now takes my breath away.

The giant red minotaur casting his glow over everyone.

"Cheers," Ben says, holding my eyes. "To breakfast."

Breakfast at home. The *crinkle sip* symphony that will never sound again. The farmhouse and Maro, our shared bottles of wine and tentative trust.

He doesn't want to speak to me. I wouldn't either, after what I said in that field. And maybe I don't actually mean anything to him. I've relied on him in these last days, have come to trust and depend on him. But he owes me nothing. We're going to part ways eventually, and maybe there was never any world in which we wouldn't. Maybe it's best to just cut it off.

I take a deep breath, seeing that teenage boy again. The holding area.

It's time to make a plan, a real one. It's time to decide what I'm going to do.

"To breakfast," I say back to Ben. I am no longer hungry.

HOW TO MAKE FRIENDS:

Join a club or community group to find
friends with similar interests.

Volunteer! You can give back and make great
friends at the same time.

Make eye contact and smile.

Ask questions about them, get to know your
new friends while making them feel special.

Follow up! Suggest a cool, hip thing you can
do together! Enjoy hangin'!

Loaves and Fishes

Ben found the library on his first day, when he snuck out of the gym, and he agrees to take me. We exit through our hidden door, Barghest padding along behind us. I scan our surroundings as we walk, taking in what I can. A series of buildings sits to our left, on the other side of which is a makeshift wall with guards stationed at intervals, dressed the same as the men who directed Maro and me here. National Guard.

"Whoa, what are they doing here?" Ben says.

Down to our right on the other side is the holding area.

In the gray light of day,

Bodies. All still now. All quiet. Bloody, pulpy. Ravaged. Ben gags when he sees them, swears and covers his eyes.

Between us and the holding area is a field, and a parking lot off to the side. The guards' backs are to us now, and they are far. Presumably they're here to keep people *out,* but I'll need to sneak past them to leave. They're all heavily armed.

"So, uh, what's up with the cop?" Ben says. He's turned away from the bodies. He's trying to think about anything else, lighten the mood. Make it through to the next moment.

"What do you mean?" I say.

He leads me up a set of concrete stairs outside, away from the holding area. The main school building is separate from the gym, and there's an administration building to the side. Barghest walks on a grassy ledge to our right, and Ben takes each step patiently as I limp up the stairs.

"I feel like I pissed him off," he says.

"No, he's just kind of like that." After a moment I try out the word, dangerous and foreign. "I feel like I pissed Helen off."

"Why do you say that?"

"She doesn't like me."

"That's not because of anything you've done."

"Yeah." This doesn't make me feel better.

"She probably feels threatened by you."

It takes me a minute to register his words. Both of us not talking about what we saw on the field. "What?"

"Well, I get the sense she's pretty shy. And obviously we've all been through . . . But this state is full of pretty blond girls—and don't get me wrong—she's pretty. Like . . . *really*. Not that it's maybe, you know, like appropriate to say, right now."

My stomach clenches.

"But you're . . . you," he says.

"What?"

"You're . . . I dunno. You just have this look in your eyes, I saw it the first time I saw you at your school."

The wind seems to wrap around my arms and neck, just for a moment. Guilt, shame. Sin. That's what he sees, that is the difference between Helen and me. A stain. "I don't think that's a good thing," I say.

He glances at me. "Well, good or not, I like it." We are almost at the door. He says in a teasing tone, "And it seems like I'm not the only one."

"Sorry?" I say.

"Well, your policeman." He opens the door, and I stop. Does he mean Maro? Maro can't even look at me.

"He's not my policeman," I say. "He just helped me out. I remind him of his sister."

"I'm not sure about that," he says, as I step through and Barghest follows. "In any case, it's tough for everyone here. Whatever Helen says or does, don't take it personally."

I'm still stuck on the last part, on everything we're not talking about. But I say, "How do you figure all this?"

"I don't figure, I know."

"But . . . how?"

He looks at me funny, and I can't tell if he's teasing this time when he says, "How do you not?"

We take another flight of stairs to a door marked SCHOOL LIBRARY.

The comforting, slightly musty library smell washes over me immediately as we step inside. If I close my eyes, I can pretend that none of this has happened, and it is just another Friday evening in which I choose my books for the week. My lonely, stifling, unremarkable life. At least I always knew Noah would be there on the other end of the phone. I always knew he was alive.

Between two sections sits a large fish tank. The light in the tank and the filter still run. Three fish eat one unlucky dead one, rip it apart and murk up the water.

I walk to the librarian's desk and open the drawer.

"Looking for something?" Ben appears beside me.

"Yeah, fish food."

"I looked before. Couldn't find any."

I exhaust the drawers and realize he's right. We watch the fish for a moment, the green water.

"It's sad, right?" he says.

"Yeah. I guess they'll just eat each other until there's only one left. And then eventually he'll die, by himself," I say.

"Well, that's a downer."

"It's the truth."

"You think this is going to happen to us. Because of the virus."

"Don't you?" This time I turn to face him. "Weren't you there last night? Didn't you just see? I mean—"

"Yeah, I did see. But I refuse to think that way," he says. A new intensity lights his eyes, a seriousness that makes me remember we know so little about each other. "Sophie, this world is a good place. Humans, for the most part, are good beings. Terrible things happen. You wake up one morning and find your mother . . ." He falters. "Life can be really hard. No one tells you how hard or how you're supposed to deal with it. But I refuse to believe that it's all for nothing or that we're only here to destroy each other. This world is not *just* about suffering." His eyes sweep my face, tracing over my nose and cheeks and mouth. He takes a long deep breath, searching me, for what I don't know.

"Of course this world is about suffering," I say. "That's the whole point."

"It doesn't have to be."

Ben and I stand close to each other, closer than I realized.

He says, "I think it's our job to find hope wherever we can. *Especially* when life is terrible and dark. It's our job to find the beauty and the light."

We stand in this library, looking at one another as the fish is cannibalized behind us. The tank casting blue-green shadows over our faces.

Ben's perfect face.

Ourdutyaswomen.

ForgivemeFather—

"We should find your things."

Ben pulls away from me and is down one of the aisles before I've regained my balance.

I am back on the highway, alone in my mother's car.

At the edge of a precipice, thousands of feet between me and the pit.

And I almost just fell in.

Beatrix

I find two different maps of the state, a *Wilderness Survival for Dummies* book, a Wisconsin travel guide, and a flathead screwdriver. Ben picks up a copy of *The Catcher in the Rye*. Barghest runs through the aisles, happy to be away from all the people. I call him over to me and pet him, lean into his great weight. He whines against me.

"It's great you two found each other," Ben says, watching us. "Like lost soulmates."

I pull back and look at Barghest. "Are you my soul—" I stop.

A uniformed man stands in the doorway. His gun is trained on us.

"Stay where you are," he says.

Ben raises his hands slowly. I hold Barghest.

"What are you two doing in here?" the man says.

"Getting books," Ben says.

The man eyes us for a long moment, looking for any sign of infection. Finally, he lowers his gun. "Last night, the cops here say a couple infected got away from them, might still be around the campus. You shouldn't wander right now."

"Who called you guys in?" Ben asks. "Are you here because of last night?"

The man blinks. "The safest place is in the gym. You should go back there."

He tells us to take a different way back, the way he came in when he found us. He stares so hard at both of us that I still feel it, even out of his line of sight.

We walk back through interior spaces. Through halls with lockers and classrooms.

Like the alternate universe of Kelly's bedroom, this alternate reality of how life could be lived. Boys *and* girls. Lockers. St. Mary's doesn't have them, we have old wooden cupboards without locks. Nothing is stolen under the nuns' gaze, but more importantly we can't hide anything from them.

I pretend, for a moment, walking through this hall with stickers on lockers, flyers for clubs, notices for events, signs and posters—**WHAT DOES YOUR FUTURE LOOK LIKE?**—**YOUR VOICE MATTERS!**—that Ben and I are not the only ones here, that boys and girls traverse these halls together, putting in their lock combinations, chatting before class. Bustling and colorful and messy.

Outside, the wind has picked up a deeper chill, and I shiver against the metal of the crutch as we step between buildings. Ben carries the books for the both of us. Barghest leaps left and right, enjoying the freedom. I call him to me on the steps, drop my crutch, and lower myself to sit under the handrail. The guard stayed inside, kept patrolling there, so we have a moment. And I need it. I have to brace myself for this.

I can make a concrete plan with the maps. A concrete plan to leave here and find my way to Waukesha. This dog and me, out in the wild together. It won't be safe. I can't ask Ben or Helen to join me, especially because I think Helen is now looking after Wyatt. And she hates me. I can't ask Maro because he has a job here, and he wouldn't want to anyway. And . . . he doesn't want to talk to me. I ruined anything there, if there was anything to begin with. I hate myself a little bit for it.

Ben stares out toward the fenced-in field down below, the one full of dead bodies. I shiver, and he notices. I left my sweatshirt with Wyatt. Ben shrugs off his jacket and hands it to me. I try to say no, but he insists. I take it, reluctant, and slip it on, inhaling his warmth, his smell. His bare arms prickle in the cold, tan and strong. He looks like a painting, here in the morning autumn light, shining and too beautiful against the simple backdrop. The leaves changing fast orange and even red. The light over Ben's face.

"What is your tattoo?" I ask.

"Oh," he says. "Nothing."

The wind claws at us, pulls at my skin, and I am so uncomfortable in this body suddenly, in this place, that I want to step out of it, peel it away and leave it for someone else to deal with.

"Will you tell me what you're thinking?" I say. I need a distraction, something.

"I'm thinking it'd be a good day to fly a kite."

I laugh, a little, but then I say, "I don't know if it's really a time for joking."

His smile falters. "Then what is it time for?"

"People are dying," I say.

"Yeah," he says, "I know."

One of the guards exits his post to speak with another, leaving a gap between them, an opening. I'll be able to leave, when I'm ready. A few hours from now, or tonight if it seems the dark would be better. But I'll be able to find a moment to sneak through.

"When I was a kid I got sick," Ben says. "Like really sick. Um, you know, like cancer. I wasn't supposed to live past ten."

Slowly I register his words. I turn to him.

"I spent a year in bed, by myself, just sort of thinking about what was going to happen when I died. I can't really . . . it was dark. My mom was always trying not to cry around me, but I could hear her at night. It's what broke my parents up, the stress of it. My dad was kind of a dick about it, but that's just how he is."

Leaves sailing through the wind.

"None of my friends know about it, it was a long time ago, and it's not, you know, easy to talk about. And I mean I lived, so it's not . . . I don't know. Anyway, I guess I never expected illness to be the biggest part of my life again. Or maybe I've been expecting it all along, in some part of myself I try to ignore. But I never expected to be the healthy one and to lose the people I love. It didn't really occur to me that that was a possibility."

"Why are you telling me all this?" I ask. It comes out wrong though, I mean why me and not anyone else. I mean why me at all.

"I don't know," he says. "I thought you'd get it."

Ben is looking for a friend and confidant. But I am hardly a person. He pushes his sleeve up. The tattoo is imperfect, more like a child's drawing. The only thing on this boy that is not beautiful and pristine. But it adds something. My chest tightens.

"It's an asteroid," he says, "or it's supposed to be. The artist didn't do a very good job. It's stupid maybe, but my mom got me a telescope when I was stuck at home, and the first thing I found when I used it was this asteroid, 83 Beatrix. I don't know. The world and the universe seemed huge, and I wanted to live. It kept me going. My mom and I got them matching."

"Mrs. Parson has a tattoo?"

"Yeah. Had, I guess. Sorry, is this lame? Didn't mean to like . . . spill my whole life story."

"No, I'm sorry," I say. And I mean it, in more ways than one. "This is all new for me too." I don't have friends. I don't know how. I say, "I guess . . . given everything that's happened, I just. I don't know how you can smile."

He shrugs, looks out over the expanse of lawn and sports field and school. All the bodies in the holding area. "The way I see it," he says, "smiling, whether or not to, is the only real choice we have left."

Riverbed

Inside, we are assaulted by noise. More than before. Eyes glued to phones. Two arguments rage in different parts of the gym. A cop runs in front of us as we enter, rushing to a guy who looks like he's going to hit one of the nurses.

In the barracks, Helen, Luke, and the new woman in the red pants stare at their screens.

We get to our cots, and a voice calls from behind us, "Sophie, Ben."

We turn and find Maro jogging toward us, unevenly. "Where have you been?"

Ben says, "Library," right as I say, "Letting Barghest out."

Maro looks between the two of us, the set of his jaw tight.

"You shouldn't be wandering around by yourself. I've told you, it isn't safe." As he says it, I see him take in Ben's jacket that still warms me.

"She wasn't alone," Ben says.

I close my eyes as he steps to my side.

Maro says evenly, "Wi-Fi's back."

It takes me a second to register what he said. That changes everything. I can search which areas are quarantined. I can actually get a proper route instead of whatever blind one I could cobble together from maps alone.

"There have been developments," he continues. "People aren't happy about it. I'd be careful right now."

"Developments?" I ask. Barghest senses my anxiety and presses up against me, nearly knocking me into Ben.

"The west coast is still okay for now, a few cases here and there, but nothing like this. At this point, seems like they're our best hope for any kind of vaccine unless some other country jumps on it, but so far they're all trying to keep this thing completely out of their labs."

"There are no cases outside of America?" Ben asks. "Still? How is that possible?"

Maro shrugs. "I have no idea. But the news is—they're finding that this combination of the NARS vaccine and the syphilis thing, it basically has a fifty percent chance of preventing infection. Obviously it can't prevent a person from getting attacked by an infected, but it keeps fifty percent of people from contracting Sylvia, even if they are attacked."

"That seems maybe like good news? Sort of?" Ben says.

"They're saying it only gets to that fifty percent efficacy after seventy-two hours total, which means people have to stay here longer if they even want a shot at this thing working."

"But they want to leave?" Ben says.

Maro nods. "And it's bad in here, but now with what we're seeing . . . it's so much worse out there. *So* much worse. I—" He swears and goes to the end of our barracks to break up a fight between a cop and a man yelling at him.

"You hear the news?" Ben asks Helen. She looks up and nods.

He sits down on my cot, leans in close to her and Wyatt.

Again, she only speaks to him, doesn't look at me. "Right now, if you're outside a quarantine zone, you're supposed to report to a vax center like this one, and inside the quarantine zones they're trying to spread the vaccines around as fast as they can, but no one can go in there without like pretty certainly getting infected. It's, um . . . there's some footage, some reports from inside some of them. It's . . ." She shakes her head, squeezes her eyes shut for a moment. "Um, also, Reverend Ansel and that group he formed—St. Michael's Crusaders. They're basically threatening to attack the vax centers. Because they think this virus is God's way of purifying the land of sinners, or something."

"National Guard are stationed here. Outside," Ben tells her.

She looks to him and then briefly to me for confirmation. Then she seems to remember she doesn't want to look at me and turns back to her phone.

"There is one thing," she says, this time looking up at both of us.

"Message boards. For different regions. You can search for names, see if anyone you know has posted that they're alive, where they are. And you can post too."

Maro comes back and runs a hand over his jaw.

"Could Sophie and I use it?" Ben asks Helen.

Helen, clearly searching the site for someone herself, hesitates.

"Here." A woman's voice. A woman standing beside me. The one with the red pants. "What's your name?" she says.

She's talking to me. "Sophie," I breathe.

"Cleo," she says. "Take mine." And she hands me a phone with sixty percent battery. She turns and walks out of the barracks.

I don't get a reply out before she is gone. But I don't waste any more time. Helen tells me the website, and she gives Ben her phone to do the same. The site has you put in all possible information, first, middle, and last names, and city of residence.

I type Noah's name.

I wait. I hold my breath, and there is nothing in the world except this phone in my hands.

Nothing except heartbeats. Milliseconds.

Please. Please, please—

No results found.

I take a breath, I won't let myself cry. I will not.

I find the place on the website to post a new update and follow the prompt.

```
NAME: Sophie Margaret Allen
LIVES: Foreston, WI
CURRENT LOCATION: Plainfield, WI
SEEKING: Noah David Allen
```

I post it, and I stare.

Maro still stands beside us, watching. I look up at him.

"Any luck?" he says. Softness in his eyes looking at me. It shocks me, makes my heart break a little. Beat faster. I don't know. I want to lean into him the way Barghest does with me.

"Um, here," I say. "You should look too, and post. If you want." I'm starting to hand the phone to him when I see a link to another site.

"Oh—" I freeze. I grip the phone tighter.

"What?" Ben says. He and Helen and Maro all stare at me, waiting.

"It's, um . . ." I swallow. Breathe. "There's a link here. A site for reported deaths. You can search them too."

We're all silent a moment.

And then I start. Because I have to.

As I type Noah's name, time stretches out in an infinite expanse. The world stands still.

The website loads. I don't breathe.

No results found.

I exhale again, and this time the tears come, and I don't care. I don't know that he's alive, but I don't know that he's dead either. I think about putting my parents' names in, but I'm not sure who would search for them except maybe Noah. And I don't want him to find out that way. I want to be able to tell him.

I hand the phone to Maro, and he does his searches. Ben is doing his. It takes them both much longer than it did for me. They input name after name, sometimes pausing to take in the information, sometimes just moving to the next. Helen asks Wyatt if there's anyone he wants to find. He shrugs and doesn't answer.

Maro has a friend he says has posted and is alive in another part of the state. Ben's cousin posted as well, somewhere up north. Helen has distant relatives who have posted. No one talks about the death list, but Maro and Helen both go very quiet when they look at it.

Cleo comes back, and I say, "Thank you, for letting me borrow it. Could I just look up—"

"Keep it."

"What?"

"Keep it. It's yours."

"Are you . . . ?"

She stares down at me as if very far away and also very, very present. An intensity and despair that scares me. She says, "That thing told me my husband died. I don't have anywhere in the world I want to be." Her words hang over all of us. "Maybe you do."

The gym volume swells, louder than before. This new commotion sweeping through all of us us all. Another infected. I turn, lift the sheet barrier so I can see below it.

My stomach sinks.

I know the woman they carry.

I know the woman now kicking and snarling, fighting the two policemen who greeted us our first day. Knocking over a table and chairs, being dragged outside.

"Maro," I say, and he must hear it in my voice.

He stands very still. "Who," he says.

I don't answer. I don't want to give him this news. I can't. Not after whatever he just saw on the phone. Not after everything.

"Who, Sophie."

And even as he says it, I know that he knows. He stares at me, one long second. Then he's up and moving.

I watch from below the sheet as Maro joins the others, asks them what happened. As he hears their answer.

Next to the downed table in the middle of the gym, rooted to the spot, Maro brings his hands to his face. The moment seems to stretch on forever. Even as officials begin to set things to rights, even as normal sound and movement resumes.

Maro just stands there with his face in his hands. Beneath the minotaur.

Everyone moves around him, and he stands still. A stone in a riverbed.

I have no idea how many people he has left in this world. I see him as the teenager he once was, his sister lost to him, just as I would be if I lost Noah.

Officer Pike's inhuman screams carrying in from outside.

I know I will never forget this image of this man, for as long as I live.

White Flag

It's early afternoon. Ben is napping. Helen stares off into the distance. Wyatt pets Barghest. Maro is off somewhere, and Cleo sits on her cot, notices Luke noticing me. I avert my eyes from them, click on a link about life in the quarantine zones.

Like the inside of the holding area. But this spans whole city blocks. A man pinning a young boy against a tree. A woman screaming, crying on her knees, blood streaming from her mouth and down her leg. Bodies, everywhere.

I click out of it. I look over the state maps and check routes against Cleo's phone, trying not to feel Luke's eyes on me. He stands up slowly and licks his lips before leaving the barracks.

A moment later, my cot shifts, and I panic, head snapping up.

Cleo sits beside me.

"Hey," she says. She smells like sweat and disinfectant, like all of us, but like expensive perfume too.

I don't know what to do. "Hey," I say, scooting over just a little.

"It's a real shit thing, being your age," she says, glancing over the maps I hold.

"Um, yeah," I say when she says nothing else.

"Maro and Ben, you good with them?"

I don't really understand what she means, and I glance back to Ben to see if he heard. But he's sound asleep. I turn back and slowly nod.

"You know how to read the bad ones yet? Like that dude Luke. You felt that? The creep factor?"

I hesitate, then nod again. I glance over to Luke's cot, but he's still gone.

She smiles a little. "There are a lot of shit dudes on this planet. A lot of shit people." She leans back on her hands. "All that climate change stuff? We're a virus. People, humans. Earth is just heating herself up to burn us out, to cleanse herself. Now she's given us an actual virus." She sweeps her hand around at everyone, laughs, "*Sylvia.* Good for her, bad for us."

I don't know what to say to that.

"How much do you know about sex?"

I am frozen, my face hot. I look around to see if anyone has overheard.

"Hey," she says, "this is serious. I'm serious. You need to use that thing and do a little research. Ignorance is dangerous in normal times, but now, you really need to know what you're up against."

I am mortified. I know I should say something, but I don't know what.

I say, "But with the earth and everything . . . what about God?" Maybe it's a stupid question. Maybe it's the only question.

She smiles with that wildness behind her eyes. I think I am afraid of her. I think I want to be just like her.

"What about her?" She says the word purposefully. *Her.*

I am stunned.

"God's a real bitch right now," she says. She smiles again as I flinch. "You Catholic?" Her tone is softer now.

"How do you know?"

She exhales, leans forward, elbows on her knees. "I grew up that way too. You can always kind of see it in people." She looks me over for a moment. "Look," she says, "I just wanted to say, it's hard enough to be a woman or even just a person in this world. All that guilt and shame and ignorance stuff, it makes it impossible. It's just baggage, and you gotta lose it if you want to survive. Got it?"

I realize she is shaking. I nod.

"Gotta run," she says. "Here." She hands me her headphones. "There's music on that thing too. Music heals. Knowledge heals. When those fail, there's alcohol and chocolate, but I haven't seen either of those around. Maybe we could find a friendly cop and bribe him to get us the goods." She winks at me, and I think of the way Maro noticed her. Has she noticed him too?

She stands, and I watch her go.

On the phone, I open the music app, and I can see there's a song that's mid-play, that she must have been listening to before she gave it to me. The image is of a woman in a black-and-white photo, smiling, a red DIDO written beside her. I lift up one of the earbuds and put it in my ear. I press play.

I don't know what I expected. Not this dreamy, hopeless song. I haven't really heard music like this. The woman sings about how she will not surrender, how she will go down with her ship, for love. It is like *The Valley of Horses,* like Eli and Fiona and the *Lovers' Whirlwind* painting. The idea of loving another so much that you will give all of yourself. Even if it is hopeless or futile. I feel that way about Noah, but I know this is different. A different kind of love.

When the song ends, a deep ache pulses in me. I don't want to leave here. I don't want to leave Ben or Maro. And yet . . .

I have to. I feel it in the wind that scrapes against the walls, the way my own heart races. If I stay any longer, with these people, I won't be able to make myself go.

With the music echoing in my ears, I think it's now or never.

I turn to Ben, and he's just waking.

"Hey," I say.

He sits up, groggy, rubbing the backs of his eyes. "Hm?"

I can't believe I'm doing this. Can't believe I am ripping myself away from this kind, safe human being. But I can't ask him to risk what I'm willing to. It's not his brother in the quarantine zone. I smile at him, and I try to put everything into it. Try to tell him *thank you and I'm sorry and I hope I see you again.*

"I'm really glad we both made it here," I say.

And before he can read it in my face, before I let something through, I stand and tell him I'll be right back. I call Barghest, and we start to walk. Slowly, achingly, we walk away from Ben. And even after just a couple of days here with him, it feels like I'm leaving a part of myself behind.

I pray I don't see Maro. I pray I do. Every step feels wrong and terrible. Every limping step hurts.

I don't see him. A crack forms in me, in my chest. But he doesn't care about me anyway. Not like that. Not in any significant way. And we've known it would come to this. I have known.

I may never get to thank him for what he's given me. But I can release him from one burden, from one ounce of responsibility. I lean against Barghest, grip my crutch tight. As we step out of the gym and into the gray afternoon. Just the two of us.

I cross the grass, scanning the grounds for guards, clocking where each of them keeps watch. They all face out, away from me, and I've identified my way through: The soccer field of bodies. They give it a wide berth. I can guess why.

I sidle around the edge of the buildings and remain in shadow. The tricky part will be cutting across the grass afterward to get from the soccer field to the parking lot, but this first part is simple. I hold Barghest's collar so he stays in tight to me. I've got the maps and book in my back pockets and the phone and screwdriver in the front.

We make it around the buildings, the wind so cold I am shivering. It was a terrible idea to leave my sweatshirt with Wyatt, stupid and even potentially life-endangering as the temperature keeps dropping. But I couldn't take it from him. And I'll find another. I'll break into a car and start it, get the heat going inside. It's only a couple of hours to where I'm going, and then I'll figure it out from there.

We stand beside the field now, ducked and hidden beneath the bleachers. Even in the cold, the stench is terrible. Rot, blood, the chlorine smell of that gas station bathroom, sweat, human waste, urine. I try to stay calm, only inhale as much as I need to. Barghest whines against me and I shush him, try to lean around the side to see the nearest guard, where his attention is.

He's focused on something. Movement in the distance.

"Hey."

I jump, turn.

Barghest growls.

Luke is here, beneath the bleachers with me.

I take a step back.

"You trying to find a way out of here too?" Luke says. His **FLAT EARTH** shirt is sweaty, and I can smell him from where I stand, even with the stench of everything else near us.

Barghest growls louder, and Luke takes another step toward me. I glance to the side. The bleachers are at my back, so the only way to move away from him is to expose myself to the guards out on the grass.

"I was just walking," I say.

"I'll walk with you," he says.

"I'm okay. Thank you."

"Your cop isn't here. That Indian kid either." I don't know what that means, but his eyes sweep up and down my body again. He's right though, no one else is around. I am exposed and alone with this man.

"Bad time to have an injured foot," he says, smiling faintly. "These days, you wanna be able to run."

The alarm bells of Will by the school sounding times a hundred. "I manage," I say.

He steps forward again, then stops. Tucks his hands in his pockets, his hips jutting toward me. "I wasn't really looking for a way out," he says, as if sharing a secret.

"Okay," I say. I take a step back. It's the last I can take. If he comes closer I'll have no choice but to step into the guards' line of sight. Barghest pulls closer in tight to me, and the low rumble of his warning continues, the vibration coursing through my body.

"You wanna know what I was doing?" Luke says.

"I'm okay, thanks. I'm gonna go," I say. "Maro, the policeman, he's expecting me."

"No he's not."

"What?"

"He's not waiting for you. I saw your cop. He's in the administration building."

Luke takes a step toward me, and I take one back, try to, but I hit the wall.

"It's pretty unrealistic, making grown men sign a contract saying they can't jerk it. You know what it's like sleeping across from you and your friend every night, unable to relieve myself?" He takes another step toward me. He's three feet away. "I'm a man, we need it. We were made this way, you know? It's just bodies." He shrugs, takes another step closer. "When you let it build up for so long . . ."

"Don't come closer," I say.

He takes another step. Barghest growls louder. I slowly drop my hand to the screwdriver in my pocket.

His voice is cajoling, matter-of-fact. "You could help me out with my problem," he says.

"If you take another step, you won't be safe," I say, fingers gripping tight.

"From you?" Another step. "Hey, listen, the world's ending, it's not a big deal, we could just do it really fast, ya know? I promise I'll be quick." He takes another step, and there are only about two feet between us. Luke reaches forward and grabs my arm, hard, pulling me to him. I grip the screwdriver tight in my hand. And—

Barghest leaps from the side.

He knocks Luke to the ground.

I step back, Luke's blood spraying already. The wind shifts, and the stench from the field overwhelms me, surrounds us, and I step out from beneath the bleachers. Just a small step, just to get air and space, and—

Luke screams. It's loud. I don't know what to do. Barghest rips and shreds the way he did with the man at the gas station. Luke yells so loudly that someone will come, of course someone will come.

It's not quick like the gas station man. This takes time, time in which I should try to step forward and stop this, in which someone is going to find us. But I don't know how to make my body move.

Finally Luke stills, and Barghest looks up at me, blood and skin hanging. I call him to me. Voices carry from around the side of the field.

I think through my options. In the shadows again, I peer around, just quickly. Six guards now in the parking lot. Why?

That was my escape. There's no way around them, not six.

The other guards draw nearer, I can hear them, and Barghest is covered in blood, and a dead man lies on the ground, and he touched me, and I can't get to the parking lot. It was the way out, the only way out unless I leave the campus through the woods, just walk until I find something, but I don't know how long that will be, if there will be cars, and the voices are getting closer, and—

The guards are going to find Luke's body. If they find Barghest and me, they'll know he did it. They might shoot us. They might put Barghest down. That's what happens to dogs who kill people, right?

They're getting closer, and there is one person I think of. One person who could help me, could maybe fix this, at least until I can escape this place.

Luke said Maro was in the administration building. I scan the edges of the buildings, the way I came. It's clear, I think. If I'm fast and quiet, I can get there.

We move as the voices draw near Luke's body. With every step I tell myself not to think about it.

In the woods beyond the perimeter, I catch movement again. A flash of red between the trees. There and then gone. I shake my head. I can't lose it now. The stench of that field carrying through the air.

A guard yells, they've found the body.

I just keep moving, just get Barghest around the corner of the administration building. We reach the front door, and I slip us inside as another voice yells out.

We close ourselves inside. An empty office. A few desks, massive filing cabinets. Barghest's tail starts wagging as soon as we step inside, blood dripping down to the floor. Luke's blood. I want to gag. Without waiting for me, Barghest heads down a short hall to a door. Tail wagging, he looks back, wanting me to open it.

I step down the hall, move around Barghest to reach the handle.

I think I hear sound inside, a rustling, and I pause. But Barghest is insistent, and Luke said Maro was here. I take a deep breath and open it.

A sound forces its way out of my mouth that might be a cry and might be a laugh.

This world. This life. Everything.

Somehow, this feels worse than the dead man on the ground. Worse than my botched escape.

Arms around waists and fingers in hair and lips on lips.

Another four-legged beast.

Maro and Cleo in the middle of the room.

Clinging to each other as if they draw oxygen from each other's mouths. As if each of them is all that's keeping the other alive. Cleo's shirt has ridden up, exposing a small tattoo of a snake on her back. Maro's hands in her hair, hers reaching for his belt buckle, the rings on her fingers glinting. She groans. Or maybe it's a sob. I'm not watching her.

I'm watching him. Maro with his hands on her. Maro with a woman.

I back away and try to get out the door. And that is when he looks up. Cleo stops too, slowly registers me there. They both stare at me, and

I at them. They don't look fevered. They don't look sick. Tears stream down Cleo's face, and Maro looks like he might have been crying too. They're not sick.

It almost makes it worse.

Cleo breaks away and turns her back to us, her face in her hands.

As though just now remembering where he is, as though he is only just remembering who I am, Maro stares at Cleo, and then around the room. He takes me in. "Sophie, what—" And then he spots Barghest. He sees the blood, and he closes his eyes, exhales long and slow.

This he understands. Danger, blood. Actions that need to be taken. "Where? Who?"

"Soccer field. By the risers. Luke. He followed me there and tried to . . . the guards found the body. They didn't see us, but—"

Concern on his face, and then rage. "Are you okay?" he says.

But stupid tears fill my eyes again. "Barghest . . . he was just protecting me."

"It's okay," Maro says. He shakes his head to collect himself. He glances to Cleo again and then to Barghest. "It's okay. I'll take care of it."

Cleo stands with her back to us, trying to take long deep breaths, but her sobs interrupt them. I can't see these adults crying. I start to say thank you, but instead I turn to leave.

Neither of them stops me.

Flames

I open the door to the outside and scan for guards, but I'm protected here if I stay in tight to the building. I hold Barghest's collar, careful not to touch Luke's blood. I take in a huge gulp of air. The wind whips my hair, slides over my face, and it smells like someone has lit a campfire. I turn to where Luke's body still lies. The guards are gone.

I step forward, stretch my neck to see the parking lot. The guards are all moving, some of them running to the edge of the woods then back, but all centered over there. Something's going on.

In the woods to my left, far from the guards, I see it again. Red, between the trees. Barghest whines, and I think it is because he wants to go back inside with Maro, but he leans in close to my body, presses his weight against me so I'm nearly knocked to the ground. I turn to him. His eyes are watering. Come to think of it, mine are too.

The air is thick, hazier than it has been, than it should be.

That campfire smell is stronger now.

More movement beyond the edges of the perimeter.

More red flashes.

A small flame not far from Luke's body, against the edge of the soccer field. A wooden plank near him, burning.

I squint to see better. Are they burning his body? Why would they—

To my right, by the library. Another large burning wooden plank.

Carried by a hooded figure in a bloodred cloak. Gliding, silent. Like a wraith.

Another red figure appears behind the first. Another, behind him. This clearly rehearsed choreography bizarre and absurd in the afternoon. And I am shaking now. Fear instinctive. Flooding me.

I turn back to where the guards should be stationed. But they're all in the parking lot. Something drew them away from what is happening, and they don't know.

Cloaked figures in the autumn leaves surround the gym from the guards' blind side, moving swiftly and silently. Smoke pours from the main school building. From the library. They're burning it from the inside.

A fire alarm goes off in the administration building. No sound from the main school building, the one that is on fire. Someone must have disabled it. The door opens behind me. Maro and Cleo step out. I don't turn to them.

These hooded figures wearing robes the color of blood with a white emblem on the back. A naked woman atop a multiheaded beast, flaming swords piercing both their hearts.

I know who she is. I try to see the figures better, but their faces are obscured in shadow. Deep black holes inside the red. Almost infinite. The figures wear black gloves and boots, no skin visible. The way they move in the robes, the purpose with which they walk, wielding their torches high. The image on their backs.

The harlot and the beast. Revelation. When God sends the angels down to enact his wrath.

When everything ends.

I make a sound, catching more movement, through the smoke to the edge of the field. They're not just surrounding the gym. Maro catches sight of them, filling in the perimeter of the campus. They surround us, and no one else knows.

And then the gym alarm sounds. Red figures on two sides of it. The guards yell, realize what is happening. They run, back to the gym, the flames in the school building. Maro drags us toward it, toward the one side of the gym they haven't surrounded yet, the one with Ben's and my secret door.

Maro calculates it all, sees a red figure round the corner, coming toward us. He turns to Cleo and me. "Get to the parking lot. Get a car. Start it," he says, already running to the gym. The smoke is thick, and I blink to clear my eyes. The gym doors open.

Pop.

A gunshot.

Pop Pop. Pop Pop.

The guards race toward the gym from the parking lot. They're almost on it, almost to the red figures when—

BOOM!

I crouch, cover my head. Barghest barks, whines, paces. Cleo swears. Debris sails through the air.

Guards, dead, on the ground. Maybe five of them, just lying there. Some alive and yelling, but the rest . . . An explosive device. These red figures—

Screams. From the guards. From the gym.

Ben is in that gym. Wyatt is there. Helen.

"Hey. Pay attention," Cleo says. She tucks her necklaces into her shirt and reaches down to tighten her shoes. "I'm gonna need you to run. Okay? Can you do that?"

I look down at my foot and the crutch. "I . . ."

"Hey," she says, catching my eye. "The answer is yes."

"The others—"

She speaks to me slowly, clearly. "These guys are no good, okay? We go now, or we might not go at all."

Half a second in which my eyes stream, my heart pounds louder.

Half a second of screams.

Ben. Ben in the gym.

Pop.

A gunshot, fired close to us. Cleo nods to me.

We run.

BOOM!

On our right, more screams. People, bodies, running, flooding out from the gym. Red figures going in. I nearly lose my footing watching them, and I yelp in pain. Barghest follows, whining and barking at every sound. The fire alarms, screams crisscrossing the campus, everyone trying to escape, the yells of the guards. These cloaked figures just silent.

"Keep moving!" Cleo yells.

More figures in red at the perimeter of the campus, advancing steadily with torches and planks, all converging on the gym. Ben, Wyatt, Helen, Maro. I cough through the smoke. I follow Cleo.

BOOM!

A massive rush of air to our left and behind us, against the administration building.

My ears ring, it's getting harder to see. My foot is half-worthless, and there are so many screams.

Pop. Another gunshot behind us.

Pop. Pop.

The smoke is so thick, the wind pushing it in one direction, then another. With all the sound, I don't hear what it is that Cleo's screaming, not until Barghest barks and growls. Until I realize he's not beside me anymore.

Through the haze, I can just make out a red-robed figure swinging a fiery torch at Barghest. *At Barghest.* Why would they—

I don't think. I rush forward, grip the screwdriver, and draw my arm back. The robed figure pauses, considers. Watches me. I can't see its face. The smoke shifts between us, and I realize. I've seen these robes before. I know them. Then the figure falls back, and I lose him in the smoke.

Cleo calls for us.

When I find her, she runs from car to car, swearing.

"What?" I yell.

"Locked!"

I scan the parking lot to see which vehicle will be easiest to maneuver out and away from everything. I do my hobble imitation of a run, Barghest beside me, and say, "This one!"

It takes a moment to get the school bus door open, but once I do, I take quick stock of what's inside. Barghest runs in after me, and Cleo follows.

I lean my crutch against the seat and bend down to inspect the steering column. This is different than the diagrams I've seen for cars, but the bus is old and that's the main thing I needed. My pulse thunders in my ears, and I pray that this works.

I stick the flathead screwdriver into the ignition and turn it. It doesn't start the bus, but it was worth a shot. I bend down again and feel for the edges in the plastic panel on the steering column, unscrewing them as I go. My hands are shaking, sweating.

Cleo swears. I look up, and another one of the red robed figures rushes at us, that silent floating run. "Just get it going!" Cleo says.

I return to my task, trying to figure out which wires are the starter and which are the battery. I think—

BANG!

Ears ringing. Disoriented.

The world is muffled.

Cleo with her arms in front of her, holding a handgun. A handgun pointed at the robed figure. The one she just shot.

She turns and yells something to me. I can't hear her. But in a daze, I turn back to my task. She has a gun. Somehow she has . . .

This is the hard part. I couldn't find wire cutters or anything I thought would work in the library. This is dangerous, and I could shock myself. I'm supposed to do it with gloves.

Cleo just shot someone.

I take the wire I think is the battery and press it up against the hard plastic of the steering column, the part I haven't removed. Taking the screwdriver, I dig into it, swiveling the metal of the flathead back and forth, wearing the wire down.

My hearing is coming back, all sound returning. Including Cleo. "Hurry! Shit, Sophie!"

I take a breath, hold steady.

The wire breaks. I do the same to the other battery wire.

This is the dangerous part. I try to strip the wires down by the same method, holding them against the hard plastic and using the flathead to dig away the outer coating. I connect them, and the bus electrical flickers to life. The radio turns on, playing some old-timey music.

You look like an angel,

Next are the starter wires. I do the same thing, break each of them, pray I don't get shocked.

Walk like an angel.

Pray and pray and pray that this works.

BANG!

I jump, and my hands jerk, nearly touching the wires together before I'm ready. Cleo in the doorway in shooting stance. Another robed figure down. Why are they coming for us?

My hands are shaking almost violently as I try to strip one wire and then the next. The smoke is so thick now I have to blink back tears.

I'm coughing, trying to hold my hands steady. Barghest whines. Sweat drips in my eyes.

I take a breath. It's now or never.

I connect the exposed wires, twist them together.

A moment. An eternity. The music playing and Cleo yelling my name. Noah yelling my name.

The engine turns over.

Cleo flings herself around me into the driver's seat. "What do I do to keep this thing on?"

I show her. Then I tell Barghest to move back. He and I take the seat behind her. More screams. The alarm. It's not letting up. None of it is. And Maro isn't here. He doesn't know what car we're in. And Ben—

I feel it from Cleo. The decision she's making. Watching me, weighing it all. Guns only have so many bullets, and she's used two. We have an escape vehicle.

We're going to leave them behind. Maro, Ben, Wyatt, Helen. Everyone inside.

We're going to leave them if we want to make it out of here alive.

"You set?" she asks me. Tears in her eyes.

And then, she looks behind me, out the window.

"Jesus fucking Christ," she says. And she laughs.

I turn to see a policeman and a young boy, breaking through the smoke.

Just them, no one else.

Cleo honks the horn and yells to Maro. They jump inside just as another huge flame erupts into the sky.

"Pull around to the front," Maro says inside the bus, once Cleo's gotten it moving.

"Are you fucking crazy?" she says.

"We can fit more people in here. Come on!"

Cleo shoots him a look, maneuvers around parked abandoned cars. Wyatt clings to the seat behind Maro.

"Police order!" he says. "Leave me if you fuckin' have to, but I can still help people!"

"First of all, fuck you," Cleo says as she slams on the gas. She turns the wheel, and the bus hurdles over a curb, Wyatt, Barghest, and me slamming against the leather seats, the old bus rattling. "Second," Cleo says, speeding out of the parking lot, "we have two kids in here, and their only shot at making it is getting out now. Third, you're not helping anyone with no gun."

I just catch sight of Maro's frantic, grim face as Cleo swings us around the corner. Maro lost his gun. Cleo has one. She turns the wheel, and Barghest falls into me. I slam into the metal. We can't see anything in front of the bus, the smoke as thick as a wall. I'm coughing, lungs burning. Wyatt is too. We can't go closer to the fire, we'll pass out if we stay any longer.

But we can't leave. Ben. Ben and Helen. All those people.

The school is on our left, the woods on our right. If Cleo doesn't turn when the entrance comes, if she continues straight, we'll leave the school and everyone in it behind. My eyes are streaming. I can't understand how she's able to see to drive. We swerve suddenly again, and I think maybe she can't.

She slows, about to decide. It's harder to breathe by the minute. I glance at Wyatt, clinging to Maro, and I know Cleo's thinking of him.

We are thrown forward as she slams on the brake. Barghest falls out of the seat, and my head collides with something, hard. I am dizzy, and Wyatt is crying now too, and Cleo and Maro are talking, and the crank of the lever and the hiss of the door.

But I am already somewhere else. My head hurts, and I think I'm going to throw up. I can't see. It's like the tornado. It's demon hands creeping through my bedroom window. It's my brother calling my name.

Voices, calling my name. I can't reach them. I can't see.

Maro's voice saying, "Drop me off up ahead. I'm going back in."

Cleo's voice, the last thing I remember.

"I don't take orders from you."

When I come to, I am staring into Noah's face. But he's younger, so I must be too. I smile and close my eyes and sink back down again into the soft pillow beneath me.

"Sophie," Noah says.

I say, "I have a headache."

"Sophie. Time to wake up, okay? You hit your head pretty hard. You have to wake up."

Slowly, my eyes open. I try to comprehend.

I am in the school bus, and it is moving. Gray sky passes outside the windows, and the wind pushes up against the outside. Noah sits in front of me. But his hair is different, and his face. He is not Noah. I reach for a name and remember. A little boy. Wyatt. Wyatt is alive.

The voice speaking to me isn't his.

"Hey. Welcome back to the land of the living," Ben says.

Ben sits beside me.

I cry out. Sit up. I throw myself into his arms. "I thought—"

He laughs a little and then folds his arms around me, pulls me in tight to him. "Me too," he says. It comes out in almost a wheeze.

I pull back and sway, his hands steadying me. "Helen?" I ask as the bus or the world spins.

"I'm here," she says, from the row behind me. Her voice is hoarse and ravaged too.

I do my best to sit up. Cleo is still behind the wheel. Maro stands beside her, watching the debris-strewn world through the windshield. I am a couple of rows back from where I sat before, and I understand why when I see what I must have hit my head on. A metal bar that was part of the roof support came loose and fell, probably when Cleo slammed on the brakes. Wyatt sits in the row behind me with Helen, Barghest on the floor between them. All our faces smeared in ash. Like mine has been so many times before.

I blink, and I smile, dazed. The world still spinning.

"I've never been on a school bus before."

Cheese Castle

W ho were those people?" Ben asks.

"St. Michael's Crusaders," Helen says.

Headache subsiding, the world still spins by. We've been driving for only five or ten minutes, the smoke just starting to lessen.

"The Reverend Ansel people?" Ben asks.

"Yeah."

"What were they doing? Why did they look like that?"

"It's like I said before. They're burning all the vax centers down. Don't want anyone impeding God's work to rid the world of sinners." Helen's voice is so hoarse it's nearly unrecognizable.

"That's insane," Ben says. "I saw one of them stab a nurse."

Helen shrugs, unsurprised, memories showing on her face. "Some people spend their whole lives waiting for the moment the rules go out the window."

"But what kind of people? I mean we're dying from this virus already, I can't understand killing each other on top of it."

"The same ones who carry hate in their hearts and call it righteousness," she says as if it is the simplest thing in the world. *"No hate in the world like Christian love."*

"Can I use the phone?" Ben asks me.

I reach into my pocket and hand it over, the headphones still wrapped around it. I still have it. That's good. I have the screwdriver too, but I realize the maps and guidebooks didn't make it. Helen's words wash over me, but I can't sort through them. Not right now.

Ben reads for a moment. "They're congregating mostly in Milwaukee for now, it looks like. We're about two hours away from there."

He holds out the phone to show a burning building with a banner staked over it in red and white. The image the same as the back of their robes. A multiheaded beast with a naked woman on its back, flaming swords impaling them both.

"Some mascot," he says.

"They come at the end," I say. "Represents . . . fornication. Sin." I blink my eyes open, trying to stay awake, but the headache pulls at me. I press my temple to the cold of the window.

The wind whips against it, almost as if greeting me.

"Who?"

"The harlot and the beast," I say.

I try to synthesize the information. Even as I can only focus on the cracked leather seat. The metal siding. The gray-orange-red-green autumn world swirling outside. The cold.

St. Michael's Crusaders. Reverend Ansel. Christian Radio. Red robes. The red robes. I focus, a little.

In the back of Mrs. Ingles's car. Sister Margaret giving one to Sister Anna at school.

They were members of this group. My congregation. How many of them? If they are alive now . . . Could one of them have been there today? Could other people that I know?

Those robed figures who were there to burn the place to the ground to stop the vaccines. Who were there to hurt us.

They were *My* people.

We drive forty-five minutes south and stop outside Portage at a Chevrolet dealership. The front door is smashed open already, so we step right in.

"Looks like someone already tried this," Cleo says. One of the car windows is broken too, glass on the floor, crunching beneath our shoes.

"Yeah. But they didn't have the code," Maro says.

He steps over to a lockbox in the office and inputs it. A flyer on the wall advertises someone's haunted Halloween cheese party at the end of the month, a block of white cheddar carved into a ghost. A small plastic pumpkin bucket with a face on it sits atop the office desk, smiling out at us. The lockbox door swings open, and Maro pulls out a set of keys, holds them up before us.

We pile in the black Suburban, Maro in the driver's seat. He slides the key into the ignition. "Buddy of mine used to brag all the time about having the code to the lockbox for the dealership he worked for. How he could use it any time he wanted if he ever got the balls. Got wasted one night and told it to me."

"And you remembered," Cleo says. Her voice is hoarse too. "Mr. Good Cop not so good after all."

"Rule breaker." Noah smiling at me on his bed.

We stop and grab items from a hardware store. Wire cutters, a few odds and ends. A gun shop called **ARMED-AGEDDON** has been almost entirely ransacked except for a few small ones, including a bright pink pistol. Maro takes it all. He's anxious to get back on the road and farther from the school. I will eventually need to go northeast, but the way the quarantine lines are drawn at the moment, we'll have to go south then west first and then north and over. Or I will, anyway.

We drive for an hour southeast before Wyatt's stomach rumbles.

A fake medieval castle sits on the side of the road, enormous parking lots surrounding it on all sides like a moat. A giant sign stands tall out front, bearing an American flag, a Green Bay Packers flag, and the words **HANK'S CHEESE FORTRESS** in red and purple neon. Two cars sit in the parking lot, and both look as though they might have been there a while.

Maro tells us to wait. He disappears inside, pink pistol drawn. After a minute, he waves us in. Cleo wants to stay in the car with Wyatt, who has just fallen asleep. She'll honk if there's trouble. I tell Barghest to stay too. Press my forehead to his.

The sky is gray still, and the temperature's dropped again. The wind hasn't died down, even a little. This wind that feels a part of this. Virus, plague. *End times.* Here to fan every flame, to hurry the spread along. This wind that I feel is saying something, though I have no idea what.

A sign posted next to the front door explains that while Hank's Cheese Fortress is the **SECOND BUILT** cheese castle in Wisconsin, it carries the **BEST CHEESE CURDS** with a **SUPERIOR SQUEAK** to any other curds at any other castle. We step inside.

Dark wood beams hang from a high vaulted ceiling, coats of arms lining the walls. Two knight-armored cows stand on hind legs on either side of the front entrance, and we are submerged in a world of cheese. Floor-to-ceiling displays of every dairy product imaginable.

The grand center display, lit from above as if from on high, is a twelve-foot-tall mountain of assorted, vacuum-sealed, packaged cheese curds. Every variety imaginable. It's been about half looted, but there is so much here still. Too much cheese I guess for any one party to steal.

"Take whatever you can carry," Maro says to us. "Food, clothing, any other supplies."

Helen immediately steps over to the clothing racks and pulls a red **EAT CHEESE OR DIE** hoodie over her sundress. She reaches for a basket and fills it with cow-print socks, cheese, cured meats, nuts, crackers, popcorn, baked goods. Ben and I follow. My eyes snag on a corner display of small branded items. I nearly trip over myself getting to them. I take everything. Travel flashlights, lighters, pocket knives, bandanas, mugs, hats, socks, and all the lip balm they have, a few small miscellaneous items. There are no painkillers that I can see. I take a new sweatshirt also. Mine says **FRIDAY FISH FRY**. Maro has pulled down all the blankets from the wall display and extra clothing, and I watch as Helen reaches for one of the bottles on the wall of wine and spirits.

She sees me watching and says, "Why the hell not." Ben and I both pause in our tasks, look at each other. Then we each grab a bottle of our own. Maro shakes his head.

On one side of the store, I stop before an eight-foot painted cartoon creature. My mind flashes back, a giant buck-toothed mouse in a fiberglass-mold graveyard. After the tornado. A closer look at the cows, and I realize they must have been made there too. That place, that fiberglass factory—two days ago? Three? A lifetime?

"Maro, look at—" I say.

Three honks sound from outside.

We move as fast as we can through the parking lot with our things. Ben carries my basket, and Cleo jumps out to help us load everything in the trunk.

"Two fuckin' freaks out back," she says. "They brought some shit out front and loaded it into those two cars. They're armed."

I throw my crutch in the trunk, hurdle over the folded seat to the very back with Barghest. Helen jumps into the middle row with Wyatt. Cleo is back in the passenger seat, shutting her door, and Maro stands with his gun raised, covering Ben, who is still not inside the car yet.

A male voice yells from the cheese fortress. Ben stops, looks up. Two men emerge from around the corner of the building, covered in tattoos, heads shaved down so close they look bald, tattoos on their skulls. One of them carries a contraption I don't recognize, and the other, the biggest gun I've ever seen.

"Get in the car now!" Maro yells. Ben throws himself in, and Maro runs to the driver's seat. "Get dow—"

We barely hear it over the spray of bullets.

Glass rains in on us. I don't feel it tearing my skin as I watch Helen, Ben, and Cleo duck down, as I throw myself against Barghest, trying to get both of us lower. As Ben yells and Maro slams himself inside the driver's seat.

It is slow motion. It is sunlight sparkling on the shards raining over us. It is magic.

As Cleo takes Maro's pink gun in one hand and her own in the other.

As she turns toward the men and lowers her window. As she shoots with both hands as if she has done this every day of her life.

Until there is nothing left in the barrel and both tattooed men lie dead on the ground.

The world. Strange, muffled, off-center.

Ringing. Confusion. Pain.

Cascading light. Heavenly, almost. Suspended. And then . . .

A crunch.

A shuffle.

A door opens. A groan from someone. A whimper from another.

One by one, heads lifting. Helen. Wyatt. Barghest. Ben. Maro. Cleo.

I look down at my body. I am here.

We are all here. We are all, somehow, miraculously, alive.

Cleo and Maro step out of the car, slow and halting. They reach in to help Helen and Wyatt out, Maro limping again.

Glass is lodged in nearly everyone. No injuries worse than shallow wounds, except one big piece of metal somehow embedded deep in Cleo's thigh, something kicked up by a bullet, I guess. She limps on the injured leg, but she leaves the piece of shrapnel there. Wyatt is the one whimpering, and Helen and Cleo help pull the small glass shard pieces from his skin.

Barghest shakes and whines. He has some cuts but otherwise seems okay. I suspect his ears hurt from the sound. I start working on his fur, feeling for the small shards. I whisper to him as he whines and touch my forehead to his, *I love you, you're okay.* I can hardly hear over anything.

Maro is gone, headed back toward the men on the ground. But Ben doesn't get out of the car. He doesn't move. Barghest and I can't move from our spots until he steps out, so we wait.

"Um," Ben says, just loud enough that I hear through the ringing, through the strangeness that has taken over this moment.

He turns, and blood is pouring down his arm.

"I think I got shot."

Maro field dresses Ben's wound, which mercifully is just a graze of the upper shoulder.

Just. There is so much blood. The two men lie dead on the ground. Maro shot them each in the head to be sure.

Helen holds Wyatt on her hip, sings a song to him outside while Cleo and I clear as much glass from the car as we can. We think about taking one of the other cars, but Cleo says we don't want the dead guys' friends to come and find us. I ask who they are. "Just another group of hateful idiots. Been around a long, long time. At least their aim was shit."

There's no first aid kit inside the cheese fortress or in the car, so we use the lip balm I grabbed to treat the minor wounds. It's not the best method, but it will help seal them and keep them from bleeding. We first treat Wyatt and Barghest, then Helen, then me, then Cleo. She tells me not to pull the metal from her leg, not until we can stitch it up. We get a shirt from inside for her to tie around it and stop some of the bleeding. We grab more food. Then we all pile back in. Ben is shaking and pale when he sits down, but he turns to Wyatt and says, "I got shot! I'm a freaking cowboy!"

"Yeah, yer a drunk cowboy," Maro says, heading around to the front. And I see that Ben is holding in his good hand one of those big bottles of liquor from inside. The label says **NORTH WISCONSIN BRANDY**.

"Everyone alive?" Maro says. "We good to go?"

He scans each of our faces and then starts the car.

Helen reaches over and rests her hand over Ben's on the bottle, squeezes it just a little. He gives her a pained smile. A moment shared between them. A feeling in my gut.

Noah's voice. *You worry about the wrong things.*

The car pulls back onto the road.

"Some aim you got," Maro says to Cleo.

"You were too slow," she replies.

He laughs, his voice hoarse. "Where'd you learn?"

"Old man," she says. "Went shooting with him once or twice."

"More than once or twice."

"Yeah. Maybe."

He nods.

"Where'd you get that gun?"

"Oh, this one?" She holds up the one she used to shoot the Crusaders, the one she used alongside Maro's new one to kill the tattooed men. She smiles. "Stole it off a cop."

Maro shakes his head with a disbelieving smile. He turns back to the road. "That's a felony, you know."

"Is it?"

"You know you're giving it back."

"But you look so good with the pink one," she says. Her words smooth like honey. "And it's hunting season, after all."

Maro and Cleo in the administration building. I close my eyes. I don't want the images. The constricting in my chest.

Helen and Ben. Maro and Cleo.

Me.

You worry about the wrong things.

Maro tosses Cleo something from his lap. She catches the blue fabric and turns to him in question. "Gettin' colder out," he says. "Thought you might need somethin'."

She opens up the hoodie, yellow with white words, **CHEESIER THAN WISCONSIN CHEDDAR**. She turns back to him, brow raised.

He smiles. It was a joke. Maro and Cleo joking, sharing it.

"Yeah," Cleo says. "Even in this shitshow, you know I'm not wearin' this."

Taliesin

A nyone have any friends or family around here?" Maro asks.
We've been driving for some time, navigating around barricades then through swaths of open road. The sun will set soon. A group of people dressed like they're from another time ambles by in horse-drawn buggies. Ben tells me they're called Amish.

We monitor the Crusaders, quarantine lines, and weather on Cleo's and Helen's phones. We've plugged them both in with chargers from the Cheese Fortress, and cell service still goes in and out. In every direction there seems to be some great danger. I've refreshed the message boards on the phone every chance I've gotten. Still no word from Noah.

"Where are we even?" Ben says.

"Outside of Cassell, heading west."

We pass a billboard with a teenage girl on it that says I REJECTED ABORTION, YOU CAN TOO, and another that says LONGER LASTING SEX CALL NOW!

No one is able to think of anyone. No one is really able to think.

"Well," Maro says. "We need to hole up somewhere for the night and get Ben's wound properly treated. That thing in your thigh, too," he says to Cleo. "And I'd prefer to go somewhere we know so there are no surprises."

"Wait," I say. "You said Cassell?"

Maro grunts yes, and I remember why it sounds so familiar. "Um . . . I don't know if this is the kind of place that makes sense or not, but . . . my father used to talk about this famous house. This architect's place outside of Spring Green. Taliesin. I've never been, but . . . maybe."

"Anyone live there?"

"No, it's just a house. For tours and stuff. I don't know."

A beeping sounds from Helen's phone.

"Service is back," she says. Then, after a moment, "Shit. Ben." She hands the phone to him, and though he's pale and swaying, he reads. He says nothing, but it's clear that it's bad.

"What is it?" I say.

"My home county is under quarantine," Helen says. "Where Ben's dad lives too." I watch her pull up the message boards, search the death list, search for new posts.

"I'm sorry," I say.

Helen shrugs, turns to the window. "My family's already gone. It's just my friends now."

"Hey," Ben says with a smile that doesn't reach his eyes, his tone more lilting than usual. He cradles the bottle against his body with his hurt arm. "We have each other at least." With his good arm, he reaches over Wyatt in the middle and squeezes Helen's shoulder.

Helen doesn't flinch beneath his touch, doesn't shy away or try to shake him off the way I would have, instinctively. They look right together, these two normal teenagers. Wyatt between them, almost like a family. Cleo and Maro up front.

Barghest is beside me though. I am not alone. I tell myself I am not. I have Barghest, and I have another half. And he is out there somewhere, still alive. I know he is. I don't know how to explain, even to myself. But I just can't believe that I wouldn't know. If something as cataclysmically earth-shaking as my brother's departure from this earth happened, I would feel it. I know I would.

Maro asks for one of the phones up front, and calls different numbers until he reaches some officers. I drift in and out, hear bits and pieces.

Hank's Cheese Fortress. Two—Yeah. Had an Uzi and a pipe bomb.

I think of home. Foreston, our church. If one person were infected and took communion, then everyone would be. It is entirely possible that every person I knew before, every person I have knelt beside, have shaken hands with during Sunday greetings, is infected or already dead.

Or they're Crusaders.

We drive through Spring Green as the sun sinks to the horizon. The shops have been looted, windows smashed, discarded items strewn on the sidewalks and small streets.

"I think I've been here before," Ben says.

The Taliesin house is the only thing in the area that looks intact. But cars are parked out front and lights on inside. After what happened at the cheese fortress, we decide it's best to move on.

Still, catching a glimpse of it . . . It strikes me how much it looks like my house, how inspired my father was by this. I feel, even seeing it just for a moment, just from the outside, as though I've seen my home again. A different version. The same minimalist and signature designs, huge swaths of glass encased in wood. The house nestled tight in among the hills, only just peeking up above the rolling green, all the autumn trees surrounding. I picture my parents driving here, my father wide-eyed in his glasses, marveling at the beauty. My mother watching him, smiling and touching her rosary in her pocket, pressing her hand to the doorway as they stepped inside together.

"Other ideas?" Cleo says.

Maro sighs. "I think we'll have to try our luck at finding a house."

"Wait," Ben says, suddenly. "I *have* been here. House on the Rock is here."

"What?" Maro says.

"That tourist thing, House on the Rock."

"Is it isolated? Defensible?" Maro asks.

"Isolated, yes. Defensible? I think. Um, I mean, it's this weird, winding, long dark place and would maybe actually be hard to defend and easy to get trapped in. Now that I'm thinking, it's probably the worst place. Never mind." He winces and takes another sip of his brandy.

"What direction is it in?" Maro says.

"Um . . ." Ben squints out the window.

And even though we all see the large wooden sign with the old-timey font on it—**HOUSE ON THE ROCK**—at the same time, he still says, "That way, I guess."

Frank Lloyd Wrong

We pull into a multilevel parking lot that is empty save for one car. "Safe bet someone's inside," Maro says. "Or they left it, but I doubt we'll get that lucky."

Bizarre giant flowerpots with dragons' faces and tiers of overflowing plants are stationed throughout the lot, thick trees surrounding the whole complex. All we can see of the house from here is a glass wall with sliding doors and a **HOUSE ON THE ROCK** sign above them. Trees on all sides, and I can't tell, but it almost seems as though the house drops off below us, though we can't see where through the trees. The wind shakes the green, orange, red leaves. I shiver.

"Wasn't this supposed to be a bad place to hole up?" I say.

Maro brushes past me, and I feel my heart stutter.

"If it's got clean running water and a first aid kit somewhere," he says, "it's fuckin' paradise."

Inside, we are greeted with an empty ticket desk in a glass, wood, and rock entry room and signs that point us to the beginning of a tour. We follow them, over low carpet, through dark rooms that explain what we are about to see. A man at one point apparently saw a large rock up high on a hill between the towns of Spring Green and Dodgeville and decided to build a house on it illegally. He modeled it after Frank Lloyd Wright's designs, but most who see it call it the evil version, *Frank Lloyd Wrong,* because of his materials and the darkness of the home. And then he added two and a half miles of indoor oddity collections for visitors to tour so he could pay the government back for the land he took. Or something like that, I may not have gotten it all. I'm only half-reading, only half-here. My eyes catch on a photo of the house, perched on a rock precipice, suspended above a forest that stretches to the edges of the photograph and beyond. I shiver.

Ben is stumbling and bleeding, Helen barely has energy to hold Wyatt, Cleo is limping, and Maro looks like he's ready to do something crazy. The good news is the power is on.

We continue inside, down long carpeted wood and white-walled hallways leading inward, downward, I don't know, featuring periodic contraptions and sculptures—wooden ships, deranged faces carved into vases—in alcoves and windows overlooking the enormous grounds. According to the map, the path will take us to the gate house, then it continues after that to the original house, beyond which lie most of the collections. Even with the map, it feels impossible to understand where we are. Knowing outside these walls, all the trees surround us.

We draw near the gate house, and we hear . . .

Polka music.

Maro tenses. We all do.

Both Maro and Cleo are armed. Helen has set Wyatt down, holds his hand. I see her prepare to pick him up again. Barghest is glued to my free side, my crutch sinking into the soft floor as we walk. Ben carries his brandy. The adults tell us with hand signs to wait where we are.

They step inside.

"Um," Cleo's voice carries to us, immediately and loudly, "what the fuck."

We join them.

A room. Red-carpeted ceiling, so low that neither Maro nor Ben can stand fully. Everything covered in red carpet or a combination of stone and dark wood. The room is round . . . ish, odd outcroppings denoting the various sections. A dining alcove, a hearth in its own red-lit stone corner that is so large I could stand up straight in it, giant pots and pans hanging all around, a small sitting area carved from the stone, sunken and tight, rock seats, rock table, rock overhang, rock floor. All of it lit in low light by stained-glass lamps, reflecting red all around.

And the source of the music. A free-standing, self-playing orchestra built into the side of the room, uplit in red. Just a group of full-sized instruments set into the wall, moving and playing themselves.

The built-ins, the deference to the wood, to shape. This space nearly like my church, the one my father designed. But it's . . . too tight, uses natural materials but is at odds with any natural order. They were right, whoever labeled the architect. It is all, just . . . *wrong*. Perverted. Barghest steps forward to sniff sculptures, idols and demons set into the rock at intervals, with wide staring red eyes. He growls at the moving instruments.

"Well," Maro says, stepping over to the sink and trying the tap. Water sputters, then runs clear. "Um, it looks comfortable enough."

"I can't do this music," Cleo says. "We gotta find something else."

"The map says the original house is up ahead," Helen says. "If we keep going."

We hesitate, then slowly move again. Every step carrying us deeper into some great otherworld. Away from any known reality.

Another shiver down my spine. That whisper in my ear. I can't hear the wind here, but I feel it, somehow, still.

The hallway spits us into the original house. It's larger. But "large" would be generous. Still entirely in dark black-browns and reds, the cave-like space has a round kitchen, a library the size of a phone booth, and too many corridors and alcoves, twists and turns, to even make sense of. All the windows are stained glass in ornately carved dark wood that barely lets any natural light in. Trees jut in and around the space, through one sliver skylight above, into the rockface of the walls.

Trees and rocks inside the house, outside the house. *House* doesn't feel right, even. Dwelling? Cavern? Subterranean-feeling, but perched up on some great boulder. The wind whistles and pummels the stained glass, here, making itself known again, and I can't understand how anything above the tree line can feel so suffocating.

More music sounds up ahead.

We continue, all of us. Wind our way through the roped-off red-carpeted visitors' walkway. Everything, even the miniature library that would normally ignite ecstasy in me, just makes me feel as though we've left the laws of our world behind. We have entered a realm that does not care about us, one whose rules we do not know. One that seems to revel in chaos.

The music swells as we edge closer, discordant and foreign, a bizarre combination of the polka from before and a lilting string music I've never heard, eerie and forlorn. We step out into another hall, this one with natural light, the last of it from the dying day. It is a relief to feel it.

The feeling only lasts a second.

Every one of us stops. My vision spins and blurs again, and I am seized with sudden vertigo. I have to lean on Barghest to keep from falling.

Helen says, "Oh god."

Ben says, "I guess we found the owner of the car."

We stand in a long, beige-carpeted space, but it is not a hallway. Or at least, it doesn't lead to anything. Dark wood frames the windows on both sides of us and above, an angled tunnel, stretching and narrowing further ahead, a glass walkway tightening and closing in, finally ending in a single convergent point like the bow of a narrow ship. Hanging, suspended, over the trees in the forest below. The claustrophobic tightening, the closing in and swallowing, the walkway jutting out and away from the rock the house sits on. Nearly a dare. A bodily protrusion of some aching beast, precarious and terrifying.

And there, at the end of it, beyond the blood and pus smeared on the glass walls and ceiling, beyond the dripping trail of it and something sticky and off-white that I wish I didn't know, lies a body. Male, and naked. His face, bloody, raw as though he tried to claw his way out of his own skin, pressed tight to the glass. Spit, blood, sweat, pus, and that other liquid all around him. Everywhere. His palm, smearing its blistered residue down to the floor where it now lies. A single fly buzzing, landing at intervals, on his body.

We are quiet for a moment.

And then Helen's voice, strangely sure. As though something has shifted.

"He saw his reflection," she says. "In the glass." And then she says another word, one that I don't understand.

Helen's voice ringing through my ears as we track back to the gate house to make another temporary home. Her word that will not make sense until I read the name of the room on the map. And then, it makes perfect sense. It makes all the sense in the world.

The fish in the tank eating their friend. Cars spilling out over the edge of the highway. A soccer field full of writhing bodies. Hellfire burning, forever.

"*Infinity.*"

We find and disconnect the power for the animatronic polka band in the gate house. The water runs, there are bathrooms nearby, full of enormous taxidermied animals who watch over the sinks, and there are enough red built-in couches in the small gate house for most of us to sleep if we curl up and share or take turns. Barghest is happy on the thick carpeted floor. I take one of the hanging pots and rinse it, fill it with water for him. We take turns bringing in supplies.

There are no doors in the space so I can't set up the keychain alarm I now have the tools for. But I do have marbles from the cheese fortress. I tell everyone what I'm doing so they don't hurt themselves. We scatter them on the floor about twenty feet out in the hallways on either side of the gate house, and we all agree to keep Barghest away from them.

Ben continues to pull from his bottle and becomes less and less helpful. Cleo finally commands him to lie down. She collapses moments after on another couch. Her face has lost some of its color, and she's switched out the T-shirt on her leg for the **CHEESIER THAN WISCONSIN CHEDDAR** hoodie.

By the time we've finished setting up, Wyatt colors next to Cleo. Ben is asleep and lightly snoring. In the strange red light, he is as beautiful as ever. His new sweatshirt reads **THE HAPPIEST COWS ON EARTH**. I want to touch his hand or his forehead. I want to touch him, to feel and know he's okay.

"Found the motherlode in that front desk." I startle at Maro's words. He holds a pair of walkie-talkies and a first aid kit. "Time to stitch up our friends."

Helen and I help Maro, though most of it just involves keeping Ben still while the work is done. Cleo sucks in air through her teeth on her turn but only cries out when Maro pours the alcohol over her wound.

Helen offers to go try to find the café on the map, in case there is any food left there. Maro objects at first, and then I volunteer to go too. Maro's eyes catch mine, just for a second, and my heart beats. Then he returns to his stitching. Cleo taking slow practiced breaths, her muscles straining where she grips the couch. It takes a moment and us agreeing to take one of the hand radios with us, but since the guy in the infinity room is most likely the only person here, Maro relents. He has to stay and finish what he's doing.

Helen and I begin our descent.

There are no windows, anywhere. It could be any time of day or night. The world could end outside, and we'd never know. Dollhouse rooms, weapon rooms, animatronic band after animatronic band. Polka, classical, and a style of music I don't know the origin of. The whole of what I think is an 1800s old-timey western town with storefronts and cobblestones and a dark sky overhead. With reaching indoor trees. The fake shopfronts lit up, animatronic shopkeepers moving around. A life-size blue whale suspended from a ceiling, fighting off a giant squid. Miniature figurines, cars, airplanes, giant Rube Goldberg machines, bones, hot air balloons. Miles of this. Giant rooms, suffocating rooms, multi-storied rooms. We walk and walk, and it all goes on. Each section a new world.

This whole plan an outward warped version of all my quiet lonely nights at home. Imagining, creating. For no purpose. To pass the time. To not hate every second of this life. My solitary, empty life projected large in front of me, surrounding and trapping me here, come to life. Projects, figurines, still life.

What if I died on my front porch and am lying there even now, next to my parents? What if this is Hell? It almost makes sense. And I deserve it.

Or is it just that something here, in this dark backward place, can see these things in me, these lonely aching memories, and seeks to draw us in deeper? If I am not in Hell yet, maybe I am about to be.

Miles of room after room and world after world. No windows, no light. Not even the wind. Down, deep down. Miles of a reality that makes no sense at all.

Helen and I don't speak. I dart around each new contraption, each new winding turn. I am terrified. Helen's eyes are wide too. But not in fear. Helen's eyes are wide with . . .

Wonder. I can't understand it.

Each new level down, each new monstrosity and cavernous or

claustrophobic space, multichambered, chasmal, dark, Helen becomes almost *more*. As though she has been searching for this place forever.

We're about to enter a new room, when—

But I hear something, behind all the music. Something that lies ahead of us.

I stop.

Boom-boom.

A great, resounding heartbeat. I hear it so clearly.

Helen, still walking, still moving forward.

She steps into the room, and I watch. The sound coming from there. Can't she hear it?

Boom-boom.

"I don't think—" I say.

But it's too late. Helen disappears inside.

I follow after.

We stand before the largest carousel I have ever seen.

Wild, vicious otherworldly animals spin round and round beneath dozens—*hundreds*—of sparkling chandeliers. Light dazzling and too bright. Animals that don't make sense—men crossed with horses, dragons with hyenas, bejeweled lions, human-faced tigers, mermaids, unicorns, half-woman-half-zebras with their breasts exposed, rabbits riding pigs—a charging horned bull, giant elephants, great cats with meat hanging from their mouths, men sneering, huge black birds with beaks wide open. All tracking up and down on their poles. Music in broken discordant patterns. Too loud. As if to burrow in our ears. As if to dig deep inside of us.

Or maybe to mask the other sound.

Boom-boom.

This room, dark, yet full of sparkling light. Gold, red, black. Decadent, terrifying. Velvet, silk, paint, glass. Music. All of it spinning. Circling. Shining, round and round, reflecting. Casting a spell on us. On me. Holding me here on the red-carpeted floor.

Boom-boom.

Boom-boom.

"Do you hear that?" I ask.

Helen doesn't answer. Her eyes wide and shining, gazing up at the dolls on the top of the carousel.

Dolls that stare out through gold-inlaid alcoves above the unnatural animals, bobbing up and down, up and down, spinning round and round. Dolls who peek their eyes out from behind each other, who watch us, who laugh behind raised porcelain hands. Gold embellishments and foreign contraptions line the walls, glint in our eyes against the glow of the carousel lights. Gold. Red. Black. Reflections. Mirrors.

Spinning. Spinning, dizzying, exhilarating. Red carpet, red walls, black sky. The carousel before us, but with the animals spinning and the dolls, and the music and the lights,

Boom-boom.

It's almost as if—

Boom-boom.

As if we are *inside* the carousel. Yes. Here we are. It spins round and round us. Us, in the middle. Creatures surrounding us, heads thrown back, laughing. Screaming in ecstasy. The lights reflected on our skin, in our eyes. Discordant music, different tunes, cymbals crashing, tambourines, accordions.

And there, to the left—

Boom-boom.

I just catch it.

Boom-boom.

Glimpses, confusion.

Boom-boom.

The source of the sound.

Boom-boom.

The heartbeat. The living center of this place. The one that wants to draw us deeper in. The one that is succeeding.

The Devil.

His mouth, stretched wide, into a passageway, eyes deranged and shining, teeth sharp and white. He beckons for us to pass beneath his teeth, step over his tongue. Plunge deep inside him. Into the next room. A portal to yet another space through his open mouth. To the *real space,* I know. The heart of this place.

I can feel it.

His eyes wild with glee. Leering and laughing. Certain we will enter.

I squeeze my eyes tight, sick, dizzy. I open them again and look up. And below the black sky above, worse than the Devil, somehow, worse than anything—

Hundreds of angels soaring above us.

Hundreds of angels crowding each other. Swarming and flocking like birds. Like the infected. Female mannequins, some naked, some clothed in tiny swaths of decadent silken fabrics. All with long hair and great beautiful feather wings. The shape of their sculpted bodies sensual beneath their clothes. Corporeal. Wanton. My heart pounds. Sweat beads on my brow.

One of them, lower down than the rest and just in front of the carousel, the soft curve of her exposed shoulder, the sweep of the cloth over her waist. One breast exposed, hair spilling down around her head, around her face. Dark, thick eyelashes and full lips, great white wings. Drawing me in. Summoning. I feel that whisper touch, the shiver down my neck.

These are not the angels I know. Angels with breasts and waists and hips, angels that beckon, that nearly scream. Piled atop one another, shrieking with lust and corporeal sin. They are not a reprieve from temptation. They are temptation itself. Everything we are meant to step away from. Everything we must not succumb to. Everything this place and this room begs us to be.

Swarming.

Immoral, luxurious, hedonistic, rich, depraved, shameless, licentious. Drowning.

Angels on angels, bodies on bodies. Heads thrown back, bobbing up and down. Their light reflected on us, through us. The carousel reflected in Helen's eyes.

I hate this room.

And yet . . .

Pulsing, spinning. All the feelings I should not have. The wants that plague me every day, that taint me. Strange and unbidden, but . . .

It almost seems transgressive *not* to pursue them here.

Want, *need*.

Panic. I touch the back of my hand to my forehead.

Time passes. Pulsing. The room spinning around me.

Boom-boom.

Here, something terrible and ancient.

Boom-boom.

But I blink.

We are not in the carousel.

We stand before it, at the entrance to the room. Did we move, or did I just imagine it?

I do not want to enter the next room, do not want to move beneath these angels or attract their painted-face gazes. But I step beside Helen, draw nearer to the carousel, the Devil's open mouth on our left, the great toothy animal faces turning as I step closer.

Helen is . . . crying. The carousel lights reflect golden on her tears so that she looks as though she might have been a part of the room all along. So that I might have just happened upon her here, another immaculate lovely frightening angel.

Boom-boom.

"Ein jeder Engel ist schrecklich," she breathes.

For a moment, I think she is speaking in tongues.

But then, "Had to read a lot of poetry . . . before all this. Learn languages. I never liked it, never thought much about any of it." She laughs. Actually laughs. But she's crying. Her tears catch in the sides of her mouth as she closes her eyes and smiles up at the carousel. Bathing in it.

"I get it now," she says.

She turns her smile on me. She is so beautiful. And she is sharing this moment of rapture. She is making me a part of it. All the eyes watch us, and I am the one she speaks to.

I can't explain it, can't excuse it. But this pulsing heart of life, and all the hungry eyes. On us.

Boom-boom.

I smile back.

I feel nearly drunk. Light, almost floating. Even on my crutch. Even in this place. Maybe I am delirious. We backtrack and find food in the café pantry and freezer. We never crossed into the devil room.

A terrible smell radiates. We can't identify it until we open the walk-in refrigerator. "What the—" Helen steps inside the room that should be cold but isn't. The lights are still on, but the refrigeration has stopped working. Her feet squish in something on the ground.

At first I think it is that horrible substance, the one I encountered in the gas station, the one on the man in the infinity room hanging over the trees. But this coats the floor in a full inch-thick drippy layer and is more yellow than white.

"Butter," Helen says. She laughs. "Butter sculptures. Look."

Two- and three-foot butter sculptures, five of them on pedestals in front of us, melting onto the floor. It's difficult to say what they were before. Maybe animals. Maybe people. Helen steps over to one and inserts her finger into it. A slow squelch, more liquid butter squirting from the hole she made, over her fingers, dripping down the side of the pedestal to the floor. A few drops landing on the bare skin of her leg.

She steps carefully around the melting statues to the shelves, lined with other food goods. "I think some of this can be salvaged," she says. "Let's see what's still cold and move it to the freezer." She brings her finger to her nose and sniffs. Then she closes her lips around it and sucks it clean.

I reach for a package of brats and close my fingers around them, feel them for temperature. "You seem . . . different here," I say.

"Do I?" she says.

"Yes. You seem . . . happy."

"Well, this place is amazing. Don't you think?"

Pulsing. Dripping.

Boom-boom.

The Devil's mouth stretching open.

I say, "It's pretty crazy."

"I think I'm just so happy not to be trapped in that school gym anymore," she says. "And getting from there to here . . . It's just nice, to have this moment, I guess."

And because she's talking to me, because I can't get enough of the shining light of her attention, I say, "You know that Luke guy?"

"Yeah, such a creep."

"Yeah, he, um . . ." I swallow. "He tried to . . . I don't know what he was going to do exactly, but I can kind of guess. Right before we left. He . . . cornered me."

Helen is silent. A package of brats in her hand. "Are you okay?"

I nod. "Yes. It was just . . ."

"What happened? I mean, how did you . . ."

"Um . . . well . . . Barghest ripped his throat out."

She stares at me for a moment, lets out a sound of disbelief. And then a laugh, a small one. "I knew I liked your dog."

The butter and spoiling meat is starting to get to me, and Helen's gaze, as wanted, maybe as needed as it is . . .

Drip.

Boom-boom.

"Um, well, I think I've gotten everything on this side," I say. "You ready?" I want to be back with Barghest, in Maro's safety, Ben's brightness. Cleo's . . . I still don't know the word for what she is.

Helen nods.

I take a step toward the door, packages in one hand and my crutch in the other. But as I set it down, the butter is too thick, too slippery.

No—

My stomach drops and my breath catches.

My crutch slips out from beneath me, and, once again, I am falling. I am on the floor, sprawled, lying down. In a pool of melted butter.

"Oh my god, are you okay?" Helen says.

I'm not used to its richness, the smell of the fatty liquid. Butter is on the list of decadent foods we no longer enjoy at home since Noah. I try not to gag as I push myself up to sit. Butter smearing down my neck, dripping. Dripping into my shirt.

"Here," Helen says. She steps over to me, feet splashing, with her hand out. I take it and lean forward to push off the ground. But it's slippery, neither. Neither of us has a firm enough stance, and—

She is crying out too, falling.

She into the liquid beside me, butter squishing and splashing beneath our bodies.

We are silent, frozen. A walk-in refrigerator in a cavernous underworld, two girls lying here in milk fat.

She will hate me now. I brace for it, the blame I deserve for pulling her down here with me, for ruining her clothes and maybe even injuring her. One brief glimpse of what a friendship looks like, and I ruined it.

After an agonizing moment, she makes a sound. Just a short one at first. And then another.

It's . . . a laugh. She's laughing.

She doesn't stop. Melodic and contagious.

I can't help it, I am laughing too. Both of us here, covered, saturated and painted in it. We are laughing so hard. She lies back, her chest shaking. "It's so gross," she says. "I can't . . ."

"It really is," I say, gasping for air.

"They're going to make us sleep somewhere else after this. Imagine their faces."

"Imagine Maro's," I say. And at this, we both lose it. We laugh and laugh until my stomach is cramped, and we lie here together in the butter. I am light and giddy and warm. Effervescent, almost.

Neither of us makes a move to stand. We stare up at the ceiling of the metal room, the steady slow trickle of the butter continuing to melt. The light flickers above.

And I feel it as it comes. Reality. Everything that's happened up to now. Everything that still lies ahead.

For a moment, laughing with this girl, I forgot. Maybe we both did. For some reason this makes it even worse now, even harder to remember after feeling anything different, any kind of reprieve.

Boom-boom.

"Do you ever wish you could just trade in your body for a different one?" she says.

Her words surprise me. "Yes," I say. "But would you?" I turn to look at her.

She tilts her head back and exhales, eyes closed. She looks a little pale. "In a second."

She trails her fingers through the butter on either side of her. "I've spent my whole life so far in these pageants. My mom's idea. It's fine because it got me money for school, but I just kept thinking for so many years, one day I'll get to just spend time with friends. One day I'll get to discover what I love, who I am outside of who I'm meant to be on this stage. And now . . . I wasted all that time. What if our world from before doesn't even exist anymore? What if there's never any school or people our age around? What if that was all the time I was ever going to have, and I just . . ."

Boom-boom.

"It will continue," I say. "It has to." I doubt my own words, and she gives me a wry smile to say she does too.

"You know, when I first met you," she says, "I thought you'd be just like the pageant girls. I'm sorry I wasn't nice." Her hands stop, momentarily. "And I'm glad you're okay, you know . . . after Luke."

"Thank you," I say. "You were nice."

She makes a sound that's not a laugh but I don't know what it is. Then some thought seems to seize her, a heavy one, a dark one.

"I get why people self-mutilate," she says. I don't know what to make of it. After a moment, she continues. "It's a nice idea, having any sort of control over this body. Making yourself into whatever you want to be. Isn't it so strange how much we assign to a person based on their looks? As if it was something they *chose,* or somehow reflects who they are? We can't separate it."

"Yes," I say. And yet I can't imagine Helen as anything but lovely. I wonder if this is a failing. I wonder if I'm doing the exact thing everyone has done to her for her entire life. "Why did you think I'd be like the pageant girls?" I say.

She shrugs. "Well, I mean you're beautiful."

"What?"

"What do you mean, *what*?"

"I don't know. Coming from you . . ." I don't know, it's stupid. I want her approval so badly, she must be able to feel it.

She turns her head to me, completely mindless of the substance on the floor. She holds my eyes. Hers are dilated in the kitchen light, and her skin is speckled with melted fat. Small droplets over smooth tan. "You are . . . very beautiful, Sophie."

Her words hang between us.

The way she says them, soft and low. Her eyes sweep my face. Drop momentarily to my lips. I know, can feel, that this moment is different.

I feel that stirring below my belly again, and a question forms. Can she mean it the way I think she does? But she can't . . . right? I mean, it's not . . . I don't know what to do or say, don't know what I am thinking. I only know that I am aware of my body. Her body. There isn't much space between us here. I want . . . something. Maybe I want to understand Noah better. The girls in the music room at school. Maybe I just . . .

We are meant to look beyond this earthly plane, meant to reject flesh

268 —— C J Leede

and temptation and physical, hedonistic pleasures. They are the Devil's work. They are designed to shine and draw us in, ignite dangerous wants. They are meant to lead us astray. I know this. I know all of this. And yet . . . I am not in our world. We have stepped into an other-realm here, an in-between. My body slippery in milk fat, hot and cold all at once. This can't be real. A dream. A nightmare. A dream. So . . . maybe I can just . . .

My heart pounds. This is sin. I know how wrong it is, and yet here are her lips, and here are my lips, and we are only inches apart. This backward place, this place that exists beyond our realm even while within it. I'm going in circles, round and round. Like the carousel. The naked mermaids, heads thrown back in ecstasy. I don't know if I want it. I don't know if she wants it. I don't know if all that I want is to *be* her. To take in what makes her shine and use it for myself. But there seems to be some kind of trance between us, a pull, her chest rising and falling, just as my own does, her breasts . . . Is she moving closer to me? Maybe I moved. Yes, I moved, and our breasts are inches from each other's, nearly touching, breathing, in and out. The smooth lines of her neck and collarbone, and only inches, nothing between us, only . . .

My stomach growls.

It is loud, loud enough to sound through the refrigerator.

Helen laughs, turns her head to once again face the ceiling.

The spell is broken.

I am mortified. I am relieved. Helen is laughing, her face flushed, eyes a little glazed, and I am breathless and staring upward too. We almost just . . . did I imagine?

"Come on," she says. "Let's take some food back."

Night falls in the gate house. I sit beside a sleeping Ben and Barghest, looking at photos of the quarantine zones and searching message boards. I can't hear the heartbeat from here. I tell myself I imagined it. The others have gone back out to explore. We've agreed to remain in two groups at all times, or at least near enough each other that if one radio calls to the other, we can all get the message. It sits beside me, as does Cleo's phone. Twice the lights flicker off, then on again. The wind hasn't died down. It traces its claws down the stained glass.

My phone buzzes, a text from the other one.

A list of article links comes in, one after the other.

Cleo, back in the school gym, saying I needed an education. I look at Ben, and my heart rate goes haywire again. I spent so much time with those useless how-tos, gaining knowledge in other areas, but not the one of my own body. This vessel that is the cause of everything. This is forbidden. I can't read these, can I? Can I afford not to?

I pull the phone closer to myself. My heart pounds as I open them. *Mechanics of Male Sexual Organs, Safe Sex, Consent, Female Pleasure, Getting to Know Your Clitoris, STD Prevention, Pregnancy Prevention, Understanding Pronouns and Gender Identity, Basic Self Defense, Kinsey Scale, How to Talk About Sex, Sex and Religion: Overcoming Shame.*

I hesitate, my thumbs over the screen. And then I click.

I devour it, all of it. I read everything and take in the images and know that Cleo is a temptress in her own right. The snake tattoo on her back, the beauty she does nothing to hide. Yet these are just how-tos. I know the how-to, I know research. And Cleo is right, we are in a pandemic, and I should know things. And I like Cleo, I trust her. She's . . . frightening. But also . . . *incredible.*

The guilt and shame grow, claw their way through my insides up to my throat, that terrifying excitement.

The Kinsey scale. The notion that Noah's magazines, the girls in the music room, that there wouldn't be a punishment for that. It's hard for me to wrap my head around the idea, and yet . . . I know Noah isn't wicked. Not in his soul. He's the greatest and truest person I've ever known. If these articles are right, if there is any truth to this way of thinking, then my brother isn't damned. If this is the world outside our community, if any of the world believes this, my brother could be . . .

Safe. It would change everything. A world for my brother. The wind gusts hard against the glass. I nearly want to cry.

I get to the last article, but I can't read it.

They are all blasphemous. But that last one is the most dangerous of all. Not only dangerous but baffling, incomprehensible. The idea of lust occurring only because of a need to perpetuate a species, and even sometimes just *because.* The idea of humans *being* animals instead of having dominion over them . . . It takes all the sin out of it. In this line of thinking, you could harbor lustful feelings outside of wedlock, and it would just be . . . *natural.*

We are not supposed to rid ourselves of shame. We are not supposed to overcome anything from our religion. It's our religion. It's the truth of the world. I feel hot and uneasy, everything I just read sitting poorly in my stomach.

And at the same time igniting new parts of my brain, pieces clicking together about reproduction and this want that threatens to consume me. About Noah. Not a sin. I think of that video Helen watched.

I search online for *Drag Queen.* I've heard this term, something our church is very outspoken about, but I never knew what it was. And Reverend Ansel saying it's part of why this is all happening.

And . . . I don't get it. I mean they all say it's unnatural, but . . . what's so unnatural about dressing up in costumes and putting on a show? Don't we do that in pageants for the holidays? And a lot of what I'm finding is them just reading books to kids. How can that be so bad? It looks actually . . . kind of fun.

I search again because I think I might be missing something. I just wonder if it hurts anyone, and it. It seems like it wouldn't. I don't know. I don't know so much.

But these articles would have me believe that we are more or less random products of organic evolution with biological imperatives and differing orientations—that's the word they use. All of that negating everything I have ever been taught. And everything I've been taught *can't* be wrong . . . right? But a world in which Noah isn't seen as wicked . . .

"*No hate like Christian love.*" That's what Helen said. Almost as if it was an expression, something people know and say. But—

The phone buzzes again. One more link and a text that says, *Have a feeling you may not have heard of her. She helped me, when I was your age. Just the idea of something more.*

The link takes me to an article on a website called **SPIRITUAL GATEWAYS**.

I scan the text, and chills run over my skin. I read it, and I think I have misread. The wind picks up, whistling and howling against the stained glass, the night nearly reaching in. Pummeling the building. Screaming.

The article tells a story. It's a story I know. The Garden of Eden. But in this version . . .

Lilith is her name.

As I read the word, the wind howls louder.

Lilith.

According to this, there is a different version of the story. One that has been redacted from the Bibles of Christians today, one they took out for a reason. According to this, Eve was not the first. Not the first woman, and not the first wife. According to this, Lilith was made from the clay at the *same time* as Adam. Not from his rib, not from anyone's. From the earth itself. Like him. An image sits to the right of the text, a naked woman with long hair and a snake wrapped around her body.

It says Adam demanded of Lilith what he demanded of Eve, what God instructed him to. Obedience, submission, devotion. He expected her, as his wife, to lie on the grass of Eden and open herself to him. It was what they were made to do. Populate God's earth with devoted children. Worship Him, forever.

But she didn't. She wouldn't.

Lilith *refused.*

She refused to be anything but an equal. She was cast out from Eden, long before Eve fell. Before Eve even came to be. In some versions Lilith went to the archangel Samael, in others to the Devil himself, pairing with them, spawning a race of incubi and succubae to torture men in the night. Demons. And in some, she was simply cast out and endured anyway. In those versions, she comes as a bird spirit of the dark. Soaring on the night wind.

Lilith, Adam's equal. Lilith, who said *no.*

The wind hits the windows, hard.

I read on. It says many believe the demon version was only written as a means to subdue women, to make her freedom seem frightening and bad, give it consequences. I work to get my head around it. To think at all about a world in which people—fallible humans—could have *chosen* which parts of the Bible would be there. The idea that it could be tweaked or contrived at all. It's history, *the* history. There can't be more than one. But . . . I guess . . . who records it? Men, humans. And humans have agendas, plans. It never would have occurred to me—to question whether the instructional manual for my entire life might be . . .

Or.

Or all of this is the Devil's work. Stories whispered in an ear, meant to deceive. Whispered in mine now. Working.

I don't know what's true, I don't know what version to believe, if any. I don't know how I'm even questioning.

But I know that I feel electricity in my veins, a spark igniting within me.

Foundations of my life shaken at every turn, all happening too fast for me to keep up.

The lights flicker out again. Adrenaline. Fear. All the time, guilt and fear. God hearing these thoughts. Knowing. I sit in the dark, the pitch black, beside Ben, willing my heartbeat to slow. Demons, this place. That great pounding heart down in the depths below. We shouldn't be here. Shouldn't have come.

I open Cleo's playlist and put in the earbuds. And I know I shouldn't, but I'm so afraid, and I am so tired of being afraid all the time. I am so tired.

So here in the dark, in the howling wind, listening to Dido, I close my eyes, and I picture this other-Eden, this before-Eden. I don't know what to make of it. The feeling rushing through me. This sense of . . . possibility. Wings soaring on a night breeze.

The wind calling out, beckoning.

The lights come back.

Ben wakes. I pause the music and put the phone away.

"Hey," he says. His voice rasping, tired.

"Hey," I say, the new ideas thundering within me. Changing nothing, or everything. I don't know. My heart, threatening to burst through my ribs.

Footsteps, down the hall, voices reminding each other to be careful around the marbles.

Wyatt and Helen appear a moment later, their faces bright and excited.

"Maro and Cleo?" I ask. I can't meet Helen's eyes. I can't meet Ben's.

"Cleo got an alert on her phone, and they got all serious and adult, said they wanted to talk about it a minute."

Helen in the butter. Fat droplets on her skin.

"This place is crazy!" Wyatt says to Ben as the two of them take their seats on the couch. He's speaking. His little voice animated and heartbreakingly sweet. "There's animals and coins and music, and cowboys, I think there's cowboys. You won't believe it!"

Ben smiles, sits up a little. "Oh man, can you tell me about it? Can you tell me every single thing you saw?" Ben, who is too good. Who has . . . parts. Boy parts.

Wyatt jumps into an excited, happy litany of everything he can remember. It's contagious. We all smile as he speaks, as he leans closer and closer in to Helen. She glances at me, once, a quick almost-sad smile, and then looks back to him. I don't dare look at Ben. My heart won't slow.

Wyatt tires, drifts off in the middle of his forever-sentence.

Helen makes him a pillow out of one of the sweatshirts and lays a blanket over him.

"How are you both?" she asks.

"Fine," I say, just as Ben says, "Never better."

It's not funny, isn't even a joke, really. But for some reason we all laugh. Barghest presses in against my leg. I reach down to pet him.

"What's the plan now?" Ben says.

Helen rubs her neck as though it pains her. "I don't know . . . sleep, I guess?"

Sleep sounds impossible. I think we all think it as we sit there, no one making a move.

"You know what?" There is a bit of color in Ben's face now where there wasn't before. I shouldn't look at him, knowing what I know. I shouldn't be around anyone, can't be trusted. "We should watch a movie."

"Where?" Helen asks.

"Well, why not here?"

She looks down at Wyatt. "He's finally sleeping. I don't want to disturb him."

"Um, we could go to the original house."

"The one with the dead body? No thanks. Besides, there's that music."

"We could go out in the information room," I say. "It's between the front desk and Wyatt, and we'll be able to hear him if he needs anything. We can leave the hand radio with him, so if he needs Maro or Cleo, he can call for them too."

They agree.

I pet Barghest and tell him I'll be back. He lies down next to Wyatt, and I kiss his head, earning a lick from him. We take our blankets and set up a little area in the information room, the history of this insane place looming all around us. Ben rests his phone against his liquor bottle, wincing at the movement. He takes one more swig before setting it up again, the phone resting against the brandy. We brought the wine too.

I take small sips only. The warmth spreads through me again, and I am back with Maro in the farmhouse. I miss him. It's strange to think it, and it comes out of nowhere, really. But now that we are with this group and traveling, the farmhouse feels like a warm safe memory. A peaceful moment.

And maybe we're having another just now. The information room is dark, only soft spotlights on the history plaques and photographs and a couple of dim lights at the entrance. Perfect for watching a movie. Not that I'd really know.

We lie down on our stomachs, Ben in the middle. Helen's body. Ben's body. My pounding heart. The movie starts. I can probably count the number of movies I've seen on one hand. When I was a child, I watched the biblical cartoons that everyone in our congregation grew up on, a blond-haired, blue-eyed Jesus and his disciples. I've seen *The Ten Commandments,* and the Christian Hallmark movies that play at the holidays.

I've never seen anything like this.

It's fun and beautiful, tragic and romantic, and I am enthralled by it. An adaptation of *Romeo and Juliet* that Ben and Helen said was made in the nineties. They both say it's one of their favorites. I've read the play, but seeing it acted out like this, with so much color, with boys in loose, unbuttoned shirts and the way Romeo and Juliet are drawn to each other, magnetized the moment they enter the same space, on either side of the fish tank, the blue light glowing on both their faces.

The fish tank. I turn, look at Ben. The map in the mall, the first time I saw him away from school, our eyes on either side of it. He gives me a small smile that tells me that is why he picked this movie. Because this scene reminded him of us, the map, the fish tank in the library at Bright Beginnings. These two free, young, living bodies playing, daring, pining, falling on the screen.

And us, here, in this strange place.

Ben did this for me.

He shifts beside me. Helen stretches out and lays her head on her arm. Ben has kicked off his shoes, and one of his toes brushes against the ground every so often. I don't know if I'm holding myself right, or if maybe I am too close to Ben, or too far away. If I smell like rotten butter. They are both so beautiful, and so perfect. Like the teenagers in the movie.

On the screen, characters move around the costume party, dancing, laughing, eating, talking. I try to imagine Ben and Helen at a party, what their roles would be with other people, what their roles must have been with friends. Ben so unaware of his body, so optimistic and confident, Helen so lithe and graceful. Who taught them this? Did their parents sit them down one day and say, "Here is how to use this body and be in it"?

Have they kissed people? If so, how many? Just as I wonder, Helen rolls onto her side and props her head up with her hand, and Ben accommodates her movement, seemingly without thinking. His foot brushes against my leg. I freeze.

After a moment, Helen's breaths come in soft waves, and I think she is sleeping. Her chest rising and falling, her chest that was so close to mine.

The movie plays on, and another question enters my mind. "Have you . . ." I didn't mean to say it out loud. But I have, and now Ben looks at me, and I have to ask, have to say it. My face is so hot. "Have you ever had a girlfriend?"

"Yeah, a couple," Ben says. "One boyfriend."

At first I think I hear him wrong. "You . . . what?"

"None of them were serious though."

Did I mishear him? I swallow. Imagining Ben and girls, Ben and a *boy*. Noah and the magazine. Helen's face inches from my own in the butter. Ben's body pressed against mine in our hugs. I glance to Helen, and she is still sleeping. I can't . . . "But which do you like?"

"Huh?"

"Girls or boys?"

"Um, I mean, it's not really like that. It can be just one or the other. But it can be both too. I mean, it can be a lot of things." He furrows his brow and after a moment shakes his head. "I keep forgetting."

"Forgetting what?"

"Just, I guess, that you were raised differently."

I try to wrap my brain around this statement. That my upbringing was the foreign one and not the norm. This outside world that at every turn seems to present new options, new ways of being. All of them dangerous and forbidden. All of them about freedom and choice.

"But what about St. Augustine's? What about the Church?" I say.

"Oh." He laughs a small laugh. "Um, I hope this isn't offensive, but the guilt and shame and sin and hell stuff, none of that's for me. And the whole, like, you get eighty years to prove you're the right kind of person to not burn for all of eternity, and only if you're born in a place where you hear of Jesus, and only if you act a very certain way. It's just . . . if that's the god that exists, he's a pretty cruel one. I mean, look what he did with that flood. All the times he leveled civilizations. Look what he's doing with all this. If you believe in him."

I am stunned. Ben doesn't notice.

"I only go to St. Augustine's because my dad wanted me to. After he left when I was sick, my mom didn't want to pull me away from my friends. So I stayed."

"But the flood was because people had become bad. God had to start over. And He gave us free will—"

"But what is bad? This whole thing of good and evil, I mean, the lion probably seems evil to the gazelle, but it's just hungry. It has to eat and feed its family. And religion seems to be the cause of wars, nearly every time, of so much death. What is evil? Like couldn't there be a version where just *because* things exist, they are beautiful? Or terrible? Or both, or neither? How can a god pick favorites among his own creations?"

"But people hurting each other, being cruel—"

"Well, God made us, in your belief, right? Why would he make us so that we'd end up that way? Why would he design us with the kind of minds that would be aberrant or cruel enough to want to hurt others? Why would he allow for other deformities to occur? This infallible god sure seems to make a lot of mistakes. Or put us through a lot of pointless horrific tests. For what? To see if we deserve eternal torture? And if he's so concerned with violence, why isn't he intervening now?"

I am stunned. "I think He might be," I say.

He stares at me. "You really think that?"

"I . . ." I trail off, watch the screen again, watch Romeo as he aches and yearns for Juliet, as he sneaks beneath her balcony. The way he looks at her. All of what Ben just said.

Mrs. Parson died. Mrs. Parson who was better than anyone. My parents died. In the most terrifying, non-Christian way possible, and because of it I'm not sure that they will even go to Heaven. After spending their entire lives living exactly as they were supposed to, as it was written in the book.

I look back up to Ben, and I say something I never thought I'd say. Something that changes everything.

"I'm not sure. What I think."

A cruel God.

For a moment, for half a second, I think, of course. Of course I have known this all along.

Aberrant. Deformities. Accidents, nature. Not cruel, not intentional. Just . . . imperfect. Just *life.*

The wind pushes from outside, howls against the glass.

Guilt. Shame. Fear. My heart.

His wrath.

I take it back. I didn't think it.

ForgivemeFather.

Too much. So many questions. The movie goes on, and I try to lose myself in it. Try to cling to this fabricated world of beauty and love and pain that has nothing to do with ours. Helen's eyelids flutter, her lips are soft. She looks a little flushed, but the room is warm, and we are all in close proximity. I don't know what to think or feel. Ben is tensed, and I wonder if he is about to say something.

He shifts closer to me, just a little. And my thoughts pause. His hip, just for a second, brushing against my hip. Just a breath.

In that one touch, that one suspended moment, the feelings, the questions. Suddenly, everything floats away. Nothing matters. Just that connecting point between our two bodies. Just us. A split second.

Then he settles. Inches between us.

Ben's foot brushes against mine. This time I don't think it's an accident.

I keep my eyes on the screen, but my heart is pounding in a new way, a way that maybe I like, that I can't admit that I like. It quiets the thoughts, all the questions. He moves his foot, a little more. One way and then the other. Light strokes. Casual but intentional, and I wonder what this means. A heat surges, and my fingertips and abdomen are alive and screaming. I don't know how a touch to my foot can do this to the whole of me, how I can be lit up in this way, all at once. At all.

And then he stops. And I think I must have done something wrong. I tense, waiting for him to tell me I am impure or disgusting and leave me here. But he pushes himself up to sit and backs up against the wall.

"Do you mind if we move?" he says. "My neck kind of hurts."

I still haven't asked about the cut on his neck, the stitches he probably received in the vax center, just before we arrived. And the new ones in his shoulder. The way his skin glowed in the red light of the gate house as Maro stitched it, as we held his body still. My hands on him.

"Yeah. I don't mind." I sit up too and back up against the wall next to him. I try to move the way he moves, try to make it seem as though I am not calculating every minute action. Helen still sleeps, the slow rise and fall of her ribs beneath the flowered fabric of her dress that smells of butter, the sweatshirt she threw on over it. I keep my legs out long in front of me because that's what Ben does.

I try to focus on just the movie, try to drown out the questions, but there is this boy body beside me, and his thighs in his jeans are like my own but different. His hands and wrists broader, surer, his forearms strong. And there is that buckle of fabric in the denim built to accommodate what a man has. What Ben has. I see the diagrams in Cleo's articles. I see the images right now. I know in my mind that I have seen it on the infected. My brain does not give me the images. It withholds them somewhere I cannot reach. They are too terrible. Too much. But on Ben . . .

Ben drops his hand down, and his fingertips brush against my thigh.

I catch my breath. I don't know if it's an accident. But he doesn't move his hand. It is there on the floor next to my leg, and as I watch, his pinky and ring finger lift just enough to brush against me again, gentle on the outside of my upper leg. The whole of my body narrows to this one point of contact between this boy's fingers and my skin beneath my jeans. Just this fabric between us.

"Is this okay?"

His words are so low I barely hear them. I nod, as much as I can. And without him taking his eyes off mine, his fingers travel slowly up the side of my thigh. My chest is full of electricity, my belly tight and charged. But it is him, and it is his eyes and his breath and his face and his nearness and his pain. His fingers move, every centimeter igniting that place below my belly. Starving. His fingers continue their slow crawl, until he stops. I am afraid he's going to pull his hand away.

He sets it down completely. His palm on my leg.

I suck in a breath. The throbbing not just in my abdomen now, but in that dangerous forbidden place between my legs, and I gasp, my lips parted, and his eyes lower to them.

His gaze pulls away first, back toward the screen. He doesn't remove his hand. Minutes pass, his thumb tracing circles on my thigh, and I need to do something because my body is screaming at me. Crying out for more, for *something*. And it is deafening. I put my hand to the ground between us, just as he did. Ben continues the motion with his thumb, looking forward.

I do as he did. First my pinky and ring finger. Just the fingertips. Just against the outside of his thigh. I think that maybe his breath catches too.

"Is this okay?" I say, and he licks his lips in a way that tells me maybe he is nervous, but maybe I misunderstand. He nods.

Just as he did, I trail my fingers gently and slowly up the side of his thigh. I am learning, and he is teaching, even if he doesn't know it. The denim of his jeans is coarser than mine, but I can still feel his warmth through them. I know I am breathing faster now, but I am mesmerized. I have never touched a boy before, not like this. I have only observed and dreamed, and even then I never allowed myself to really think about . . .

I glide my fingertips, just as I do with the library books, down the side of his leg, to his knee. I trail them up the side to the top of his knee. I run them slowly, so slowly, upward. I watch my fingers make their trail, and I try to imagine the skin beneath this fabric. His hand is still on my leg, and the heat between my thighs, the throbbing there is nearly unbearable. Does Ben feel what I feel? How could he possibly?

My fingers want more, and I am not myself, and I don't want to be anyway, and Romeo and Juliet do what they want on the screen, and we are alone here in the dark.

Almost alone. My eyes flick to Helen. My fingers move up further, closer to that buckle in the fabric, the zipper and button and what lies beneath them. His skin is hot beneath, I can feel it, and I move my fingers within an inch of that place. His thumb stops its movement on my thigh, and I wonder if I've done something wrong.

"Sophie," he breathes, and I'm sure he is going to tell me to stop, that I am wicked and sinful and—

His thumb resumes its movement.

I am full of desire, and I am so curious, and I am so wanting, and I look at him, and he is looking at me, and his breath is coming fast too, and his lips are parted, and I need to know. I need to just feel and know and understand.

I barely touch the fabric, barely graze it, as I run my fingers over the zipper. Ben makes a sound and says my name, and I think it's a warning, but I don't know and I don't want to stop. Maybe I *am* wicked. Maybe I can't be anything but shameful and bad. Maybe it doesn't make sense to deny it, to deny myself anything.

There it is, beneath the coarse fabric. This thing that boys have. This is Ben's. This is Ben's, and I run my fingers over the length of it, the denim, the still-closed zipper. I am here and somewhere else entirely, I am not Sophie Allen. I am a girl with a boy who wants me, and here is the proof of it, and touching this thing, feeling it, it makes me want more. It makes me want to open myself to him, to feel without the fabric between us, to know and explore . . . everything.

I move my fingers, and the movie plays on the screen, and this thing between Ben's legs, this thing that I am stroking, it comes to life. It hardens, grows more and more beneath my fingers, and—

It is the thing from the man on the highway.

It is the thing on my father.

I push myself away from Ben and back against the wall.

"Sophie?"

I am back in that car on the highway, I am back on my front porch, and I am shaking, and my eyes are squeezed shut, and my father is coming after me, and my mother, and the gas station attendant, Luke, the bodies on the field, pushing, shoving in, pinning, trying to crawl away, hands ripping hair, my mother, the man on the road, my mother, and my father, and—

Ben is saying my name, and it's not a whisper now, it's loud. He touches my arm, and I flinch away from him. He drops it. I bring my knees into my chest, and I try to breathe, but it's not working. I can't stop shaking.

"What happened? Is she okay?" Helen's voice.

My father running at me. My mother tearing my sweater.

My father pinning me to the ground. His hand, sliding over my leg.

"Sophie, I—"

His skin on my skin, pushing my skirt up, tearing my shirt.

"Give her a minute. Did something set her off?"

My father's bare skin on mine. His blood spraying over me.

As I stab him.

Ben doesn't answer. I am here and not here. I did this. I am not worthy of anything.

Ben or Helen stops the movie. And a scream sounds down the hall. It's the scream of a little boy.

DOES MASTURBATION MAKE
YOU GO BLIND?

No. Masturbation is perfectly safe and natural.

Masturbation is even good for your mental and physical health! Stress relief made easy!

DID YOU KNOW?
  One theory regarding the origin of this old wives' tale is that a man ejaculated so hard he burst blood vessels in his eyes, making him, in fact, temporarily blind!

Touching yourself is safe and normal.

Night Terrors

We run.

Wyatt's voice in the night and my foot and crutch alternating down the hallway. Ben and Helen run ahead, and when I turn the corner to the gate house, Helen is already there beside Cleo. Cleo holding Wyatt tight in her arms, Barghest whining, pacing beside them. When he sees me, he bolts toward me and knocks over one of our food bags. Maro looks furious, and Cleo works to calm Wyatt, but everything seems okay. Everything seems . . . fine.

"What happened?"

"Nightmare," Maro says.

Cleo holds Wyatt tightly, and Helen, beside them, strokes his arm. She says, "We're here. We're not going anywhere." She looks up at Ben and then me. Her eyes are a little unfocused, and she is flushed from running. We probably all are.

"We should have been here," she says.

"Where were you?" Maro's stare is hard, focused on all of us.

"Watching a movie," Ben says.

Maro looks me over, and I feel . . .

I missed him. I wanted to feel his presence again. But not like this. Maro looking at me with disappointment in his eyes. My gut tightens. I want to be angry at him, want to lash out with something, but I know it is only because I want to see any look on his face that is not that. I know it is only because I know I deserve it. So I keep my lips closed and say nothing.

They fill us in. New developments, Crusaders, fires. Maro and Cleo think it's possible we will only have the night here and then have to move on. They recommend we all try to sleep, and they give us the living room. Wyatt and Helen on one couch, Ben on the other. Me on the floor with Barghest. Maro heads toward the front to keep watch, and Cleo goes to a different corner of the gate house to sleep, a few rooms in. She leaves a hand radio with us. Maro has the other. I can't stop seeing Maro's face. He looked at me like I was a child, like he didn't know me at all. Or maybe like he didn't want to.

Ben, what almost happened with us. And Helen. That I could be doing any of this even in normal times, but *especially* now.

Maybe Noah would be better off without me. Maybe the world would. I lie in the dark and hear Helen's voice over and over, even as she now sleeps, as Wyatt does.

We should have been here.

Wyatt alone, in this terrifying place, and Ben and me doing what we were doing. Next to Helen. While she was sleeping.

Cleo's articles would have me think that there is no shame in this body and what it wants. I know the truth, and I can't let myself forget. Not even for a second.

It will be taught to us, my mother said, *and not gently.* I have been a temptress, a serpent.

Ourdutyaswomen. ThewordofGod.

This flesh is evil, and it will lead to our destruction.

"Sophie, you were having a nightmare."

Lying in the gate house, moonlight now streaming in through the windows. Ben sitting on the foot of my bed.

I'm in a bed.

Ben leaning forward, his hand beside me on the sheets, leaning down close to my face.

His other hand sliding up my leg, my hip, my stomach, to my chest.

His lips inches from mine. One of his legs between mine. Heat.

But Ben is Maro.

Then he is Helen. Then Maro, then Cleo, then—

Pulsing, throbbing.

Radiating.

Burning.
So much heat.
So hot.
So hot.
I am so hot.

My eyelids flutter, and I move to push the blanket back, but something prevents me. I open my eyes. Faint red glowing light, and . . . a shape.

Suspended above me. The light, flickering in and out as the shape blocks it from sight. Red, then black, then red.

Breathing.

Moving. Moving on me. I think I am still dreaming. A curtain of hair hangs down over my face, brushing my cheeks. Black-and-gray splotches of flowers hovering above my chest. Flowers that in the light are pink and red. Flowers on a dress that holds in two heaving breasts, inches away from my own.

Helen.

I tilt my head back. Two light blue eyes. Fevered, demonic in the red-black night. One full-lipped mouth, exposing white teeth in a hungry smile. Inches from my own.

Helen's glazed eyes.

Helen on top of me.

Sylvia.

Fever. Hot from a fever.

This is no dream.

Helen. Helen is infected.

I scream.

I free my hands of the blanket and put one between her mouth and mine just as her lips press down. She sucks one of my fingers into her mouth. I use my other hand to try to push against her ribs, but she is impossibly strong.

She lets out a half-snarl, a feral animal sound, pulls herself closer to me and growls against my throat. I cry out again, for any of the others. Where are they?

I press the sole of my foot to the carpet and try to shove Helen away with my knee. She wedges her body between my legs, her hips moving in a rhythmic motion, one hand reaching down to the hem of her dress to pull it up high.

I turn my face to the side, brace myself, and shove, hard, with my good leg against her hip. She falls back.

I waste no time getting up. I can't find my crutch in the dark, and Helen is blocking the way to the exit. I run, move.

Away from the exit, deeper into this place. Back down below. Limping, jumping, half-blinded from the pain. Helen is right behind me. Seconds behind. And—

I yelp, scramble for the railing as I slip on one of the marbles, but catch myself just in time and clear them. I do not see Barghest, Ben, or Wyatt. I don't know where they are, where anyone is. I left the hand radio back where we were sleeping.

It's just us.

Just Helen and me.

She slips on the marbles behind me, I hear the thunk of her body hitting the ground. A snarl rips free from her.

Helen's hot breath. The glazed look in her eye. She's sick. Helen is sick.

Of course. How did I—

I move, ignore my foot. I am adrenaline. I am fire. I am a girl desperate to stay alive.

She's back up. Her feet pound behind me on the carpet, through the halls. The animatronic dragon band plays its lilting tune. The lights flicker as I run over the walkways and paths, red, then white.

And then they are gone.

There is no light. The music comes to a sputtering stop.

Quiet. Pitch black.

Boom-boom.

I hit something, hard. The railing. The power's gone out. I don't allow myself to panic, there's no time. Helen is sick. I scramble, grope in my mind for how-tos, for anything.

Cicero's mind palace. I didn't have time to read the book, to learn the method, before all this. But I think I can remember the layout of this place. I have to.

I am sweating, and my foot is screaming. I think there is a sharp left turn just up ahead. I can't tell how far Helen is. I take a hard left where I think it should be. I grope blindly, and I hear Helen miss it. The collision with the outcropping. The thump of it, her stumble. It might have bought me only seconds.

Maro is out front. I should be able to get to him if I can skirt around her somehow. But I hear her again, coming up fast. I can't outrun her, I can't get around. The information room on the way is zigzagging, and I won't have the space to maneuver. If I go deeper into the building, I will have straight shots.

But so will she.

Helen snarls. It's close, she's close. Nearly directly on my left.

I make my decision.

I move deeper into the labyrinth, down farther into the chaos.

When I know the hall will jut right, I take the turn. She hits, again, in the dark. She slips, slides to the floor. My friend. My friend who is infected. It's pitch-black. So dark that I know this is a mistake. I know this is—

Lights. Lights flicker back on. And sound, music somewhere ahead, the giant music rooms. I sprint over the cobblestones of the fake old-timey town. My steps are uneven, my foot refusing to hold this weight.

I pray. This can't be the end. Not in this place.

I cut right, through the music rooms. The giant Austrian symphony and the foreign orchestra I can't place. My heart is pounding, so hard I can barely breathe. Helen isn't far. I know she isn't. Even with the halting jerky run the infected move with, she'll be on me in no time. The lights flicker when I turn the corner. It might save me. If I can remember, if I can just—

Black.

Once again. Darkness. The music stops.

Boom-boom.

My own breath.

I close my eyes, then open them again. It does nothing. A total absence of light. My breath in my ears, my heart pounding. Nothing else. Annihilation.

And then a sound. Not much more than a whisper.

To my left.

No, my right.

It echoes off the instruments. Travels through the space, circling me. I can't locate its source. I stop, and I turn. I shouldn't turn. But I've done it, and I turn back, and I think I know which way forward is, but now I . . . don't know. I *can't* know. I've lost the path. I can't think.

Another sound. Behind me on the right? In front, on the left.

Straining to quiet my breaths. But they're loud. So loud in the space. And then . . .

I hold my breath. The sound continues, rasping, in and out.

She is here. In this room with me. Her breaths echoing, ricocheting off hollow metal, above, below, all around. Us in this room together.

She could be ten feet from me, she could be two, I can't tell.

Her breaths stop.

There is silence.

There is nothing.

Boom-boom.

A flicker, the pulse of electricity. Light flashes.

Helen right beside me.

The music returns.

She grabs my sweatshirt.

I spin, try to keep moving forward, but it is black again. She loses her grasp. I am disoriented. I move forward, I think. Stumbling, moving. Music all around. Too many types of music. So much sound echoing, clanging.

And then there is light.

I turn another corner, this time to the carousel room.

The demonic spinning animals, the giant gold and red and black space. And only one way forward.

Helen's been this way before, with Wyatt, deeper and farther down. But I haven't. If the lights go out again . . .

Helen enters the carousel room behind me.

Boom-boom.

So I run. The only way I can.

Boom-boom.

Through the Devil's mouth.

Organ Room

Vertigo. So overwhelming, so wholly consuming, I might even welcome death. This room, through the Devil's mouth . . .

It's Hell.

The red carpet continues, but nothing else makes sense. All my surroundings, red and black, as far as I can see. Stairways, paths, twists and turns, leading nowhere, leading everywhere. Too many directions to go in this senseless unending place. Somehow it is so much higher and so much lower than the carousel room. So many levels, so much sound. Above, below. All around.

This room, one giant organ, full of organs. The others branching off from the one great instrument. Organ pipes taller than trees, taller than my house, even my church. And actual trees. Branches, drum sections, too many organs, everything stuck in between all these narrow precarious walkways suspended high above the ground—the ground so far below that I can't see it. Staircases and ramps, weaving over and through and around each other. Angels and demons perched above or beside them, watching from the ceiling and walls. Holes in the walkways for giant wheels with spokes, taller than I am, taller even than Noah or Ben, turning. Organs and drums, gears, as if we are trapped inside a living clock. As if we are stuck in Time itself, in God's own mind as He determines it for us. Everything curving, rotating. This giant mechanism, this demonic orchestra pit. Everything sparkling. Everything red.

And if I take one wrong step, one wrong turn, I will plummet. Down into the darkness below. One wrong move, and I might spend eternity here.

I run. The drums and cymbals clang, the great organ chimes, haunts, and echoes, urges me forward. As though it had been built for this very moment. The music plays. The Devil laughs. I run, and I stumble, and Helen's breaths come fast again. She is here. And there is a railing ahead of me, a turn. A narrow walkway down with no side rails, and I can't see what's on the other side. I'm going fast, too fast.

The lights flicker out. The music comes to a stop.

Heartbeats.

Boom-boom. Loud. So much louder in here. Beating through me, around me.

Boom-boom. Breath.

I take the turn. I can't run. I have to slow down or I will plummet.

Silence. Darkness. *Boom-boom.*

Forgive me, Father, for I have sinned. Forgive me—

The music starts again, before the lights. A too-slow, off-key *Glory, Glory, Hallelujah.*

The chorus of sound. The barrage, a great sea of it. Its waves cresting and swallowing. I've stepped through the mouth of the Beast, and now I will burn and decay and expire in his belly. I grasp and grope as I shuffle forward. I don't hear Helen. I can't hear her over the organ. The deafening, droning, resounding sound.

The lights back on. A gong before my face. A hanging branch, reaching out as if to grab me. A smiling winged demon.

I don't see her.

Helen isn't anywhere.

I pause, turn, heart thundering in my ears with the terrible song. *Boom-boom.*

Is it possible she fell, that I didn't hear it over the sound of the music?

I peer down below, over the railing on one side of my walkway. I still can't see the bottom.

A drop of something lands on my shoulder. *Boom-boom.*

A drop. And then another.

I turn my head, slowly, to it. As if in a dream.

Spit. There is spit on my shoulder.

I look up.

Helen, drooling, suspended above me. *Boom-boom.*

She plunges down.

Helen's fingernails dig into my skin and hair, and the momentum propels us.

She drags me with her, down over the edge.

More sound, pain, as we collide, hard, with cymbals, organ pipes, branches. My side hits a drum, a railing. I groan. Helen clings to me. The girl who was Helen before. Her nails piercing the skin of my neck and my lower back. I try to push away. She's so strong though, is holding me so tightly, I can't separate myself from her.

We fall into pipes, into steel. More pain. I cry out, but it doesn't matter. It does nothing. This room and this realm made for this.

I push, and she pulls, and we fall through time, discordant church hymns egging us on, the music playing faster now, faster and louder as we fall.

A halting, excruciating crash.

A broken drum set beneath me. A metal rod digging into my lower back. I can't move. Am in so much pain I can barely breathe.

Helen tears at my clothes. She pins me with her legs and rips my sweatshirt over my head. She hovers above me. On top of me, holding me down. I can't fight her, I can't—

A clang sounds up above, something different. As Helen rips at the button on my jeans, as she reaches for the belt loops.

Boom-boom.

I am so hot, and Helen's movements, her body between my legs,

Boom-boom.

Her breasts against mine,

Boom-boom.

Heat. Fear, but also . . .

I am infected. I must be infected too.

Another sound up above. One that I recognize. The bark of a dog. I open my eyes.

Helen smiles down at me, and she is the most beautiful thing I have ever seen. The most frightening. An angel.

There—distant, above us, somewhere—Maro's voice. Cleo's. I—

Helen bends to press her lips to mine.

Boom-boom.

The power goes out again. Darkness. Silence. I close my eyes. And I wait.

Boom-boom.

But her kiss never comes.

Her weight lifts.

Helen's weight is gone. Helen is.

No one touching me. Only darkness. Pain. Fear.

Loss.

And then a bright light shines.

A sweeping beam of light. I can just see Maro and Cleo holding, fighting Helen, the girl who used to be Helen. Their hands on each of her arms. She flails against them, her dress still hiked high. Tears burn my eyes again, and I hate them. I zip up my jeans as fast as I can. I hate this body. I hate it.

The power comes back. The music and lights. *Glory, glory, hallelujah!* This place is a nightmare. It is everything I will face from here on out, and I know it.

But it is nothing compared to this body, to the cage that tricks and traps and never releases until the very end.

A large furry body brushes against my shoulder, a familiar whimper. I barely feel it. I haven't moved from this spot, but now Ben and Barghest are here with me. Ben with the flashlight. He helps me up to sit, helps me move off the broken drum and onto flat ground. But I don't want to stand yet. I would do anything to be out of this room and this organ dirge, but I can't move on my own, and I don't want anyone to touch me.

The others are gone. Ben sits on a step a few feet away. He rests his elbows on his thighs and hides his face in his hands, his knees bouncing up and down, his body shaking as much as my own. He turns his face toward me, and his eyes are shining the way Helen's were last night. Every sign of Helen having a fever. There was every sign. And none of us saw it. Or maybe we just didn't want to.

"I'm so sorry," Ben says. "I couldn't sleep."

"What?"

"I took Barghest outside for a walk. Wyatt had gone to sleep with Cleo, and Maro was out front, but I was just gonna be gone for a minute. I didn't think . . . I shouldn't have taken him. I'm so sorry. I shouldn't have left you alone. I'm sorry, Sophie. I'm so sorry."

"It's okay."

His face is back in his hands, his knees bouncing faster.

Boom-boom.

"Ben, it's not your fault," I say.

His legs twitching, shoulders moving with uneven breaths.

"Helen's infected." I inhale. It's hard work. I might have bruised a rib. At least that. "We need to calm down and think," I get out. "Is there any way that you might . . . also be?"

His head shoots up, and he looks at me as if I'm insane. "Of course not."

But I could be. We've been in close proximity, Helen and me. Twice now. Her skin on my skin. Her spit on my shoulder, my finger in her mouth. Could any of it have gotten inside me? We didn't share wine bottles while watching the movie, each drank from our own. But . . .

"Sophie, we never . . . I didn't . . . How could you think that?"

"Okay," I say. It's more of a whisper, but he hears it.

He doesn't stop shaking, doesn't stop moving his legs.

Boom-boom.

"Ben."

He doesn't answer me.

"Ben, stop."

I say his name again. I reach my hand out and set it on his arm. Barghest leans into me from behind.

My touch seems to help bring him back into his body. But it also brings me back into mine, brings the memories back. The feelings that seconds ago I did not feel. It is excruciating, but I make myself keep it there, just for a minute. Just enough for him to be okay.

"I just never would have known, you know. You just—it happens so fast. One minute they're there and normal and fine, and then the next . . ."

"We should have known," I say.

We sit for a long time like that. Barghest, Ben, and me. Bathed in the red glow of the hell room. The infernal organ droning on and on all around. Us deep inside it. I lean on Barghest and press my face to his.

The three of us, here, alive. When so many others are not. How has God has chosen me and Ben and Barghest to live but not the others? How could He do this to Helen? My friend.

Boom-boom.

A cruel god.

"Sophie, I . . . it's so fucking brutal, and senseless, and . . . that it was Helen. That she . . . But—" He runs his fingers together, his brow knit and his eyes on the broken drum set before us, tears shining in them, his chest rising and falling. "When I heard the scream in the hallway . . . when I came in and saw something was happening . . ."

He shakes his head again, and his eyes finally focus as he takes a deep gulp of air.

He says, "I'm so glad it wasn't you."

Helen

Maro can't do it.
Cleo has to.
In the carousel room.
Beneath the angel swarm.

Devil's Lake

Did you know there's a supermassive black hole in the center of our galaxy?"

Noah, on the phone at Sacred Hearts, me sitting in my bedroom.

"A what?"

"A black hole is a part of space-time with gravity so strong that no electromagnetic waves have energy to escape it. And supermassive means it's, well, really big."

"What's inside it?"

"Matter. But matter that's compressed to an infinitely small point. There's no space or time, gravity just overwhelms everything."

"No space or time?"

"Yeah."

"But how?" Even Heaven and Hell have space and time. Even Eden did.

"Because . . . that's the universe."

"That sounds terrifying."

"Why?"

"Because . . . what would happen to us?"

"We just wouldn't exist, I guess. Not in the way we do now. But no one really knows."

"And that doesn't scare you?"

"It makes me feel small, but it's, I don't know. Indifferent, I guess. It doesn't have an agenda, or human feelings. It's so huge that we have to realize the vastness, the limitless possibility. It's just . . . I guess maybe it could be terrifying. But it's beautiful too."

"I think I know where we should go," Maro says.

We stand beside the packed car. It's morning. Gray. Bright. Maro's hands are blistered and dirty. Blistered and dirty from digging another grave. We've read that the Crusaders are moving again, in our direction. Helen is gone.

Barghest leans against me. Ben watches me from where he stands on the other side of Cleo. Wyatt has gone silent again.

Maro shows us his phone, a place that is reporting as safe right now, a name that I have not heard in a very long time.

Think Mom and Dad will ever take us?

"The Dells?" Cleo says. The first words she's spoken since last night.

"What do you think? A lot of folks are congregating there. We might be able to find people, or at least get you all somewhere safe." Maro. The look on his face. He is barely a person. Barely holding it together. His gaze doesn't meet mine anymore, not even for a moment.

Distantly, through the haze of everything, a mind that was once mine thinks there is a chance Noah could be there. That if he had broken off somehow from the others, the Dells might be where he'd choose to go. Because maybe I would think to go there too.

We stop in a state park to relieve ourselves in the woods.

It's peaceful. The oranges and reds that have taken over the land, the lake shining in the evening sun. The autumn trees mirrored there. It is fall now, in full force. Even with the gray sky and hazy smoky air, it feels cruel for this much beauty to exist. Or maybe it makes perfect sense.

A cruel god.

"Indifferent, I guess."

On the way in, we passed these large not-quite hills. Burial mounds, they were called. Ben was surprised I had never heard about them, said they were a big thing in Wisconsin, in this whole part of the country.

All of us trying. Trying to speak, trying to breathe.

"Is it satanic?" I asked.

He looked at me like maybe he was insulted by my question, or maybe even hurt. "No . . . it's Native."

"Oh," I said, "Sorry."

I stare down at my feet, the bandaged one and the one in the sneaker. I stand in the grass, the wind carrying the leaves on the air, drifting them to the ground around me. Barghest sniffing and circling.

When we were little kids, you were really afraid to step in the grass. Remember?

A throat clears maybe fifty feet from me, in the trees. I know that it's Maro. His being here, his presence. It maybe isn't good, how much I need him. How much I have grown to rely on someone I have no real ties to. And yet I don't fight it. Not now. What's the point? What's the point of anything?

"It's fine, I'm dressed," I say.

A moment later he steps out. Barghest running to greet him. Maro looks even worse than before. His eyes swollen.

"Hey, I, um . . . I just wanted to make sure you're okay," he says.

Sitting in that farmhouse together. Meeting on the highway and eating at the supper club. Eli's house, the tornado. He's protected me, even when I was horrible to him, even when he deserved it. There's so much I want to say, so much I need to say, and yet when I open my mouth I find I don't really know what it is. A feeling tugs at my chest, writhes there the way the guilt always does in my stomach.

But it's not guilt. I know guilt, and I know what this is. I've felt it before. For Noah. Even now, after so little time, for Barghest. Maybe when I was young, for my parents. But there are so many types, so many variations, and I . . . I don't know. I just know that when I stand here across from this person I only met not so long ago, now, I feel . . .

"I'm sorry," I say, hoping he can't read my thoughts and hoping he can, needing something I can't identify. "For what I said in the fiber-glass place, about you not saving those teenagers. It was selfish and not true. You did what you were asked to do, and you do so much for everyone. You didn't deserve that."

He runs his hand through his hair, feels in a front pocket for a cigarette that isn't there. Inhales deeply and sighs. "Maybe I did though."

"Are *you*?" I ask.

"Am I what?"

"Are you okay?"

"No," he says. "But I'm here."

We stare out over the water together. We could be back in the parking lot of Millie's Supper Club. We could be standing in a hundred places doing this very same thing.

"That house," I say. "The one we stayed in before the tornado hit. You had been there before, hadn't you?"

This catches him off guard. His face goes blank. Then,

"Yes," he says.

"Why did you take us there? And why didn't you tell me you knew it?"

He puts his hands in his pockets. "Well . . . for one, it was close. You needed clothes, and I knew there would be some. And I wanted to see if the people who lived there were okay."

"Who were they?"

"Well, one of them was very . . . special to me. I just needed to make sure she was alright."

"The girl? The one whose room I was in?"

"No, God no, it was her mom. I was seeing her mom for a long time."

A pang in my gut, for some reason, at that. I think back to the pictures in the hallway, the shiny-haired woman in the photographs, the kind eyes, pretty smile.

"She sprained her ankle about six months ago. It's how I knew to look for your crutch." He reaches into his pocket and pulls out a gold chain with a locket. "I got her this. Found it, in the house. It's why I was taking so long, when we first went in. I . . . it's stupid, but I was sad. To see that she left it."

Maro sitting on an elephant in the fiberglass-mold graveyard, staring at something in his hand.

"I'm sorry," I say, ignoring the pang I feel.

He shrugs. "I got bigger fish to fry these days."

"She's so much older than you."

"Only eight years," he says. "She had her daughter really young." Only eight.

"She's married," I say, a little breathless.

He gives a half shrug. "Not to the best guy."

"Do you love Cleo?"

He gives me a look. Surprised and then maybe . . . amused? Relieved. For the distraction. "Do you love Ben?" he says, a mischievous glint in his eye.

I scratch behind my ear and drop my eyes.

"Hey, I was just messing with you. It's none of my business."

The way he says that brings the sadness back. I don't know what I wanted. What I need. My body hurts from our fall. Helen's and mine. It hurts from everything.

Helen in the ground. In the woods, surrounding that terrible place.

"Hey," he says. "Come over here."

"What?" I wipe my eyes with my sleeves, try to make myself into a human being.

"Come on," Maro says. I don't know what he's going to do, if . . .

The air blows in a huge gust, and it sweeps leaves up and around us, rattling against our legs, scraping against each other on the ground. Some fly into the lake and land on its shining surface, obscuring the perfect image of the trees reflected there with ripples. Barghest leaps and plays in them. One sticks to Maro's shoulder. I step toward him, a chill snaking down my spine.

"Okay. I've been thinking. I can arm you better, teach you how to defend yourself. I think . . . I think it'd be smart. You're not gonna have much of a stance with that thing," he says, indicating my crutch. "But we can make it work. So. Ready? Hold your hands up in front of your face, above your chin."

I think he's joking. But after a moment, it's clear he's not. I look around the forest clearing, and the wind blows again.

"Come on," he says. It sounds almost like a plea. He needs this. One thing he can do to feel useful, not powerless.

I do as he says.

"Elbows in. Good. Now right foot back and crutch a little in front. Bend your knee."

I try it, and he looks me up and down. His eyes catch on mine. That pull again. Heartbeats.

"Right," he says, blinking back some feeling that threatens to break through, looking away for a moment. He clears his throat. "So basic jab. Watch me. See, you want to turn and use your shoulder for more power. Return right away to block your face. Now you try."

I do what he says, leaves crunching beneath me, cold wind sweeping through my hair. It hurts to move, but I do it anyway.

"But this time like you mean it."

He shows me how to feint, tells me how to work with balance, how to size up my opponent. I'm not good at any of it, and the crutch and foot make it nearly impossible. But I listen, and I feel . . . here. When his hand touches my arm or my shoulder, his warmth in proximity to me. A steady presence, after everything.

I try for an upward thrust at his nose, and he catches my arm and holds it there. He tells me what I did wrong, how I would have been able to properly disable or distract my opponent.

I don't hear him.

We are standing close, Maro and me. His hand gripping my wrist but somehow I feel like I am clinging to him, a lifeline. He finishes speaking, waits for me to say something.

And then his look changes, and he sees. Sees me looking at him. How close we are.

He is . . . with Helen and Ben, it's . . . urgent, strong. Or, I don't know. I wanted this with both of them. Proximity, their heat on my skin. I still want it. I know I still want both of them. This body does. Ben, so handsome it's almost absurd, so perfect and good. Helen . . .

But with Maro, it's a sort of *ache*, I think, somewhere deep within me. That recognition. That knowing. A line comes to me from one of my forbidden books I read months ago, alone in my room. Before any of this.

"*Whatever our souls are made of, his and mine are the same.*"

It might be stupid, and it might be childish, but I feel that somehow, my soul changed the day I met him. Somehow, in a world dark or light, I still think I'd find him, at one point along the way. I let my eyes meet his, and I see in the way he swallows, in the uncertain furrow of his brow, that he sees it too. Maybe it's because of Helen, because of what happened. But I feel a strange clarity, here, now. I start to speak, but I'm surprised when I say,

"Eight years."

"What?" he says, voice soft and hoarse, that frown still on his face.

"You said eight years, between her and you. The woman with the crutch."

His eyes sweep over my face—nose, cheeks, chin, lips. His hand still holds my wrist. *Whatever our souls are made of.*

His eyes on mine again. "It's not the same," he says. "When you're older. When you're both older."

"Isn't it?"

His eyes on my face. They linger on my lips, for half a second longer than the rest. His brow furrowed, mouth tight, breaths coming fast through his nose. So much happening inside him. And in this moment of strange clarity, I see it. Want, shame, guilt, fear, self-revulsion, and that deeper thing between us. That night in the farmhouse, in the middle of all this. A bond that grew in that house and that storm. That maybe was there anyway. Maro feels it too.

He swallows. I once again watch his Adam's apple bob up and down. He takes a breath, eyes on mine. "I—"

"Hey, Sophie—"

Barghest barks, jumps and runs to greet him.

Ben at the edge of the trees.

Ben standing there.

Maro and me like this.

Maro lets me go. Takes a step back, then another. He rubs at his jaw. "Yeah," he says, voice strained. "So if anyone tries anything on you, you, uh, at least you know some basics."

"Everyone's in the car," Ben says. "We're ready."

He doesn't meet Maro's eyes, or mine. I hate the look on Ben's face, and I want to reach out and touch him, and I want to touch Maro, and I am very distant from all of it. As if everything is underwater, as if nothing in this world is real anymore.

"They're going to have to wait," Maro says. "Still got one more thing we need to do."

Maro and Cleo unload all the guns and set them on the ground in front of us. We can't waste too many bullets. But they teach us. Ben is left-handed, something I didn't know. He's a decent shot with the handgun, even with his injured shoulder, but he can't hold any of the rifles right now. I'm not good with either, but I listen and commit it to memory as the shots ring out through the forest. Cleo drives Wyatt and Barghest away to protect their ears. Ben keeps his eyes solely on his task and doesn't speak a word, only nods in acknowledgment of instruction. He doesn't look at Maro, or me. Not once.

We load back up in the car. Service is down again.

Ben stares out the window, away from me.

We break through the forest and leave the trees and the peace of the park behind. It won't be long before all the leaves fall, before the snow comes. This transitional season always brief here, a mere moment between hot summers and brutal winters. Just a fleeting glimpse. A sign flashes by, seeing us off and into the night.

Thank you for visiting Devil's Lake.

The Dells

Today, I am finally going to the Dells. So many years after Noah and I discussed it in his room, prayed for it for our birthday. And this is it.

What I learn is that the Dells is a region, but there is a town too. Situated on a broad swath of the Wisconsin River, with a number of small lakes. High cliffs on either side of the river, and a downtown built for tourists. Waterparks scattered all around the area, tourist traps of all kinds up and down the main street.

I learn all this from Maro, whose tired voice answers my questions, Maro who pretends it didn't happen. The moment in the forest. I do the same. All of us who don't speak of Helen.

But we are not driving into the Dells yet. Instead, we're stopping in Baraboo, at the Ho-Chunk Casino, now a vaccination center and, supposedly, a place that will be safe to stay. In moments of cell service, our phones tell us that more and more casinos and hotels are functioning this way, especially since Milwaukee and now Madison are unsafe. The people there who haven't been infected or aren't joining the Crusaders or some group like them have been forced out, and the vaccination centers keep getting hit. The Dells region, apparently, is much safer than the rest of the state because a lot of the cops and medics who've been displaced have gone there to help out.

The parking lot is packed.

Maro takes the keys out of the car and eyes me as he does it. I don't know what he's thinking. Cleo steps out and tilts her head up to the sky, eyes closed. We all head in.

The Ho-Chunk Casino complex is enormous and very nice. Entering the lobby, we are met with a bluer sky than the one outside the building today. A faux sky inside the large atrium, bright blue with white puffy clouds, eagles soaring below it. Beneath them are trees and waterways, greenery and rocks. A kinder, gentler version of reality. Maybe one that used to exist. Maybe one that still exists, somewhere.

The hotel is nicer than any I've ever been to.

A handful of officials stand in different places near the entrance, and they watch us as we enter. A few feet inside, I hold my breath as one of them takes our temperatures from our foreheads. But we're all okay. One person works the reception desk, and we answer a series of questions about where we've been, if we've received the shots, if we've come into contact with any infected.

The man asking the question, dark skin and hair and white teeth, smiles. "We have to ask that, but if someone somehow *hasn't* met any infected, I want to know what they've been doing. You're welcome here. Only thing we ask is no swimming since we're still not totally sure about fluids. And, you know, wash your hands and all that. Vaccines are at the far end of the casino. We're doing breakfast still, but we're short on staff, so it's kind of like honor system—take and make what you need and clean up. But there's more food in town still open. You can take this room, it should be clean. If it's not or if there's an issue, come back down, and we'll get you sorted out."

"Just one room?" Ben asks.

"Oh, it's a suite. If you're traveling together, we'll try to keep you together, so we have space for more people."

"This place is . . . How are you holding it together so well?" Maro asks.

The man smiles. "Rest of the state keeps losing power. The plant is on tribal land, we run it. We're keeping this open and getting people what they need until somebody makes us stop."

"Has there been trouble?"

"Yeah. People who don't like that we're giving out the vaccines. We're not forcing it on anyone either, just offering." He shrugs. "But so far we're standing."

"How much for the room?"

"Credit card machines are down. Don't worry about it."

"Really?"

"At a certain point, you just gotta help each other out."

Cleo reaches into her bra and pulls out a money clip, hands him a hundred-dollar bill. "It's not enough, but . . . something anyway. Thank you."

The man nods and puts it in a drawer with a key. His eyes catch on Ben. He opens his mouth to say something, but Ben ducks away before he can.

We settle into our room. I grabbed a map of the region downstairs and now lay it out on the coffee table. I asked at the desk if they'd heard Noah's name at all, to no luck. But I have these paper maps and lists of the nearby hotels so I can find out which ones are also still functioning and go by and check.

"Hey," Cleo says to Wyatt. "Want to go play some slot machines?"

"What's that?" Wyatt says. They're the first words he's spoken all day.

"A game with big bright letters and numbers and pictures, and you can win money. Sound fun?"

He shrugs one shoulder.

"Right. We're off. And when we get back, we are both taking *long* baths."

She shot someone last night.

She put our friend down.

That fragile look, behind her smile, in her eyes.

Cleo and Maro agree that the best thing for all of us to do is to keep meeting back at the room. We have three keys between us, the two hand radios, and two cell phones.

We unpack our food bags and eat. I fill a paper cup with water four times for Barghest to drink, and eventually we just fill the bath with cold water and let him drink from that. The room is unthinkably comfortable. A gas fireplace in the living room, another in the bedroom. The bedroom has one bed, the living room a pull-out couch and a cot in the closet. I find the science museum on the map. If Noah is in the Dells but isn't in one of the hotels, maybe he'll be there. Anything's worth a try at this point.

Ben goes in to take the first shower. Maro speaks on one of the cells to different people, telling them where he is, asking where he can be of most use. We've drawn the curtains, and I sit in a chair by the fireplace. Warming myself by a fire in this safe, quiet place. My dog curled up beside me.

Helen in the ground.

I sink down on the floor and bury my face in Barghest's fur. He pushes back against me, seems to be transmitting love to me. He whines softly, and I try to transmit it right back.

Ben steps out of the bathroom, and Maro tells me I can shower next, if I want. He returns to the bedroom to make another call. He shuts the door. Ben's had to put his dirty clothes back on, his jeans and his shirt. He's missing his sweatshirt, and now that he's clean, the cuts and bruises are so stark against his skin. He moves as if in deep pain. As I look at him, his wet hair, his perfect face, something comes over me, and I don't even think before I stand and go to him, and I wrap my arms around his waist, press the side of my face to his chest, and hold it there. He says nothing, as shocked as I am, and I don't say anything either. I can't. I step back, chin lifted to see him. His face that is here, that is alive. I am breathing heavily now, and I know what is coming.

I don't want to do it in front of Ben, don't want to cry in front of him again. I close the bathroom door behind me. I peel my clothes off, and I don't look in the mirror. I see and feel the bruises, the cuts and scrapes that will soon become scars. None of it matters. Just in time, I turn the shower water as hot as it will go, and I get in, lower myself to sit beneath the spray. Just as every image, every moment, all of it bubbles up through my chest and into my throat. Just as all of it comes rushing out of me.

Helen and me laughing on the floor.

I tuck my knees in and drop my forehead to them.

Helen beneath the angel swarm.

That heartbeat I wish I'd never heard. That still clings to me.

For the hundredth time, I cry.

Cell service goes down again. Maro takes a shower. I fall asleep in the chair. Ben stares out the window through the space between the curtains at a gray sky. When I wake, I tell Maro I'd like to go to the science museum, and he says we'd be better off sticking around here. Then he looks from Ben to me and back and sighs.

He says, "I'll take you both if you swear you'll be smart."

I nod. Ben does too, though he looks like he might be happy to never get off that couch. He still doesn't really meet Maro's or my eyes.

"I mean . . . if you're up for it," I say to Ben. An offering, a hope.

After a second, he nods.

"Alright, I need another twenty minutes and to let Cleo know, and knowing you two, you'll be off somewhere even in that amount of time. Meet me at the car, and if you're even a second late, I'm sounding an alarm. Understood?" Maro says.

"What alarm?" I say.

"Sophie."

"Yes," I say. "Okay."

Ben and I head downstairs. There aren't too many people around, just a handful here and there sitting in the alcoves or the booths of the closed restaurant or in lobby chairs.

We find Cleo and Wyatt at the slot machines. Wyatt smiling the way he did when he first saw House on the Rock, pulling down the lever. The blue, yellow, purple glow on his face. And I think I'm starting to understand what Ben meant back at the school. About smiling, about it being important. Ben's not smiling now.

We tell them what we're doing. Cleo gives us a handful of bullets and says, "Be stingy with these. We don't have too many. But I bet they'll buy us somethin' good."

We continue to explore, Ben still refusing to speak, until we come upon a book with the history of the casino and the Ho-Chunk Nation, photographs of them, adorning the walls in one of the sitting areas. I didn't know anything about them before now. I learn there are other tribes too, more Native people, and they've been here. They were here before any Europeans came, long before.

I haven't learned this. I don't know how I never learned this. Not at home, or in church or school. Not even in any of the books I've read at the library. I want to turn to Ben and ask him if it's true, but I think of the burial mounds and some of the signs we've seen along the way. I think of the look on his face and him saying, *I forgot you were raised differently.* As if it was something terrible. More and more, I think it is.

"Hey there," a voice says. We turn, and it's the man from the front desk. He looks more tired than he did before, and though he still smiles, it looks like work. He says something to Ben that I don't understand.

"I'm sorry," Ben says. "I don't . . ."

The man squints his eyes as if trying to solve a puzzle. "What tribe?"

"Um." Ben rubs the back of his neck. "I'm not really . . . I mean, I don't know anything."

"Who knows anything about anything?" He smiles at both of us. I like him. Maybe I do like anyone who can smile in these times. I glance back to Ben.

"Chippewa," he says. And I try to understand what he's talking about. Then I think . . . he's talking about himself.

I realize once again how little I know about Ben. How we have lived through so much together but are still strangers in many ways. It is a crazy thought, how much more we might be able to learn about each other still, if we survive.

How much we might have still learned about Helen.

The front desk guy nods and smiles. "Anishinaabe."

"Yeah, I guess," Ben says.

"You guess or you know?"

Ben doesn't want to answer him, I can tell he doesn't, so I ask, "Do you live around here?" It's a stupid question, but I don't know. There's so much I don't know, it's overwhelming.

"Nah. But I worked here, before."

"Are you part of the tribe?" I ask.

He laughs a little but nods again, glances at someone behind us.

"I'll catch you two around," he says. Then he looks at what we were reading and gets a thoughtful mischievous look on his face. "You know, we've been here through three ice ages. We were here before. We'll be here after. We're gonna get through this too. And so are you." He claps a hand on Ben's arm. His good arm, but he winces anyway. "Keep your head up."

He walks away. I glance in the direction he's heading. A woman, happy to see him. He slings his arm over her shoulders, and they kiss as they walk.

𝔇𝔦𝔡𝔬 𝔞𝔫𝔡 𝔈𝔳𝔢

Maro takes us to the Dells and parks next to some cop cars. Barghest jumps out first, then waits for me, his big black eyes trained on my face. He can feel how anxious I am, how hopeful. This animal so attuned to me. I am overwhelmed with love for him, I nearly want to cry. I kiss his head and scratch his neck and ears. I tell him I love him so much.

The streets look mostly clean, and at least half the shops are intact. A jewelry store's front window is broken, and blood spatters the ground in a couple of places. But the brightly painted shops and museums are just as wondrous as I thought they would be. Police are stationed at intervals, mostly outside the few cafés and restaurants that are open. Maro instructs us to stay within four blocks of him, and he tells me three times to call him if anything happens. He's brought the hand radios. I raise mine in answer, and he goes off to join the other cops.

Ben, Barghest, and I go to the science museum. It doesn't seem to have been looted or destroyed, just left sort of empty. An entryway leading to interactive exhibits, diagrams, images, specimens. Everything Noah would have loved as a kid. The cosmos and physics and the laws of the universe. That phrase is printed on the wall. **THE LAWS OF THE UNIVERSE**. None of this fits what we were taught. But Noah never believed that anyway. I try to see through his eyes, take in all the stars and planets and galaxies. Noah's heavens.

Indifferent. But it's beautiful.

He's not here. I don't know why I thought he would be, at the exact moment I was, or at all. It was a stupid idea.

I pause outside, not sure what to do or where to start. I check my phone, but service is out again. I won't get discouraged. I won't cry. I will find him.

Ben suggests we step into the bakery. It's been mostly picked over, but there are a few good items left. The woman behind the counter holds a rifle cocked on one hip and grabs our pastries with the other hand. She waits for us to give her something in return, and we offer a bullet. She waits, and we offer another. She hands the pastries over.

"That a rescue?" She means Barghest.

"Sort of. Yes," I say.

"Right thing to do." She hands over an extra bag to us, and as we thank her, a treat for him too.

"Hey!" Ben says, when we step outside again.

"Oh," I breathe.

It sits just ahead of us. A bookstore. Completely untouched by anything save for one long smear of blood on the pavement outside.

We step in slowly, but there's no one here. And other than the cash register being gone, the store is just normal. I mean, normal the way I think a bookstore would be. I've actually only ever been to the library and the one church bookstore at Holy Hill. To be surrounded by something as dependable and familiar as books in this, to get to breathe their air again . . .

Neither of us moves. We are exhausted, truly exhausted. I'm no closer to finding my brother, and we just put a friend in the ground. Even here, maybe especially here, I feel it.

"I don't know how to pick one now," Ben says. "It just feels insane. That we're here, and there are these pristine books. All written before this, about a time before this. It's just . . ."

"It hasn't been that long," I say. "I left home five days ago, I think? Five days. Eight or nine days, since we were in the library. The one at home."

"What an eight days."

I know what he means about the books. The most normal things from before are the most foreign now. In so little time, our world has completely transformed. Time has no meaning anymore, even as we all have less and less of it. He reaches out a hand to take one, holds it in front of him, wincing at the movement.

"That's a good one," I say. He's got *Dune*.

He laughs softly. "I forgot. You're the only person I know who might be a bigger reader than I am. Did you ever get around to reading *The Valley of Horses*?"

Barghest sits at the door, his back to us, keeping watch.

"I, uh . . . I may have read it multiple times. Before the world ended," I say. "I haven't read any of the rest of the series yet. I loved it though."

"They might have some here."

"Um, as much as I want to, I'm not sure . . . if that's the kind of book I should be reading right now. In this well, *climate*."

He rubs his ear. "Yeah, I guess it's a little . . . steamy, or whatever."

In another world we might have both laughed at this. A day ago we might have.

"Did you get to read any of the others you checked out, before it all happened?" He leans against a bookshelf, and I feel him watching me.

"No. Except the chickens one. It wasn't great."

He smiles, a little.

The science museum is still bothering me. Cleo's articles. How we can exist on this planet with such vastly different views. Noah and me. The rest of the world. Noah, who isn't here. "You're really not religious?" I ask after a moment.

"I mean, I'm not Christian. Does that bother you?"

"No. It doesn't." And I realize that I mean it. It should bother me. I should be doing everything I can to get him to believe, to save him, but . . .

"Life is short," he says. "Clearly. If it brings you comfort to believe in a spiteful sky king, then I'm all for it. But if it doesn't, then I don't see a need to impose more rules on yourself and everybody else than the world does already. And especially not the kinda fucked-up ones that just exclude, condemn, and hurt people for things that are so arbitrary."

"But what about the afterlife?"

Something crosses his face. And I think of him as a little boy contemplating his own death. Alone in his bed. Watching his mother die before this.

"Well," he says, "there's no guarantee that there is one, right? So I think we should live however we want. I'd like to believe there is an afterlife, but . . . we can't know. And we know we have this one life here, so I just think that's what we focus on."

"You don't like rules," I say.

"Some are important. Maybe. I don't know. A lot are important. But knowing when to break them is important too. They're all just made up by you or someone else. We're all just humans." Ben looks me up and down, crosses his arms in front of his chest, and eyes one of the shelves. "So, on a more important note, how is it that you pick out your books again? I can't seem to remember."

I give him a half smile. He's forgiven me for earlier, at least a little. "I'll show you." We can have this. One moment of reprieve. I can allow myself this, before we go. I limp over to one of the aisles, and he moves to stand behind me. "Whatever book your finger lands on, you have to read. No exceptions."

I lean against the opposite shelf and watch Ben move. The funny way he steps, so tentatively, with his eyes closed, how unused to it he is. His shoulders under the thin fabric of his shirt. That dangerous feeling again spreading through my abdomen, intensified by everything that has happened.

I don't know where the thought comes from, but I want music. I want to hear that song again, the one from Cleo's phone. "White Flag." I take out the phone and hit play, set it on a shelf beside me.

Ben opens his eyes, his hand on a book and a smile on his face. "What is this?" he says.

"I like this song. You know it?"

He laughs. "Yeah, everyone does. Or, I don't know, my mom liked it. It's an old one."

"Is it silly?"

"No, it's nice to hear music. Really nice."

"There was music at House on the Rock."

Ben makes a face. "You know, I'm okay maybe never thinking about that place again."

His eyes meet mine, and we are both remembering.

The music has cleared the air of nothing. If anything, it has given voice to everything I want, everything we need to escape. Ben's expression changes. He must see something in the way I am looking at him, because he slides the book back on the shelf and takes a step toward me. I watch his mouth, imagining what his lips feel like. I bite my own.

I can't be here, can't allow this. There is too much at stake, and I can see that he wants the same thing that I do, the same lethal thing. To continue what we started. But the feeling deep down in me, the wanting, it renders me motionless. The wanting is a living thing, like the wind, a separate self from me. Maybe it is all that I am.

I back against the bookshelf, my breath shallow and quick. I am aware of every inch of my body, my fingers, my toes, the back of my neck. Ben steps directly in front of me, looks down, his face only inches from mine. My hand tightens on the handle of my crutch, the other reaching behind to steady myself against the bookshelf.

"Sophie," he breathes, studying my face, looking for something that I can't imagine he will ever be able to find in me. "Is this . . . ?"

My lips part, but I can't form words. Despite everything in me that knows this is the worst decision, my head nods, just a little. Just enough. I need this. Noah isn't here. Helen is dead. I need something that isn't darkness and grief. Just a moment of not thinking, not remembering.

He grazes my arm with his fingers, starting at the little prick mark from the vaccine. But this time it is bare skin on bare skin. I shiver. He hesitates and then continues, his fingers trailing down my arm to the inside of the joint. Down my forearm and to my hand. He takes my fingers in his, intertwines them. My breath catches. Our fingertips held between us, playing off each other as if in a dance. So many nerves in the fingers. Thirteen hundred per square inch, I think.

Ben releases my hand. We stand apart but crackling. Not a single inch of his skin touches mine now. Only his body heat, and breath.

Before he can pull away completely, I whisper, "Why do you like me?"

The question takes us both by surprise. "What do you mean?" he says.

"Is it just because I remind you of before?"

He pauses, then says, "Sophie. I liked you before all this, when I saw you at school."

"But . . . why?"

Again that look, as though this is the dumbest question. But it isn't to me.

"Because. You listen and learn, and you're your own person. You read books I'm sure you're not allowed to read. Mom told me you would sneak them into your bag so your parents wouldn't see. You think for yourself. In the real world hardly anyone forms their own ideas. Religion or what everyone is saying is the *right thing* to think in any given moment on social media, or Reddit or Tumblr or the newspaper, or whatever. Or even like people who go and get the same kind of dog they grew up with, end up living in the same town they grew up in, voting the same as their parents without questioning it. It's nearly everyone. People just think what they're told to. There's always something you're supposed to believe, and always consequences if you don't. And I know you struggle with this stuff. But you at least ask the questions. You at least leave room for possibility and a life other than the obvious, easy one."

"But I'm not good like you." I swallow, needing to pause this moment, needing to catch my breath. "That asteroid you saw, 83 Beatrix, your tattoo. I think it was named for Beatrice in Dante's *Divine Comedy*. She was all good, all light. She reminds me of you, or you her, or—"

"Sophie," he says, taking a half step forward so that there is so little space between us that if I took a breath, my breasts would touch him. He puts his good hand back to the bookshelf beside me. Grief is written all over him, and the same want I feel. So much pain on this boy who was so bright, so much brighter and lighter and better than anything I could ever be. I feel it. His heat and his sweat and every moment that I have not touched him, that I have watched him and wondered and pretended not to want.

"I'm not that good," he says.

My heart is beating in my ears, electricity over my skin.

Ourdutyaswomen.

ThewordofGod.

I watch his lips, and he watches mine.

I'm so glad it wasn't you.

I press up onto the toes of my good foot.

My lips meet his.

Ben's eyes shoot open, and he pulls back to look at me. My lips tingling. My first kiss. He is tired, exhausted, full of pain, but not fevered.

He doesn't look sick. Still, I might have just infected him. I might just have doomed this perfect boy in front of me. For what? A second?

"I'm so sorry," I say. My first kiss. My lips. "I can't believe I . . ."

He removes his hand from the bookshelf, and I am filled with shame and anxiety. I have done the unthinkable in the worst of times, and I am not worthy of anyone's love. I wait for him to step away so I don't have to do or say anything else, my eyes lowered so he doesn't see the tears filling them. But he doesn't step away. He takes his hand and slowly, so slowly, tucks a strand of hair behind my ear. I don't move. I hardly breathe. He pauses, and there is nothing but our breaths, nothing but Ben and the body that is me as he slowly, so slowly, traces an invisible line from my ear, over my jaw, and down my neck.

"Hey," he breathes.

I keep my eyes down. He says it again, and I look up at him. He is as uncertain as I am, as terrified and wanting, and bereft. He slides his hand behind my neck, shivers wracking me. He holds the back of my head with his hand, fingers twining in my hair. I suck in a breath.

An infinite moment.

A threshold. A precipice.

We jump together.

He leans forward, and his lips meet mine. Stronger now, stepping closer so that I can feel his entire body, every hard line. His heart beats against my chest just as fast and hard as my own, and I want everything, everything this body can give me. I am not a person. I am not Sophie. I am a vessel that is meant for nothing other than to pair with this boy in front of me, to come together and shine and lose ourselves in the union.

I meet him. This kiss, awakening and feeding a hunger and need and ache and euphoria that is so much more than intoxicating. I arch instinctively against him, my body taking over, knowing what to do even when I don't. He is sweet and sweaty and delicious and male, and I know this maleness somehow, have been waiting for it forever. It is wrong. It is dangerous and foolish. There is guilt, and there is shame, and there is terror and grief, but they are so far outweighed by the hugeness of this force.

Now I know.

Now I know.

After some time—a second, a millennium, too soon—he pulls away, our lips slow to part. He rests his forehead against mine.

He smiles, and it's a real smile. There is pain behind everything now. It is the main fabric of our lives, and it is supposed to be. But here, now, Ben lets out a gentle laugh on an exhale, and I let myself smile too. I am changed, and I am new, and in the darkest darkness of my life, we stand in lethal color.

The song plays on. I think of the space between us, all the things we could do and discover if we eliminate it. We have that ability. He leans down and kisses me again. It erases everything and heightens it and makes me swim the way the wine did, and it is delicious and excruciating, and I think of angels and mortals and God, and I reach my hand out and run it over the hard planes of Ben's chest. His tongue finds its way into my mouth, and I part to let it in, to meet it with my own, to explore every way we can taste each other. I pull him closer by his shirt, and a sound escapes me as his hips almost press against mine, just almost.

The light we generate. Light that no priest, Sister, or parent can control. And the way Ben looked at me, the way he *wants* me. There is power in this. So much power.

This is the power my parents wanted to hide with boxy clothing, sequestering me. This is the power the Sisters have shunned and the priests have forgone in the name of something pure. This is the power to fell a nation, to move an empire. The power of Lilith in the story. And I have it within me. I tilt my hips forward, cross that final inch, and I feel all of him, virile and wanting and alive.

This is *power.*

This is—

"Sophie. Do you read me?"

The radio. Maro. I pull back.

Ben before me is breathless and flushed. My chest rises and falls, and we are still so close. Barghest lifts his head.

Maro's voice sounds again.

Birthday

A t the casino, Maro asks if he can talk to me a moment alone. Ben gives me a small secret smile then gets in the elevator. A family nearby plays the slot machines, the son telling the father about a serial killer's skull he saw at one of the museums. Maro watches me a moment and then says, "Hey, look, so it's none of my business, but I just want to make sure you're being careful."

"You're right, it's none of your business," I say, my face hot.

"Yeah, I know," he says. "And normally I'd . . . It's just . . . dangerous right now. What Cleo and I did, what you saw us do . . ." He clears his throat, runs his hand over his head. "It wasn't smart. Anyway, I've been trying to be this example, and I know you and Ben and Wyatt don't have parents around now, and I just . . . I don't know."

The thought upsets me so much, makes me almost furious, or . . . "Maro, you're not my *parent*." A look between us. Full of so many things. Confusing, conflicting things.

"Yeah, I know, I just. You don't have adults around, and . . ." His fingers search for a cigarette I know won't be there. He sighs. "My sister always lived like there was no tomorrow. And that was fine, for her, you know. Maybe the way she went was the way she'd want to go, having fun. Still young. But if there's no tomorrow for you, there's still a tomorrow for all the people who care about you. I can tell you, Sophie, it's a real shit thing to be the one left alive."

"I know it is," I say.

"Well, I'm just reminding you, in case you need it. Just because all this is going on doesn't mean you should put yourself at risk or throw your life away."

"You think any of us are really going to make it through this?" I ask.

He stares at me, and I can't read the expression. I shift on my feet, nervous about what he sees.

"Funny," he says, eyeing me over the slot machine lights. "I thought I had a pretty good read on you." He pulls out a cigarette. He had one after all.

"What do you mean?"

He lifts it to his lips and stops, looks me in the eye.

"I just thought you were a fighter."

I look down at my feet. I don't have an answer, for him or me.

"You're planning to leave," he says.

I think about denying it, but I'm tired. It doesn't seem worth it to have the same fight over and over with one of the few allies I have in this world, one of the few people I have left. I don't want to fight with him. I don't want him to think of himself as an adult and me as a child.

"I'll look for him here first. The other hotels. But if he's not here . . ."

"I have to stay," he says. "I gotta try and help these people keep this place running. Or find the next place where someone needs help. I can't go with you to find him."

I knew that leaving meant leaving Maro. I knew, and yet . . . hearing the confirmation, I realize now maybe I hoped in some part of me that it didn't. Leaving him, losing him . . . It is hard to breathe. But we knew. I knew. I say, "I wouldn't ask you to."

"Okay," he says.

"Okay?" I ask.

He nods. He holds my eyes for a minute, and there is so much in that look, so much that I know I will be piecing it out maybe for years to come. If I live that long. The fact that anyone I have known for this amount of time could mean so much to me. We can't parse through this. We won't. But still, to have it. To know it, even for a second.

"I hope you like your life, Sophie," Maro says. My name on his lips and a chasm stretching between us. Eagle screeches and music from the slot machines. "You just get one."

————

Ben on one chair, Cleo and Wyatt on the couch. I still half expect Helen to be with us.

"Any news?" I say. The casino's Wi-Fi is up and running again. I check the boards, still nothing.

"Another tornado, in Indiana. Weather's insane everywhere. Crusaders have gone quiet for the moment. Hospitals are fucked," Cleo says.

Ben and I hand out the pastries, and we lay out a dinner from our other food items. Maro was able to get us painkillers in town, and we all take them.

"Does anyone know what day it even is?" Ben asks. "I don't. I feel like it's all just . . . like maybe time stopped when we left home."

"It's October 8."

My head snaps up.

"Something wrong?" Cleo's focus is on me, and when she asks, so is everyone else's.

"Oh, no. I mean . . ." And I shouldn't say anything, don't need to bring attention to something so silly, but the fact that time just continues forward. "Um . . . it's my birthday."

It's Noah's birthday.

There's silence, and I know I shouldn't have said anything. Then Cleo squeezes Wyatt's shoulders and says, "I think we need a party."

Cleo and Wyatt make posters from the coloring book. Ben disappears into the bedroom, and Maro is out somewhere. Barghest jumps and leaps, playing with Cleo, Wyatt, and me, joining the new excitement, nearly knocking everything over.

But I don't feel it. I wish I hadn't said anything. Birthdays are hard, have been ever since Noah left. My birthday has never been my own, and to celebrate it, or live through it, without the other half who was supposed to be there with me is always its own kind of misery.

Helen died the day before my birthday. My parents died a week before.

But Wyatt is happy. He's occupied and smiling. A fragile breath of life seems to have infused everyone. Maro returns, having found candles and tape. We've eaten the pastries already, so we decide to

322 — CJ Leede

open one package of cheese curds and stick a birthday candle into the middle of each one. This becomes a game for Wyatt, Cleo, and me as we try to keep them from rolling or falling over to keep the candles in. Wyatt laughs, and his boy laugh is so like Noah's when we were young.

Cleo teaches Wyatt and me how to tear out the colored pages and fold them into paper party hats. Noah making origami animals for me.

Wyatt takes the candles out of enough cheese curds to feed them to Barghest that we open a second package and set them up again. Maro joins us too. We have one bottle of wine still, and he fills the hotel plastic cups with enough for everyone. In the last cup, the one for Wyatt, he puts a piece of candy he's scrounged up from somewhere. Then he sits on his knees across the coffee table from us and helps us with the crafts. Cleo has a game called Questions, in which someone asks a question, and everyone answers. Favorite colors, favorite movies, what kind of animal we would be.

I've never been asked these questions. And it's fun to try and think of what I like, of what I would want to be. Who I am, I guess. All the time I've spent alone, and I don't really know this about myself.

"A bear," Maro says.

"Scary," says Cleo.

"No, one of the nice ones. Black bear maybe." He winks at Wyatt. My heart flips, a little.

"I think I'd be a hyena," Cleo says.

"A hyena?!" Wyatt is appalled.

"What, you don't think so?"

"They're scary too."

"But they get to laugh and laugh, all the time. That's what I want to do. Plus, they have fabulous hair."

Wyatt contemplates this.

"What about you?" she says.

"Lion! And I'd ROAR!" Wyatt lifts up, his hands in claws, and strikes at the air.

Cleo joins his roar, tickling him at the same time, and his roar turns into peals of laughter. Ben is still in the other room, and I don't know what he's doing, why he's not with us. An image of him with sweat on his forehead, glassy eyes. Panic seizes me, and just as I think I won't even be able to stand to check on him, the door opens.

"What's so funny out here?" he says, in a teasing voice directed at Wyatt.

"I'm a lion, and I'm going to eat all of you," Wyatt says.

"A lion?!"

"What about you, birthday girl?" Maro asks. *Birthday girl.* Those words in his mouth, in his voice. My eyes flick to his, and again, that feeling, that constricting in my chest. Everyone is watching.

"I think..." I say. What do I think? I picture the skies, forests, plains, deserts, mountains, oceans. Mostly from books, mostly described in words and sometimes images. What would I want?

Noah's voice, the wind beating against the window. *Birds are always chirping after a storm, telling the world they've made it through. Finding each other.*

"I'd want to be a bird," I say.

"Why a bird?" Maro again. Maro's eyes on me. Ben takes the other chair and watches what we're doing, holding something in his hand. Watches Maro and me. I don't look at either of them, and the words that come out of my mouth surprise me.

"Just once, I'd like to feel it. Soaring on the wind."

Cleo whispers in Wyatt's ear, and Wyatt nods and smiles. He sets to work coloring one last thing on one of the hats and then holds it out to show us. He's put a bird on mine.

Maro gets the lighter for the candles, and Cleo unclasps her necklace, the one with the red gem. She gestures for me to come closer, and I suck in a breath as she fastens it around my neck, warm on my skin, from hers.

"I can't—" I start to say.

But she winks at me and whispers, "Looks better on you anyway. Happy birthday."

We crowd around the table in our party hats, candlelight glowing on our faces, and they sing the birthday song. I don't know how long it's been since I heard it. My parents don't sing it, not since that night, and they don't do it at the church or school. It was too painful to celebrate with Noah gone, I think even for my parents. The memory of the sound, the words, the love of these people, fills me with so much, and Wyatt and I blow out all the candles. We toast with our wine and candy, eat our cheese curds, and we laugh. Tell stories.

I step into the bathroom, and when I come out, Ben gestures me into the bedroom. I glance over, and the rest are too busy to notice.

He and I go to the other side of the room so we won't be seen.

"I, uh." He rubs behind his ear. "It's not much, but . . . Happy birthday."

And he holds something out between us. An envelope, with something inside.

A gift. A present from Ben. Again, these stupid tears, but . . . "Do I open it now?" I say.

"More cheese curds!" Cleo calls from the other room.

"Maybe later," Ben says. He's so beautiful I can barely breathe. He smiles down at me, and he wipes a tear from beneath my eye. "You deserve it. And a lot more."

Cleo sets Wyatt up in the bedroom, a kid's movie about adventure and sword fights, and the sounds of it carry to us in the living room. The wind is here, but it feels softer now, less insistent. The world beyond these walls unable to reach us. The fireplace. Cleo and Ben on the couch, Maro and me in the chairs on either side. Barghest on the floor beside me, leaning into me, and my legs resting on his back. *My* dog's back. My hand on his head, my heart nearly too full.

This room, the people in it. The feeling in my chest and gut that is separate from the guilt and fear, from the loss and longing. The warm feeling, the one that makes me feel this life might be worth it after all.

We've continued Questions, and I've learned so much about everyone. Cleo grew up doing ballet six days a week, but she didn't love it anymore when she went to school for it. She discovered she was good at coaching people, helping people find their way, and she became an agent for bands. She was visiting one of her bands on tour when everything happened. She lives in Chicago, and that's where her husband was. She grew up going on hunting trips with her dad once a year, and they practiced at the gun range all year long. She loves every genre, but punk music is her favorite, whatever that is.

Ben plays lacrosse and knows every word to all the Lord of the Rings movies, and Maro hiked the whole twelve-hundred-mile Ice Age Trail when he was eighteen.

"Well, I knew this one was a Catholic girl the moment I set eyes on her," Cleo says, following a train of thought I've missed.

I smile, shrug, feel embarrassed somehow.

"What do you fear most?" Cleo asks me.

Maro snorts, takes another sip.

Cleo rolls her eyes. "Only if you want to answer," she says.

I think about it. Try to sift through all the horrors we've witnessed this week, everything from before. "Hurting someone I love," I say. "Hell. Someone I love burning in Hell. Possession. Being bad. Being wicked."

"See, right there," Cleo says, leaning forward in her chair. "That's how they get us."

"What?" I say.

"Why do you think possession is so frightening?"

"Because you lose control over yourself, you lose free will." Because a *demon* enters you.

"You wanna know why I think possession scares you?" Cleo says, elbows resting on her knees, looking at me intently. "It's the same reason they want it to. Because on some level you feel that you've already given up your free will. God and Jesus and the Devil and angels and demons have already infiltrated your thoughts, your whole being. The church has. They make us so afraid of possession, of doing wrong and being wrong, because they don't want us to see they've done it to us already. That fear, guilt, and shame, *that* has possessed you your entire life. And they put it there. Now tell me who's the one who deserves to go to Hell."

Tears fall from my eyes again, silly stupid tears. But I do not move. I see her, seeing me.

Seeing me.

Maro and Ben are silent.

"You might struggle with this your whole life," she says. "You might never get out from under it fully. You probably won't. But you'll have moments. Moments when your thoughts are yours and yours alone."

"What does it feel like?" My words a whisper.

She smiles at me, and I know I'll remember it for the rest of my life.

"Like wings on the wind, baby."

Cleo, Wyatt, and I take the bed, Ben the couch, and Maro the cot. In the dark of our room, I wait until the soft sounds of Wyatt's and Cleo's breaths even out, until there is no more movement in the other room. Until there is me awake, and the wind, and Barghest on the floor beside me. I slowly and carefully reach to the bedside table where I've set Ben's gift, and I open it.

The makeshift envelope surrounds a card. I blink in the dark to see it, and after a moment I understand what Ben has done. He must have taken the guide to the Dells that I brought upstairs with us and ripped out letters and pictures from it, collaging them with tape into one image, and one message. Tape that Maro got for him. Water and trees and blue sky for the background, and in front of it, in mismatched letters pasted together, it says,

I'm luCkY tO KNow yOu.

And at the bottom right, beneath them all, he's cut out and taped in a heart.

I can't help it. My heart beats fast, and I am filled with the same tingling from when his lips touched mine, when his hands were in my hair and on my neck.

"He's a good one," a voice whispers. I turn to find Cleo is awake, still lying on her pillow, but watching me. I start to put it away, but she's seen it anyway, and I don't want to yet. It's my birthday present, and I want to look at it.

Cleo is smiling, gently.

"Thank you for the necklace," I whisper. "I've never owned anything so beautiful." I touch the gem and feel as though it thrums beneath my fingers. "And . . . for that other thing. For what you said."

Wyatt stirs a little. She rubs his arm, and he settles again. I sense there is more Cleo wants to say, so I wait, watch as her expression turns thoughtful. My necklace and this card.

She bites her inner lip, weighing something, then says, "What we were doing when you saw us back at the school, Maro and me, it wasn't smart, and it wasn't safe. But . . . I'm not sorry." She holds my eyes for a long moment, as if this is very important for me to hear. As if this is not the most dangerous idea of all. "They call this thing Sylvia," she continues, her whispers just loud enough to make out over the wind. "They made her a woman. Like storms. Wind and rain and destruction. I get the sense no one's ever said this to you before, so whatever it's worth, I'm gonna say it now. Your other gift." Her eyes, that knowing look.

"You don't carry a precious thing to give away only once, and you do not lose value as a human or a woman once you give it. *You* are a precious thing, *you*. And you get to do whatever you want. You *matter*, and you have to live your life as though you matter. Now and always. I'm not sorry," she says again and smiles. "Not at all. Happy birthday, little bird."

With this, she turns away from me and settles in for sleep.

Maro's words. *You just get one.*

Too many earthshaking, reality-bending ideas, too much to sort out. And the wind blowing so hard I feel the thrum of it in my veins.

I admire my gift a little longer, the card that was made for me. I am full of giddy warmth. Ben in the other room, sleeping. Ben who made this. Then I slowly tuck it away and reach down to stroke Barghest's fur. He looks up, and I stare into his eyes, soulful and full of uncomplicated love.

"*I love you,*" I whisper to him. I wish he could fit on the bed with us up here. The next place we stay, I'll make sure he can. I never want to sleep another night without him. He leans into my hand. I am overflowing with love.

Barghest. Ben, Maro, Cleo. Wyatt.

I got a party, I got a birthday and gifts and love and acceptance. Even if there are dangers, ideas that threaten to destabilize the whole of my world. Even if there is no Helen. Even if her absence is louder than the wind.

But I am here, surrounded by love.

And my brother, my person, is out there, maybe with no one.

As far as I know, tonight, Noah got nothing.

𝕴𝖓𝖋𝖊𝖗𝖓𝖔

Every young girl and boy is born into sin. Does anyone know why that is? Yes, Sophie.

Because of the Fall.

Very good. And why is it that little girls are born into more sin than little boys?

Because Eve took the fruit from the Serpent and gave it to Adam to eat.

Very, very good. And why did the Serpent give the fruit to Eve, and not to Adam?

Because girls are more easily tempted than boys.

Yes. Girls are more prone to temptation. We must remember. We are the wicked ones.

A tree, so beautiful. Lush and full with leaves. Tan parchment awash with black. Words. Pages. Hundreds of pages leafing the tree. Words beneath the bark, words lining the branches. Words on the fruit I now hold in my hand.

Where did this come from?

A voice. Familiar. Close. Ben. He is naked. Why are you naked?

I should ask you the same.

I am naked, standing here before him, and—

The fruit in his hand now.

Sophie, is this a gift? For me?

No. I didn't give it to you.

It's so beautiful, Sophie. Thank you.

No! Leaping forward, trying to knock the fruit from his hand. Toppling over, landing on top of him. Naked flesh on naked flesh.

Oh. I didn't—

His lips silence mine.

Rolling over, looking up into his face, the grass soft beneath my back. Kissing, feeling.

Heat.

Heat coursing through my veins. Heat radiating between our bodies. Heat coming from the tree. What's happening?

A snake slithering away in the grass.

Flame salamanders licking at the base of the tree, climbing higher and higher. Crawling their way up.

Branches burning. Pages burning.

Ben! Ben, where are you?

Ben is gone. The fruit is gone.

Just me beside a burning tree.

Flames. Salamander flames, licking at my ankles. I squint my eyes open, and I'm in the hotel. I can't quite wake, can't shake the dream. I reach for Barghest, but he isn't there. I sit up and blink to bring the room into focus. Why won't it come into focus?

My eyes burn and water. The air is thick and full. My brain is slow to piece it together. Smoke, again, that campfire smell.

But it's not outside the windows.

It's coming from inside.

The room is filling from floor to ceiling with thick gray smoke.

No alarm.

I blink in the dark, glance to the bedside alarm clock. The power's out.

Still, if there was a fire, there would be a backup generator. I've read about it. A place like this, the alarm would go off, sprinklers, even without the power. I must still be dreaming.

Unless someone knew, or thought, to disable a backup generator. Someone who wanted the place to burn. Someone—

I sit up and feel the burning in my lungs, choke out a cough. This is real.

"Hey, hey! Everybody wake up! Fire! There's a fire!" My words are cut short, another bout of choking. I reach over, still coughing, shake Cleo and Wyatt. Cleo's eyes flutter, but Wyatt is not waking. Why is no one waking up?

I find Cleo's arm and shake it harder.

Finally, she stirs, her head rolling over to look at me. I shake her again. "Put your hands over your mouth!"

Something snaps into place in her awareness, as she takes in the room and she rolls onto her stomach, pulls her shirt up over her mouth and nose. She reaches for Wyatt, scoops him up, and uses her other hand to put on her shoes. I grope for my crutch, the smoke obscuring my vision. Shouting now, some voices close, some farther away. My hand closes on the metal. Maro runs in, hair disheveled from sleep, shirt half on. He yells that we have to move.

"Where's Barghest?" I ask.

"What?"

"Where's Barghest, I can't find him!"

Ben chokes in the other room. "Here! He's not waking up. Sophie, help, come here!"

"I gotta get Wyatt out," Cleo says. "We'll find you."

I follow Maro's voice and the vague shapes I can make out through the smoke, and finally touch fur with my outstretched hands. I can feel Ben shaking him awake, and I join in. "Barghest, wake up! It's time to go! We have to get out of here!"

The dog raises his head and then drops it back down. I take off my hoodie and put it in front of his face. "Come on, buddy! Wake up! Please wake up! It's time to go!"

Ben produces a cup of water from near the couch, pours it over his face and the fabric of the hoodie. Barghest stirs, then blinks awake. He scrambles to his feet. I hold the fabric to his muzzle and tie it around the back of his head. Tears stream down my face, and Ben's, and Barghest snorts and shakes his head to clear it.

"I'll get him, you worry about your crutch."

We trip toward the door, stooping low, faces covered. Fighting for each painful breath. Now, belatedly, a fire alarm erupts, screaming through the confusion. The door handle is hot. There's fire in the hall. But there's no other way to go unless we jump out the window, and we're on the fourth floor. I pull my sleeve down over my hand and open it.

Frantic bodies stream down the hall. Fire leaps up from the open stairwell to the right, and two adults aim fire extinguishers at the blaze. The flames keep coming.

We join the stampede running to the left. Making sure Barghest follows, I stagger through the smoke toward the stairwell that isn't on fire. Someone rushes past, pushing me down to the floor. My lungs burn, and I cough as I scramble back to my feet. A hand on my arm, Maro's I'm sure. We reach the stairwell. Shouts from behind us. We need to get down quickly, but with my foot and the crutch and the smoke, everything feels impossible.

Ahead, an old woman struggles to move. Maro tells Ben and me to stay together and lifts her off the ground. He carries her down the stairs ahead of us. I start the descent, and turn to Ben, frantic bodies pushing in close behind. "Take Barghest. I'll meet you outside."

"No, we'll stay with you."

I shake my head. "Please."

The look in his eyes says he doesn't want to leave me, would rather do anything else. But it also says trust, and he passes me with a quick nod, taking Barghest with him, and disappears into the crowd. I stick close to the railing and let the rest of the people pass on my left, taking each step carefully. They shove past, shouting, tripping over each other. Someone kicks my foot. I cry out.

There is only one flight of stairs left. The heat grows behind me, the smoke so thick that the door at the bottom is just an outline. Someone shoves at my back, and I can't grab the rail in time, can't get my footing. I'm thrown forward. My hip knocks against concrete, my elbow, knees. Something is rammed into my stomach. I slide down, am shoved forward again. Out the front door and into the night.

My skull collides with the doorframe. Once again, it all goes dark.

———

I open my eyes to a world on fire.

Every building on the casino compound emanates a red-orange glow, a blistering heat. Stone-clad buildings burning from the inside. Burning wood outside too, in bonfires set all around. Everyone running, trying to find loved ones, trying to find safety, rushing toward the parking lot. Ash flakes raining down from the dark sky overhead.

Devils.

Red demons bearing torches, cornering innocents, moving so effortlessly it looks as though they are gliding. Red robes with a white emblem on the back. Hoods shadow their faces and conceal them from view. I can see one of them through the crush of bodies and smoke and flames, retreating toward the others.

There are so many, too many to count, moving through the night as if they own it, as if it was created for them. A flag flies high above the place where they converge. The Harlot and the Beast.

A hand grips my elbow.

"Sophie! We need to get away from the building!" It's Ben. He and Barghest are here.

Smoke streams from the windows and doors, flames fighting to gain traction on stone, licking out from the windows. Sweat breaks out all over my skin as heat pours in from every direction, the ceaseless wind fanning the flames so that they spread to the treetops.

Maro isn't here. Neither is Cleo nor Wyatt. I don't see them.

I follow Ben and Barghest away from the building.

Pop, pop.

Two gunshots, close enough to set my ears ringing. All my senses dampened, everything impeded. The smoke incapacitating us. Ben coughs, is seized by it, has to stop and wait for it to pass. My throat burns, and I desperately need water. I am dizzy. Barghest pants and whines. We struggle forward, dodging people left and right, branches falling from trees. Barghest is slow. He limps alongside Ben, barely keeping pace.

The wind whips through, fanning the flames, but it clears the air too. Alternating between seeing and groping, so much sound and smoke. So many people.

Gunshots. Yells. Screams. Crackling flame. A giant branch crashes to the ground right before us.

And there, in a break in the smoke, beyond the branch and down the lawn, I catch sight of Maro. Helping evacuate people from the building, telling them where to go. Passing children to other officers. He looks up briefly, and our eyes catch.

Then the smoke passes between us again. I lose him.

I see them in flashes, in shifts in the breeze. Crusaders. Not just with torches this time. Knives, guns, metal glinting against the flame.

"Ben," I say. "They—"

Barghest suddenly lifts his head and sniffs the air. One of his ears perks up, and he is up on his feet and bolting away from us. Not in the direction of Maro, but to the left, farther from the building. Ben and I call to him. Ben swears. We have no choice but to follow.

Barghest runs until he reaches another tree. He stops abruptly and whines, noses something on the ground. I can't see what he's doing until I drop down on my knees beside him.

No.

Red pants and gold jewelry.

No.

How—

I was just sleeping beside her. I don't—

Cleo lying here in the grass. Blood on her stomach. The sound, the horrible rattling sound . . . it's coming from her throat.

Cleo. Singing me happy birthday. Cleo, straining to breathe. Blood now spilling over her lip, painting it red.

No.

No, no, no.

I pull her shirt up. There's so much blood. She's been stabbed in her abdomen. Someone has stabbed Cleo. I tear the fabric and bunch it up to press to the wound. I give Ben orders, as if I know anything. Barghest whines and paws.

Cleo grabs my wrist with a shaky hand and says, "No."

I think it is my own voice repeating it. *No. No, no, no.* She reaches beside her and groans. My eyes track her movement, see what she's pointing toward as the smoke clears again.

No.

A striped T-shirt. Jeans. Little-boy sneakers.

He is still. Here on the grass.

Wyatt is still.

No sound, no laughter, no roar.

No breath.

Ben drops down beside him, touches his wrist. As if he could do something, as if he could do anything. But there is no how-to to fix this. There is nothing that will undo what has been done.

Wyatt's throat sliced open. Slit like a sacrifice.

This little boy, this *child*.

Cleo.

None of this is real. It can't be.

A jewelry-laden hand grips my wrist, again. For the last time. The final time.

The field, the flame and screams. Cleo's hand on mine. She holds my eyes, wheezes through a word I can't understand. The most powerful woman I've ever known, lying here on the ground. She heaves and tries again, and it is excruciating, watching her fight her own body to get the words out. Watching her understand that this is the end.

"Why?" I say. It's all I can say.

"Shot. One of them. Another. Came after me. Us."

Too much blood. Covering Cleo. Covering Wyatt.

Wyatt's sleeping face that is not sleeping. Wyatt's sneakers are dirty. They are dirty, and I could have cleaned them. Any of us could have.

We told him everything would be okay.

Cleo's words, her last words, break through everything. Through the disbelief and shock and grief and despair and rage. Through the smoke and screams.

"Fight. These. Motherfuckers."

She pushes the gun toward me.

Pop.

Pop, pop, pop!

Gunshots, getting closer.

Ears ringing, smoke filling every part of me. Cleo's eyes on mine, and my hand on her hand.

I don't know who is shooting, don't know who wields the knife that felled Cleo and Wyatt.

Her heart beating beneath my fingers. Beating, and then,

And then it stops. I feel it. There, and then gone.

I search her face, the space around her. Try to find where she possibly could have gone. But there is nothing. No glowing orb floating up from her as her soul travels elsewhere. No sense of peace. Just a light snuffing out.

Just like that.

Ben is saying something.

We have to go. They're coming. The men in robes are coming. The hooded men. The ones who did this to Cleo. The ones who did this to Wyatt.

St. Michael's Crusaders. My people.

The tree will not give us cover. Ben is saying it again and again. He is begging me to move.

Fightthesemotherfuckers.

I let him pull me from her. From the two of them, still lying on the ground.

My crutch is gone, and I lean on Ben to walk. I hold the gun, and I hear her words.

Barghest barely keeps up, coughing and wheezing. I won't move ahead of him, insist on holding contact. My hand on his head. Cleo's blood. Wyatt's blood.

We reach a clearer section of lawn, step over a small ledge that separates a higher grass area from a lower one. We duck behind the ledge to rest, protected by the shadows. I run my fingers under Barghest's eyes where they are watering. He whimpers and coughs again, leans into me. My forehead to his. Transmitting love. Pulling all my strength from him and trying to give him some of my own. *Shh, I love you, it's okay.*

Ben holds his hand out to signal danger. A rustling behind us, then footsteps on the stairs leading down from the ledge. I feel the vibrations in Barghest's belly as he begins to growl but hold my hand over his mouth to quiet him.

One of the red-robed figures hurries along the lower lawn toward the parking lot, holding a torch in one hand and some kind of container in the other. He only looks behind him once, missing our huddled figures in the shadows.

Ben, body tense, muscles coiled under his skin. I feel my own tense up, Barghest rigid beneath me.

Fightthesemotherfuckers.

We watch as the Crusader rests his torch against a metal bench and unscrews the cap of the gasoline canister, like the one Maro used to fill up at the gas station. That's how they were able to get it to blaze so fast, they're splashing fuel all over the place. And those long giant planks so many of them carry.

Maro. Where is he?

The Crusader walks to the end of the lawn and begins tracing its edges with gasoline, making a sweep all the way around this section of grass. A blaze shoots up not far to our left. We could go to the parking lot, get a car and drive away. But Maro is here, somewhere. And even if he weren't, even if it was just these men in red robes with their gasoline canisters, I'm still not sure I would run.

These people who killed Cleo and Wyatt. These people who have done this.

Pop.

Another gunshot.

Screams.

Ash falling through the smoke, coating the lawn in gray.

All these people. Choking, running for their lives from the one safe place they had. Because one religious group doesn't believe in offering medicine. Because one religious group has seized on an opportunity to make the world what they want it to be, at the ultimate expense of others. A religious group who are supposed to be my people.

All the cruelties to Noah, all the pain he has endured. The loneliness of my whole life thrust upon me because my parents thought my brother was something sinful, because they feared him. Mrs. Ingles watching me fight for my life, having to stab my own father to survive. Mrs. Ingles with a red robe in the back seat of her car. The Sisters with the red robes. These Good Christians. These Kind Christians.

Cleo.

Wyatt.

Fightthesemotherfuckers.

I am up.

I am crossing the lawn to the robed man with the gasoline. He sees me. Confusion passes over his face. An injured young girl, limping toward him.

A girl full of unseen fire.

We are both fifty feet from the torch, in opposite directions. I pick up my pace, not feeling my injuries. I will beat him, even if it breaks me. He realizes what I am doing, what I am moving toward. We both run. I do not listen to Ben yelling to me. I see but do not see another hooded man coming from behind and Ben intercepting him. I do not feel the pain in my foot or the raspy shallow breaths in my throat, the smoke in my nose and mouth and eyes. All I see is the torch in front of me—a beacon, a guiding star, the one thing I can do for this place against the people who are trying to destroy it. *My* people. My people doing this.

Then I am there, next to the torch, my arm stretched toward it.

The man in the robe is here too, feet from me.

He grabs it first, and I lift Cleo's gun, point it at his head. He shoves his elbow into my arm, and the gun drops to the ground. He kicks it away from us.

He smiles, holds the torch between us so I can see his face in the firelight.

And . . .

Pale skin. Soft. A beer belly beneath the folds of his robe. He has no facial hair, no hair on top of his head. He wears thin metal glasses. He sweats in the heat, his forehead and his lip. The kind of man I could have seen at church a hundred times, the kind of man whose hand I would have taken. A limp handshake, a short-sleeved button-down.

Peace be with you.

Not some terrible harbinger of God or the night. Not scary or powerful. Not anything.

"Why are you doing this?" I ask.

He mumbles something in Latin, too quiet for me to make out, and steps toward me.

"Why are you doing this," I repeat, louder.

He holds the torch close to me so that the heat burns my skin, the bitter smell of burning hair singes my nostrils. I shoot my hand out to grab it, but he takes hold of my wrist before I can reach the flame. The canister he held moments before falls to the ground with a clang and liquid glugs, spills out all around, splashing up onto my jeans and my arms.

I try to pull away, but he holds my wrist tight. His face remains serene. Pious, smug. Moral superiority. Generous pity. My parents, the Sisters, the priests, the nurses at Sacred Hearts, nearly every adult I've ever known.

"God's plan will always prevail," he says. His voice is higher than I expect. This man, so painfully ordinary. So cruelly mediocre.

What would Jesus do?

What would Cleo do?

"There is no way in Hell that this is God's plan," I say, and I elbow him in the gut.

He grunts, staggers back, but before I can take the torch, he shoves me hard in the ribs where I am bruised already. I stumble, and he throws me onto the grass. I fall outside the gasoline puddle in which he stands. He towers over me, torch held high, and leans forward.

To light me on fire, to tell me something, I will never know.

Because at that moment, a giant black shape leaps through the air and tackles him to the ground.

Barghest pins the man, gasoline splashing up on both of them.

I watch in horror as Barghest tears out the Crusader's throat.

As the Crusader drops the torch.

"NO!"

It happens in slow motion.

The torch flying through the air. Landing right in the middle of the liquid. Barghest's teeth tearing into the man's flesh and ripping it away.

The flame surging to life and speeding toward him.

I push myself up on one arm and get to my feet just as the blaze spreads to the red robes.

And then to Barghest's gas-soaked fur. I scream.

I take a step forward, but my foot gives out, and I collapse onto my hands and knees. Then I hear it, the agonized whines, and smell, the acrid smell of burning hair, fabric, and flesh. I watch in horror, crawling. As his giant shape twists and writhes in the flames that now are an extension of him. As though he is some great luminous beast of the night. Not my Barghest. Not—

I reach the edge of the flames, reach my hands forward to grab him, to save him, to stop his suffering. This can't be real. This can't—

A figure runs at me from the side. A woman. A woman holding a bloody knife. I reach for Barghest, and the fire singes my skin. I can smell his body burning, can hear it crackle and sizzle and char. My hands blister. I am sick, and I am screaming, and the woman is calling out prayers and scriptures into the night, running toward me.

She raises the knife high. Feet away. Almost on us.

I don't have water, I don't have anything to put the fire out. My clothes are soaked in gasoline.

But hers aren't.

Fight. These. Motherfuckers.

I turn just as the robed woman reaches me, swipe my leg under one of hers and pull on her robe as hard as I can, gritting my teeth through Barghest's yelps. She falls to the ground. Her hood falls, revealing dark hair and makeup. At first I think, that is me. The smoke shifts, and I think, no, this is my mother. I blink, and she is not. My mother is dead. My friends are dead. I am nothing like this woman.

She swings at me with the knife again, and it catches my forearm, but Maro's lesson plays through my head, another how-to. I thrust my palm into her nose. The bone cracks, and she drops the knife, her hands shooting up to her face, palms together over her nose as if in prayer. I try to pull the robe from her but I can't as long as she is on her back. She reaches for the knife again. I take it before she can, and without thinking, I shove it into her chest. Cleo and Wyatt. I shove, hitting bone, hitting flesh, until I am covered with her sacrifice. I roll the woman, wheezing her last breaths, and rip the robe from her body. Barghest, I have to—

I turn just in time to find Ben's attacker running for me, Ben on the ground behind him.

Ben on the ground.

I throw the robe over Barghest, and I think maybe it is working, maybe it will be okay. I push myself up to stand, try to think of what Maro said even as all I know is the sound of Barghest, the smell of his flesh. Ben on the ground.

I feign collapse, and the man slows his pace. I am an injured sinner, a pliant lamb.

He steps forward, and I can see he is handsome. Young, a boy. He might be my future husband in another life. Mine to obey and dote upon, to give that most sacred of gifts that can only be given once, to bear the fruits of his seed.

He steps toward me, so sure of himself, so confident in his faith and purpose. Every second of his slow progression is wasted time. Every second is Barghest's pain. But maybe one more robe, maybe it will fix this and save him.

Barghest howls. The boy closes in.

I plunge the knife into his groin, but I miss, and it lodges in his thigh. I pull it free, as his face registers shock, then rage. He swings his own knife toward me. It swipes my cheek. I barely feel it, barely notice the drip of blood and sting of the metal. I stagger back, and then I come at him again. I use strength I have never possessed, and I slice down through his wrist. His knife clatters, falls, and he grasps his hand, red and bloody.

He runs forward and shoves his body into mine, taking me down to the ground. I struggle beneath him, beneath his weight that overpowers me, and he is my father, and he is Luke and the man on the highway and the man in the gas station, and his wrist sprays blood. I thrust my shoulder upward, and it hurts so much that I can barely see, but it is enough to free the knife from beneath him. I reach around his side, and I stab again and again and again, into the flesh of him, into this Man of God, this Son of Christ. Until he grunts and stops fighting.

Nothing but flesh, nothing but dead weight.

I drop the knife, and push and wriggle and strain until I free myself of him. I pull at the fabric of his robe and finally take it.

I turn to Barghest. I can't stand, but I crawl. He is howling, screaming. The woman's robe didn't help. It didn't work. I throw the other robe on top, and it ignites too. It didn't work. It didn't work, and Barghest writhes in the flame, and I reach forward, into the fire, pushing through the heat and the pain to this creature that I love. Who loves me, and he is howling, whining, pain so terrible that it is as though I can feel it. I want to tear this world apart to save him. My hands and forearms blister, the flame dances inches from my face.

I reach for him.

Hands pull at me. I fight them. I do not turn around.

I didn't fight for Noah, not hard enough. Didn't fight for Wyatt or Cleo. But now, for Barghest, I fight.

I fight against arms holding mine. Barghest who saved me. Barghest who is burning alive because he loves me. After so little time, and he—

A voice speaking, yelling. Heat and smoke and flame. Hands hold me back, and I reach out for Barghest, and I can't reach him anymore, and I am sobbing, and the voice doesn't stop.

"You're covered in gasoline, Sophie, you can't! Oh God, Sophie, oh my God. It's—it's too late. I'm so sorry. I'm sorry." Holding me tighter and tighter on the grass, rocking me back and forth, holding me back as I fight, whispering to me. Again and again.

Ben's voice, Ben's words. *Don't look, it's too late, oh God, don't look.*

I watch every second. I watch as he howls and yelps and struggles. He can't stop the burning. It doesn't stop.

More yelling, something happening to our left. I don't see it. Someone coming for us. Running at us. It doesn't matter. None of it matters except these flames and the howls echoing through the night. I fight Ben, and he doesn't let me go.

Until the howls stop. Until they are finished and quiet. And there is only the crackling of flame. There are only useless tears and fire.

I scream.

A bullet flies.

A burning on my cheek. I bring my hand to my face and remove it to find blood there. A bullet grazed my face.

Up, to our left. A gun is trained on us, ten feet away. While Barghest burns.

No time at all passes. An eternity. A Crusader will end us. Right now. Barghest, dead on the ground before me.

I don't know what the end will bring, but I know in this moment, and with every part of my being.

I will carry my vengeance with me.

He pulls the trigger.

The shots ring out through the night. Two of them.

The smoke is thick again. I can't see.

Or maybe this is the last of my vision leaving. The last thing I see on earth this hooded Christian with the gun.

But the sounds don't stop. Nothing around us stops. I look down, and I am not shot. I turn to Ben. He isn't either. Neither of us understands. We are not dead. I can't stop crying.

Then the smoke clears.

Maro and the shooter. Both of them, down on the ground.

Maro shot him. The shooter lies still, and Maro sits beside him. Upright, like he is just waking. Staring at Barghest, trying to understand.

I can't understand. I am sobbing and screaming, and I will never understand.

That's when Maro looks down at his chest.

When I do.

The dark red spreading there.

Barghest's cries echoing in my ears. Fire raging over his body. Blood on Maro.

Blood spreading from the center of his chest.

The wind rips through, carrying smoke with it, shoving it into our mouths and eyes.

I crawl toward him. Maro who is swaying.

I say his name. Call it like a prayer.

I get to his side, and he sways again.

No. Not—

I help him lie down. I prop his head up on the dead man's robe. I don't know what to do.

"Sophie," he says. It sounds funny. Wrong. Weak and too low.

"Hey, you're going to be okay," I say through my tears.

"Cleo, Wyatt?"

Cleo and Wyatt. Barghest. I have to stop crying. I swallow, hard.

"They're okay," I say, my voice breaking, barely my voice at all. "Don't worry, we just gotta take care of you." Tears are falling from my face. I can't stop them. They mean so little in all this. My tears mean nothing, have stopped nothing.

He smiles. "Ben?"

"He's okay too."

"You?"

"Well, that depends," I say, my breaths coming in too fast, his skin getting too pale.

Barghest. Cleo. Wyatt.

"On?"

"On you getting up."

He looks at me a long second, wincing at the sounds. I can still smell Barghest's hair and body on the air. Maro's eyes losing focus.

"Maro, you have to get up. I need you, okay? You were right, I need you."

He coughs, a terrible sound. "You don't need me."

"Yes, I do. I really do. Please."

"You . . ."

Maro trails off. His eyes go distant. As though he sees something new, through me, above me. I turn, but there is nothing there. Ben sits with his head in his hands a few feet away. But it is just us.

"I never thought I'd see you again," Maro says.

I don't understand. The way he's looking at me.

With such love. With so much pride.

"Mom and Dad always talked about you being in Heaven," he says, "but I knew you never left. I always knew you were right here. Somewhere just beyond my . . ."

I don't understand, can't understand.

And then I do. "No. Hey. Maro, stay with me, okay? Please, just stay with me. You can't leave yet. I need you."

He smiles again, coughs up a little blood. He doesn't stop smiling. "Saved you. This time. I finally . . ."

"Maro, please!"

Barghest.

Cleo.

Wyatt.

He exhales.

A loud keening wail fills my ears, joining all the other sounds of Hell.

It isn't until Ben pulls me away, until he tells me we have to go—it's time, and we have to go if we are going to survive—that I realize the voice is my own.

𝕳𝖔𝖑𝖞 𝕳𝖎𝖑𝖑

We take a red SUV we find parked by the exit. A rosary hangs from the rearview mirror. A reusable cup in the cupholder says ROADIE SOADIE on the side.

Everyone is dead.

Ben gets us away from the casino.

Ash smeared on his skin like the strangest of tattoos, like the ash we smudge on ourselves. Remind ourselves that we come from dust and will return to it. Ben's hands unsteady on the wheel. He's shaking all over.

Everyone is dead.

The landscape littered with former lives and broken futures. The state of Wisconsin looks like a war zone. A billboard hangs halfway off its pole: YOUR SUBURBS ARE NOT SAFE: SEX TRAFFICKING IS ALIVE AND WELL. Another, still intact, says LIFE IS SHORT, HAVE AN AFFAIR, ASHLEY MADISON. A third is a condom with a face. Crusader flags in front of a couple of houses. By the time we pass through Arlington forty minutes later, our tank is running low, and Ben is shaking so hard that it's not safe for him to drive anymore.

He cuts the engine at the next gas station we see.

We don't move.

We sit, and we stare into a night slowly fading to another gray day. Impossible, for the sun to rise again. The wind shoves against the sides of the car. We are covered in gasoline and the blood of others. I killed people today. I am seventeen.

Barghest, Cleo, Wyatt, Helen. Maro.

BarghestCleoWyattHelen—

Ben's hand on my hand. Ben's hand in my hand, and I take his too. I grip it tight.

A mourning dove calls from somewhere up above. It is the worst sound I've ever heard.

Ben manually siphons gas, something he knew how to do. I check our one phone, refreshing the boards, searching to see if there are any others. I can't believe there's cell service.

There is cell service, and everyone is dead.

My face stings. Bullet graze on one side. Knife swipe on the other. I pull down the mirror to check and then put it back up. I don't want to see myself.

Down the street, a body lies face down beside a truck.

Behind it, fallen from its post and half-torn on the road, a billboard that says GOD ON HIGH. The image, a church that everyone knows, one we've been to so many times.

Holy Hill.

The only place Noah and I ever went together away from home.

And . . .

I open the browser on the phone. I search *Holy Hill*.

A lot of unhelpful things, and then,

A post comes up, one of the social media websites Ben showed me.

Holy Hill is safe, and we welcome all with open arms. The post is dated four days ago. I search through the comments, people saying they are on their way.

Holy Hill. The largest Catholic church in the region, and the one that all the smaller parishes flock to annually to drink the free-flowing holy water.

I search *Sacred Hearts Holy Hill*.

It comes up first thing.

Another post. Another parent on the same social media site.

The Sacred Hearts kids will be moved from St. Joseph's Hospital to Holy Hill. Can't think of a better place to stay safe and out of harm's way in Christ's love. We're headed that way to meet him.

The giant hill towering over the rest of the state. It's a fortress. The most revered place for every Catholic in the region.

Why didn't it occur to me before? Of course they would all move there.

The question is, would Noah have gone with them?

BarghestCleoWyattHelenMaro.

Ben gets back in the car. I tell him to drive east.

We pass lootings, violence, abandoned cars. Burned and burning homes. People crying, screaming in the streets. Desperate people. Bodies. Fast food restaurants. We are shot at, once, but the shot flies high, and they don't shoot again.

His grip tight on the wheel.

We see Crusader flags raised on poles in front of houses, more of them.

"How many Christians *are* there?" Ben asks.

"I think in America, it's maybe sixty percent." More trash. Another body.

"How many followers does Reverend Ansel have? I know Helen was on it, but I don't watch his videos."

"A lot."

"I just . . . can't understand it," Ben says. "What god would want you to kill other people for him? People *he* made. It's all just . . . fucking insane."

A Baptist church's front sign reads THE MOST POWERFUL POSITION IS ON YOUR KNEES. Someone has hung a red robe from the side of it.

"Yeah," I reply. "But not to the ones who believe it."

We see Holy Hill miles before we reach it, looming above everything else. GOD ON HIGH.

I might be driving toward my brother.

BarghestCleoWyattHelenMaro.

We stop half a mile out from the road up the hill. Cars trail down from it, bumper to bumper, parked and left by all the others making the same pilgrimage before us.

We slowly limp out of the SUV. Ben carries a handgun.

All the cars are empty. Branching out in every direction from Holy Hill, abandoned vehicles. Bumper stickers bearing a fish, one saying A CARPENTER DIED AND LEFT YOU A FORTUNE, another LOVE THY NEIGHBOR. Another says I'M OLD FASHIONED and has the image of a cocktail.

"They've all come here," Ben says. "To be on Holy Hill."

"Are you alright to walk?" I ask.

He glances at me. "Are you?"

We pass car after car as we make our way up the hill. No overwhelming signs of violence or struggle. Just, seemingly, people coming here, together, to ride out this storm. I lean on Ben as we climb, and a couple of times he winces or groans at my weight, and I try to walk on my own. Then he reaches his hand out, and I lean on him again.

An enormous basilica sitting on Wisconsin's highest hill, home to a group of Carmelite monks and surrounded by Kettle Moraine forest. The forest where Maro hiked as a teenager, the one the Ice Age Trail passes through. Old woods, ancient forest. Red, orange, green. Probably more of those burial mounds around. The ones I never knew to look for. The ones from people who were here before us.

The church can be seen from miles in every direction, towering over the treetops. There is a feeling on Holy Hill. Something greater than us, primordial. I've always felt it.

"There's a little stream, at the top," I say. "It pours out of the rock, natural water, holy water, as they bless it. People come to fill their bottles with it. It's supposed to have healing properties. Some say they've been cured of paralysis, blindness, just from drinking the water and sleeping here overnight."

"Maybe we need some of it," Ben says.

It's a joke. Neither of us laughs.

"I've heard these woods are haunted," Ben says. "The state park."

Everything is haunted now. Maybe it always was.

"It's important, though, I think," Ben says, between labored breaths. I realize I don't even know what all his injuries are now. What mine are either. "Believing in miracles."

"Do *you*?" I ask.

"Yes."

Ben, who doesn't believe in God. Ben, for whom every answer comes easily. "But do you really?" And I mean it, I really want to know.

We clear the middle of the hill and make our way closer to the top. It hangs here between both of us.

This hope I have been carrying all along. This precious thing I hold inside me, that feels more fragile by the minute. Everything leading to this moment, that never should have looked like this.

BarghestCleoWyattHelenMaro.

We reach the parking lot. The sun is just beginning to glow from below the horizon. Noah could be here. Why not? It would make sense. My brother really could be here, and I might be about to see him.

For the first time, I wonder, and it feels unreal, what Noah and Ben will think of each other. I am nervous. I don't know why, don't know if I can trust it, but . . . I do. I feel him. Here, in this place.

The wind lifts my hair, tosses it around my face. I want to turn and spit in it. I want to scream. *What? What are you trying to tell me?!*

BarghestCleoWyattHelenMaro.

Barghest on the ground. Maro beside him.

The wind shifts again, away from me.

The parking lot at the top of the hill is packed with cars, all of them empty, autumn forest lining the hill around them. It's quiet, the wind making most of the noise around us. I don't know what I expected. Voices or song? Ahead of us sits the basilica, and off to the side a number of buildings, gift shop, café, boarding and guest houses.

"Where is everyone?" Ben says. His voice is wary.

"Let's try the boarding house first," I say. "I remember a lot of bedrooms there. Seems like where Sacred Hearts would go."

We cross the parking lot, and still no one appears.

We reach the boarding house. I open the doors.

Ben makes a choked noise behind me.

Inside, it's like the soccer field. Worse. The smell hits us, and we both take a step back.

Ben says to be careful, but I don't hear it. All I hear are my own breaths and my own heart, my own silent prayer.

People. Human beings. Adults of every age, teenagers, some children. So many red palms. Pus and blood. They're all naked, or half naked. Missing skin, smeared in red. Chunks of hair ripped out, clenched in fists.

So many atop one another, clinging to one another. So much flesh housing nothing now. Empty casings. Cleo. Helen. Wyatt. Maro. Barghest. So many tangled limbs.

I scan the faces, praying. Begging. We step through and around them. Bodies in the halls. Bodies in the old monastery. Bodies in every bedroom, in every sitting room. Tears stream from my eyes, but it doesn't matter. I have to scan every face. The Shrine Chapel, the St. Therese Chapel. The café and conference rooms. Bodies everywhere.

Between buildings, on the grass, on the grounds. At least a hundred people, maybe two hundred. Maybe more. So many. But not Noah. Not my brother.

Finally, we go to the basilica.

We step inside the giant space, the beautiful, vaulted, glorious space. So many of us flocking here every year, so many coming to see this grandeur and glory. And it is stunning. It really is. Painfully beautiful. And . . .

There are people in the pews.

People sitting upright. Facing forward, facing away from us.

The great basilica door closes behind us with an echoing bang. We stand very still, waiting for a response, waiting. For something.

No one turns around.

No one moves.

"Sophie," Ben whispers, holding his arm out to stop me.

I continue forward, my uneven footfalls echoing through the cavernous space. There is the sound of my movement, and ragged breaths. Nothing else.

Red streaking the ground. I reach the first row of pews, and I turn to them.

My hand covers my mouth.

They are mostly clothed, though the clothing is torn and bloody. Some of them missing flesh from their faces or throats or chests where others bit it off. All their eyes are closed, every single one, their hands placed in each other's, creating a link. In silent prayer.

Row after row, pew after pew. Everyone sitting in this church, hands held, eyes closed.

Silent. Still.

Dead.

But there is another sound. I stop, and Ben stops. The ragged gulps of air continue. Someone in here is alive.

We continue forward, careful, Ben with the gun drawn, until we see him.

At the end of the aisle, slumped against the steps leading to the altar, there is a monk.

His eyes are glassy, sweat on his forehead. He sees us and startles, his breath catching and then coming again in a gasp. "Stay back," he wheezes. "Please." He holds his chest and scrapes in breath.

"We're not here to hurt anyone," Ben says.

"No," the monk wheezes. He is young, I realize. He looks to be about Maro's age, maybe only a couple of years older. Not so much older than me. Someone has clawed the side of his face. "Me," he says. "Sick."

"What happened here?" I say.

"Tried. To cover them. To give them . . . peace."

The skids on the floor, the smeared blood.

"You dragged all these people into the pews? You put them like this?"

"Thought." He coughs hard for a moment. "It was better. Dignity. Together."

"Did anyone escape? Anyone get out of here?"

"Yes. We all . . . had to leave. Many . . . of us. Got out." Another great wheezing inhale. "I . . . came back. See. If I. Could help."

"And someone attacked you."

A jerky nod. He coughs, smiles. "One left alive. Attacked me. God's plan . . . I guess."

"Was Sacred Hearts here?" I ask.

His eyes wander. Like Maro. Maro looking past me and seeing his sister. Maro dead. The monk blinks a slow blink then looks back at me. I repeat the question.

"Old. Monastery," he says.

"What can we do for you?" Ben asks, a tremble in his voice.

"Took . . . something. A doctor here. Gave . . . in case. Not to . . ." His hand unfurls, and a pill bottle rolls out on the ground.

"Not to spread it," Ben says.

Again, the shaky jerk of a nod.

"I pray . . . not . . ." He inhales a deep rasping breath, and I see blood on his neck that I didn't see before. It looks like his skin has been ripped there. Enough that I can see muscles or tendon beneath.

His eyes move to the crucifix hanging above us, to Christ Almighty. The monk releases one long final exhale.

Silence in the space.

His last words hang in the air around us, his final wish. He didn't need to finish them, not for me to understand. To know exactly what he meant. Every Catholic would know.

He took his own life. He did it to save anyone else he might encounter, but he did it all the same. His final wish, his final prayer, when he came back to help and no one else did.

He prayed his act of compassion was not a sin. And he knew by God's rules that it was.

We lift him onto the pew. We set his hand in his neighbor's. But when Ben moves forward to close his eyes, I stop him. The monk is looking upward. He's looking to God.

The sun fills more of the sky, and early morning light streams in through the cathedral windows, illuminating swirling dust motes and the whole of the congregation. Still silent. We stand before them, this congregation of the dead. None of these people wearing red robes or setting anything aflame. I turn and look up at the cross, at a crucified man who was flesh and never was. All these people at my back, all of them came here. To worship, to find safety. Not to burn or hate.

And here they all are, beneath Christ's sorrowful eye. Here. In Heaven. Someplace else or nowhere at all. Dead.

BarghestCleoWyattHelenMaro. Mrs. Parson. Mom. Dad.

"We should wash ourselves off," I say.

Before we reach the doors, my eyes catch on something. I step over to the alcove in the wall. Crutches and boots, wheelchairs, canes, eye patches, hearing aids, and glasses. These items left by supplicants who drank of the holy water, supplicants who were cured. They came in crippled or blind, and they walked out whole. I stand before this display, this testament to the will of God, to the might of the Lord, to belief itself.

I reach inside and take hold of a pair of crutches.

I walk out on them.

Birdsong

Now that it's brighter, now in the light of day, I expect to see more evidence of outbreak, expect people to have tried to flee and crashed or tried to step into their cars before being ripped out. But there is none of that. I suspect no one made it past the buildings. I suspect they all drank from the same chalice of His blood, were all infected at the same time.

Ben says, "We'll find him, Sophie. We'll keep looking."

"I should just be grateful he got out." If he was here at all.

Cell service is out again. I set my crutches down and sit on the step. Ben sits beside me. I drop my head in my hands.

"I just had such a feeling, you know? Like he and I would meet here, and this would be it. It just felt . . . right. I felt like maybe he knew I was coming. I don't know, I know it doesn't make sense."

"If he has you as a sister, I'm sure he knows you're coming. No matter what." He puts his hand on my back.

I freeze beneath Ben's touch.

"Did I say something wrong?" he says. He pulls his hand back.

"No."

If Noah knew I was coming, even hoped that I was coming, he might have left something. A note, or . . .

I stand, barely getting my footing.

"He said Sacred Hearts had been in the old monastery, right?"

"Yeah, but Sophie, no one there is—"

"Right." I can't think. I can hardly breathe. "I have to—"

I set off on the crutches. Ben follows. At the door I turn around, my mind whirring, all my thoughts circling in a whirlwind.

"Ben," I say. "You have done so much for me. You've been more than . . ." I take in his face, and also I am not here, my mind sifting through the possibilities. "I need one more favor. If . . . if you're up for it."

I stand in the first bedroom. One body on one of the twin beds, the other on the floor. I take a breath. Ben is in another room, doing the very same thing. For me.

We don't know which room was Noah's. If he was here. We can't be sure. We have to lift up every mattress, every single one, until we find something. Or until we don't. Because he might not have left anything. But if there's even a chance, if there's even a sliver . . .

Every room.

Getting close to these bodies, these naked sick infected bodies. Touching them. Blistered, torn, brutalized. Every one of them, a life. Every one of them, stories. Families. Friends.

Not people anymore. Just husks, just decomposing material.

We check every mattress, every room.

Until there is one room left.

We stand before the open door together. This room has no bodies in it. If I find nothing, if he's left me nothing, I don't know where to go. I don't know how to find my brother. It's the only thing I can think of.

We step inside, and Ben lifts one of the mattresses. I watch, wait, as he feels beneath it. And again. After a moment, he sets it down.

"I'm sorry," he says. He means it. The look on his face . . .

My heart sinks, as it has with every room up to now, as it has a hundred or a thousand times since the start of all this. There is one bed left. One more to try, and then that's it. I stand, lifting the pathetic mattress away from the spring.

But there is nothing there. I stare at the empty space.

I drop it back down. It was a stupid idea. I was so stupid for thinking, for believing. I can hardly hold myself upright. I don't know what to do. I sit on the mattress, and it squeaks beneath me.

I lean forward to drop my elbows on my knees, and I am about to let myself sob. We just watched everyone die. Barghest's howls in the night. Barghest who will never again be in my arms.

A sound.

Tiny and nearly insignificant. I think I must have imagined it.

Just a small rustling.

Ben is up and moving. Reaching beneath the bed.

He holds the item out to me.

In Ben's hand is a folded-up piece of paper. The same kind Noah and I used to leave for each other in the secret compartments under our mattresses.

In Ben's hand is an origami bird.

It must have fallen when I moved. This most precious thing. I can hardly breathe.

I reach out, and I take it from Ben, hold it in my hands and feel him. *I feel him.* Noah.

I try to open it as carefully as possible, my fingers fumbling on the thin paper. Ben sits again, and I cry out when I see the writing.

I cry out because this is real, it is not some fantasy. My brother is here.

I found you, Noah.

I found you.

⁓⁎⁓
Ark

Sophie,

I've left these notes every place we've been. I don't know if you will find them or if you are alive, but I know that if you are, you will try to find me. And . . . I don't know if it's stupid or crazy, but I just kind of know that you're alive. I don't know. You have to be.

They sent us with these psycho guards, some of the Crusaders. Insane to think that they'd worry about what we could do if we got loose in the world, given what they're doing. Given what's happening with the infected people.

There's something I didn't tell you before, and I should have. I've met someone, found someone. His name is Tyler, and he grew up the way we did. But he's smart and funny, and he doesn't believe everything they shove down our throats. He thinks for himself.

There are too many people here. Everyone's going to get infected. We know it. Tyler and I are leaving. We've found a way to get past them, and we've found somewhere to go. We have another friend, they sent her to Sacred Hearts because she was pregnant. She found a place where she can safely deliver the baby, and Tyler wants to stay with her and make sure we can get her there. I can't come to where you are, but I hope you'll come to me.

I know you'll find me, Sophie. If you are alive. And I can't explain it, but I just know you are.

Twin islands. You will find me.

The world from before is gone. It's a good thing. It's time to start over. Tyler doesn't believe, but he's always talking about guilt. He's like you with that. It makes no sense, but it's clearly messed him up. But he and I talked, and he said you probably felt guilty, for what happened that night. For Mom and Dad bringing in the priest, for them taking me away. I told him that was crazy and you couldn't possibly. But in case you do, in case there is any part of you that is guilty about anything having to do with me, please don't be.

Please know you are my person and my other half. I wouldn't be me without you. Please know you are everything.

This virus isn't going away. And I know there's been so much darkness, so much bloodshed. But I can't help but feel that maybe it's not a bad thing. That maybe we were due for some sort of reset. Not like the Crusaders think with God killing everyone off to lift up the righteous, but maybe just with our society. I don't know. Maybe it was time for some change.

Tyler talks about sin too. They all talk about sin. All this world obsessed with it, obsessed with keeping us obedient.

This is the last thing. You're so smart, Sophie. But sometimes you really just don't see what's right in front of you. So in case you need to hear it, in case it's the last thing to push you closer to me. In case it gets you through even one day of this chaos.

Sin is made up and stupid. It doesn't exist.

I love you.

HOW TO RECOUNT THE
END OF THE WORLD:

Realize that somehow, you have made it
through. Somehow, even if you don't deserve
to be here, you are.

Don't spare any details, no matter what the
cost.

Rethink everything, because you might have
been wrong all along.

The end of the world might in fact be the
beginning.

Revelation

I read it ten times through, twenty. I am wrung out and ravaged and so angry that he would leave and not tell me where he was going.

I read it again.

Noah has fallen in love. That's what he was saying.

He's fallen in love with a boy. Tyler. To speak freely about who he is, what he wants. The way he speaks out when I have been so afraid to misstep, so terrified of every wrong thing, every day of my life. I marvel at my brother's bravery.

And his friend, their friend who is pregnant. Who gave away her virginity. Our parents would have me view them as broken, as fallen. Noah and Tyler and this girl. Cleo's words. The idea that this girl's whole value can be tied to this one thing that she gave away and will never get back. This one thing that in the scope of someone's life, all the choices we make, all the pain and trials we endure, everything we experience, all the people we love and lose, seems to mean almost nothing. Maybe actually nothing. And Noah and Tyler. They have each other. Noah has someone in this world. After so many years of pain and isolation, my brother is not alone.

Virginity, chastity, purity, men only being with women, women only being with men. How can these things possibly matter when people die, when storms tear walls off homes? When a ten-year-old boy tries to come to terms with the fact that he might not make it to eleven, when another is ripped from his home because he is just a little different. And when one is left bleeding on the ground next to a woman who isn't his mother by the hand of someone who calls himself righteous.

Ben watches me. Patient, kind. Good. What is good anyway? When the people who are supposed to be the ultimate embodiment of Goodness seem to be those who hate and fear the most.

I don't know anything. I have no faith in anything.

Except Noah. Helen, Barghest, Cleo, Wyatt, Mrs. Parson, and Ben. Maro. I believe in them.

Noah has given himself over to the very thing I have been so afraid of all this time. He and this boy, Tyler, out in the world together now. No restrictions, no daily prayers or punishments.

Noah is free. Free to live whatever life he wants. There are dangers. There is infection, there is violence, there is weather and the problem of currency and a million forces that could work against them. But maybe none of that matters because he chose it.

My brother made it out. And I have to believe he is still alive. I have to believe, like he does, that I will find him. My brother, who is braver and runs faster than anyone I know. My brother, who, despite everything, still believes in me.

We scan to see if there is anything else useful for us to take on the way out. The water taps don't work, but we find some disinfectant wipes to scrape over our already-dry skin.

We head outside to the holy water stream, but when we arrive, it is dry.

We drive until we find a house that looks abandoned and isolated, an American flag on its road-facing side. I pick the lock.

Ben puts on a kettle for tea. The house must have belonged to an old woman, everything covered in lace and macramé. We discover a treasure trove of canned goods and nonperishable foods. A grandchild's illegible drawings are held by magnets to the front of her refrigerator. We find water bowls and a litter box, but there is no cat.

Barghest isn't with us. I fall to my knees in the kitchen and press my forehead to the floor. I sob, for hours. Until I think it might kill me.

We sleep through the night.

We wake to another bright midwestern morning.

This brightness, though, is new. The world is illuminated through the cloud cover, alive in its grayness, vivid in a way it never was when the sun beat fully down upon us. God's light, meant to warm and protect us. The wind. Smoke. A world set ablaze.

We spend days in the old woman's house. Recovering, tending our wounds. Occasionally, when service comes, we check the phone. Sometimes I use my crutches to walk. Sometimes I lean on Ben. This proximity, so perilous before, is still dangerous now. And yet everything is different. The world is different. Or maybe the world is exactly the same, and I am the one who is changing.

On the bookshelves, I find religious titles. *Marry Him and Be Submissive. Made for This: The Catholic Mom's Guide to Birth. The Supreme Vocation of Women.*

I dream of my parents every time I close my eyes. My parents. Barghest, Helen, Cleo, Wyatt. I dream of Maro and Barghest the most. I can't believe they're gone, that any of them are gone. But with Maro, I dream that he is here still. I dream that we meet when we're older, I dream that I keep him safe this time, and not the other way around. I dream that I feel Barghest in my arms. I dream of Mrs. Parson in a room full of books.

Waking, I can't think of any of them, can't face it.

Barghest's howls, Wyatt's throat. I hear Barghest's phantom footsteps on the floorboards, I wait for him to brush up against my leg, lean his weight into me.

But at night, I visit them. They visit me. The wind is steady and almost comforting, a constant companion, a reminder that there is a world outside the four walls of this house, this in-between space we have found. There's a chicken coop outside, and I tend to the chickens. One hen didn't make it, and I bury her at the edge of the property.

The blisters on my hands are healing. I am beginning to feel a new relationship to this dirt, to this earth. Some kind of understanding between us. Just tentatively forming. Just the very beginning.

We wash, help ourselves to the selection of old magazines and paperback mysteries. Neither of us reads. Mostly we just stare at the pages. We sleep in the main room of the house, on different couches. It is safer to be able to see the front door.

Sickness still spreads. The Crusaders are growing.

I wonder if I will ever feel able to sleep alone again, and Ben says, "I don't know." I said it out loud. I didn't realize.

I find a copy on the shelf of *The Divine Comedy*, the same cover as the one I read, right before all this. I set it aside and then . . . I take it in my hand again.

Ben makes us coffee in the kitchen. A bird chirps, somewhere outside.

"I loved my birthday gift," I say.

He pauses in his task, raises his eyes, his face maybe a little red. He clears his throat. "I didn't know if you'd ever opened it."

"It was one of the best things anyone's ever given me," I say. "Thank you."

He smiles, a little, and fills our mugs. He steps over the creaking floorboards to sit opposite me, and again I expect Barghest to come barreling from behind him. Maro's voice, from the other room. Tears burn, and my chest hollows out. I breathe for a moment until the worst of it passes. These waves of grief like knives to the body. Constant, unrelenting.

"I think my mom would be proud of us," Ben says. He stares out the window at our new world. "Maro, too," he adds, glancing to me once and then looking down into his mug.

I don't have words. He doesn't need them from me. Ben, who understands.

"You know, you're kind of like her. In some ways. Not that I . . ." He clears his throat. "I mean, my mom had a kind of complicated relationship with her upbringing too."

"What was it?"

"Well, I mean, she left the rez to marry my dad, and she never talked about it again. We never went back. She might have gone without me a couple times when I was young, but once I got sick and my dad left, she just . . . didn't. I keep thinking I should have asked about it, should have tried to learn more, but she never brought it up. Sometimes, every now and then, she would get this look in her eye though. Like she could see the water and the cliffs, like she was back there again. I think . . . I don't know. Can't change anything now. But being in the casino, and that guy asking about it . . . I've just been thinking, is all."

"I'm sure she was happy with what she chose, if she chose it."

"Yeah, but I don't think she chose it for *her*. I think at first it was for my dad, and then for me. And I think . . ." He swallows. "I think she never went back because it was too painful, because she missed it so much, and she didn't want to. She didn't want to uproot my life, and I think she felt that it was better to try and forget it ever existed in the first place."

"Why do you think she missed it?"

"She told me stories, back when I was sick. About cliffs and red rock and ice caves, about lakeside beaches and the sound fresh water makes lapping against rock, mist over the surface."

"Where is it?" I ask.

"Hm?"

"Where is the rez? The . . . reservation. Where was she from?"

"Oh, um, up on Lake Superior somewhere. Red Cliff."

I stand and head to the bookshelf, scan through the bird and field guides until I find what I'm looking for. I sit down beside Ben and open the map on the coffee table.

"Can you show me?"

He hesitates, then leans forward and flips through the different map pages until he finds the one he's looking for. He points to a section of the Bayfield Peninsula on the lake. I mentally calculate.

"We'd have to check again on the fires, but with the Crusaders mostly moving south, if we can get around the quarantine zones, I think we can get there within a day," I say. "If you want to go."

He thinks. "We'd have to go through quarantine zones, I think," he says. "I don't see a way around."

"That might be true for going anywhere."

"Don't know what we'd find there, at this point."

"I don't know what we'll find anywhere."

"Would you want to? I mean, does that work for you?" His voice sounds different, and I glance up at him. He looks . . . nervous. He is watching me for my reaction, and I realize what I see there that I didn't before.

Hope.

I consider his words.

"Well," I say, "since I don't know where Noah is right now, I guess heading to new places anywhere is kind of the best bet I have. And if your family's there, it might be safer for us. At least as a place to start. Ride out these fires and this weather."

"I mean, I don't know them, not really, but maybe . . . maybe there's a place for me there. If I tell them who my mom is, who I am. And you with me, if you want to, I mean. And obviously only if—"

But I don't hear the rest of what Ben says. My eyes have caught on something I've never seen before. A grouping of islands off the coast on Lake Superior. Twelve of them, just beyond where Red Cliff is. They are labeled *Apostle Islands*.

Noah's letter. That line that didn't make sense.

Twin islands. You will find me.

I pull the letter from my pocket and reread. I read it wrong before. I was so stupid.

I laugh, and I am crying again. I can't help it, and I don't even try.

Twin Islands.

"Yes," I say to Ben, who is now watching me. "It definitely works for me."

Two islands with names that mean everything, that change everything. Noah wasn't saying something about us. He was telling me where he was headed. Two islands in the Apostles. Two islands right by Red Cliff.

North Twin and South Twin.

We load up what we have and what we want to carry from the old woman's house under cover of dark. We have enough food to last us weeks, months even. We have blankets and water and all manner of supplies. We will have to be careful, people will want to steal it. We will have to protect it or be ready to part from it. People might want to do us harm, for any number of reasons. We have guns. We know at least the basics of how to use them.

There is hope and a plan. There is so much loss. Everyone not getting in the car with us.

The ghosts of them, lingering. I beg them to linger forever.

The weather has turned again, another storm on its way. Flames spreading throughout the region, fires set off on all sides, burning away all the old-growth forest, buildings, towns. Razing this country to the ground. We see the flames, orange and yellow, glowing on the horizon.

The wind claws at us. We lean into it. We are learning how to move with the wind, how to coexist, how to use it. Maro and his sailing.

When the car is loaded, I set my crutches inside and hop away from Ben to stand on my own.

The two of us. The red car. The wind licking. Sweeping over this land as though to wipe it clean, erode our monuments and our temples to nothing.

Bodies in a whirlwind, so many bodies in a torrent.

As though to ignite something.

These days and nights of recovery have passed as if in a dream, but now that I stand outside in this vast and strange world that I still do not know entirely, I feel I can see clearly for the first time in a very long time.

Maybe death does that to you. Maybe hope does.

I think of my mother driving me to school, telling me I needed a new uniform. I think of my father and the *crinkle, sip* symphony and a time in which I knew nothing of the world outside our home. I think of a sealed bedroom window and a little girl who was afraid of the wind. My heart is beating, my throat is raw.

I still hold the book in my hand, *The Divine Comedy. Inferno.* I have carried it around for days. Considering, trying to understand. The wind laps at us, kicking up dust.

"Wasn't there wind in Dante's Hell?" Ben asks, nodding to it. His voice surprising, and not. In the wind, in this moment. His voice more than a lifeline. He leans against the car in his stained but washed clothes, his hair overgrown. I'm not sure I've ever seen anyone so beautiful.

I say, "In the second circle."

"Which one was that?"

"Lust."

He narrows his eyes at me in what I know is a smile, the only sort he can give. But that spark is there, in him. The same one that's in me. I can see it, can feel it between us.

"So if we're in the second circle," he says, "does that mean all the others lie ahead of us?"

I chew my lip. The scar on the side of his neck, the slight bulge of the bandage on his shoulder beneath his shirt, the set of his hips, and his chest. He lets me look at him. I let me look. We deserve beauty. Ben, and me. We have held so much death. These bodies don't last long, and it takes very little to break them. It takes almost nothing. And we might both be driving toward the end.

"No," I say. "I think this is the only one that matters."

The American flag on the side of the old lady's house flaps in the wind. Dante in my hand. Figures, parallels. Cleo, Dido, Hellhound, *Lovers' Whirlwind*, Paolo and Francesca, Virgil, Beatrice. Maro. Ben. It could be the answer. We could be in Dante's Hell. If Reverend Ansel is right, we are on Earth, and these are God's smiting winds and plague sent here to punish us. And maybe the Christians have been raptured. Maybe their bodies remain, but they've gone on to Heaven, been taken there. Or it could be that demons have finally taken over this deviant world, have possessed all the wicked and now drag them down to the depths of Hell.

Maybe we are in Hell now. Maybe we are headed there.

Or maybe, for the first time, it occurs to me.

This burning place of eternal punishment and damnation, the one we fear our entire lives.

Maybe there isn't any Hell at all.

Maybe it was a human who made the whole idea up.

That whisper in my ear. The brush up against my neck.

"So," Ben says. His voice is stronger now. I think, looking at him, that this boy is nearly a man. He might already be. Did that happen since I've known him? I wonder what it makes me. "Are we ready?"

My eyes catch on his lips as I consider. All the words run through my mind, all the lessons and prayers and strictures. But only two sound for me now. Only two voices play through my head, overwhelming and eradicating the rest.

Noah's. And Maro's.

Sin is made up and stupid. It doesn't exist.

I hope you like your life.

"I don't know," I say. The way Ben's face has thinned, the smell I know is uniquely his. My want for him, despite everything, *because* of everything. So loud that it drowns out the wind. It drowns out everything except Noah's and Maro's words, repeating again and again.

This wanting, this growing blazing fire inside me.

The wind surges, whips my hair and skin, throws dirt into my eyes. And I lean in.

I lean all the way in. I know exactly who she is.

The power that Cleo had, the power of Helen and Fiona, the girls in the magazines, Ayla in *The Valley of Horses,* the Harlot on the back of the Beast. Cleo's necklace on my throat.

Lilith.

Are we ready?

"I don't know," I say again, to Ben, to the night. "But I'm driving."

Ben throws his head back and laughs, actually laughs, and the sound sets me on fire. He tosses me the keys, and I catch them. He turns, to get in the passenger seat, to get on the road.

"Hey, Ben," I say.

He turns back. And he sees it in my eyes. What I am about to do, who I've become.

I watch him take me in, for just a second. I watch the hitch in his breath, understanding. I make sure we see each other. He nods.

I throw myself into him. And he catches me.

He smiles again, and my lips are on his. And we are *here.*

We're not okay. It is so clear that we are not okay. We will never unsee or unfeel or unknow any of what's come to pass. There is so much I will never forgive myself for, so much I will carry with me, forever. We are broken and battered and not the same people we were. We hardly even know ourselves at all. We are drowning in a grief so terrible and ripping and profound we might not live through it. I have so many questions, never ending. So much to learn. But I know I *choose* this. I choose this again, and again.

Noah said that the old world was finished, not that there couldn't be room for a new one.

The wind swirls around us. And I know her.

She is standing, eyes closed, beneath an open sky. She is every possibility and freedom and power and *life.*

She is the night bird, letting us begin again. Letting us soar.

She is me. Finally letting go.

I cling to Ben, and he holds me so tight.

My skin and his. Our heat, our breaths coming hot and fast. But nothing is fast enough, nothing brings us close enough.

I feel the eyes of Jesus, God, the Devil and all the demons, all of them watching, all of them witnessing my fall. As Ben and I let ourselves just feel, just be. Together. This life of choice and freedom.

I *choose* this.

As flames set the horizon aglow, as Ben and I refuse anything but this, as I give and take and I *live*. I can almost hear laughter in that whisper on my neck. Can almost feel her smile.

The world, this world, *our* world, is only just beginning.

And when we head north, toward our families, toward the unknown, but side by side, together, if Jesus and God and the Devil want to watch, well . . .

I can at least give them a good show.

I pull back, and look into Ben's eyes, glazed from pleasure. From what we have done, and will do again. Us, in the wind. In the night. Us in a ravaged earth.

I grab for his hand, and he grips mine, and we hold so tightly to each other. Maybe I have lived to know my first love. Maybe this is everything.

Sweat lines both our brows. The wind touching every part of us. Both our eyes glazed in pleasure.

This is power.

This is freedom.

Or maybe, I think, delirious, tears streaming down my face and the wind on my neck,

Maybe it's a fever.

A Letter to the Reader

I thought my dog dying was going to kill me.

If I'm being honest, I still think it, some days. Most days. If I'm being honest, I still think it every day.

Soul-mutt. Best friend. Not everyone understands, or will. That's fine. I've never been one to want to share in grief, never been one to share much of anything. Only child, writer. A dog removes itself from the pack to lick wounds clean. A dog goes off, alone, to die. But we all know it—a family member, a friend, the sudden glazing of the eyes, the feel of a heart stopping beneath our hand. Our souls and selves dropping pieces each time someone exits this earth. Our identities, foundations shaken. Even sometimes bulldozed to nothing.

This one brought me to my knees. At the time of writing this note, I can honestly say, I have never felt anything like this. I am truly surprised it hasn't killed me.

I always knew Barghest was going to die.

Barghest's death was (with the deaths of the others) the worst thing I could think of, and my job as I see it is to explore all the worsts. And all the bests, too. This book, or more accurately, an early, now unrecognizable version of it, was the first thing I ever seriously wrote. It was also what got me started on this path of Writer. Someone read this early snippet and believed in it, in me. This was a story that I wanted to tell from day one, ideas that hounded me then and have for all the years since.

It's taken ten years, an education, all the events of a decade of life, and more drafts than I'd like to count for me to tell this story in a way that felt right. In a way that is (I hope) befitting of you, most precious reader. And these dogged questions of guilt, shame, faith have nipped at my heels through everything.

Funny, how they always draw just enough blood to keep us from running full tilt.

But now. In the wake of a loss that has shaken me more than any I've lived through before, in a moment in which I find myself, like Sophie, questioning everything, questioning what the point of being here is at all, I have to say,

It all feels very human and very small to confine and bind ourselves to anything that seeks to diminish us. This world and universe and existence is so expansive and evolving, and we choose to let ourselves be crippled by someone else's *ideas*.

We share life with mortality. We will die. Everyone we love will die. We will all face the dark. Together, or separate. We just don't know. There is no self-help book, no textbook, no how-to that can tell us, definitively, what comes after. By the time any of us has the answers, we won't be here to write them. *None* of us knows, even if we think we do.

But here is what I do know: We live with death. And horror chooses not to turn away from it.

Horror looks the darkness in the eyes. Horror dances with the absence, the loss. Explores ways for us—you, the reader, and me—to take it in our arms and spin around together. Ways to embrace the centrifugal force that is human striving, human searching. *Mortal* life.

Dogs die. Humans die. We live with it, whether we want to or not.

But from choosing to look, choosing not to turn away, from our embrace in the darkness, I hope that guilt and shame and any idea invented to hold you down in this glorious, nearly blinding existence, will seem, at the end of it all, very, very small.

You, and me, spinning too fast for them to catch us.

Thank you for continuing on this journey with me. With my characters, who are of course, now yours. These questions and worlds that I humbly share with you. That now belong to you.

And while we keep hurtling through the unknown, as we spin round and round, I want to say,

Here's to dancing, book by book, question by question, through this vast, shining existence.

Together.

CJ Leede
January 2024
Los Angeles